Egan, Lesley
The Miser

18008

THE MISER

THE MISER

LESLEY EGAN

DOUBLEDAY & COMPANY, INC.
GARDEN CITY, NEW YORK

All of the characters in this book
are fictitious, and any resemblance
to actual persons, living or dead,
is purely coincidental.

This one is for
Elaine Bechtel
because she likes Jesse best

Perverse disputings of men of corrupt minds,
and destitute of the truth, supposing that
gain is godliness: from such withdraw thyself . . .
For we brought nothing into this world, and it
is certain we can carry nothing out.
And having food and raiment let us be therewith content.
But they that will be rich fall into temptation
and a snare, and into many foolish and hurtful
lusts, which drown men in destruction and perdition.
For the love of money is the root of all evil:
which while some coveted after, they have erred
from the faith, and pierced themselves through
with many sorrows.

                                    I Timothy 5–10

THE MISER

CHAPTER 1

Jesse had seen the old man only once, and that had been six and a half years ago. That had been in the rather dingy old office out on Vine Street, with Miss Williams ineffectually pottering around pretending to be a legal secretary; and in those days he had sometimes taken Saturday morning appointments, still building a practice. It had been a Saturday morning he had seen Jan Vanderveer.

When Miss Williams had peered into his office and said, "The eleven o'clock appointment's here, Mr. Falkenstein," he had gotten up automatically to welcome the new client. In the little anteroom was a tall old man and a youngish woman.

The old man stood up promptly; the woman half-rose and he turned on her peremptorily. "You just wait, Dulcie."

"Yes, Papa." She was perhaps in her early thirties, a plumpish brown-haired young woman, round-faced, nondescript.

The old man came into the office and sat down abruptly in the client's chair. He was tall and gaunt, once a powerful man but stooped a little with age; he had a keen hawk-nosed face, and his voice was sharp and sure. He was shabbily dressed in an old-fashioned gray suit with a vest, his shirt collar frayed. He regarded Jesse sardonically and said, "I'll bet you'll never guess why I picked you. Haven't had any dealings with a lawyer in years. Tried nine of 'em, see? Your gal quoted me the lowest price—thirty-five dollars to make a will."

Jesse returned the sardonic grin. "That's for a simple straightforward will, Mr. Vanderveer. Anything complicated, it might be more."

"Better not be—I got the firm quote. It'll be simple, all right." Vanderveer scowled and passed a hand over his largely bald head. "Howie said I ought to have a will, and he's right, but dammit, it's hell to know what to do. It is hell to get old, and nobody sensible to leave it to. If the wife had ever had a boy—but she never, just the two girls, and women are all fools about money. Hen-brained, the lot of them. I want it all left in trust, only thing to do, dammit."

Jesse prepared to take notes. "Damn it," said Vanderveer, interrupting his first question querulously, "it wouldn't make sense, appoint Howie—partners for thirty-seven years we were, but he's only five years younger than me. If he and Flo had ever had a boy—but they never had any at all. I don't trust banks more than halfway, but I know Semons at Security, he's an honest man and only forty-odd. Thought about it, and I guess that's the only thing to do. Everything in trust, that branch of Security-Pacific—Hollywood Boulevard." He sounded dissatisfied. He told Jesse the names of the legatees absently: his wife, Myra, his daughter Dulcie.

"You mentioned another daughter, Mr. Vanderveer?"

"Marcia. Hah. She needn't expect anything, running off with that damn lah-de-dah college professor. She's provided for—made her own bed."

Jesse regarded him soberly. "I'd advise you to leave her a token legacy at least," he said. "If you pass her over entirely, it could be grounds to contest the will—a direct blood heir." People did come all sorts.

"Hah!" said Vanderveer with a rather wolfish grin. "Marcia'd know better than that. But come to think"—he gnawed at a thumbnail thoughtfully—"could be that damn prissy professor might not. You think so, hah? Leave her a hundred dollars and it'd have to stand? All right, make it like that."

Jesse got the name, Mrs. Marcia Coleman, an address in Claremont. The Vanderveer address was on Kingsley in Hollywood. "And a list of the property—exactly what does it consist of?"

"None of your damned business," said Vanderveer testily. "You just put down, 'everything of which I die possessed'—that's the legal phrase, isn't it? Good enough?" Jesse admitted it would be legal, if not altogether desirable. "All right, you put it down like that. And that's all." His thin lips worked a little. "Hell to get old," he muttered. "Never made a will before, but Howie said I ought not to leave it. Otherwise the state taking a piece—damn government."

It would be a very simple will. Jesse told him it would be ready to sign on Monday. Vanderveer was annoyed at the delay, and had it pointed out to him that it was noon on Saturday and Jesse's secretary had other work to do. He got up stiffly and Jesse escorted him out. In the front office he said, "Say, one o'clock on Monday, we'll have it ready for you to sign."

"If that's the best you can do," said Vanderveer sourly.

The young woman spoke up placatingly. "I can't take a day off to drive you, Papa. Mr. Klein's expecting some important calls on Monday—you could take the bus."

Vanderveer said grudgingly, "Will say you're a conscientious gal—'s right, when you're working for a man, got to give full value." He gave Jesse a rather baleful stare. "The damn D.M.V. took away my license last month—said I couldn't pass the eye test. Damn nuisance—been driving sixty years without any trouble. All right. Monday." He stalked out, the young woman pattering after him, and Jesse went back to his desk to start drafting the simple will. People did come all sorts; but Mr. Vanderveer struck him as the prototype of the fellow of whom it was said, if he couldn't take it with him he wasn't going. Except that that was beyond the control of a mere mortal.

Vanderveer came in that Monday, read over the formal phrases carefully, and carefully signed the will in the large childish scrawl of the uneducated men unaccustomed to penmanship—Jan Willem Vanderveer. Jesse said routinely, "It ought to go in your safe-deposit box, if you have one—or if you prefer you can leave it with me."

Vanderveer ruminated. "I suppose you might as well keep it," he said. "Less trouble. All right." He handed the pages back and stood up.

Jesse had never seen the man again after he shuffled out of the office that day. And a good deal of water had flowed under the bridge since then. He and Nell had been married, and eighteen months ago David Andrew had been born. They had met that old reprobate Edgar Walters, who had died last year and left Jesse quite a respectable amount of money. And Nell had found the sprawling old house on an acre of ground up Coldwater Canyon Drive, and had been amusing herself remodeling and redecorating. These days Jesse was established in the new, larger office in the new building on Wilshire Boulevard, and pampered by his extremely efficient twin secretaries, Jean and Jimmy (Jamesina) Gordon. Clients and cases had come and gone, some dull and some interesting, and in his office safe reposed the wills of a few other clients who preferred the lawyer to have custody; and the name of Jan Vanderveer had faded from his mind.

Until last Monday when Jean had briefed him on the various appointments for the coming week and mentioned it. "The earliest I could fit him in was at three on Friday, there's that divorce hearing, and the Saunders' damage suit—you'll probably be in court on that up to Thursday."

"Vanderveer," said Jesse reflectively.

"He wouldn't say what it was about."

Jesse vaguely remembered the old fellow, wondering if it was the same one, and forgot about it. As he had expected, they had to postpone the court date on the Lenhoff divorce—Lenhoff's attorney was being sticky about the settlement. He was pleasantly surprised when the damage suit went to the jury early on Thursday afternoon—he had rather expected it to trail over into Friday.

As it was, he found himself at loose ends after lunch on Friday, with only one appointment—another client who wanted a divorce— at four-thirty, after Vanderveer. He was studying the latest counteroffer of Lenhoff's attorney—dammit, the man was worth five or six million, and Rose Lenhoff had put up with his drinking, womanizing, and physical abuse for twenty years, he wasn't going to fob her off with token alimony if Jesse could help it—when William DeWitt came in. He looked wet and annoyed. Southern California was evidently going to have another early wet year; at the end of October the second rainstorm had arrived yesterday, and it was drizzling again today. DeWitt, as tall and dark and lean as Jesse, divested himself of his raincoat and dumped an account book on Jesse's desk.

"Go through the motions," said Jesse, eying it. "There's never anything in it, William. Very modest little operation, yours is."

"Have to abide by the law," said DeWitt grumpily. He had finally severed professional connections with the Parapsychology Foundation and formed his own psychic research association; with some personal wealth and a few solid backers, he was happily engaged in, as he put it, redoing the basic research of a hundred

years ago, with a couple of fairly gifted psychics; and Jesse had
taken on the official job of treasurer. To maintain nonprofit status,
the financial reports had to be made, but there was little work to
it, the sums involved minuscule. Jesse shoved the account book to
one side of his desk, and DeWitt sat down and lit a cigarette.

"People," he said. "People! I have had it with this Finch
woman. Dammit, I'm sorry for her, but why do these people have
to come wasting our time? Well, I can't say that exactly—"

"What about her?" asked Jesse. "You haven't mentioned that
one before."

"That's right, she only showed up about three weeks back. Yesterday was her third session with Cora—no, fourth." Cora Delaney
was one of the psychics working with him. "And an intelligent
woman, too—she's a lawyer in Santa Monica—but the absolute ma-
terialist. She's lost a daughter—only child, girl in the teens, hit-run
by a drunk driver—and she's divorced, alone, it hit her hard.
She—"

"Wants some communication, proof the daughter's still there
somewhere. Haven't any of your tame psychics brought anything
through?"

"Dammit, it's never one hundred percent evidential—or seldom,
as we both know. But both Cora and Wanda have given her some
good solid stuff, better than you often get. An unusual pet name,
childhood memories, a couple of dogs they'd had—what I'd call
pretty evidential. And the damn woman—first she's in floods of
tears, darling Lottie, and next minute it's no, I can't believe it, it's
just telepathy, she's reading my mind—"

"People," said Jesse. "As if telepathy was all that common or
easy. Makes you tired."

"At least we've got the records for the files," said DeWitt. "But
it's annoying. Puts the medium off some. I brought along the transcript of yesterday's session, in case you're interested—really quite
evidential when you analyze it—" He brought out an untidy bundle
of typescript. Miss Duffy's copy from the tapes was impeccable,
but DeWitt would cram it into his pockets instead of a briefcase.
Jesse eyed it dubiously and said he'd look it over when he had
time.

After half an hour or so DeWitt said he had an appointment
with a psychologist at UCLA, and reluctantly took himself off into

the rain. Jesse looked over those figures again, told Jean to get him Lenhoff's attorney, and spent forty minutes arguing with him, getting a few grudging concessions. When he put the phone down he glanced at the clock; it was twenty past three. He got up and looked out into the front office.

"Didn't we have somebody coming in at three?"

"Mr. Vanderveer," said Jimmy. "I wish people would be punctual—it throws all the routine out."

Jesse sat thinking about the Lenhoff settlement, and an unspecified time later Jean looked in and said, "He hasn't shown up yet. Should I call to remind him?"

"Who?" asked Jesse.

"Mr. Vanderveer," said Jean patiently. "It's a quarter of four, and sometimes people do forget appointments."

"Oh—yes, you'd better, I suppose," said Jesse absently.

She went away, and past the open door he heard her on the phone. Presently her voice went up in excitement. "Oh, yes, sir. Yes, sir, I see. . . . It's Mr. J. D. Falkenstein, Wilshire Boulevard, and of course— Oh, yes, sir, I'll tell him. . . . Jimmy! You'll never guess—" They both appeared at the office door, and Jean said, "Oh, Mr. Falkenstein—he's been murdered! That Mr. Vanderveer. That was a police officer answered the phone, and he said Mr. Vanderveer had been killed yesterday, and the police will want to talk to you. Of all things!"

"Well, I'll be damned," said Jesse mildly. But of course the crime rate was up, and a lot of innocent citizens were getting killed these days, with the violent ones running around loose. At that moment he wasn't greatly concerned over the murder; what entered his mind was that will. "It was Jan Vanderveer? Jan Willem?"

"Yes, that was the name—"

"And when he made the appointment, he didn't say why he wanted to see me? Well, I don't suppose it matters now. But dammit, it'll be some more paper work. We've got his will on file. I'll have to see the family, set up a date with the IRS and so forth, get the thing into probate." He felt the first stirrings of curiosity as to how the old man had gotten himself killed. "Murder?"

"That's what the officer said."

"Be damned," said Jesse again.

There wasn't anything more he could do on the Lenhoff thing today; he'd have to talk to Rose Lenhoff tomorrow, or, no, Monday, see how she felt about the latest offer. He had three divorce hearings set for next week, and there should be a court date set for that other damage suit, the Osborne thing, any day—that was going to occupy some time. It couldn't be helped. He could probably get some information about Vanderveer from Clock. He looked at his watch and decided he might as well go home, and left the Gordons chattering about the murder.

The new house was on a street called Paradise Lane, up Coldwater Canyon, and it was farther to drive from his office. The street was isolated, with only two other houses on it a distance away from the big old two-story house at the dead end. The house was on an acre of ground, with a chain-link fence all around it; Nell, expecting him home, had left the gate open, which meant that Athelstane was in. Jesse drove through the gate, got out and shut it, parked the Mercedes in the garage next to Nell's, and went in the back door to the generous old-fashioned service porch.

David Andrew, having mastered the art of walking six months ago, these days usually proceeded at a run; he came pounding across the kitchen excitedly. "Daddy! Kitten!" He hurled himself at Jesse. "Kitten!"

"Oh, my Lord, not now, Davy. Later." Of all the nursery rhymes Nell recited and sang to him, David Andrew had seized upon the three little kittens and their mittens as his all-time favorite and demanded repetition endlessly.

Nell straightened from the kitchen table and came to kiss him, his lovely Nell with her bright brown hair in its usual fat chignon on her neck, her cheeks a little flushed from the oven heat. "For once," she said, "he's not talking about those kittens. You'll never believe it, Jesse, but I've discovered Athelstane's secret."

They had moved in a month ago, and it was only last weekend that Jesse had finished shelving all the books and stereo records. Gradually they were settling in, and Nell had nearly stopped changing furniture around in the living room.

At first, when Athelstane, the mastiff, had taken to vanishing for hours at a time, they had supposed he was simply investigating his new domain. There was lawn and shrubbery at the front of the house, a good-sized covered patio, and a little more lawn at the back; but a good half acre there had been left wild, with a tall old stand of eucalyptus trees, a place any dog might spend time investigating. But Athelstane was a people-oriented dog, and when he continued to disappear for most of every afternoon, they had begun to be curious.

This afternoon it hadn't started raining until about one-thirty, and Nell had gone out after lunch, while Davy napped, to plant some bulbs she'd brought home yesterday. She was on her knees, working assiduously with a trowel, at the edge of the eucalyptus grove, when in the silence up here on the hill away from the city she heard Athelstane grunting. When Athelstane was feeling particularly happy and contented, he emitted soft little whuffles; and somewhere there in among the trees he was telling the world he was happy. Amused, Nell got up stealthily and began tracking him. Stepping softly, she followed the whuffles in the tall underbrush; and when she spotted him, for a moment she didn't believe what she saw.

Athelstane, for all his huge size and heft, was something of a retiring personality. He was scared to death of the Clocks' black Peke, Sally; he had never been on terms of friendship with another dog. But here he was now—Nell peered incredulously—uttering little pleased rumblings, and lovingly licking something between his enormous front paws. The brush was thick; Nell stepped closer, wondering if he could have caught and killed something—there'd be gophers up here, mice—and then suddenly she burst out laughing.

Athelstane had evidently made a friend. The object between his paws was, incredibly, a cat—by the glimpse she had, a Siamese cat, blissfully snuggled up against the great brindle chest. At her burst of laughter, the cat leaped convulsively and shot away under the trees, and Athelstane looked aggrieved.

"The big baby," said Nell now, telling Jesse about it. "You can't imagine how funny it looked. Quite a handsome Siamese from the little look I had, it must belong to someone around, one of the houses down the hill." Athelstane had pressed up to welcome Jesse, who pulled his ears fondly.

"Never know what the monster'll think of next. Queer, all right."

"Kittens!" said Davy insistently. "Fee kittens." He tugged at Jesse's trousers.

"Later on, Davy. Before bed."

"We've got time for a leisurely drink before dinner, after I get him to bed," said Nell. "Come on, big boy."

They had the leisurely drink, and dinner, and it was eight-thirty when Jesse settled at the desk in his study and picked up the phone. Just as he'd promised himself, in this house there was a comfortable chair beside every phone. He leaned back comfortably in the high-backed desk chair and dialed, and in a moment his little sister Fran answered.

"So you're feeling better?" asked Jesse.

"I'm always all right by evening," said Fran crossly. "It's the damned morning sickness—everybody says I should have been over it months ago, but the doctor says it's just my metabolism or something and not to worry. So easy for him to say. The longer this goes on, the more I'm thinking this is going to be an only child."

Jesse laughed. "Wait till it's here."

"I can hardly wait. Two more months to go! And I look worse than I feel." Of course Fran was normally svelte and slim and fashionable, and she didn't appreciate maternity clothes.

"Is Andrew home?"

"I'll get him." And a minute later the deep rough voice of Sergeant Clock, LAPD, Hollywood Precinct, replaced hers.

"That damn doctor," it said. "I'm worried about Fran, Jesse. She's feeling like hell, this damned morning sickness or whatever, and that doctor—"

"Now, Andrew. He's supposed to be one of the best around, I suppose he knows what he's doing. Preserve patience and keep the fingers firmly crossed. I want to know something about a homicide. It's your beat"—the Vanderveer address was Kingsley Drive—"so you probably know something about it. One Jan Vanderveer."

"Oh, that," said Clock. "What's your interest?"

"He had an appointment with me this afternoon. I don't know what was on his mind—I'd only seen him once, years ago, made a will for him. When he didn't show, Jean called, and found the fuzz in possession."

"Oh," said Clock. "Well, I'm on it, yes—Petrovsky and I got

called right at the end of shift yesterday. The daughter came home from work and found them—both Vanderveer and his wife dead. It looks like a run-of-the-mill thing—and that's the hell of a comment on modern city life, but there it is. There doesn't seem to have been a break-in, but I suppose the old man could have opened the door, and he or they just bulled their way in. Right now I'm betting it was juveniles, maybe a pair."

"Why?"

"There wasn't any ransacking of drawers and so on. The lab's still poking around dusting for prints, something may show. Of course the daughter was pretty shocked and shook up, but we asked her to look around for anything missing and she didn't come up with anything. My bet is that it was juveniles, maybe with petty records or no records, and they panicked and ran when they realized what they'd done. It has that kind of smell."

"How were they killed?"

"Banged around and beat up—we won't see autopsy reports for a while, but that was obvious. And I don't suppose it would have taken much, they were both elderly and frail. Kind of thing that could happen without intention. The old woman was evidently partly crippled, she used a walker. She'd been knocked away from it against a wall. It looked as if he might have tried to put up a fight. The poker out of the fireplace set was alongside him with blood on it—maybe he grabbed it up and somebody got it away from him, or when he tried to put up resistance they, whoever, went for it as a weapon. There were things around could have been hocked for a little loot—portable TV, typewriter, but none of it was missing."

"Yes, I see," said Jesse. "And I suppose not a hope in hell of any leads on it."

"All up in the air. That's a working-class neighborhood, not many people at home during the day, and it was raining like hell most of yesterday. We'll go through the motions, but it'll probably end up in Pending."

"The hell of a thing all right," agreed Jesse. "But what I'm really calling about—I'll have to get in touch with this daughter. Immediate family. Find out about his bank, start the red tape. Do you know if the daughter—"

"Well, she was all shook up, naturally," said Clock. "We got a policewoman up, and she called some relative for her—a sister, I think—and then a Mrs. Griffin showed up and took her off. I meant to talk to her sometime today, but we had a gang rumble go down at Hollywood High—just a second, I've got both addresses in my notebook." There was a hiatus. "Lessee—the Griffin woman lives in West Hollywood, Harratt Street. The sister's Marcia Coleman, it's an address in Claremont. Mrs. Charles Coleman."

"O.K., thanks. I think you're supposed to be coming to dinner some night next week, if Fran feels up to it."

"I tell you, I don't like it at all, she's seven months along and she shouldn't—" Jesse heard Fran in the background sounding annoyed; and then she came back on the line and said, "If you're finished with Andrew I want to talk to Nell."

"All right." Jesse put the phone down and called Nell, who said she'd take it on the kitchen extension.

While he waited for the girls to finish chatting, he slid farther down in the desk chair and reflected, the hell of a thing indeed. Inoffensive old people peacefully in their own home, set on suddenly by the violent ones. Killed for nothing and no reason—and that could have been the juveniles, not yet quite hardened enough to go on and rob when they saw they had done murder. A very elderly couple indeed, they'd have been—Vanderveer had probably been in his mid-seventies those years ago.

And the odds were, no leads on who had done it. And he thought, Kingsley Drive—a very plebeian address. The chances were the old man hadn't had much; it would be a piddling little estate to settle, just the red tape and paper work.

When the phone finally hummed blankly at him, he dialed the number in West Hollywood, explained. The voice on the other end was high and girlish. "Oh, what did you say your name— Are you police, or— Oh, the *lawyer!* Oh, yes. Isn't it the most dreadful, dreadful thing—I just couldn't believe it, but the awful things that happen nowadays—when Marcia called, I just couldn't take it in—I went *right down*—that police station on Fountain Avenue, you know—of course it would take Marcia nearly two hours to drive up—but she and Charles *came,* of course, but of course they took Dulcie back with them—the house—the police were there, and Dulcie said there was blood—oh, it's just too dreadful— What? Oh,

I'm actually not a relative, just an old friend, my husband and Johnny Vanderveer were partners and of course—"

Jesse got away from her at last and called the Claremont number. Here he got a very different female, who sounded tired but crisply efficient. Mrs. Marcia Coleman. She also sounded surprised. "Oh, yes," she said. "You said Falkenstein? But I don't— how did you know? There isn't anything in the papers—" Jesse explained about the appointment, and she said, "Papa had an appointment—I don't understand. It's very odd you should call just now, you know, because it wasn't half an hour ago that Dulcie remembered Papa had made a will, but she couldn't remember your name."

"I'll want to see both of you, Mrs. Coleman, when it's convenient. We'll have to sort out the estate, start probate. There's no special hurry, I realize you're both upset— Do you know if your father kept a safe-deposit box?"

"Yes, probably. He must have, of course. He banked at Security-Pacific, I'm not sure which branch."

"I'll have to set up a date with the IRS, you see. I know this seems like an intrusion at such a time, but—"

"But," said Marcia Coleman dryly, "life goes on and the red tape has to get tied up. Yes. I understand that."

"Your sister would know definitely which bank?"

"Mr. Falkenstein," she said, "I'm not going to wake her up to ask her now. She's been through a very bad time for the last year or so, and she's exhausted—the shock of finding Mama and Papa murdered was just enough to put her right over the edge. I got my doctor to prescribe some sleeping capsules for her today, and she's knocked out. The police want to talk to her too, naturally, but it'll just have to wait. Maybe Monday we can come to your office."

He didn't know offhand what appointments he had on Monday; if there was a conflict one of the Gordons would have to sweet-talk another client. He agreed to a suggested two o'clock meeting, and she thanked him and rang off briskly.

When they came into his office at two o'clock on Monday afternoon, he thought at first glance that they were very unlike to be sisters; and then he realized that they were alike—it was the contrast of clothes and manner that differentiated them. Marcia Coleman looked to be in her mid-thirties, and was neatly and smartly dressed in a well-cut navy suit with an ivory tailored blouse. Her dark brown hair was smoothly, smartly cut, her makeup discreet; she was a good-looking woman, with regular features, intelligent blue eyes, a generous mouth. Her sister might be a few years older, and she had the same regular features, small straight nose, brown hair, and blue eyes; but she was plumper, and gracelessly dressed in a dowdy-looking beige knit dress, low-heeled oxfords, a too-large camel's-hair coat. She said correctly, "How do you do," in a dull voice, and obediently took the chair indicated. Marcia Coleman sat down beside her.

"We'd better get right to business," she told Jesse. "But I'm afraid neither of us can be much help to you. We don't know at all what Papa had, how much, or what it was in—except for the houses he owned. But I expect you'll find accounts or something in the safe-deposit box."

"He kept an account book at home," said Dulcie. "I've seen it. I don't know where he kept it, though."

"His desk probably," said Marcia. And then, unexpectedly: "Oh, God, it's Mama—to think of that happening to her— And didn't we tell him! Didn't we try to tell him!" She drew a long breath. "Going on living in that neighborhood—but nobody could talk to Papa." She opened her bag, got out a cigarette, and lit it before he could reach for his lighter. "Oh, I suppose you think it sounds pretty cold and crude, Mr. Falkenstein, but Papa—he just wasn't a man anybody could be fond of, he didn't—"

"Except Uncle Howie," said Dulcie.

"Oh—" Marcia shrugged. "Yes, of course, but they'd known each other so long, they'd been young together."

Dulcie looked at her and a large tear slowly slid down one cheek; she got out a handkerchief and wiped it away. "Oh, Marcia, it's just—I can't stop thinking about it—how sort of pitiful it was. He aged five years when Uncle Howie died, and ever since then—you know how I've told you it's been, the last couple of months—he just hasn't been himself—Uncle Howie was really the only close friend he ever had—and how he kept saying, we'd be better out of it, your mother and I—and Mama—" She put the handkerchief to her mouth.

"Oh, God, I know," said Marcia.

Dulcie raised her eyes to Jesse's. "I don't know how many times Mama's said to me, I wish I could die and be at rest—but to have it happen—like that—"

"It's no good talking about it, Dulcie. It happened. And, my God, it's a terrible thing to say, Mr. Falkenstein—it's a terrible thing even to think—but at least it is a solution. We'd been feeling rather desperate—and after that awful row a week ago Saturday, the things Charles said to Papa—of course just the plain truth—I've had nightmares about it." She fumbled for another cigarette; she'd stabbed the first one out half-smoked; this time Jesse held his lighter for her.

"It wasn't anybody's fault," said Dulcie tiredly. "Just how Papa was."

"That sums it up neatly," said Marcia. "I suppose you think we're pretty—unfilial, if that's the word. That I am, anyway. But another month of it and Dulcie'd have been in the hospital with a nervous breakdown or whatever it's called now. What the situation was, Mr. Falkenstein—Papa must have been a very wealthy man. I don't mean a multimillionaire, but there must be quite a lot of money somewhere. He and Uncle Howie—Howard Griffin—had their own construction company for over thirty-five years, and they bought and sold land, apartment houses, I don't know what all—with the building boom after the Second World War they must have made a lot of money. But Papa never spent a dime more than he had to—he was always tightfisted and of course he just got worse as he got older." She gestured fiercely. "Uncle Howie used to—to kid him about it, but—men!—he never realized how it was for us, and anyway even he couldn't change Papa. He—Uncle Howie, I mean—that's how you can judge it, because they were equal partners until they dissolved the business about fifteen years ago, and retired. Uncle Howie and Aunt Flo had that beautiful house in West Hollywood, and good furniture, and nice cars, and they went out to theaters and—oh, Uncle Howie wasn't extravagant, but they always had nice things and—lived like civilized people. Anybody could tell there was money, big money even. And Papa must have had just as much, maybe more, because I've heard Uncle Howie say Papa was a smarter investor than he was— and what did we have?" She was wound up now, her tone bitter. "Nothing! Even when Dulcie and I were kids, Aunt Flo had a cleaning woman and her own car—and when I think how Mama had to slave—the fuss he made about buying a washing machine! And that house on Kingsley—my God, most of old central Holly-wood running down for years, the crime rate up, but he wouldn't hear of moving. The house was good enough, taxes cheap compared to anywhere else, he had good locks, and what did it matter where you lived?

"You just summed it up, Dulcie—just how Papa was. But it was all his fault, obviously." Marcia drew strongly on her cigarette. "You see, Mr. Falkenstein, they weren't young when they were married—Mama and Papa. Papa'd been married and divorced before. He was forty, and Mama was only a year younger. Papa would have been eighty-two next month. And his parents were old country, and Papa was pretty old country too. Females just for waiting on men, and doing housework. My God, when I wanted to go to college—foolishness for a girl, he'd never gone to high school and he'd gotten on all right—I stood up to him, and when I got my first job I got out. And then when I worked to earn my own way at LACC, and met Charles who was a college *teacher,* you'd have thought I wanted to marry a queer or— But forget about me. It was Dulcie who came in for the brunt of it.

"Papa's arthritis was getting worse all the time—he could hardly get around some days, and he would go on trying to take the bus, too cheap to take a cab, he'd had a couple of bad falls lately. Lucky not to break a hip, I suppose. But Mama—she had her first stroke five years ago, and then another last year, and she had arthritis too, and when Papa found out Medicare wouldn't pay for the therapy, he said she didn't need it. They'd gotten her walking with the walker, but she couldn't do much. Dulcie had it all, you see? She works a regular job, and on top of that she had all the housework and cooking and taking care of Mama—I was no help at all, I'm an hour and a half away on the freeway, Charles is at Pomona College, and we've got four children, fourteen down to six—I've got to be at home. I couldn't help at all. And Mama needing more and more attention—and he couldn't see it—"

"It was just," said Dulcie, "that I had to be up with her so much at night. She couldn't help it. We got the bedside commode for at night, and the last six months I slept in her room, Papa moved into the den—she couldn't help getting me up three or four times a night, she didn't sleep very well."

"And try to talk to him!" said Marcia. "Oh, Dulcie could manage! She always had! They had the visiting nurse coming in—you know that county service—three times a week, to give Mama a bath and a hot lunch, do a little cleaning up—that helped. But it couldn't have gone on—Mama could manage to get to the bathroom, even make a cup of coffee, but she was getting worse, it was obvious that there'd come a time she'd be bedridden—it was just the week before last that that nurse, I forget her name—"

"Mrs. Gibson," said Dulcie. "It was just, you see, I didn't feel it was fair to Mr. Klein. I've worked for Mr. Klein for twenty years, since I was nearly nineteen, and he's been good to me. Sometimes I felt so queer, as if I wasn't all there, if I'd been up a lot with Mama, and I made mistakes in taking phone calls and writing orders—"

"This Mrs. Gibson," said Marcia, "called Dulcie and said we should realize that Mama would have to be in a convalescent home pretty soon, she'd be helpless and need attention around the clock—but Papa simply wouldn't listen. And what could we do? He said those places cost too damn much money and he wasn't going to pay for any such folderols. With Dulcie about to die of exhaustion—and I couldn't do a thing—and we know he had plenty of money to take care of her properly, what's money for except to keep you comfortable, buy necessities? But you just couldn't talk to Papa!"

"I see," said Jesse. "Frustrating."

"Oh, for the Lord's sake, water under the bridge," said Marcia, leaning back. "I'm sorry for the tirade. And it's a terrible way for it to end—but maybe you can see why I said it's a solution. Except for Mama—" She leaned forward to stub out her cigarette.

"I could have managed awhile longer," said Dulcie.

"My darling idiot, you were managing yourself to death. Look, Mr. Falkenstein. Neither of us knows much about what Papa had, or where it was, except that he owned two houses down there, one on Kingsley and one right behind his house, on Winona, and an apartment up on Fountain. He always went to collect those rents himself. The bank's the nearest Security-Pacific on Hollywood Boulevard." She stood up. "And you'll want to go through his desk, look at his account book. The police called this morning to say they were through at the house, and they sent back everything Papa'd had on him—when it happened. We can let you have his keys. You just go ahead and do whatever has to be done. I'm keeping Dulcie with me for a while, and you've got the address."

Jesse verified the safe-deposit box and duly contacted the local IRS office to set up a date for the official opening on the following Thursday afternoon. He had, by then, had a further annoying session with Lenhoff's attorney, and was about to leave the office for a quick lunch before foregathering with an IRS man at the bank when Jimmy put through a phone call.

"Oh, Jesse," said Clock. "I thought it'd be only neighborly to let you know that the D.A.'s office is probably going to charge one of your clients with homicide. At least I suppose you could call her a client."

"For God's sake," said Jesse. "Who the hell are you talking about?"

"Miss Dulcie Vanderveer," said Clock. He sounded irritated. "For once I seem to have been wrong. Some very funny evidence has turned up. I haven't had the definite word yet, but the assistant D.A. I talked it over with bought the case. It's offbeat, but—considering human nature—what you might call persuasive. If they bring the charge, it'll be Murder One, I think."

"My good God in heaven," said Jesse blankly. "What in God's name is the evidence?"

"I'll be happy to discuss it with you," said Clock. "Something very funny, Jesse."

CHAPTER 2

Jesse was still feeling somewhat stunned when he got to the bank; he'd hear what Clock had to say later. The IRS man was waiting for him, a fat middle-aged fellow by the name of Dobson. On Monday, Marcia Coleman had handed over the official little bag containing the effects from Vanderveer's body, including a ring of keys: a Yale house key and the long, narrow, warded key to a safe-deposit box marked 1370. On Monday, Jesse had duly verified the rental of safe-deposit box 1370 at this branch of the Security-Pacific bank and notified them of Vanderveer's death.

He fished the keys out of the little bag now, handed them over to Dobson. A blond woman led them into the vault incuriously.

It was everyday routine to the IRS man. The blonde used her key on the little door, he handed over the other, and she pulled out a good-sized steel box—one of the larger ones available. They took it into one of the cubicles and opened it.

"A very nice little pile," said Dobson five minutes later and opened a notebook and began to write busily, making a list.

Jesse regarded the loot in some fascination. It was a nice pile indeed. There was a fat sheaf of stock certificates, mostly preferred stock, and in respectacle blocks of a hundred, five hundred, a thousand shares—IBM, Sony, General Electric, Southern Pacific, New England Electric, Pacific Telephone, General Telephone, Texaco, Mobil Oil, Royal Dutch Airlines, Toyota— "Beautiful," said Dobson gratefully, making rapid notes.

There were deeds to four pieces of property, two houses on Kingsley Drive, one on Winona Avenue, one on Fountain Avenue. Which said that the property was free of mortgage, clear. There was a marriage certificate dated May of 1940, for Myra Ellis and Jan W. Vanderveer. And that was all; it seemed to be enough.

"I'll have to get current quotes on the stock," said Dobson, "but I'd estimate it as at least upwards of a million at current prices. All such very solid stuff, blue-chip, it'd have been paying very well."

"In spades," said Jesse. He shouldn't be feeling surprised about Vanderveer; that kind of careful, shrewd old fellow, the sort who did amass the money—and now and then got murdered for it. Dobson made copious notes, gave Jesse a copy of the list of contents, and an official release of the box to the estate. They proceeded upstairs to see the bank manager and request a look at Vanderveer's current account. The manager was a friendly-faced middle-aged man named Olderson, cooperative and amiable. This kind of thing was routine to him too: bank patrons died every day. He offered them cigarettes, then got on the phone to the chief teller.

Jesse reflected that at least he had put a clause in that will making Dulcie Vanderveer the residual legatee if the mother predeceased her— Dulcie. He conjured up the plump little figure with the oddly innocent eyes, feeling incredulous. But the most unexpected things did happen; and Clock knew all about the rules of evidence.

The chief teller was a sedate man of about fifty, rotund and bland and bald; his name was Parker. He acknowledged introductions with a nod and laid a manila folder on Olderson's desk.

"I hope this wasn't too much trouble," said Olderson pleasantly, meaninglessly.

Parker leaned on the desk and brought out a cigarette, eying Jesse and Dobson thoughtfully. "Oh, no, it's a very simple account. Always has been. Old Vanderveer's dead, is he?" He looked at the cigarette. "Natural causes, as they say?"

"As a matter of fact, no," said Jesse.

"Is that so? I'm not asking any questions," said Parker equably. "But—well, have a look at that latest statement, and I'll tell you something." It looked like a simple account indeed; there were just the latest posted figures here. Vanderveer had had only a checking account, and at the moment there was slightly under three thousand dollars in it. In the last month—they were coming up to the first of November—there had been just three checks written on it, in the sums of $67.10, $19.47, and $17.40.

"Yes?" said Jesse. "You've got something to tell us about the account?"

Parker blew out a thin stream of smoke. "I don't know if it means anything, but—well, I've been chief teller here for fourteen years. We've got a lot of customers, and the average account just gets posted and recorded automatically, nothing to notice, if you take me. But I could tell you something, not so much about the account, but the old man. Vanderveer used to deal in quite large sums of cash—you see, the girls would have to come to me for verification, pay out that much—or take in that much, come to that. I've known him to come in here and hand over ten, twenty, thirty thousand for a cashier's check."

"You don't say," said Dobson interestedly. Olderson sat up with a jerk.

"My God, man—did he ever offer any explanation, or—"

"Well, look," said Parker, "it was unusual, but what could I say to him? The first couple of times I said to him that walking around with that much cash wasn't very safe, and he snapped my head off—it was his own money and he'd handle it any way he damn well pleased." Parker shrugged. "It was his business—but naturally I wondered. He'd bring in dividend checks, other checks, and take cash—quite sizable amounts. Walk out of here with a couple of thousand on him in twenties. I just thought," said Parker cynically, "it could be he was one of those types—you read about one in the paper every so often—found dead of starvation or something, with a hundred grand in a suitcase in the closet."

"I will be goddamned," said Dobson avidly. Jesse surmised that Vanderveer's record with the IRS would be examined with a fine-tooth comb.

"You remember the last time anything like that happened?" he asked.

"Oh, I couldn't say exactly, it'll show in the accounts, but sometime back in the spring he bought a cashier's check for something like thirty grand, and paid for it in cash."

"My God," said Dobson, scribbling.

"Had he banked here long?" asked Jesse.

"Before my time," said Parker. "Probably. He had a big loan with us too, the records came through on his statement every month. I don't know anything about that."

Who did know was one of the officers in the loan department, Peter J. Metcalf. He was a spare elderly man with the banker's proverbial gimlet eye, and at his word a pretty, dark secretary conjured up the records in short order.

The loan had been applied for and granted seven years back, and it amounted to just under a million dollars at the time. "Probably appreciated in value since," said Metcalf, "the property that is—in that location, Trousdale Estates." The property consisted of a twelve-unit apartment building in that very exclusive area, and Vanderveer had put down a tenth of the purchase price, getting the rest from the bank. The entire profit was applied to the loan monthly; the bank was handling it as a routine matter, billing for rents and paying the taxes, maintenance, and so on. "Of course it made a useful tax shelter," said Metcalf, eying the figures. "Interest and depreciation, et cetera. The principal wouldn't have been paid off for another twenty years, but meanwhile it was money in his pocket."

Dobson went off with a notebook full of figures. And Jesse should sometime see the officers of the trust department here, about that will; but until he knew exactly what was going to happen about that will, there wasn't much point.

It was four o'clock when he found a slot in a public lot up on Fountain and walked back to the new precinct station.

And his head was still full of figures—the monthly net take on that apartment house was fourteen thousand bucks; the house property in Hollywood would bring in a more modest return, he'd have to investigate that too, but together with those very solid dividends which would have been coming in from all that blue-chip preferred stock— A very cute old fellow, Jan Vanderveer, and Jesse could appreciate how Dulcie and Marcia had felt. Such a lot of nice money, and the old boy too tightfisted to hire a practical nurse or pay for his wife's care in a decent rest home. Well, they hadn't known how much he had, just that it was probably a tidy bundle; and so it was. That stock—Jesse didn't follow the market, and it had been up and down for the last year or so, but still—that kind of stock—

Where moth and rust doth corrupt, he thought, going in past the desk sergeant. Indeed, what was it but a medium of exchange? Hoarded for its own sake, it was meaningless, you could say; he thought of Marcia Coleman saying, what's money for?

What indeed, he thought ruefully. They had spent quite a lot of money, the money the old man had left, on Nell's house up on the hill; Jesse would rather have old Edgar back; but he knew how old Edgar would feel—money was to enjoy and use.

The big communal detective office at the rear of the precinct station, overlooking the parking lot, was starkly lighted with overhead fluorescent strip lighting. It was at the moment nearly empty; only Clock and Detective Petrovsky were there, heads together over a report.

"Well, I expected to see you sooner," said Clock.

Jesse pulled up a chair from a nearby desk and sat down. "I had an appointment with the Gestapo. But now suppose you give me chapter and verse on your funny story." He lit a cigarette and leaned back.

"It is a sort of queer one at that," said Petrovsky. His shortish rotund sandiness was in direct contrast to Clock, whose broad figure filled the desk chair. "But it hangs together, Mr. Falkenstein."

Clock passed a hand over his prognathous jaw and said, "You can say so." He looked annoyed. "Damnation, it looked like random violence—God knows we see enough of it—until a few funny things showed up. All right, you want to hear the evidence, it's easy to read. We talked to both the daughters at the time—Saturday, wasn't it, Pete?—not at length, but enough to get the picture. The unmarried one, Dulcie, was in a difficult spot, the mother to take care of, working a regular job, the old lady getting more helpless. That was just background, because of course at the time it looked like the possible juveniles, the random thing. But—"

"Yes," said Jesse, "and all the more frustrating because Vanderveer could have afforded the best hired help. He was loaded."

"Oh?" said Clock interestedly. "And everything left to the family?"

Jesse gave him a mirthless grin. "Depending on your evidence, I suppose the D.A.'ll be pleased to hear that most of it goes to Dulcie. And it won't impress you that I doubt very much if she knows it. What, for God's sake, have you turned up to tie her in?"

Clock said, "You don't say." He took up a large manila envelope centered on his desk and reached into it. "I've just got this packaged up to send to the D.A.'s office, don't suppose there's any harm in your seeing it. The first thing that showed—the lab men were still at the house poking around, you know what a hell of a time they take—was this." He handed it to Jesse. It was a small sheet of cheap stationery, with one typed line roughly in its center: *We are better out of it.* Jesse cocked his head at it. "The paper's from a box in Dulcie's room, and it was typed on her portable typewriter there. The note was under the grate in the fireplace. You know, that was a cold rainy day, and there'd been a fire lit there. It looks as if she thought it'd be burned, but it drifted under the grate and wasn't. But that's getting ahead of the evidence. When we got the autopsy reports, we did some rethinking. What it comes down to—usual bunch of six-syllable words—they'd both had an O.D. of the old lady's pain-killer prescription. It's some stuff called Ban Cap codeine capsules—the doctor prescribed it for her arthritis. The prescription had been renewed four days before the murder, so there was plenty available. Dulcie had gotten it refilled the previous Monday, at a pharmacy on Fountain. Both the old people had had a hot drink—eggnog for the old lady, cup of coffee for him—the glass and cup were still there, and used utensils in the kitchen, eggbeater, spoon, saucepan. The lab found traces of the stuff on everything. Both drinks had been laced with enough to kill. As a matter of fact that's what the old lady died of. Him, no. But you know, Jesse, we might have bought it, she might have gotten away with it. There was a little suggestion that the old man had thought of suicide. That pharmacist—sometimes Vanderveer got the prescription refilled, and the pharmacist said he'd heard him say people could live too long and they'd be better out of it at his age. This Griffin, Vanderveer's oldest friend, had just died in a convalescent home a couple of months ago, and apparently Vanderveer missed him, had been hit hard by that—he used to visit him every day. Of course it says nothing that Dulcie's prints were on the eggnog glass—she was doing the housework—but for what it's worth there they are, one good one, one not so good."

"Now really, Andrew—you're calling this evidence?"

"Just some. You see, we've got her placed there," said Clock. "She usually left home for work about eight-fifteen, got home a little after five-thirty. But that day she was seen to come home about ten-thirty in the morning. She works for a Bernard Klein, office down on North Spring, he's a salesman of some kind and it's a one-girl office. He's in and out, and he was going to be out most of that day, and she knew that. The other office people on that floor don't mingle—nobody would miss her. It was a dark rainy day, and a lot of people on that block on Kingsley would be at work—the Vanderveers didn't neighbor with anybody there, it isn't that kind of neighborhood. The chances were she wouldn't be noticed at all—but she was, just by a fluke. There's an apartment building next to the Vanderveer house, and this old fellow Richard Eberhart lives in the rear ground-floor unit on that side, his back door overlooks the Vanderveer drive. He says he saw her drive into the garage about ten-thirty that morning—swears he recognized her and her car."

"You can see how it was supposed to look," said Petrovsky. "She comes home with some excuse of Klein giving her the day off, and neither of the old folks pay any attention to what she's doing—she fixes the eggnog and coffee, slips in the overdose, and types out the suicide note. Intending to leave it propped up somewhere, and go back downtown, find the bodies when she comes home at the usual time. Only the old man must have realized what she was up to, maybe got a look at that note—and there was a struggle, and she snatched up the poker and hit him. The old lady"—Petrovsky sniffed thoughtfully—"from the photos we can deduce she was in the bedroom—where the eggnog glass was— maybe she heard the fight, was coming to see what was going on, and either fell from the walker and knocked herself out against the table or the girl knocked her down too. They both had O-type blood, which was on the poker. But she died of the O.D., anywhere between one and four. He died right then of a skull fracture. Call it eleven A.M."

"And," said Clock, "seeing the suicide setup was ruined, she threw the note in the fire and ran. Hoping, probably, that we'd put it down to the daylight burglar—but I'm inclined to think that by then she was pretty well unnerved, which would be understandable, or she'd have at least tried to fake a break-in. As it was, she just panicked."

"Now I will be damned," said Jesse. "It hangs together—but queer all the same, Andrew. No prints on the poker, I suppose."

"Not a hope."

"No, but that prim little soul—don't tell me, murderers don't conform to any type. And human nature, yes—what the sister said —maybe she wasn't altogether responsible. Tired out, going without sleep, not seeing any way out of the tangle—and resenting the old man's attitude, also understandable. Naturally. The girls both seemed fond of the mother, but not of him. With good reason. And—another thing she said—mother wishing she could die and be at rest— It could all have boiled up in her overnight, and she saw how it could be set up—not in her right mind, maybe. A psychiatrist might say—"

Clock laughed. "Is that the defense you'd put to a judge?"

"Not much criminal practice," said Jesse, brooding over his steepled hands. "I don't know if I'd take on the job of defending her, Andrew. But I can see that happening all right. A damnable thing. And what has she got to say about it? Have you questioned her since all this showed?"

"No," said Clock. "We just got the autopsy reports yesterday morning, and kicked it around with the lieutenant, and went out looking around Klein's office—"

"We heard Eberhart's story on Tuesday," said Petrovsky, "but it didn't seem important until we heard about the times of death. We'd been out asking any neighbors at home if they'd noticed anybody at the house that Thursday, naturally—drew a blank until we got to Eberhart."

"We'll be talking to her to get some answers," said Clock. "I'm bringing her in tomorrow morning. And you never know—she might come apart and admit it right off the bat. But I think the D.A.'s office has more or less decided to bring a charge. It might be Murder Two, of course."

Jesse drove home feeling sad and also uneasy. Thinking of those two women in his office last Monday—Dulcie's reactions just what anybody might expect, perfectly natural— But he didn't know the woman, after all; and most women were born natural actors. But she hadn't struck him as a very complicated woman— of course it hadn't been a very complicated crime. And it could be, as Clock said, that confronted with the evidence, she'd admit it readily. Didn't know what she was doing—or claiming a mercy killing. Human nature, he thought. And that shrewd single-minded

old man, supremely unconscious of his narrow despotism, bringing
it on himself—

He was late. Nell had just gotten the baby to bed; and it was
cool enough for a fire in the living-room fireplace. They had a leisurely drink before dinner, and Athelstane leaned his bulk on
Jesse's legs and had his ears fondled. "He was out there all afternoon again," said Nell amusedly. "I think he's fallen in love with
that cat—it's too absurd." Jesse agreed absently, and she cocked
her head at him. "You're worried about something, or just mulling
over a case?"

"Just brooding on human nature." He told her about Vanderveer, and she was horrified.

"But what an awful thing, Jesse—the poor woman—"

"Yes, you can see how it could have happened, in a way. Without excusing her. And dammit, even if she's convicted on a lesser
charge, second or third degree, nobody can profit by a crime—
there may be some litigation over the old man's loot. Marcia
Coleman would have to get that will set aside as the next blood
relative. It's a hell of a thing all right."

He had two divorce hearings on Friday morning, but both were
straightforward and brief; he was out of court by noon, and back
at the office by one-thirty. Fifteen minutes after he came in,
Jimmy put through a call, and it was Marcia Coleman. Her voice
was frantic, with overtones of panic.

"—got to see you, I never in my life expected anything so wild
as this—the police think *Dulcie* had something to do with it—stupid
cops—but she ought to have a lawyer—and Charles says—I don't
believe this, but—Charles said to—"

Jesse was just about to start drafting a new will for an old client, but he hadn't any appointments the rest of the day, and
agreed to see them. They landed there hardly an hour later; whoever was driving must have broken some speed laws on the freeway.

Charles Coleman shook hands formally and said with a forced
smile, "Shall we say a family crisis seemed to warrant canceling
my afternoon classes." He was a tall fair man with a quiet voice, a
quiet manner; his eyes were watchful.

"But it's just wild!" Marcia burst out. "I don't believe it—sending a police car, they kept her there all morning—those stupid cops —when she told me what they said, what they asked—"

"Marcia," said Coleman, and she subsided. "I must say we can't understand this at all, Mr. Falkenstein. This is supposed to be a competent police force, I shouldn't think they would act without evidence."

"No," said Jesse. He got them to sit down, offered cigarettes. He opened his mouth to tell them something about the evidence, but Dulcie, silent until then, forestalled him. She was looking more animated than he had seen her before, with color in her cheeks, and her voice was fuller and stronger.

"Mr. Falkenstein," she said, "I just want to say that they're wrong. I couldn't take it in at first, what they were talking about, why they were asking me all that—but when I realized what they were thinking, I was just so surprised. Not even frightened—just surprised. How could anyone think such a thing? That I could ever do a thing like that? I just don't understand it. But that big officer kept asking the same things over and over, and he kept saying, clear evidence—they asked all sorts of queer things, about my learning to type, and Mama's prescription—"

"Yes," said Jesse. He sat down in his desk chair. "You'd better hear about the evidence—I've talked with the sergeant." He told them about the autopsy reports, the fake suicide note, Eberhart. Against his expectations, it was Marcia who began to cry and protest incoherently. Coleman just looked wary and more watchful.

And Dulcie just sat and looked at him. She was dressed a little more smartly today, in a dark-blue dress. He hadn't noticed how square her little chin was, or the firmness of her rather wide mouth. And she said, cutting across his voice without apology, "But I didn't do that, Mr. Falkenstein. Believe me, I'd never, never have thought of doing such a thing. Do they think I'm insane, even to think about such a thing?"

Jesse said equably, softly, "That could be a line of defense, Miss Vanderveer."

She thrust her chin at him. "For heaven's sake," she said, "I'd been awfully tired, never enough sleep, but I knew what I was doing all the while! I'm not so crazy or plain wicked as ever to have thought of that. I don't know anything about that note, but I certainly didn't come back home that morning, and I don't know anything about what happened." Her voice was strong and sure and oddly calm.

"What about Eberhart's story, Miss Vanderveer?"

"They kept on and on about that, they told me I'd been seen coming back—they didn't tell me who'd said so, and I'm afraid I was just confused at first, all the questions about different things—those two officers, the big man with the big jaw and the other one, they kept asking the same questions and after a while I began to see what they were thinking, and I was just so surprised. But when they kept saying that, that I'd been seen coming back that morning, all of a sudden I remembered—a couple of days before that, it was Tuesday, I'd forgotten my keys to the office and had to come back. I got all the way downtown, I'd changed handbags the night before, and I had to go back for them. Mr. Klein wasn't coming in that morning, but he'd remember because I mentioned it to him later on. But it wouldn't have been as late as ten-thirty, it'd have been more like nine-thirty when I got back home. I thought maybe whoever it was who said he'd seen me had just confused the days. That could be, couldn't it?"

"Oh," said Jesse. "Did you tell the sergeant about that?"

"I most certainly did, as soon as I remembered it myself," she said sturdily.

"What car do you drive?"

"It's a two-door Ford, tan, it's ten years old." She was sounding indignant now.

"But they can't really think—just this rigmarole—I can't believe anything like this could happen—" Marcia was in a panic.

"It isn't any use to cry about it, Marcia," said Dulcie a little impatiently. Whether fear or righteous anger had animated her, today she was the stronger of the two. And she sounded as if she were telling the flat truth. He wondered how Clock felt about Dulcie now, after hearing her answers. "Mr. Falkenstein," she said, and she flushed deeper and leaned forward. "I don't suppose it's any good my saying it, because anybody can say anything. Papa wasn't at all religious, but Mama'd been brought up in the Presbyterian Church, and she sent us to Sunday school. I haven't been to church in ages, well, I haven't had time—but I'm a Christian. I believe in the Commandments—about doing no murder, and honoring your father and mother. I just couldn't have done—what they seem to think."

Jesse was interested in this woman now; the colorless personality had burgeoned into something more forceful. With animation in her expression, the resemblance between the sisters was more strongly marked. And he thought, indeed, she might always have been the stronger of the two, the one who had for those long years withstood the monotonous daily grind, staying home with the old people. The warm sincerity in her tone was unmistakable.

He said slowly, "Well, this may put a little different complexion on it, you coming up with an explanation of that witness—a possible explanation."

"But all the rest of it," said Coleman. "The autopsy results—that's very odd indeed, isn't it? It makes it look—" He stopped, and Jesse finished the thought for himself: like an inside job. Yes.

"But what can we *do?*" burst out Marcia. "They can't possibly—"

"We wait and see what happens," said Jesse. "All we can do at the moment."

Clock and Fran came to dinner that night. In spite of bulging considerably in the middle, Fran looked her usual pert dark gamine self, and said it hadn't been so bad this morning. Over dinner, with Athelstane scrounging for tidbits, the talk was general; but when Nell and Fran retired to the kitchen, and later upstairs to look at the new bedroom drapes, Jesse asked Clock how he was feeling about Dulcie now.

"I heard about the keys this afternoon."

"Oh, yes," said Clock. He massaged his Neanderthal jaw. "Well, I sent another report to the D.A.'s office. It's something on the other side of the ledger, Jesse, but not all that much. I saw Klein this afternoon, and he said he remembered her mentioning it. Yes, she sounds quite honest and straightforward, but you can't get away from the evidence, you know. The note, the overdose. Who else knew those capsules were there? They weren't social people, seldom had anyone come to the house. Who else knew the old man's phrase, better out of it? Who else could have arranged the overdose so quiet and easy? And we can't shake Eberhart's story. He's absolutely certain of the day, and he's got good reason

—it was his late wife's birthday, he wanted to go and put flowers on her grave, and he kept looking out to see if the rain was letting up. He's sure of the time because he always has a second cup of coffee about ten-thirty, and he was in the kitchen getting it."

Jesse said ruminatively, "There's some evidence that Vanderveer's mind could have been running on suicide, Andrew. One thing that occurs to me—what that visiting nurse said. There was a family row about it, I'd like to hear more about that—they were trying to get across the truth about his wife's condition, persuade him to put her in a rest home. He just wouldn't listen, Marcia said, but he must have taken some of it in. It could have been working away in him, and he decided they'd be better out of it indeed. He could have arranged the overdose just as easily."

Clock made a derisive sound. "Oh, now, Jesse. Coincidences happen but that'd be one hell of a long one. And the same day, nearly the same hour, he inadvertently lets in a violent burglar who bangs them both over the head and then runs off without ransacking the place? And another thing, that note—I talked to Questioned Documents again yesterday, and they say it was typed by a professional. Even touch and no errors. Vanderveer had probably never used a typewriter in his life, but it's how Dulcie earns her living."

"And that, of course, is another thing," said Jesse, but his voice was dissatisfied. "They knew he must have a good bit tucked away, if not how much, and that when he shuffled off they'd get it. But at that, could they be sure? He was a secretive old gent, and funnily enough, I don't think the money had much to do with it. And you'd better hear about that." He told Clock what they'd come across at the bank, and Clock whistled respectfully.

"That would be a dandy extra motive."

"By the way, did somebody say he kept chains on the doors? How did she say she expected to get in that night? She couldn't—no, I'm not thinking straight, of course."

"She told us," said Clock, "that he knew what time she generally got home and unhooked the chain for her—there was a TV program he liked to watch at five-thirty. So she didn't think a thing about it, walked in as usual. Well, of course she couldn't very well hook the chain after herself when she went out after killing him. That's all perfectly natural."

"But—well, of course, yes. But that girl—I really don't think she did it, Andrew."

"For God's sake," said Clock. "You've let the baby face and innocent look convince you?"

"I think she convinced me this afternoon," said Jesse.

"Just tell me who else could have done it, then."

"Yes, that's the difficulty." And about then Fran and Nell came back, and Nell began telling Clock about Athelstane's love affair, and the conversation became general again.

It had drizzled for an hour or two on Friday afternoon, but Saturday was clear and cold; they were in for an early winter. Jesse drove down into Hollywood and started hunting the address on Kingsley. When he found it, he pulled into the empty drive of the Vanderveer house and contemplated the house, the block.

A good many years ago, this part of central Hollywood had been a generally good middle-class area; never anything fancy, but safe and respectable. But it was an old area, and there were houses and apartments scattered around these sixty square blocks that would date fifty and sixty years back. After the war, this whole area had started running down, and the character of the population had changed. Ten years ago most of the residential blocks off the main drags here had been shabby, slatternly, sinking toward something not quite a slum. Where once most of the single houses had been lived in by owners, by then a majority of residents were tenants. Then a change had come, with developers tearing down the oldest places to put up garden apartments, smartening up a block here and there, so that now many streets like Kingsley were a combination of old and new.

This block on Kingsley was one of those. Jan Vanderveer's house must be one of the oldest on the street, a little frame California bungalow with a wide front porch, a narrow drive made of twin strips of cement with grass between, an old single garage with old-fashioned double doors. It could have stood a coat of paint; its once white walls were faded to a grayish tone. It probably dated from the twenties.

On the right of it as Jesse faced it was another single house only slightly newer; it was a cracker box of a pseudo-Spanish stucco, with no front porch at all. To the left of the Vanderveer house was a garishly modern small apartment building, its stucco painted bright yellow with brown trim. It was built in two wings running front to back, with a walk and strips of lawn down the middle, and a driveway adjoining this one. Jesse measured it mentally and decided that each wing might contain eight apartments, four up and four down.

He fished in his briefcase again for the little bag Marcia Coleman had handed him: effects taken from the body, handed back by the police. Now, reaching in for the keys, he dumped out what else was there. There wasn't, he discovered, very much. An old man at home on a rainy day wouldn't have had much in his pockets. An ancient dime-store address book; he'd look that over later. Thirty-seven cents in change. A dirty handkerchief. A ballpoint pen.

He thought about that safe-deposit box, looking at those things. —*brought nothing into this world, and it is certain we can carry nothing out,* he thought sadly. He had a brief memory of the gaunt old man in his office that day, suspicious, grudging, prejudiced.

There had been a police seal on the front door. And he thought, the crime rate up, leaving a house empty is inviting the burglar: not that he supposed there was anything of much value here that either Dulcie or Marcia would miss.

There hadn't yet been a burglary, and it was a dingy tired house full of dingy gimcrack things. The narrow combination living-dining room ran straight across the front, with a hall going off the living-room end, which gave onto two bedrooms with a bathroom between. The kitchen, large and square, adjoined the dining area, with a service porch and a back door on the driveway. All the furniture was cheap and old. Sometime after the house had been built, a third bedroom had been added at the rear; the floor level was uneven where a door led straight from the end of the hall into a box of a room about twelve feet square. That was Dulcie's room: there was a narrow wardrobe, a single bed, a thin rug, white organdy curtains at the one window looking out on a bare backyard with a long-unpainted picket fence around it. There was a portable typewriter on a tiny metal table opposite the bed, a narrow mirror over a dressing table. The typewriter was an old Smith-Corona.

The middle bedroom had been turned into a den. There was an

ancient scarred rolltop desk, a studio couch, a vinyl-upholstered recliner with some stuffing coming out, and one metal file cabinet. Here, and in the front bedroom and long front room, the carpeting was wall-to-wall, much worn, a faded beige.

In the front room he looked at the marks left by murderer and detectives, and read the simple story. The fireplace was at one end of the living-room area, on the side wall: a conventional red-brick fireplace with a painted mantel. Under the front window was a couch, and at the other side of the fireplace a fat square chair and ottoman faced a portable TV on a metal stand in the corner. There was a rough chalk outline of a body between those two, and rusty marks on the carpet: where the old man had died. Just down from the door to the hall, the cumbersome metal walker lay on one side, and there was another chalk outline: the woman had fallen, or been struck down, close to the old-fashioned round oak table, and there were more old bloodstains.

He wandered back down the hall, remembering that Dulcie had said she'd been sleeping in her mother's room; in the front bedroom was a pair of twin beds, in one corner the ugly necessary bedside commode, a metal affair with its plastic bucket concealed by a plastic lid.

The odd thing was, of course, while this house, or anything in it, was worth very little, the land it was sitting on in central Hollywood might add a respectable sum to the estate.

—*or anything in it.* The chief reason he was here, of course, was what that chief teller had said. From what they knew of Vanderveer, he'd have been exactly the type to keep the wads of cash at home; indeed, with that modest checking account, what had become of all those nice dividends?

He started looking in the old man's den, the obvious place. He looked behind the three pictures, tore the paper backing off. He went through the desk quickly, not stopping to examine anything in detail, and came on this and that: a box of current-year bank statements, a large account book. The drawers were sparsely filled. He found a steel cash box in a bottom drawer with sixty dollars in cash in it. The pigeonholes were stuffed with meaningless odds and ends: paper clips, old pens, rubber bands. When he had been through the drawers he took them out one by one and looked at their undersides: a favorite place to tape valuables. There was nothing.

The file cabinet was no more productive: there were a few long-out-of-date construction contracts, statements and receipts from seven different local brokerage houses, the most recent dated last spring. Nichols-Neuman, Meyer and Salmon, Rettig and Rettig—all respectable well-known houses. He took down the addresses. The statements, dating back a good many years, listed sales and purchases of stock very different from that solid blue-chip stuff in the safe-deposit box now. He abstracted the whole wad to go over at his leisure.

He looked into the narrow built-in wardrobe. It held a collection of shabby old clothes, slacks, jackets, sweaters, shirts; the narrow shelf was stacked with old cardboard boxes, which were neatly packed with old copies of *The Wall Street Journal*—the bottom box went back to 1942.

"And didn't Solomon have the word for it," said Jesse to himself. *"Riches profit not in the day of wrath."*

He turned the file cabinet upside down, and found nothing. He removed a collection of old shoes and stacked clothes from the wardrobe floor and looked for evidence of a trapdoor or concealed recess: nothing.

It was very unlikely that Vanderveer would have hidden anything where the women might have come across it, but just in case, Jesse investigated the tiny coat closet beside the front door and discovered several boxes of Christmas ornaments, a collection of umbrellas, and a silver-headed cane. He looked behind all the pictures through the rest of the house and went through the old woman's room methodically, but it was going through the motions. If Vanderveer had had a hidey-hole for the wads of cash, it would have been in his own domain.

Frustrated, he stood on the front porch and ruminated. To hell with the chief teller: that was just imagination. Whatever else you could say about him, Vanderveer had been an eminently shrewd man; he had made his money work for him, and been smart and lucky in investments. Was it so likely he'd be so foolish to keep the hoard at home? So he'd liked to deal in cash, he was an old-fashioned, cautious fellow. What it came down to, had he had another safe-deposit box? Somewhere? Or—another thought—had all that dealing-in-cash, with the anonymous cashier's checks, been something to do with a tax dodge? He could imagine what Vanderveer had thought of the Gestapo.

And he thought, *Where moth and rust do not corrupt—* It had turned a good deal colder and he hadn't worn a coat; he shivered suddenly.

About one o'clock Nell went out to the garage to empty wastebaskets, and was surprised to find it so cold. "Climate's changing," she said to Athelstane, who had accompanied her.

The chain-link fence ran beside the garage, with a tall growth of shrubbery against it, and when Athelstane uttered a pleased whuffle and started over there, she looked after him.

The Siamese cat was huddled under the thick shrubbery there, barely visible, motionless. This time she could see that it was a dark seal point. But Siamese were generally pampered by owners; on a day like this it ought to be inside, she thought. She said coaxingly, "Pussin—come, pussin—" Nell was fond of cats and had never had one since long before her father died.

The cat fled away, long and low, and disappeared behind the shrubbery. Athelstane uttered a minor whuffle.

CHAPTER 3

When Jesse turned down the walk leading between the wings of the apartment house next to the Vanderveer house, he was reflecting: a working-class neighborhood, but it was Saturday. He could see a row of garages at the rear of the property. On the front step of the first apartment to the right in from the street, a rather blowsy-looking woman with dyed red hair was taking mail out of one of the two boxes between the doors.

On the forlorn chance that Clock had missed her, Jesse stopped to ask questions.

"You another cop? I already told the other one, I wouldn't have noticed nothing that day, I was at work. I wouldn't have noticed nothing at that house anyway, living upstairs like I do. But a murder right next door—it's scary these days, killers and robbers all over. What? Oh, the people live downstairs here, I told the other cop that too, they wouldn't have noticed nothing—the Lutzes —they've gone off on a trip somewhere, I think they left that day or the day before, I don't remember."

Jesse went on down to the rear units, and found the name slot in the ground-floor front door. R. J. Eberhart. The chief reason he wanted to see Eberhart was to gauge what sort of witness he might sometime be facing in court.

Eberhart looked at his card and invited him in, listened to his questions. "About that business next door," he said. "Siddown. That's short answered, sir. Sure I'm sure. What I saw and when." Eberhart was a peppery, perky little man around seventy, with once fiery red hair turning gray; he had a pugnacious bulldog face, shrewd little blue eyes, a quick sharp voice, and he was obviously in possession of all his faculties. "Look here," he said to Jesse, "I don't know those people—don't know anybody along here—I got my own friends and family. I only moved over here from south

Pasadena when my wife died five years back, so as to be closer to my daughter, she and her family live up on Outpost Drive. But you can't help noticing people, just casual. Roundabout five-thirty or a bit later, I'll usually be in the kitchen fixing something to eat, and the window and back door give on the driveway and the driveway of the house next door. I didn't even know the people's name, see, but three-four times a week I'd see that young woman drive in. About that time. So when I saw her drive in that morning I recognized her. Naturally."

"And you're absolutely sure of the day and the time?" asked Jesse.

Eberhart said exasperatedly, "How many times do I have to say it? Look, son, I may be seventy-one come January, but I've still got all my buttons and my eyes are as good as they ever were. I only retired a couple of years ago—worked for Kellogg Plumbing and Heating in Atwater for nearly forty years, and you can ask Jack Kellogg, Jr., if I showed any signs of senility."

"Nobody's suggested it," said Jesse.

"It's nothing to do with me," said Eberhart, "one way or the other. But I know what I saw, and when. Didn't take but casual note of it at the time, but I noticed it. The young woman next door driving in there. Drove right into the garage. It was around ten-thirty that morning."

"And you're positive which morning."

"Certainly I'm positive. It was Alice's birthday, October twentieth. She died five years ago, she's buried out at Rose Hills, and I never missed taking flowers to the grave, her birthday and Christmas and Memorial Day. But it was raining cats and dogs that day, I was hoping it'd let up. Kept looking out to see. It never did, and I finally went out anyway."

"And you're sure of the time," said Jesse.

"Well, I am." Eberhart looked at him belligerently. "Like I told the cops, I always have another cup of coffee along middle of the morning. I was in the kitchen fixing it, only reason I saw her drive in. Ten feet off across the apartment drive. That old tan Ford. She drove right into the garage."

"Mind if I take a look at your kitchen?"

"Help yourself."

The little apartment was neat and clean, the kitchen spotless and uncluttered. The window over the sink was a generous size, with a clear view past the driveway on this side to the Vanderveer drive and part of the Vanderveer garage.

"Do they think she did it?" asked Eberhart at his elbow. "The daughter? Did the murder?" He sounded avid. "Will I have to go in court?"

Jesse looked at him thoughtfully. He wore an eager expression. "I couldn't tell you, Mr. Eberhart. Possibly."

"Oh. Well, all I could do is tell the plain truth," said Eberhart. "What I saw. What I'm sure of."

And Jesse was thinking about witnesses. Good, bad, and indifferent. Eberhart was one kind: dogmatic, stubborn, arrogantly sure of himself. Sometimes judges and juries were wary of that kind, and sometimes they were quite right to be. Of the man convinced he couldn't make a mistake.

He stopped at a coffee shop on Sunset for a sandwich, and went to take a look at the other places Vanderveer had owned. Owned outright, and always collected the rents himself. One of them, a block down on Kingsley, was nearly a twin of the Vanderveer house, but its front lawn was greener and neater and there were rose trees lining the front walk. The other house fronted on Winona Avenue and was back to back with the Vanderveer house. It was an ugly square stucco house with a neglected front yard.

The apartment house on Fountain was one of the newer garden apartments, square and modern and brightly painted. There were sixteen units on two floors, and considering rents now, and that he'd owned it clear, it would be paying a very respectable profit. But none of these tenants would have known Vanderveer personally; they wouldn't have seen him in a month. Yes, and those rents would be due on Monday, and somebody would have to attend to that. A nuisance; have one of the girls type notices to leave in mailboxes, send checks to his office.

He drove on up Fountain until he spotted a public phone and called the Claremont number.

It was a pleasant wide street, Redwood Drive, in a neatly manicured residential area, and the house was a rambling ranch type on a wide lot, with a stretch of lawn and flower beds in front. Dulcie Vanderveer opened the door to him. "Is there anything— different?" she asked anxiously. "When you called I hoped maybe—"

"Just a few questions," said Jesse. Her face fell a little but she welcomed him in, to a comfortable homey living room furnished in early American. "Marcia had to take Jay to hockey practice, and Charles is out working in the yard— Sit down. What do you want to ask?"

"The day you forgot your keys," said Jesse. "When you got home, did you drive into the garage? And if so, why?"

She thought. "Yes, I did. Of course I was going right out again, but if you remember, it was raining. At least it was then—it hadn't been predicted, it started when I was driving downtown, and I didn't have an umbrella in the car. So I drove into the garage because it's closer to the back door. I had an awful time making Papa hear me, to come and unhook the chain and let me in."

"He always kept the door chains up?"

"Yes. Except when he knew I'd be coming home, at the usual time."

"Would you have any idea," asked Jesse, "whether he was in the habit of keeping much cash in the house? And where?"

"Well, I don't know," she said doubtfully. "Some, yes. Just for expenses. He gave me thirty-five dollars every Saturday to go marketing with—"

"For God's sake!" said Jesse. "A week's marketing?" He thought about the bills Nell reported, and she wasn't an extravagant shopper. Inflation—

Dulcie laughed a little bitterly. "Papa was supposed to be smart about money. Investing it, maybe. But I don't suppose he'd been in a grocery store for years. It wasn't any use trying to tell him. I used to put some of my money with it, to get enough—and little treats Mama liked, like fresh strawberries and Roquefort dressing. But about the money—I think he kept some in the den. If there wasn't enough in his wallet when I was ready to go to market, he'd go in there and get some. I don't know where he kept it, his desk probably. He never told us—Mama and me—anything about his money, he thought women were all fools, you know, about that kind of thing." Her little smile was mirthless. "He used to pay the newsboy in cash, before he stopped taking the paper—it got too expensive, he said. He used to subscribe to *The Wall Street Journal*. He stopped that too when the subscription rate went up—he used to go to the library and read it there." Suddenly Dulcie let out a huge sigh. "You're all thinking he was an ogre," she said unexpectedly. "He wasn't really, Mr. Falkenstein."

"Well—"

"No, really." She looked down at her clasped ringless hands. "He was lonely, you know—especially after Uncle Howie died, really his only close friend. We always called them aunt and uncle, but we really never saw much of them, even when we were children—Aunt Flo is pretty social, bridge and things, she hadn't the same interests as Mama, and of course Mama didn't drive. But you mustn't think he was a—a tyrant, Mr. Falkenstein. It was just the last few years—since he'd retired from business, he hadn't much to interest him, you see. Marcia's right, he wasn't always so bad—I can remember, when we were growing up, he was more cheerful, he'd make little jokes, even bring home little presents sometimes. He never liked to go out places, movies or restaurants, but Mama and Marcia and I did sometimes—he'd fuss about the money but we did. And after I was driving, that was after Marcia left home, Mama and I used to go out shopping and to movies, while she was still getting around all right. But the last couple of years, he was lonely," said Dulcie sadly, "and he hated getting old. He was so cross-grained he'd snap at you if you looked at him—but he wasn't always like that. Fighting with everybody."

"Had he had any—er—fights with people recently? There was something about a row in the family, when the nurse—"

"Oh, that," said Dulcie. "That! He didn't want to believe it, you see, that Mama was getting so much worse, so he wouldn't let himself listen. I hardly know Mrs. Gibson, she's the visiting nurse who'd been coming most of the time—sometimes they change around, you don't always get the same one, but it was her mostly. She came Mondays, Wednesdays, and Fridays to give Mama a bath and so on, and Mama said she was nice—and when she talked to me on the phone she sounded, well, efficient. I should have had better sense, but I talked to Marcia and we thought if we all went at him—you know. Of course he just shouted us all down. He didn't want to listen. And he was furious because Charles was there—"

"Why?" asked Jesse.

"Oh, he always hated Charles. You see, Mr. Falkenstein, he always blamed Mama for not having a boy—he didn't think much of girls—but at the same time, we sort of belonged to him and he'd, well, always have found some reason for—for hating anybody who tried to take us away. He wasn't really—prejudiced or—" She blinked. "He sort of despised what he called fancy education, he said Charles was a prissy old maid. And the children—you'd think he'd have been glad to have two grandsons, but it didn't work out that way. It was sort of impossible. Whenever Marcia brought the children, Mama loved to have them, but he'd be forever saying they weren't being raised right, indulged too much, given a lot of fancy ideas—it just made trouble, and Marcia just gave up. She'd come to see Mama when she could, and we talked on the phone—"

"I see," said Jesse. All that was expected.

"You can't help the way you're made," she said. "He never had much education, he started out as a carpenter. And after he retired from the business he didn't have anything to keep him interested. You asked about anybody he'd argued with lately. He'd had trouble with some of the tenants in the apartment house on Fountain—they were always late with the rent, and he told them to get out, and they left the place in a mess. He was trying to get damages from them—the place needed a lot of repairs, the stove and dishwasher. And about a month ago he had a terrible fight with somebody who came to the house, I don't know who it was. Mama told me about it. She'd been taking her nap when she heard the doorbell, and Papa let somebody in, and then there was a lot of yelling and shouting—but it took her a while to get herself up and into the walker, and she said when she got out to the living room Papa was just banging the door and yelling something like, 'Don't you ever dare try that again, goddamn liar'—and he just told her it was some drunk—but why would he have let him in? And he was mad at one of the other tenants, I don't know who that was either. It was just after the other thing. I answered the door, it was in the evening, and it was a young man, very polite, he had a little accent, I think he was Mexican. He just said he was one of Papa's tenants. I'd been busy getting Mama to bed, so I

don't know what it was all about, but after he left I could see
Papa was just furious about something. And then," said Dulcie
resignedly, "he had a fight with the gardener because he was raising his price. It infuriated him that he couldn't cut the lawn anymore, had to hire it done, and the same man took care of the
apartment house, the lawn and bushes there. He's a Mexican fellow, sort of excitable, and I thought they were going to kill each
other. Oh, it all sounds so silly. But the least little thing would
upset him, lately. I know he stayed out all day that next day, and
he forgot all about that TV program he always watched."

"Did he watch TV much?" Jesse was still thinking about the
money.

"Oh, not much. There isn't much worth watching anymore, and
I never had time. There were a few things Mama liked. But he had
three or four programs he usually looked at—not anything Mama
and I liked, they were, well, what I'd call a little risqué, if you
know what I mean."

Jesse felt vague surprise. "Did he go out very much? Do you
know where?"

"Not as much as he used to, it was getting hard for him to get
on and off the bus, and cabs are so expensive. He'd go to the bank
for the housekeeping money, I suppose, and he went to the library, the one up on Santa Monica—and of course he went to the
rest home a lot. Where Uncle Howie was. He had diabetes, you
see, and they finally had to amputate his leg and it never healed
properly—Aunt Flo couldn't take care of him at home and he had
to go there, he was there nearly two years. Papa used to spend a
lot of time there—he'd get me to take him on weekends, and the
rest of the time took the bus. He was still going there sometimes,
he'd gotten friendly with a couple of other old men who live there
and went to see them even after Uncle Howie died. You know, it's
sort of frightening, Mr. Falkenstein," said Dulcie soberly. "How
people get when they get old. Changing, and at the same time
more—more like themselves. And sometimes—like Uncle Howie—
That was pathetic, it really was, Marcia and I both said. It was at
the funeral, I took Papa of course, and Marcia came—sort of a
mark of respect—and after it was all over, Papa said to Aunt Flo,
I'm glad Howie's gone, the last while he wasn't the Howie we

knew, just a childish old man, he's better out of it. Mr. Falkenstein."

"Yes?"

"That—that queer note. I've been thinking— Do you think Papa
could have done that himself? Planned to take Mama with him—
like that—and then something went wrong, or—?"

"Well, it is a thought," said Jesse noncommittally.

"I've wondered." And then she looked up, turning her head.
"There's Marcia back." Automatically following her gaze, he saw
a middle-aged tan Chevy parked in the drive, and Marcia Coleman and a teen-aged boy getting out of it.

He spent Saturday evening poring over Vanderveer's account
book, a big stiff-covered ledger. It was evidently the latest one in
use; it had been started on January first four years ago, and was
about half used.

The old man had hardly been a trained bookkeeper, but he was
painstaking and methodical, and had his own method of record
keeping. Everything was scrupulously entered, from utility bills,
grocery bills, medical fees to the occasional large purchase or sale
of stock. Income, outgo—once Jesse figured out the system it was
easy to follow; but mathematics had never been his strongest
point, and he sat scribbling figures, hunched over his desk, mutter-
ing as he tried to add and subtract.

He went back over the year before this, and this year, and
wished he had a calculator. The wastepaper basket accumulated
discarded sheets as he multiplied and added, made mistakes and
did sums over.

When Nell looked in and said, "Are you coming to bed? It's
nearly midnight," he muttered at her, "Presently." He sat back
and looked at several pages of figures rather incredulously.

The real property, modest though it looked, had been bringing
in a very healthy income. Both the little houses rented for three
hundred and fifty a month. There were sixteen units in the apartment building, the singles renting at two-fifty, the doubles at three-
fifty. Of course the taxes and maintenance took a bite out of that,
but it had still been a nice income. And the dividends from the
blue-chip stock had added a pile to that. The gross income would
have put him way up there in a high tax bracket, but of course

there were convenient write-offs in real estate—Jesse remembered that there had been some 1040 and 540 forms, copies of tax returns, in that file cabinet, he'd have to take a look at those—and that heavy loan at the bank, a sizable write-off there, would have lowered Uncle Sam's take.

He gave it up half an hour later. It was a job for a CPA. But as far as he could figure it, if the amounts were true ones, there was anywhere between fifty and a hundred thousand dollars unaccounted for. Twenty-eight hundred in his checking account. Sixty dollars in a cash box at home. And where the hell was the rest of it? Where the hell?

If he knew IRS men, Dobson had been ferreting out Vanderveer's back records. See if he had come up with any attempted evasion to suggest where Vanderveer might have channeled the money. Turn the whole mess over to a CPA, and see what the trained mind made of it.

He opened his briefcase to put the big ledger into it, and as he did so encountered the little bag that had held the effects from the body. He hadn't looked at that address book, and took a minute to glance at it now.

It was very old and worn, and had been a cheap one to start with. Riffling through it, he realized just how obsolete it was; it must date from the years before Vanderveer's retirement, for it was largely filled with the names of realty companies, building-supply firms, and the like; there were very few personal names. But here and there through the little book he came on cryptic notations. They didn't seem to mean anything.

The first was on the first page, printed minutely at the very top. A Archer 1459. The next under B—BC Brown 730. The next under C—C Canning 1240. He studied them, frowning; they said nothing to him.

He found himself yawning, and put out the desk light and started up to bed.

On Sunday morning he went back to the house on Kingsley to pick up those tax records, and being in the vicinity wondered if he could track down the young man with the accent who had annoyed Vanderveer: what had that been about? The tenant of the house on Kingsley was listed in the ledger as Roberto Renaldo; the tenant of the place on Winona was R. Perez.

He got no answer at the first place; the doorbell chimed emptily. He drove up a block to the ugly little house on Winona.

The woman who opened the door was in the forties by her face, a once-pretty rather vapid little face, but she had kept a good figure. She had golden blond hair. She was chewing gum, and wore a fluffy pink housecoat. "Oh," she said to Jesse's self-introduction. "It's about that? Yeah, I heard about the old man getting killed. Who owns this place now, do you know? The rent's due tomorrow. And I'll bet the old bastard asked for it, too, whoever did it. I'll bet he left a bundle of money. He'd raised the rent on me twice the first year I was here, and it's tough to find anything much cheaper now—and I got two kids to raise and that no-good Mex husband of mine ran out on me four years back."

Jesse regarded her with interest. "Why should you say he asked for it?"

She pressed her lips together and then said drearily, "Oh, I don't suppose it matters now, only I still wouldn't like Bill to know about it. That dirty old bastard—that Vanderveer—just a nasty old man like they say. He hadn't ever done that before, but along last April or May, when he came to get the rent he said it was going up again, and I said I couldn't pay any more, and he laughed sort of funny and he started pawing at me—said if I was nice to him he'd be nice to me and not raise the rent. Dirty old bastard—what I had to put up with—every time he came since, pawing and slobbering over me, and I had to stand it. He couldn't do much more, he was about a hundred, but he sure had the urge. And all the time, I was scared to death Bill'd find out—my boy—he's got a temper on him, he'd have knocked the old bastard into the middle o' next week, and he could do it too, he's over six feet now already. When I heard that old bastard was dead, I just said thank God. Do they know who killed him yet?"

Astonished, he stared at her. And then he remembered the dirty TV shows. There hadn't been a hint at this facet of Vanderveer's character; had the old man started to go senile? Just along that line? Or just a little queer? And if in one way, maybe in another.

He handed her a card and explained that she could pay the rent to his office until the estate was settled. He wondered about Bill.

He got back in the car and started for the apartment on Fountain, and halfway there he suddenly slid the car in to the curb and switched off the engine. He asked himself what the hell he was doing. He wasn't a private eye. And it didn't matter a damn who Vanderveer had had arguments with, how many people had had some reason to hate him or to want to be rid of him—the same difficulty was still there: the difficulty of setting up that inside job. That very funny inside job. Of having the knowledge to do it. Conceivably, Vanderveer would have admitted the gardener, one of the tenants, almost anybody he knew even slightly who claimed legitimate business—even the meter reader, whoever—and how wild could you get? But, obligingly fetching the eggnog, the coffee, prying into the medicine cabinet—

Woolgathering, he thought disgustedly. And he wasn't a detective. He sat up to start the car, and idly noticed that he was parked across from a little cluster of shops, one of the neighborhood blocks of small independent places that might eke out a modest living from local residents. There was a pharmacy on the corner, a cleaner's, a variety store, a beauty salon. The door of the pharmacy was open, and it struck him suddenly that this would be the pharmacy where that codeine prescription had been on file. Clock would have heard about dosages from the coroner's office, but Jesse felt he could bear to know more about that, and also whether that last refill had been at a usual time.

He walked across to the pharmacy and went in. It was an old building, high-ceilinged and dim, and very untidy, with counters piled all down the center. He didn't locate the pharmacist until he had penetrated to the very rear of the store and came on him behind the prescription counter, a thin bald man in a dirty white smock.

"I'd like to ask you a few questions about that prescription of Mrs. Vanderveer's—" He reached for a card. "I expect the police asked you about it last week."

"That's right." The man looked nervous; he clutched the card without looking at it. He was about fifty; he had pale china-blue eyes behind metal-framed glasses. "It was all in order, the doctor's office said it could be refilled whenever she needed it. I told the police before—"

"How often was it refilled as a rule?"

"Oh, it varied. There were a hundred capsules to a bottle. The dosage is no more than two every four hours. She'd usually use up a bottle every couple of weeks, around there."

"And when had it been refilled the last time? I mean, before Miss Vanderveer got it refilled a week ago last Monday?"

"I had to look it up for the other officer—it was about two weeks before. The old—old gentleman called the order in that day, said his daughter would pick it up on her way home from work."

"Oh, said Jesse. "By the way, I'm not police—I'm the lawyer. What are you nervous about?"

The man stepped back a pace and said angrily, "I'm not nervous—but that's a dirty trick to pretend to be a cop, mister. You might have come right out and said what you were after. All I can say is, you can't get blood out of a stone, like I told the old man— I'm sorry, I'm an honest man and I like to pay my debts, but the way business has been—I said I'd pay him something as soon as I could—"

"You owed him money," said Jesse softly.

"As if you didn't know." The pharmacist was sullen.

"As a matter of fact, I haven't come across any record of it yet," said Jesse.

"Oh, sweet Christ—and I have to open my big mouth—"

"Of course I haven't been through everything."

"He took an IOU," said the pharmacist. "He offered it. He was in here, an old customer, I was just telling him about it—that fire inspection, how I had to have the whole building rewired. I own this block of stores, and they all had to be done, or we'd lose our business licenses. It was going to cost over five thousand and I didn't have it. He offered. Said he'd give me half percent less interest than the bank. That was way last year, I was supposed to pay so much a month, and he was here on the dot to get it too. But the last six months business has fallen way off, I just couldn't squeeze it out, and he'd been nasty about it."

"Well, well," said Jesse. "That's interesting, Mr.—"

"Schultz."

"Mr. Schultz. It'll be a while before the estate's settled, we can sort it out. Nobody's going to harass you about it." But he thought, back in the car, such a canny old man. Such a secretive old man. And just getting more so as he got older. And still busily

raking in the money wherever and however he could. That IOU
had to be somewhere. That rolltop desk—there could be a secret
drawer somewhere? Damn the old man. And that funny business
with the Perez woman—that really rocked him. Nobody had
suggested that sort of thing about Vanderveer up to now.

Suddenly he remembered that Vanderveer had made that appointment with him, wondered about it again—and then at least
one thing fell into place with a little click. Those tenants at the
apartment who had been kicked out. Vanderveer had wanted
damages out of them and had probably decided on legal action.

But he was wondering now just how many people there were
around who, hearing that the old man was dead, had said a fer-
vent thank God.

He had to be in court on Monday, on that other damage suit,
but the bench was either bored or lazy and dismissed the court at
four o'clock. With any luck it would go to the jury tomorrow. On
his way back to the office, Jesse stopped at the CPA offices on the
second floor and talked to a young fellow named Thurlow. He
handed over the ledger, the bank statements for this year and last,
the copies of the tax returns. Vanderveer had figured his own
taxes, and to give him credit had had everything filed quite neatly
by year. He explained what he was after.

"I'm no good at figures, and besides I'm busy. You've got all
the handy calculators. By all I come up with, this old boy was living on a pittance and raking it in with both fists, and what the hell
he's done with it is a mystery. I've got to settle his estate, and I'd
like to know exactly what there is to settle."

"Don't worry," said Thurlow with a grin, "Uncle Sam's Gestapo will locate it for you, Mr. Falkenstein. I'll see what it looks
like."

Reminded of that, when he got to the office he called Dobson,
who said they'd been back through Vanderveer's account with
them and he seemed to have an absolutely clean record. "Never
delinquent a day, never been audited, never any suspicion of any
fiddling. But considering that bank account, and a few other
things—"

"Yes, I know," said Jesse. "Where is it, and how much? Well,
it's more my worry than yours."

"You can say that six times," said Dobson. "I suppose it's occurred to you what sort of inheritance tax will be slapped on all
that gold-plated stock, and the heirs with just that checking account to pay it."

"The thought had entered my mind," said Jesse irritably.

Jean had left a memo on his desk. Lenhoff's attorney had called
and wanted to set up a meeting on Wednesday. "Damned
shyster," muttered Jesse, but he supposed he'd better see him. At
least Rose Lenhoff was out of town somewhere. And ten to one, if
that judge decided to quit early tomorrow, the damned court case
would drag over into Wednesday and he'd have to postpone the
meeting.

It was one of the days when he wished he'd gone in for anything but law.

He got home just after six; but of course they'd gone off daylight saving time last Saturday night and it was pitch dark. Up
here at this end of the canyon the street was unlighted; the first
thing he'd insisted on was a couple of good bright lights at the
gate, at the front door. He could see the lights at the gate as soon
as he swung onto Paradise Lane, shining out a welcome; and as he
turned into the drive the twin floodlights on the garage glared at
him. The gate was open: Athelstane was in. As he slid down the
drive, something small and light-colored fled across his path and
he slammed on the brakes.

Nell was just setting the table in the dining room. "Athelstane's
friend was out in the front yard," said Jesse, bending to kiss her.

She looked concerned. "At this hour? Cats ought to be in by
dark, and a Siamese—"

Athelstane came bounding up with Davy hanging onto his collar. "Daddy! Fee kittens!"

"My God, how long does this phase last? All right, all right,
we'll read about the three kittens just once, and then it's bedtime."
And as he swung the sturdy little figure up in his arms, he thought
of crabbed, suspicious, despotic old Vanderveer, who had exchanged all his chances of love and respect for the bundle of
money.

"I'll be in to bed him down in ten minutes," Nell called after
them.

*   *   *

When the phone rang at nine-forty he was getting on with the job of cataloguing all his records and knocked over a stack of Bach fugues getting to the desk. "Oh, Jesse," said Clock. He sounded very tired. "This is the first chance I've had to call you, sorry, but we've got two men off sick and we're all doing overtime." A sharp yip in the background cut across his voice, which suddenly turned fatuous. "That's my sweet girl, you just wait a minute and I'll get out your brush—"

"Just wait," said Jesse, "until your offspring arrives, and that hairy floor mop will get her comeuppance. And you won't be sounding so doting. Get a little education."

"What are you talking about?"

"Fee kittens," said Jesse darkly. "Do you want anything?"

"Just to break the news. The D.A.'s office is going for a charge of second degree. The warrant's applied for and will probably be waiting in the morning. We'll go out to arrest her as soon as it comes through."

"I was afraid of that."

"You still think she didn't do it."

"I can't know for a hundred percent sure. I just feel it's—out of character."

"You don't deal with crime by using intuition," said Clock. "It's out of my hands now. Red tape set in motion."

"Yes. Well, thanks for letting me know. And dammit, I've got to be in court— Look, Andrew, will you just tell her I'll get there as soon as possible?"

"Will do."

The case went to the jury at eleven o'clock, but what with the nice free lunch at an uptown restaurant, they didn't bring in a verdict until nearly three o'clock.

He got down to the Sybil Brand Institute, the women's jail, at three forty-five, and a few minutes later a wardress brought her in to him in one of the visitors' rooms, a bare little cubicle with a square table and two straight chairs. She looked quite calm, but the square little jaw was in evidence.

"That sergeant said you'd get here as soon as you could. Isn't that the queerest thing, him being your brother-in-law. I thought— you know—I thought if it ever happened—I'd be frightened, being arrested I mean, but I wasn't. It just all seems so awfully silly. That anyone could think I committed murder. Mama and Papa. Mr. Falkenstein, what happens how?"

"You'll be brought up for arraignment," he told her. "Probably the day after tomorrow. Later on you'll be indicted. You do know that there's no bail granted in homicide cases, you'll have to stay here."

She nodded. "The sergeant told me. It's all right—just like a little room, and very clean. But—do you think"—she leaned forward, her hands tightly clasped—"Mr. Falkenstein, all I can do is say it again—I didn't do it."

"If you plead guilty," said Jesse deliberately, "it'd just be a hearing before a judge, and the sentence very probably something like three to five years. You know all the evidence seems to be against you."

"I couldn't do that," said Dulcie. "Are you advising me to do that? As a lawyer? You don't believe me?"

"Against all common sense, I guess I do," said Jesse slowly. "Look. Can you tell me who would have known your parents' routine, have been admitted to the house—would have been able to arrange—what was done?"

She said helplessly, "But there's nobody—I mean, nobody who'd have done that! The family—Aunt Flo—Marcia, Charles— There weren't many visitors the last few years. Some of Mama's friends had died, and the ones left didn't come to see her often, they're all old too and don't get around much. Mrs. Fellowes went back East to live with her daughter—Mary Bright's in a rest home —and after Alice Hope moved to Long Beach, Mama used to write her letters, until her hands got so crippled— Oh, there might be a lot of people who knew things about us, but nobody we knew, you see. We didn't know any of the neighbors—most of them out all day, and not old neighbors."

"What do you mean, lots of people knew about you?"

"Oh, you see, Mama was just starved for talk," said Dulcie. "She hadn't anybody to talk to all day, she'd never been one for reading—I could sit and read all day, only I never had time—and if anybody came to the door when Papa was out, she'd talk to them as long as they'd stay. If I know Mama, tell them what time we had dinner and anything came into her head! She was so pleased when the Avon lady came, but she hadn't been back in a while, because Mama never could buy anything."

"Something else," said Jesse. "You knew your father had money somewhere, but you don't think he kept a lot of cash in the house—just what he gave you for shopping and so on—"

"Well, I don't know, but there wasn't a safe in the house like the one Uncle Howie had at home. Papa was smart about money, and he knew about the crime rate. I don't think he would have kept a lot around." She was silent, looking down at her hands, and then she said, "I know how it looks, Mr. Falkenstein. As if nobody else could have done it—that queer note—and no door broken in or anything. But I didn't, I don't know anything about it."

"All right," said Jesse. "Now I'd like you to go over that day in your mind, and think about this. Could there be anybody who might be able to testify that you were in your office downtown, say, between ten and noon?"

"I've already thought about that," said Dulcie. "The office door was closed, naturally, and Mr. Klein didn't come in that day until about two o'clock. I always took my lunch, there's no place right around there to get a sandwich, and we've got a little refrigerator and a coffee maker off the front office. But that day— I went down to the ladies' room about, maybe, a little after ten-thirty, and there was another woman there, just washing her hands before she left. I don't know if she'd remember it. I'm pretty sure she works in the tax office at the end of the hall—a blond girl about twenty-five, she's thin and always wears a lot of jangly bracelets—I don't know her, but of course everybody in the building would run into each other occasionally, see each other in the halls and so on—and maybe she'd remember. Of course I'm alone in the office a lot, Mr. Klein out seeing customers—"

"What's the business?" asked Jesse to keep her talking.

She brightened a little. "Oh, it's a very interesting business, Mr. Falkenstein. He's a wholesaler for fabrics, we deal with all the big department stores, furniture stores, upholsterers, dress factories, places like that. Most of the textile mills are in the South, you know, and Mr. Klein's the middleman supplier. I've gotten to know a lot about fabrics since I've worked for him—and he's always been so nice to me, he's a nice man."

"Well." Jesse stood up. "I can't tell you not to worry, Miss

Vanderveer. The court calendar's always full, I don't know when the trial might come up."

"It's funny," said Dulcie, "but I'm not worrying. Maybe I'm just being naïve to say I know I'm not guilty so it'll all come out all right. It was Marcia who went to pieces when they came with that warrant. And I'll be all right here, I've got my own things, clothes and like that. When I called Mr. Klein—after it happened —and told him, he was kind and said to take a couple of weeks off. And Marcia packed some clothes for me to take while I stayed with her, and they let me pack a bag this morning." Suddenly she yawned widely, and said, "Oh, excuse me. It's awful—I don't think I've caught up on my sleep yet. All I seemed to do at Marcia's was sleep, and right now that nice clean bed is all I can think of. I must be a funny client, Mr. Falkenstein. But I'm not worried."

CHAPTER 4

"What the hell are you giving me?" asked Bernard Klein incredulously. "Dulcie arrested? For homicide? That's ridiculous. This I've got to hear about."

Jesse had found him hunched over a typewriter in this rather cramped two-room office in an old building on North Spring Street at ten o'clock on Wednesday morning. Klein was a middle-sized stocky man about fifty, with thinning dark hair, a big crooked nose, a prominent gold tooth, an incipient paunch, and cynical dark eyes. His herringbone suit wasn't off the rack, but he was the kind of man whose tie went crooked ten minutes after he put it on. "What the hell?" he said blankly.

Jesse rather liked the look of him: a plain man, a man without any subterfuges. He sat back, lit a cigarette, and told him all about it. Klein listened, and commented with one succinct four-letter word.

"Dulcie!" he said. "Dulcie'd never in God's world have done that. 'S ridiculous."

"Well, she says she didn't."

Klein swiveled around in his desk chair and lit a cigarette with an angry snap of a disposable lighter. "My God," he said, "do I know my Dulcie! Better than her own family, I swear— God knows she spent more time here than at home! She's a good girl, Falkenstein, a nice girl. With me nearly twenty years, God, how the time goes—a green young girl when she came to me, but she caught on fast, she's a smart girl. Hell, I'm out calling on customers, showing samples, most of the time—I just need a girl here to answer the phone, take orders, do a few letters. I cover the whole damn county, all over, I'll be in maybe a couple of hours a day and that's all. But twenty years—you're telling me the law thinks Dulcie did a murder?" He used the succinct word again.

"There's evidence," said Jesse.

"You can shove the evidence," said Klein. He looked at his cigarette. "She never said very much about her home life—but sometime last year, around there, I figured she wasn't having it so easy, she'd mentioned about her mother's having another stroke and having to use a walker, and getting worse. And the last couple of months she'd been looking like hell, all tired out. I told her to take a couple of weeks off if she wanted, but she wouldn't. Said she'd had the usual two weeks in May, she'd be all right." Klein stabbed out his cigarette and got up to stand at the window, looking at the view over the city, gray and bleak and cold-looking.

"It hadn't been easy for her, certainly," said Jesse.

"That's a rough one, what you say about the way things were— that old bastard of a father." Klein laughed sharply. "My God, we're supposed to be the misers and skinflints, hah, but at that, there are a couple of things Mosaic law has to say about it—"

"*He who maketh haste to be rich shall not be innocent,*" said Jesse sleepily.

Klein laughed again, sharp and high. "I don't remember that one. Talk about biting off your nose to spite your face— What the hell did he think he was piling it up for? That's damn foolishness. All very well to stack it up, take care of it, but when it comes to going without necessities just to sit and gloat over the damn bank balance—" He turned to face Jesse. "I'm sorry for that girl. A good girl, Falkenstein. I always have been sorry for her. When I thought about it. Come to think, she never had much. Stayed at home, looked after the old folk, looked after my office. You could say sort of thankless jobs."

"She never said much to you about her home, you said."

Klein shook his head. "Not a complainer, our Dulcie. Always bright and cheerful. A good girl. God, I can't take this in. But an old bastard like that—all the work, her mother— But I'll never believe she could do a thing like that. No way. It's a funny word to use, maybe, but she's a gentle girl, Dulcie. A nice girl. She wouldn't be capable of a thing like that."

"Rather what I thought. Don't know her as well as you do, of course."

"Like I say, maybe better than anybody else," said Klein. He turned abruptly and sat down at the desk again, lit another cigarette. His dark eyes were sad. "Nice to think there was some rhyme or reason to things. People getting what they deserve, good or bad, eventually. God. A thing like this—I'd felt so damned sorry for her, you know, when Dan Wolfe showed up so unexpected—I thought she was going to pass out when he walked in, I happened to be dictating a letter to her—but Dulcie's a pretty game girl, she pulled herself together and put up a good show. I'd always thought there was something there, on her part anyway, and the way she looked, after all those years, I guess there was, in spades. I thought at the time—"

"Who's Wolfe?" asked Jesse.

Klein was staring out the window again. "Oh, he used to work for Wechler Brothers, down the hall, they're candy and novelty brokers. God, how time gets away, that's twelve or fourteen years back. He and Dulcie had dated some, back then. God, how old would Dulcie be now?—getting on to forty, I guess, it doesn't seem possible. She wasn't ever a spectacular beauty, you know, but— pretty. Nice skin and hair and eyes. Pretty in a quiet sort of way. A quiet girl. I know at the time I was kind of surprised at a young fellow like that having the sense to appreciate her."

"Oh," said Jesse. "Serious on his part?"

Klein met his eyes. "Well, I kind of had the feeling it was. Nothing definite said, but she— Well, I had an idea it was serious. Then all of a sudden it was kaput. Wolfe went into business for himself about that time, wasn't around anymore, and Dulcie never mentioned his name again, never said anything. Not a girl to talk about her troubles. I hadn't laid eyes on Wolfe since, but he turned up one day last month, seems he had some business with somebody down this way and dropped in to see his old boss—he came in here to see me and Dulcie."

"I see," said Jesse thoughtfully.

"About this trial," said Klein abruptly. "I don't suppose she can lay her hands on that money. Now or ever. It's a goddamned shame. And you don't work for love. Just take it that I'll guarantee your fee, Falkenstein. Nobody gets rich at the rag trade, any part of it, what this business amounts to—but Dulcie's a good girl, I'd like to see her through this. Do you think you can get her off?"

"I've got no idea," said Jesse. "There'll be enough money—however things turn out—but thanks for the offer. Any idea where I'd find Dan Wolfe?"

Klein looked curious. "Sure. He's in candy, novelties, souvenirs —he'll be in the phone book. Can she have visitors?"

"Anytime."

"I'll go and see her. She's a nice girl, Dulcie."

Down at the end of the hall from Klein's office was a door with a frosted glass top which bore the legend c. p. BAKER TAX AC-COUNTANT. On his way down the hall Jesse had noticed the door with the LADIES sign on it, sandwiched between Mason's Moving Service and W. F. Gunn Insurance.

Past the frosted door was a front office with a counter halfway across, two females, a row of file cabinets, and two desks with typewriters. Beyond an open door at the rear was a glimpse of a larger office where a broad-shouldered dark man in shirt sleeves was bent over a desk.

One of the females was plump and dark, the other thin and blond; the blonde was wearing a purple sheath and an armful of charm bracelets.

"Yes, sir? Mr. Baker's busy right now, but if you'd like to make an appointment—"

"Think it's you I want to talk to." He gave her a card. "I'm looking for a possible witness, Miss—?"

"Mrs.—Mrs. Linda Orley. What's it about? You're a lawyer?"

He told her what it was about. "It was October twentieth. A Thursday. If the date doesn't mean anything, the day it rained so hard for the second time. It would have been between ten-thirty and eleven, when you were in the ladies' room down the hall. There was another woman who came in just as you were leaving."

Her gaze was blank. "Heavens, I wouldn't remember."

"The woman who works for Mr. Klein in one-ten. A woman about thirty-eight, short, plump, brown hair. Miss Vanderveer."

"Oh, I know her. I never heard her name before. But goodness, I just couldn't say—I don't remember. Any of the girls working on this floor, we'd run into each other occasionally in the ladies' room, but it isn't a thing you remember particularly. If you know what I mean. I just couldn't say—yes, I'd seen her there some-times, but I couldn't swear to the day or the time, anything like

that. If it came to going into court or anything." She looked
vaguely alarmed. "One day's like another in this place. I just
couldn't say."

Jesse hadn't really expected anything else; but it was frustrating.
He thanked her and started back for the elevator. And it wasn't at
all relevant—or was it?—but he found himself curious about Dan
Wolfe. Anything about Dulcie Vanderveer interested him at the
moment.

He was in the book, at an address on Olympic Boulevard. It
was an old office building, middling rents, nothing fancy; Wolfe
was on the top floor. The hall door led into a tiny front office
where a freckle-faced red-headed girl asked his business briskly.
"Mr. Wolfe? If he's in, like to see him."

"Well, I'll see, he's on the phone." She went into the inner
office. In a minute a man appeared in that doorway.

"What can I do for you?"

Jesse handed him a card. "Few minutes of your time."

"Well, all right." He led Jesse into a small square untidy office
with a littered desk, a couple of straight chairs. "Am I getting
sued, or have I inherited a bundle?"

"Neither. You remember Dulcie Vanderveer?"

Wolfe's half smile vanished. "Well, sure. What about her?"

Jesse told him economically, and Wolfe said, "Oh, my God. My
God, what a—what a hell of a thing. I'm damned sorry to hear
about it. Damned sorry." He looked as if he meant it.

And Jesse looked at him with interest. Wolfe would be about
Dulcie's age, a year or two older. Twelve, fourteen years ago he'd
have been a very handsome young fellow; he was still handsome
in maturity: a tall, dark, well-built man with sharply chiseled features, thick eyebrows, a head of gleaming black hair, a firm well-
cut mouth. He looked back at Jesse blankly and said, "The hell of
a thing. I hadn't seen her for over thirteen years—just happened to
be near my old office one day last month, and dropped in. She
hadn't changed much—I was a little surprised—but what—"

"What's it got to do with you? Nothing at all. And you'll think
I've got a damned nerve to ask you," said Jesse. "But back there
quite a while ago, you'd dated her a little. Klein thought it might
be serious. Was it?"

Wolfe got out a cigarette and tapped it slowly against the desk top before lighting it. "I don't know why the hell I should tell you anything about that."

"Neither do I. Just take it, it wouldn't go any farther."

"What the hell?" said Wolfe. "It's ancient history, it doesn't matter now. Dulcie was a nice girl. Not the prettiest girl around, but that isn't everything, and when you got to know her— You could say I was halfway serious about her. I thought she liked me pretty well. She'd never had any boy friends, she was a shy sort of little thing. We had maybe half a dozen dates, and I was thinking —well, put it that I was getting serious about her. Then—well, she'd always asked me to pick her up at the office, and then she finally told me that her father didn't like her to date, he was old-fashioned, but we'd have to meet sometime, and she asked me— that next date—to come to her house. I did. It was a place in Hollywood—old house in the middle of town. That old bastard," said Wolfe. "How the hell do people get that way? She introduced me, and right away he started in yelling—I thought he was going to jump me—he wasn't having his daughter going with any dirty Jew, and all the rest of it. You can fill in the blanks for yourself." He shrugged.

"Oh, yes," said Jesse. And he remembered how she had said, anyone who wanted to take us away—and, he wasn't really prejudiced. The excuse. Even the useless daughters had belonged to him, part of his possessions.

"Well, for God's sake," said Wolfe. "Even if I'd been all the way serious, there's no profit in that sort of thing, is there?—hardly the basis for a settled marriage." He laughed shortly. "I was planning to start my own business about then, I don't think I stayed with Wechler more than a month after that. I didn't see Dulcie again. Hadn't seen her since, until that time last month. End of story."

"Short and sweet." Jesse looked at his own cigarette. "Are you married, Mr. Wolfe?"

"Yes, Ruth and I got married the year after that, we've got three kids now."

"Well, sorry to have raised a ghost," said Jesse, getting up. "It was just a loose end."

"I'm very sorry to hear about this," said Wolfe formally. "I don't suppose there's anything I can do, but—"

No, there wasn't, thought Jesse in the elevator. That surprise visit to the old office probably a pure impulse. And maybe he'd showed some proud pictures of the three kids. He thought of Dulcie saying so steadily, I don't know anything about it— A last straw? The only man who'd ever acted serious about her, that could be inferred, and a handsome man, a virile man. She could have been deeply in love with him. And the irascible, reasonlessly jealous old man driving him away. The long dull years going by. And lately, coming home day by dreary day to the increasingly helpless old woman, the fierce despotic old man—

That chance meeting with Dan Wolfe last month just could have waked some slumbering passions.

He had believed her. He'd like to go on believing her. But he hoped the D.A.'s office would never hear about Dan Wolfe.

Lenhoff's attorney came into the office at three o'clock and to Jesse's surprise brought a counteroffer which nearly matched the settlement Rose Lenhoff was asking. It was probably the best deal they could get, and Jesse accepted it provisionally. He told the other man he'd contact her and let him know. But it appeared that Mrs. Lenhoff was still out of town, and the daughter who answered the phone when Jean called couldn't say when she'd be home.

Jesse felt annoyed with the wayward clients.

And it was out of his way, but he left the office early and drove into West Hollywood to see Florence Griffin. He had nearly forgotten her; he had discounted her as irrelevant to the case. But Dulcie had reminded him that she was indeed one of the relatively few people who would have been admitted to the house without question—an old friend—would have been given the freedom of the house. But what possible motive could she have had?

It was a block of older homes, in a quietly elegant neighborhood of manicured lawns and solid wealth. The house was French Colonial, on a wide lot; he contrasted it with the mean little bungalow on Kingsley.

She answered the door promptly; he remembered the high girlish voice on the telephone that night. She was a small, neat woman with fluffy silver-gray hair, a peaches-and-cream complexion, and she greeted him warmly. Not ever an intellectual woman

in any sense of the word, he judged her, but she had a warmth of
personality, she was friendly—and a talker. "Of course Marcia
called, I just couldn't believe it, there must be some mistake—as if
Dulcie would do a thing like that! I don't know what the police
are thinking of—but"—she regarded him with her head on one side
—"you look like a very good lawyer, Mr. Falkenstein, you can
show them how wrong they are. Do come in and sit down and tell
me how I can help you."

"Well—" He wasn't sure what he wanted to ask her. "When was
the last time you saw any of the Vanderveers?"

"At the funeral," she said promptly. "Howie's funeral. It was
really awful of me that I didn't go to see Myra oftener, but time
goes by—Johnny came to the funeral, of course, with Dulcie and
Marcia, and they said if I felt up to it Myra'd like to see me, so I
went over there for an hour or so afterward. Of course I'd seen
Johnny nearly every day at the rest home. Howie liked Johnny to
come—of course they'd known each other so long, and been partners in business. Frankly, I always detested the man—it's funny, I
suppose men see something in other men that makes them friends,
but they weren't at all alike—oh, Howie was ambitious too and
liked money well enough, but at least we enjoyed it—not being extravagant, I don't mean, but just living nicely and being comfortable, and trips and theaters and things like that. Oh, I was sorry
then—that day—that I hadn't gone to see Myra oftener, I was sorry
for her, you know. What with Howie so bad, I hadn't realized—
But Myra and I never had much in common, she was so much
older. And Dulcie looked just terrible. It was killing her—taking
care of them. I hadn't seen Dulcie in ages—but she just looked
exhausted." She accepted a cigarette with a little nod.

"What did—" But she had flown on.

"When the children were small they were told to call us uncle
and aunt, but we never actually saw much of them socially—Myra
and Johnny I mean— He wasn't so bad back then, more talkative,
if he always was an old grouch—but then he had the business to
give him an interest in life, men need that the way women need
bridge and shopping, it's funny. I wasn't surprised when Aline left
him, his first wife—you knew he was married before—"

"I didn't realize you'd known her."

"Oh, yes. Let's see, Howie and I were married in 1935—we

wanted a family, of course, but I guess it just wasn't meant to be. He and Johnny were both working for Keene Construction then, and lucky to have jobs at all, but things were awfully slow—the Depression was still on, you know. It was a couple of years later that Howie's father died and left him a little money, and Johnny had some savings, and they decided to start their own company. Johnny and Aline had gotten married the year before we did, and she was a lot younger than Johnny—he was five years older than Howie, you see—she was about my age, and I was twenty-one. She left him about six months after Howie and I were married, and as I say I wasn't surprised—all his penny-pinching and ordering her around. I said money was tight—the Depression—but you could still have fun and enjoy yourself—movies twenty-five cents and there was always the beach—but Johnny always grudged every penny. And then there was his chasing around—"

"Oh, did he?" asked Jesse.

"Well, I couldn't prove it but I know in my bones he did. Men are funny," she said ruminatively. "Whenever I mentioned it to Howie, he just laughed. Now, Howie'd never have played around on the side, he wasn't that kind of man, but I guess a man can overlook that sort of thing in another man—it was like Johnny telling the dirty jokes, but not in front of women unless it was by accident, and Howie'd never repeat them to me. But Johnny had an eye for the girls—only I don't suppose he did *much* about it because it'd cost him money. And he only married Myra to have a cook and housekeeper. She was nearly his age, he was forty then, she'd never been married, worked in an office somewhere. I always thought she was so grateful to be able to call herself Mrs., she just put up with him, but maybe I misjudged her. I don't know how she did put up with him. She was a good mother to the girls, I will say, but he never let her forget she ought to have had a son."

Jesse remembered that that was nearly the first thing Vanderveer had said to him.

"Poor Myra—I ought to have gone to see her oftener, but it was all pretty depressing, you know—that horrible little house, and the walker, and Johnny grumbling around like a bear. It was the girls I felt sorriest for—I always thought Myra could have stood up for them better. Of course Marcia was the rebellious one—she stood up for herself. When she wanted to go to college Johnny had a fit, what good would college do a girl, he never finished high school and he made out all right, and Marcia just got herself a job and moved out, started to go to LACC part time, and of course that's where she met her husband. It was poor Dulcie got the short end of the stick, ending up taking care of them both, but then she's the kind— Well, Howie always used to say, there are two kinds of bravery, you know. There's the kind that makes you rescue somebody from a fire, or stop a dog fight, and then there's the kind that makes you able just to stand things, however bad it is, just grit your teeth and bear it. "

"That's perfectly true," said Jesse.

"But when I saw Dulcie that day—as bad as I was feeling about Howie—I could just have cried for her. She looked awful. It was killing her, all that work and no rest. And of course Johnny would never even notice it." She put out her cigarette and looked at him seriously. "You've just got to make everybody see that Dulcie would never have done such a thing—*killing* them. It's just impossible. But"—and suddenly her light voice sounded almost fierce— "I'll say one thing, Mr. Falkenstein. If I thought Dulcie had done it, I'd say Johnny Vanderveer just brought it on himself."

The arraignment was set for ten o'clock on Thursday morning; there wasn't any need for him to be there, but he showed up to give Dulcie a little moral support.

And he intended sometime today to talk to some of those stockbrokers; but he'd just gotten back to the office when Jimmy came in and said the Colemans were here.

"Oh, Lord," said Jesse. "All right."

They came in and sat down, looking very grave and miserable; but Marcia was in control of herself, her voice was steady. Coleman was looking very worried. "Mr. Falkenstein," she said, "we thought we'd better come and talk to you. About money. Dulcie's got some savings, but we haven't got much at all—the children, and it's expensive to live now, and—"

"Oh." Jesse was surprised. "I wouldn't worry about it, Mrs. Coleman. It'll all be all right."

"All right!" said Coleman roughly. "You'll want some sort of retainer to defend her—I know these things don't come cheap. I'm not sure how much I might manage, but—"

"But there's money available, or will be. You knew that your father had a bundle," Jesse said to Marcia.

"I know we always suspected it. But what he did with it, how he left it—"

Jesse said, "My God, that's my fault—I should have known, of course it wouldn't have crossed his mind to tell anybody. I should have told you about the will."

"Dulcie remembered a will. His making one. But—with all this going on—I'd forgotten about it. Is there a lot of money?"

"Quite a bundle. But it'll be tied up." He told them about the will, and Marcia shut her eyes and leaned back in her chair.

"Oh, isn't that typical. Just exactly what he would do. Stupid woman with not enough sense to handle money, appoint a bunch of men to do it for her. And he always resented my getting out from under his thumb, of course." Coleman was looking very relieved. "Why will it be tied up?"

"Well, you see, legally nobody can profit directly from a crime. If your sister is convicted, that will can't be proved. It'd be a little legal mess, I'm afraid. The estate was left in trust, so the trustees at the bank would have some say—but it might take a while to straighten it out."

"What would have to be done?" asked Coleman interestedly.

"Mrs. Coleman would have to petition the court to set the will aside and award the estate to her as the next blood relative. I think it'd go through without much trouble, but it'd take time. Maybe a lot of time—the law's like the mills of the gods, doesn't get things done overnight."

"That's if—if Dulcie's found guilty. What happens if she isn't?"

"Why, then the will goes into probate and she gets it all. Except for your hundred bucks. But that's another tie-up, you see, because as matters stand I can't put it into probate. We'll have to wait until we know the outcome of the trial."

"I see," said Coleman.

"Either way we'll get the money, you mean," said Marcia. "Both of us. Because I know how Dulcie'll feel. If she got it all she'd share with me. If I get it all, I can give her half, can't I?"

"If you want it that way."

"But you might have to wait quite a while before you get paid for your services," said Coleman.

"Don't fuss about that. I can stand it. Lawyers get used to that sort of thing."

"Mr. Falkenstein," said Marcia in a small tight voice, "what—what do you think is going to happen?"

He didn't pretend to misunderstand her. "I think we've all got to realize," he said gently, "that the chances aren't very good for your sister to be found innocent. It may seem to you that it's rather vague evidence against her, and mostly what's called circumstantial evidence. But what a lot of people don't realize is that circumstantial evidence is perfectly valid. In this case—well, you can see it for yourselves, it isn't so much a question of her possible guilt as the near impossibility of anybody else having done it. Maybe that's oversimplifying, but you see what I mean."

They looked at each other in wretched silence. "What kind of sentence would she get?" asked Coleman.

"Well, it's second degree. It's barely possible that a judge might hand her a ten to twenty, but I'd be more inclined to expect something like five to ten, and that would mean she'd probably get parole in about two years."

"Two *years*," said Marcia, and gave a little dry sob.

"Better than the other," said Coleman shortly. "When do you think the trial might come up?"

Jesse shrugged. "The calendars are always full. A couple of months—it could be longer."

"Oh, my God," he said.

"There was a story in the *Times*," she said. "Not much, and on a back page— But there are the children, you can't lie to them, and Jay and Ann are old enough to be sensible, but—"

"Excuse me," said Jesse, "for prying, Mrs. Coleman. Just an academic question. Your sister doesn't seem to have any close friends. Any friends period. I mean, rallying around as it were. I realize she'd been living a restricted life lately, but surely—"

"Oh, for heaven's sake," said Marcia. "Excuse *me* to say that's just like a man. Of course she had friends—at school, and later on. Good friends. If not a squad of them— Dulcie's not the kind to have a lot of friends. But all the other girls went on to get married, some of them pretty young, and they started their own families, and married women have different interests, different concerns, and not much time for gadding around. For a while there'd have been the phone calls, the occasional get-together—and then when Dulcie had to be home most of the time she wasn't working, they just—dropped away. I know exactly how it would happen. First it'd be, I haven't seen Dulcie in ages, I really must call her, and later on it'd be, I wonder what ever happened to Dulcie, and then they'd stop thinking about her."

"Yes, I suppose so."

"It's just, I feel so d-damned guilty," she said suddenly. "I could have helped more than I did—gone to spell her once a week or something—"

"Now, Marcia," said Coleman.

"I could have. And now this—I don't know how she can be so—so calm about it. When I saw her yesterday—that enormous jail, and guards—"

Coleman got up. "We'd better not take up any more of your time, sir," he said heavily.

Before he could get away, Thurlow called him from the CPA office downstairs. "Say, I've been over all these figures, and very interesting they are. I wish the old boy was alive to tell me how he lived so cheap. But what I come up with, adding up his gross income and subtracting expenses, property taxes, and income taxes, he should have come out on the right side of the ledger—I'm talking about this year—by eighty-nine thousand, six hundred and seventy bucks and ninety-two cents."

"For the Lord's sweet sake," said Jesse.

"Did I understand you to say you don't know where he was putting it? It's just gone?"

"That's about the size of it. Oh, there's a lot of stock, and real estate, but this'll be the net income derived from that, and it doesn't seem to be anywhere visible. My God. As much as that?"

"Last year it added up to more—the market's been down. Let's see, it came to a hundred and five thousand, seven hundred something. Net."

"Thank you so much," said Jesse. "Send me your bill, and all those figures."

"Oh, I won't forget."

He got down to Meyer and Salmon, one of the oldest and most conservative brokerages in town, at one-thirty. It was housed on the ground floor of a newly refaced office building on Spring Street, and it was a large busy place with a lot of smartly groomed secretaries and young executive types. After talking to several of those, he was finally introduced to a Wallace Halliday, who took him into a private cubbyhole in a row of those at the rear of the office. Halliday was in his forties, with a cheerful round face and bland dark eyes. He was the broker here Vanderveer had dealt with.

"Oh, yes, I remember the old boy, Mr. Falkenstein. He'd been dealing with the firm since before my time—Brett was handling his account, and when he retired and I took on some of his clients, Vanderveer didn't think much of me at first." He laughed. "What do you want to know? You said you're settling his estate?"

"That's right. There's a lot that isn't very clear, evidently records missing. When was the last time he did any buying or selling?"

"Oh, a good five years ago," said Halliday. "He never did much speculating, chopping and changing around—we didn't see him all that often. Sometimes he'd hang onto something just awhile and then sell, usually did himself some good too, but mostly he just bought the stuff to sock away and sit on—the blue-chip stuff. He never asked me for advice, he knew just what he wanted to do. I remember the first thing he bought through me was a block of Pacific Telephone, and he never let go of it."

"How did he handle the transactions?" asked Jesse. "Personal checks or what?"

"Well, when I first had his account it was checks—that was about fifteen years ago. He was still in business then, and able to drive. He'd drop in here once in a while, talk over the market, tell me what was on his mind—sell this, buy into that—and if there was anything due, he'd hand over a personal check. Later on, I suppose when he was older and not feeling so spry, he'd do business by phone. I'd get him a current quote if he wanted to buy anything, and he'd mail me a cashier's check. Or if he was selling, we'd mail him ours. But he hadn't done any business with us in a good five years. I could check, but I think it was along in the spring of 1976, might have been 1977. I was thinking of that, oddly enough, just the other day," said Halliday thoughtfully. "He wanted to sell a block of G.M. common, and I told him he was crazy. Let me look it up." Halliday rummaged in the bottom drawer of the tall file cabinet behind his desk. "Inactive accounts—never know when they'll come to life—R, S, T, U, here we are—" He straightened with a manila folder in one hand and sat down again. "Yep." He riffled through statements and found what he wanted. "G.M. common, like money in the bank, I said he was nuts. He knew me then, and he just laughed. He said, wait and see. He just had a hunch that pretty soon the American manufacturers were going to find themselves in trouble, it was time to get out. And wasn't he right indeed, if it took a while. He was a smart old boy, Vanderveer. But he was pretty old then, he'd been retired for some time, and he couldn't drive anymore. He hadn't been doing much dealing for a few years before that—" Halliday had been leafing through the statements and now clicked his tongue again rapidly. "Oh-oh, there was that—I'd forgotten that. Yep. 1965. He sold off a great big parcel of stuff, different bundles of stock—some good stuff too—and took it all in one big check. He said he was buying an apartment building with it, paying it off clear. It came to a hundred and seventy-seven thousand, six hundred odd. I said he was crazy then too, and he laughed and said, a good rule always was to diversify your holdings, and real estate was always the first thing to go in a depression and the first thing to come back."

And that would be the apartment on Fountain, Jesse surmised. At today's inflated prices, it might change hands for nearly double that. He said, "He'd dealt with other brokerage firms. Rettig and Rettig, Neuman—"

Halliday's eyebrows shot up. "He had?" He sounded incredulous. After a moment he laughed. "That's damned funny. Damned funny. As a rule, an investor picks one broker and stays with him —unless, of course, he's the kind of investor who takes the broker's advice and it turns out to be not so hot. There's no difference in commissions, what's the point of going to two or three?"

"Could you suggest any reason he shopped around?"

Halliday passed a hand over his round well-shaven face. "Old Vanderveer," he said thoughtfully. "He was a queer old codger all right. He had some funny ideas. About women, for instance. Old-fashioned. Now you take my wife, she's got quite a nose for the market—a smart girl. But that old boy—I'd lay a bet he was pretty secretive about his private business. You know? He was what they call a self-made man—liked to boast about it—told me how he'd started working at fourteen, got to be a master cabinetmaker and went on to start his own business—construction. It just could be that he didn't want any one broker knowing all about what he held, all his assets. All I can think of." Halliday grinned. "Uncle Sam would know, of course, but that he couldn't avoid. Like not putting all his eggs in one basket."

"Um," said Jesse. "Do you think he was an honest man, Mr. Halliday?"

Halliday looked serious, and massaged his round cheek again. "Now that's not a thing always easy to guess about another man. But I'd say he'd have been honest to the letter of the law. He might cut corners a little—always a way to beat the devil round a gate—but it'd all be perfectly legal. On the other hand—well, he was mighty fond of money, that old boy."

"Yes," said Jesse. "Well, thanks very much for nothing."

"All the same, you have to admire a fellow like that. Pulled himself up from nothing and died worth a small fortune."

"*The hand of the diligent maketh rich,*" said Jesse, "so Solomon says. Thanks very much." He got up.

He stood in the entry beyond the elegant smoked-glass front door with the gold lettering and reflected dismally that he'd have to see every one of these brokers personally. He hadn't looked at those statements in Vanderveer's file cabinet. Vanderveer hadn't had any dealings with this house in over five years, but he could have had with others; and if he had been starting to go a little senile, he could have destroyed statements; it wouldn't say anything if the statements in his files weren't recent.

That IOU of Schultz's was somewhere. That secretive, sly old man—not putting all his eggs in one basket—

No, of course he'd have to report everything all honest to Uncle. Uncle had so many snoopers now—the automatic reports of all bank dealings sent to Uncle, any other deals—all the duplicate paper work— He couldn't have gotten away with keeping other bank accounts. Even bank accounts in different names, because he'd need different addresses for the statements—and come to think of it, different Social Security numbers. Social Security numbers didn't appear on bankbooks, weren't recorded by the bank, but all bank reports and tax returns, ending up in Uncle's hands, got tied to Social Security numbers, and when there wasn't one on file for the fictitious name, no tax returns, Uncle would investigate. The mills of the gods— Vanderveer couldn't have hidden away any of his take that way. And that, he'd know.

And what Halliday had said—the letter of the law. And maybe not, too.

The phrase ran teasingly across his mind again, not putting all his eggs in one basket. Jesse swore, fumbling for his car keys as he started for the parking lot. Vanderveer always close-mouthed, a loner, and secretive—but— As he came up to the car he amended that in his mind. Vanderveer had discussed his affairs with Halliday, probably to a much greater extent with his former partner and close friend Howard Griffin, very possibly with other men, while he was still active in business. It was women he thought were stupid about money—he hadn't wanted the foolish women to know anything about his cache of cash in the house, what business deals he was into, how much he had— And something else. Liked to boast a little, said Halliday. Lonely, said Dulcie. Yes, he'd been in the habit of a busy active life, mostly among other men, and when he retired he hadn't had much to do with himself. Reading *The Wall Street Journal* at the library— And Dulcie had also said, Uncle Howie at that rest home for two years, and Papa friendly with a couple of other old men there.

It was a thought. And it was five minutes past three, and he had an appointment with a new client at four.

On Thursday afternoon Nell started out to the market about three, with Davy strapped into the seat beside her. When she went past the nearest house, a quarter mile down the hill, there was a woman bending over a flower bed near the street, pulling weeds. Impulsively Nell braked and got out.

The woman stood up and Nell introduced herself. "We just moved in last month, and we do like it up here so much—it's so quiet, isn't it? You really feel as if you're away from the city." The woman was about forty, thin and angular, with a narrow jaw and a thin-lipped mouth.

"Oh. You're the people bought Miss Spicer's house. I'm Mrs.

Tidwell. We didn't know her at all, she was a sort of peculiar woman, an artist, you know."

"Yes, I know." The realtor had told them that: Miss Bertha Spicer had been a well-known illustrator of children's books. "What I stopped to ask you—"

"Artists are always peculiar," said Mrs. Tidwell.

"Well, what I wanted to ask you, do you have a Siamese cat? Because—"

"Heavens above, no," said Mrs. Tidwell. "I can't abide cats and neither can Martin. Nasty sly dirty things. Have you seen it up there? I don't know where it belongs—it's come into our backyard hunting birds, I'm always chasing it off, I called the pound once but they said I'd have to get it in a box before they'd send a truck, and of course you can't lay a hand on it—not that I'd want to—cats always carry germs."

Getting back into the car, Nell reflected that at least Mrs. Tidwell didn't live nearer and wasn't inclined to be neighborly. She stopped at the only other house at the bottom of the street, but there was nobody home.

CHAPTER 5

On Friday morning a new client had a damage suit in mind; it would be a rather complicated business, and Jesse took a couple of pages of notes in his finicky copperplate. The client left a little before eleven, and Jesse swiveled around in his desk chair and stared unseeingly out the window, wondering what he was going to say to a judge and jury about the deaths of the Vanderveers.

Call Klein as a character witness. Such a nice reliable girl, she'd never do such a thing. Very useful. And there was Eberhart—Eberhart the dogmatic, couldn't have made a mistake, know what I saw. Oh, yes? Jesse sighed to himself.

There was Dan Wolfe. Could have been the unwitting spark that triggered her—Dulcie, meekly looking after the old people, efficient at her job, all those dull years, reminded of what she had missed.

Eberhart could easily have confused the days. Tuesday when she forgot her keys, Thursday when the Vanderveers had died. But he didn't have any idea what story he might spin to a judge and jury.

Just before he went out to lunch, Rose Lenhoff called. "I know you've been trying to reach me, Mr. Falkenstein—I'm sorry, I've been in San Diego, my sister had an emergency operation—but thank God she's going to be all right, everything's fine. I just got back." He told her about the offered settlement, and she was pleased. He explained that they would have to get legal evaluations of all Lenhoff's property—he was into land development, had holdings all over—and after that it might be a while before they got a court date.

"I think what we're looking at here is sometime in early February. I know it's already taken some time—"

"So long as it's settled," she said. "I'm very grateful, Mr. Falkenstein. You'll be in touch then."

He started out for lunch, and as he came into the front office Jean was saying, "Well, I wish he had a twin brother to date me, it was just your luck I backed out of Gina's party and you got to meet him first—"

Jesse regarded the Gordons suspiciously. "Neither of you thinking of leaving me for the rich husband?"

They laughed at him. "Not yet," said Jimmy. "They don't grow on every tree, Mr. Falkenstein."

After lunch he went to see another stockbroker. Rettig and Rettig was another respectable conservative brokerage, not as venerable as the other one, or as large. It was out on the Sunset Strip, in a newish high-rise office building.

He got passed around a little, but ended up with Mr. Anthony Rinaldi, who belied his melodious name by being square and phlegmatic and businesslike, with a New York accent. "Oh, yes, I remember Mr. Vanderveer," he said. "I handled his account, but it didn't amount to much—he bought and sold stock infrequently. What exactly did you want to know?"

"When was the last time he did any business with you?"

"Oh, it's been some time ago. Five or six years at least." Rinaldi brought out a thin cigar and squinted at it before lighting it. "Oh, yes, I remember him. He dealt with us for ten or twelve years, just now and then as I said. A very decided character." Rinaldi looked thoughtfully at the cigar. "The last time I saw him —your asking about him just reminded me—well, I wonder if he was right."

"About what?"

"To the best of my recollection it was early in 1977. He came in and wanted to sell a block of some preferred stock, I forget what it was, and I tried to persuade him into buying some South African gold stock. A very sound investment and paying quite well, but he just laughed at me and said I'd lose my shirt, go in for that." Rinaldi looked a little disturbed. "Five years ago, but the headlines yesterday— Vanderveer said that was the next Communist goal, reason for all the trouble there, and anybody fool enough to invest money there could kiss it good-bye."

"Oh," said Jesse. "And doesn't it look as if he was right. He hadn't done any business with you since then? Well, thanks so much."

When he left there he was thinking again about that convalescent home and Howard Griffin. Had anybody mentioned which one it was? He stopped at a public phone and called Mrs. Griffin to ask; but nobody answered the phone. He called Marcia Coleman and she couldn't remember, had only been there twice. He finally had to chase all the way down to the jail—they wouldn't summon a prisoner to the phone on the mere claim that it was her lawyer—and Dulcie told him that it was the Golden West Convalescent Home on Vermont.

It wasn't very far out on Vermont. There were a couple of big hospitals in that area, a Kaiser hospital, the Hollywood Presbyterian Medical Center, and there were several convalescent homes not far away; this was one of them. It occupied nearly half a block, a tan stucco building with a red tile roof, and had its own small parking lot.

Beyond plain double doors he found himself in a little lobby with a counter built halfway across at the back, vinyl-covered banquettes, a couple of low tables spread with magazines. There was a vacant-eyed old lady strapped into a wheelchair sitting on one side of the lobby, and a stout young woman with sandy hair behind the counter.

She listened with perfunctory interest and said, "Well, most of the old people are always pleased to have visitors, whatever kind. I'd better let you talk to Mrs. Seager." She led him out of the lobby into a wide hallway.

As such places went, this one seemed to be a nice enough place. It all looked very clean and bright and tidy. As he followed her along the hall, he had glimpses into rooms with open doors, small rooms with two single beds each, but airy and neat. They passed a cross hall, and down there to the right was a double exit door propped open, beyond it a neat quadrangle of lawn and trees and brick walks. Not inviting today, with an overcast gray sky and a chill wind moving the trees, but in nice weather it would be a pleasant place for the patients here.

Patients. Euphemisms, he thought. The majority of people here, as in most of these places, were the old people—senile, or just physically incapable, or without responsible family, for whatever reason sitting here waiting for death.

Up the hallway another cross hall cut through; they passed a uniformed nurse's aide pushing a wheelchair with an old man in it. There was an L-shaped counter, a desk with a telephone, and a couple of uniformed nurses.

"I don't want to disrupt any routine," said Jesse meekly.

Mrs. Seager regarded him benignly. "Don't worry about that." She was a rather tall thin woman in her forties, with a plain no-nonsense face, defiantly gold-tinted blond hair, an inquisitive long nose; she looked very efficient. He noticed her severe little cap, the gold badge on her uniform, remembering that these places had to have a fully trained RN for every so many rooms or patients. "Of course I remember Mr. Griffin very well," she told him. "And his friend—I'd forgotten the name until you said it—Mr. Vander-veer. He used to come nearly every day while Mr. Griffin was here. We were sorry to lose Mr. Griffin, such a nice old man, and he always tried to keep cheerful in spite of all the pain he had."

"I understand Mr. Vanderveer had gotten friendly with some of the other patients here. I'd like to talk to any of those."

"Oh?" she said a little blankly. "Well, of course the ambulatory patients sit in the TV room a good deal, and on his good days Mr. Griffin would be there—I know he was friendly with a few of the other men, I suppose he could have introduced the other old gen-tleman. I wouldn't know about that, it's the aides and LVN's who have the most to do with the patients, you see. But you can ask, of course—it's just down this hall." She slipped off her high stool and led him down the cross hall. "We call it the TV room, but actually it's more than that—we have card tables set up and various amuse-ments for the ones still able to function. There are a couple of church groups who are very faithful about coming in, and we have a director of hobbies who supervises little arts and crafts projects and games, to give them some interest in life. That's very impor-tant, of course." They passed a wheelchair with an ancient wrinkled man sagging to one side, mumbling to himself, and came into a very large room, vaguely like a hotel lobby. It was at least forty feet long, and well furnished, if not expensively, with couches, chairs, low tables. There was a color TV in one corner, and an old lady in a wheelchair was hunched in front of it watching a soap

opera; the sound was turned low. There were a couple of old ladies in wheelchairs talking animatedly to three women sitting on a
couch. At the opposite end of the room four men were sitting together, two in wheelchairs, one flanked by a couple of heavy
canes.

"Oh, there's Mr. Ott," said Mrs. Seager cheerfully. "He and
Mr. Griffin were great friends." She led Jesse up there and introduced them, and went away with the air of washing her hands of
him.

Ott was the man with the canes. He had once been a big man,
but he had shrunk with age; he had bright little blue eyes and his
mind seemed to be working all right. "Oh, sure," he said at once
to Jesse's question, "Griffin and I were good pals, had a lot in
common, I was in construction too if not one of the bosses. He
was a nice fellow—shame he had to have so much trouble with
that leg of his. His wife's a nice woman, came to see him every
day. It makes a difference when you have people coming, my
daughter and son come as often as they can, a'course I lost my
wife last year. Sure I know Vanderveer, Griffin's old partner, he
was here most days and he's come back a few times since Griffin
died, that was the end of July." He introduced Jesse to the others:
Fischback, a big fat man in a wheelchair, Perloff, a smaller man in
the other wheelchair, a Mr. Nettleton. "He's not incarcerated
here, just our visiting preacher." Nettleton was a middle-aged man
with a thin face and fine gray eyes with a twinkle in them.

They had all known Vanderveer. They were surprised but not
shocked to hear he was dead. "Of course he was older than
Griffin," said Ott. Jesse didn't elaborate on the death and nobody
asked questions. "Do I remember what he used to talk about?"
Ott repeated doubtfully. "Well, Griffin and Vanderveer talked
about old times mostly, guess that's what old people usually do
talk about, isn't it? Jobs they'd done when they had their own
business, deals they'd made—they'd both done pretty well, I gathered—"

Fischback said somberly, "And families and wives and good
times when we were all young. Like that."

"Why do you ask?" asked Perloff curiously. Jesse explained:
settling the estate, and some records not clear. "I just wondered if

he ever mentioned much about what he owned, how much he had and what it was in—anything like that."

"Oh," said Ott. "Well, I dunno. I know Griffin told me that Vanderveer had parlayed his take into quite a pile, investing in the stock market—me, I was never smart enough to fool with that even if I'd had the money. Griffin said Vanderveer used to give him lots of tips, he'd made quite a bit too. Now I do recall that Vanderveer said he owned real estate too, I think he had quite a bit tied up in that."

"I guess he was pretty damn smart about making money," said Fischback gloomily. "The way he talked. And what Griffin used to say."

"He thought we're heading for a big economic crash," said Ott. "Something real bad. He said he figured there'd be bank failures and a lot of businesses going down the drain. Oh, I don't know if it'd mean anything to you, but he said once that he used to keep a big savings account at the bank, but when the government was going to slap the withholding tax on savings, and seeing you get such piddling little interest, he closed it out."

"Yeah, I remember him saying that," agreed Fischback. "Must be nice to have money, all I can say. That much money." He sounded envious and angry. "He said that—about another depression, and the banks—he said anybody had very much was a damn fool to leave it all in one bank. Something about diversifying, he said. My God, I got little enough in one bank account—"

"My God!" said Jesse. "Oh, yes, I see. That's enlightening."

"He was a queer mixture—an interesting man, Vanderveer," said Perloff. "He was actually quite proud of the fact that he'd had very little formal education—oh, excuse me, I'm a retired schoolteacher, you see, I taught math at Marshall Junior High for nearly forty years. But he had a very quick mind, it was rather remarkable at his age. I always did say, if one has to end up incapacitated, I'd rather have it physical than mental," and he looked ruefully at the blanket across his legs. "I'm very thankful my mind's as good as it ever was. Do you know, I taught him to play chess—Mr. Nettleton very kindly comes in to give me a game when he has time—and Vanderveer took to it right away, even beat me a few times. But I don't think he'd have talked about his private affairs to us, except in general terms. He probably did with

Griffin. The days when Griffin wasn't so well they'd be in his room, not out here."

"Griffin had old Ortiz in with him mostly, didn't he?" said Ott. "Well, he died before Griffin did, so that's no good. He didn't speak very good English anyway. It was that temporary patient was in with Griffin just before he died—Dickey, that was the name, Adam Dickey. Had his knee crushed in an auto accident, he was here a couple of months having therapy. I remember they moved him the night Griffin died—I never saw that Mrs. Seager ruffled before, but she was then—I guess Griffin started to pass away before they rightly expected it, and they don't like a patient in the same room—" Ott sighed sharply. "Not a thing anybody likes to think about, but we all come to it. I guess we're not much help to you, sir."

"Well, have to keep poking around," said Jesse. "I just wish he had thought some about dying, and realized somebody'd have to do the tidying up."

"Left things in a mess, did he?" asked Fischback. "Must be a nuisance for the family."

"Yes. *We brought nothing into this world and it is certain we can carry nothing out*—isn't it the truth—"

Nettleton coughed and said, "Excuse me, but I have always thought that that line is much misinterpreted, Mr. Falkenstein. That's not strictly true at all. We bring a good deal into this world with us—what brain we have, our physical bodies to use at useful work and play and procreation, what talents we may have, what characters we develop. And we take a good deal with us when we leave, too—all that's eternally important to us, the good or evil we've done, the love we've given, kindnesses done, the whole results of how we've employed our characters, our lives, what we've given our children of moral training, the responsibilities we've borne. The least important thing about any person is what material possessions he may control while he's here—that is so ephemeral. The most important is what we take with us when we leave."

"And that's true too," said Jesse soberly. "*His own iniquities shall take the wicked himself, and he shall be holden with the cords of his sins.*"

Nettleton beamed at him gently. "*The Wisdom of the Torah.* Oh, yes, indeed that is true."

That damned wily old sinner, playing both ends against the middle, thought Jesse as he drove home. Not dreaming up any tax dodges at all: just hedging his bets. Expecting some banks to fold, maybe the big ones shored up later, just protecting his assets—scattering money around in different banks, and my God, there were ten thousand in the greater L.A. area—what a hell of a job—but there must be some way to narrow down the hunt. And where were the bankbooks, the bank statements? It wasn't likely he'd have used banks out in the valley, or down at the beach, probably nearer home—

Oh, yes? Those accounts would be inactive, he wouldn't have had occasion to visit the banks—he could have done the whole thing by mail. Yes, and according to that woman at the apartment the other day, the mail was delivered about eleven o'clock, and Vanderveer would have been the one to take it in; and the chances were that on Saturdays, even if Dulcie was home and not at the market, he'd get it then too. What the hell had he done with the statements?

Trying to second-guess the old fox, Jesse felt halfway certain that he'd had a hidey-hole of some kind at home—and more than sixty bucks in it. Emergency provisions, for when the banks shut up. The stray thought slid across his mind—that visiting nurse, he forgot her name, Gibson—how long would she be there when she came? The old man used to her coming and going in the house, and he didn't pay much attention to women anyway—except, Jesse amended, in one way, and he marveled again at what the Perez woman had said. Would the nurse possibly have noticed anything? By God, he'd go over that house inch by inch, in case there was a hidey-hole of some kind. He couldn't get at the banks until Monday anyway.

The gate was open. He drove through, got out and closed it, drove into the garage and went in the back door. Nell was taking something out of the oven. He said to her, "You've got duplicate keys to the office, and access to the safe-deposit box and checking account. You know where my will is, and where to find the combination to the office safe. You do know which insurance company we're with, don't you?—well, it's in my address book at the office. I can't think of anything else—oh, don't forget we're both members of the Neptune Society—cheap disposal, cremation, and ashes scattered at sea. Very hygienic."

Nell stared at him. "You've suddenly found out you've got an incurable disease?"

"I feel fine," said Jesse crossly. "But I tell you, these damned secretive people can leave utter chaos behind, without intending to. What a mess. Come and sit down and hold my hand and I'll tell you about it."

"You sound as if you need a drink," said Nell sensibly. "For once the offspring's peacefully playing in his room. He can have another half hour before bed."

He felt a little better for the drink and dinner. It was getting on for eight o'clock when he called Clock and brought him up to date.

"Tomorrow's your day off, and you're the expert on where people hide things, after covering all the burglaries. You can come and help me hunt."

Clock swore. "It's not a police case any longer, it's all your own baby."

"Listen," said Jesse, "I keep reminding you, I've got a lot of money, maybe to leave some to a niece or nephew. You'd better keep on good terms."

"Oh, hell," said Clock and laughed. "O.K., I'll meet you there at nine o'clock. And Fran's feeling a lot better, she hasn't been sick in a couple of days."

"Good. I'll see you in the morning."

"I'll tell you one thing," said Clock on the front porch of the house on Kingsley on Saturday morning. "If there's anything here worth anything, you'd better locate it and take it away. An empty house in central Hollywood is a standing invitation to the burglars."

"The thought had crossed my mind. None of the furniture would be any loss, but I'd better ask the Colemans to pack up all Dulcie's things. Now look, Andrew. I think the chances are that if he had a little hidey-hole here, it'd be in the den. Under his own eye. I think we start there."

They went down to the little room and Clock surveyed it dubiously. "I'm not all that much of an expert. The carpet's fastened down, that's no good." They took everything out of the wardrobe, tapped the floor and walls. They emptied the file cabinet—Jesse wanted all the contents anyway—and looked at the undersides of its drawers. They took the studio couch apart to look under the mattress. They turned the old-fashioned desk chair over.

Clock stood in the middle of the room eying the rolltop desk. "My grandfather had one something like this, and it had a secret drawer in it. I remember him showing me the trick. Let's see. It was at the back of one of the pigeonholes, a place you pushed—" He fumbled around in the pigeonholes, one after the other, without result, finally found an old steel letter opener and prodded with that.

Suddenly part of the ornamental carving below the pigeonholes shot out with a little click, revealing a small drawer about an inch deep and four inches long.

"Not very secret or very big," said Jesse.

"Don't be so ungrateful."

The drawer held just two pieces of paper. One proved to be Schultz's IOU on an ordinary piece of bond typing paper. The other one was another piece of Dulcie's stationery with one line printed on it in a crabbed hand. *G. W. 411-0219.*

"Now what the hell?" said Jesse.

"He couldn't stash away much cash in there," said Clock. He was looking around the room. "Now I do wonder—places this old don't usually have too many electric outlets." There was an overhead light with a switch by the door; an outlet behind the desk; and one across the room under the window, with nothing plugged into it. "Well, let's have a look." Clock kneeled down in front of it. "There's this new gadget out—of course it's not very big either, handy place to hide jewelry, little items like— Ah. There you are." The electric outlet wasn't an outlet at all, but a little box built into the baseboard; it tilted out under Clock's questing finger. The inside was about three inches deep and a couple of inches wide.

Crammed into it, tightly folded, were ten hundred-dollar bills.

"Well, very pretty," said Jesse. "The man was a carpenter, he could have installed that quietly while his wife was taking an afternoon nap. But my God, nobody knowing." He tucked the money away.

"Could be little caches like that all over the house for all we know," said Clock. Fired with the hunt, they carried it to the rest of the house. But all the other electrical outlets were just ordinary outlets. They took everything out of the front closet and sounded the floor, walls, and Clock got a splinter in his thumb off the shelf. They rummaged through the Christmas ornaments. They looked under the cabinet beneath the sink in the kitchen—"A good place to put a trapdoor," said Clock; but there wasn't any loose board.

"My God," said Jesse suddenly, "those boxes of *Wall Street Journals*—there could be bills tucked between every page—"

Clock emerged from crawling under the sink and stood up, brushing at himself. "At least we can look at those sitting down. I've had a rough week, and I'm beat. How you get into these things, Jesse—"

They dumped all the old *Journals* out of those boxes and went through them thoroughly page by page, but didn't find any more money hidden there. It took a while.

They gave up at two o'clock and went out for a belated lunch.

Jesse had called that Visiting Nurse service and gotten the name and address of the woman who had gone to the Vanderveers'. She was Mrs. Amelia Gibson and she lived on Courtney Avenue. Clock had gone home after lunch, claiming that he was entitled to half a day's rest. Jesse found a public phone outside the restaurant and tried her phone number. She was in. No, she wouldn't mind talking to him.

It was an old apartment building on an old street on the border of West Hollywood; probably these places were larger and more comfortable than a lot of the jerry-built new ones. She lived on the second floor, and when he'd pushed the bell the door opened on a chain, and she took his card through the crack before asking him in, unhooking the chain.

"Sorry, but you can't be too careful these days, the things that go on." Amelia Gibson was a plain woman in her fifties, with a sallow horseface and short gray hair. The living room was neat, plainly furnished, with no frills, utilitarian. She offered him a chair, sat down in another, and rather to his surprise accepted a cigarette.

"I don't know how I can help you," she told him. "I never knew the daughter at all."

"I know that. You'd been going to Mrs. Vanderveer how long, Mrs. Gibson?"

She thought. "About a year. I went Mondays, Wednesdays, and Fridays for a couple of hours. I think before that she had Miss O'Hagan. And sometimes the schedule gets changed, with temporary patients turning up, there were a few times I was sent to somebody else and another nurse substituted. The permanent patients usually get the same nurse, of course. Poor woman, she was getting more helpless all the time. It was a terrible thing her getting killed like that, I could hardly believe it when Mrs. Borchard told me, that's our supervisor—so much violence these days, but her own daughter—"

"Do you remember," asked Jesse, "any time you were there, Mr. Vanderveer having any visitors? Or maybe you happened to overhear something he was saying on the phone—not to suggest that you'd eavesdrop deliberately, but maybe you couldn't help hearing—"

She didn't acknowledge the invitation to gossip. "He was a crusty old man, not very sympathetic to his wife." She glanced at Jesse, and away, hesitated, and went on, "They couldn't have gone on like that much longer, she would have been bedridden before long, and needed a lot more care. I'd told him that, or tried to tell him, that they should make other arrangements. Put her in a rest home, or have more practical nurses in. I couldn't make him understand it, he just said his daughter would manage, she always had. I talked it over with Mrs. Borchard, and she said I ought to talk to the daughter. I never saw her, you see, because she was working all day. So I called her on a Saturday, and talked to her about it. I must say," said Mrs. Gibson uneasily, "she sounded quite sensible. She said she knew her mother was getting worse, but it was going to be difficult to make her father see it, that she'd try. Well, it was the family's business after all, nothing to do with me. Of course I was annoyed"—she drew down the corners of her mouth—"but that wasn't her fault—"

"About what?" asked Jesse.

"What? Oh, she happened to mention that my supervisor had called to ask if I was satisfactory and coming when I was supposed to—really I was very put out at Mrs. Borchard, of course she checks up on new nurses who haven't worked for the county before, but after all I've been with the service for nearly ten years, she knows I'm quite reliable. I didn't say anything about it, of course, but I was annoyed. But you were asking about any visitors or— He was really a most unpleasant old man. I remember once, quite some time ago, there was a young man came to pay his rent, Mr. Vanderveer owned rental property, you know, and he was quite ugly to him, Mr. Vanderveer I mean, shouting and threatening him because it was overdue."

"Mmh," said Jesse. "Remember anything else?"

"Well, yes," she said. "It was your mentioning phone calls that reminded me, and at first I wasn't going to say anything, but maybe I'd better. I did hear something once, something that really did disgust me." Her mouth drew tight. "You're quite right, Mr. Falkenstein, I wasn't trying to hear, but I'd be going back and forth from the kitchen to the bedroom and bathroom, you know, and of course it's not a large house. And the phone was on his desk in the den. This was just a couple of months ago, by the way. He was talking on the phone, and I couldn't help hearing what he was saying as I came past—and he was talking to a woman named Gloria, sounding like an old lecher—he was actually making a date with her, of all things, saying about the usual place on Saturday afternoon."

"Well, well," said Jesse. So Flo Griffin had been quite right.

"And him eighty if he was a day!" She sniffed. "They do say, no fool like an old fool."

That was all she could tell him, and it was interesting, but hardly helpful on any of his problems. He sat behind the wheel of the Mercedes and got out that little old address book—there hadn't been any general address book at the house—and hunted through it again. He realized again just how obsolete it was, most of the ink faded; all the old building-supply houses, names of realty companies—he recognized the name of one well-known developer whose obituary had been in the *Times* a couple of years ago. There were few personal names and no women's names at all. He puzzled briefly again over those cryptic little notations; no rhyme or reason to that.

And then suddenly he thought about that other paper in the little secret door of the desk. G.W.—G. for Gloria?

*   *   *

"You know, Jesse," said Nell, ladling out lima beans and passing the dish to him, "that cat. I don't think it has a home—I think it's lost, or abandoned. I asked the other people down the hill today, and they don't know anything about it either. Where it belongs. And we're so far from any other house—I suppose it would be attracted up here by all the underbrush, mice and things on wild land. That Mrs. Tidwell is a horror. I got another look at it this morning, it was sitting by the side fence, and it looks awfully thin. Siamese are usually pampered pets, but something could have happened, someone died or— And people do just abandon cats, the kind of horrible people who think cats can fend for themselves."

"It's a five-hundred-dollar fine in this state to abandon an animal," said Jesse. "You'd better start feeding it, then. Can't have Athelstane's friend going hungry."

"Oh, I will. I always liked Siamese, and if it ever had a good home it might make friends with people again."

Ensconced in the study after dinner, Jesse looked at that slip of paper curiously. G.W. Well, you never knew where something might show up.

He dialed the number, and after three rings a voice answered: a pleasant woman's voice, sounding educated and mature. "Is Gloria there?" asked Jesse.

"Who is this?"

"I just want to talk to Gloria, set up a date."

"I think you must have the wrong number," she said remotely. "This is the Worth residence."

"Sorry," mumbled Jesse, and hung up. Worth. G.W. He picked up the phone book. He had all six of the books covering Los Angeles County, but he was pretty sure that that prefix was local and tried the west central book first. And there it was as big as life. Robert Worth, an address on Glentower Terrace, and the same phone number. That would be up in the Hollywood hills, up near Griffith Park. Quite a classy address. What was this? He sat back and wondered.

But like Mr. Kipling's Elephant's Child, he was always curious, and whether this was relevant to anything or not, he'd like to know what the hell it was all about.

Early on Sunday afternoon he looked up the address in the *County Guide* and drove up there. It was one of the short streets curving off Beachwood Drive, and when he found the house, it was a handsome old Spanish place with a smooth lawn and rose beds in front, and past the end of the drive a hint of a pool behind. It said money, it said class, and just what its connection had been with Vanderveer he couldn't imagine. Well, you didn't get answers if you didn't ask questions. He parked in front, went up to the door, and pushed the bell.

The woman who opened the door might be in her late forties, not looking it. She was an attractive dark-haired woman with a fine fair complexion, a professional coiffure, smartly dressed in a navy sheath and tasteful costume jewelry. She had a very nice figure.

"Mrs. Gloria Worth?"

She looked at him in small surprise. "Why, yes."

"I think," said Jesse gently, "that you were acquainted with Mr. Jan Vanderveer."

Terror filled her eyes, stark and sudden. "No. I'm afraid I don't know anybody by that name."

"He had your phone number in a rather special place," said Jesse, watching her.

"What do you want?" she demanded sharply. "I don't know you—either."

"No, but I'm perfectly respectable, Mrs. Worth." He handed her a card; she didn't look at it. "Did you know he's dead? I'm the lawyer settling his estate, I'm just clearing up loose ends, that's all."

She said dully, after a long moment, "It was you—on the phone last night. So it starts up—all over again. You'd better come in. Thank God, Robert's out, he and the children went riding."

It was an elegantly furnished living room, expensive furniture, everything in excellent taste. She didn't ask him to sit down. She faced him coldly, and asked, "How much do you want?" And her voice was sharp and contemptuous.

Jesse said, "My God. He was blackmailing you? That old bastard— Look, Mrs. Worth, it's all right. I'm just tying up loose ends, as I told you."

She stared at him for a full minute, as if she were trying to see into his soul. "Oh, my God," she said in a strained voice, "I saw in the paper that he'd been killed, and I was never so thankful for anything in my life. Please, please—I have a husband and family, it would kill Robert to find out—Johnny didn't tell you, leave anything written down, did he? Oh, my God, haven't I paid enough in —in being so ashamed, for something twenty-eight years in the past?" That was passionate. "I've got a good decent husband, a son and daughter—I couldn't stand it if they knew—please, please don't—"

"Now calm down," said Jesse. "Take it easy." She was shaking all over; he took her by the shoulders and walked her over to a chair, made her sit down. He sat down on the couch opposite. "It doesn't matter what he had on you, there's no record. I don't know anything about it and if I did I wouldn't put an ad in the *Times* about it, or write your husband an anonymous letter. Everything's all right now, Mrs. Worth."

She stared at him again, and this time he saw her beginning to believe him.

"Oh, my God," she said, and drew a long unsteady breath. "I nearly died when I saw him—I hadn't seen him in twenty-six years— And of course it had to be that day my car was in the garage, and I had to keep a dental appointment—I had to be on the same bus. And he had to see me, and recognize me. I was—on my way home—and he followed me. Saw which house. I nearly died when I saw him on the porch—like an old dried-up mummy, he was old when I knew him—back all that time ago—standing there grinning at me like a fox, saying, you've got a nice house, Gloria, maybe a husband with money, a nice family—you think your husband 'd like to meet one of your old cust—" Her hand went to her mouth and her eyes were terrified again.

"Oh, I see," said Jesse. "Don't look so scared—I'm safe. That old bastard. Do you mean to say he—well, what did he want?"

"Money," she said bitterly. "Oh"—and she gave a hard laugh— "he'd be past wanting—anything else, wouldn't he? I've been paying him fifty dollars a week out of the housekeeping money, I couldn't manage any more, Robert's easygoing but he'd wonder if I asked—" Her voice had gone dull again. "Just a silly stupid kid, I'd gotten into drugs in high school, pot was just starting to be the 'in' thing then—and one thing led to another—it was only a couple

of years, I straightened up and pulled myself together—but it
would kill Robert—"

"Well, by God," said Jesse, "I wish the old bastard was alive to
get his teeth kicked in. That's the damndest— Whoever did kill
him deserves a medal, all I can say."

She managed a bitter laugh. "Amen to that."

"Look, don't worry. This won't go any further, I'll forget all
about it. Sorry to upset you all over again."

And she was glad to see him go, if she did believe him. But as
she shut the front door on him her eyes were still anxious.

He got into the car consumed with seething contempt for his
late client. You'd think the man would have been more concerned
with his immortal soul, as close to death as he was at eighty-one,
instead of still fanatically concentrating on raking in the pennies
and dimes wherever, however he could. The old bastard.

He sat at his desk on Monday morning and thought, how the
hell to track down those probable bank accounts? Banks didn't
give out information about their customers for the asking. Clock
could do it, but Clock was a busy cop—the police weren't concerned in the case any longer.

I'm a fool, he thought. The statements. It was just past the first
of the month, and the statements ought to be coming in—what the
hell had the old man been doing with them? Such a convoluted
mind—and Jesse could swear that they had searched that house
thoroughly, there wasn't another hidey-hole, but—they hadn't
looked in the garage, dammit. Never mind, the old man had had
somewhere to keep the statements—if he'd kept them at all. Very
likely the inactive accounts, though if he destroyed the statements
you'd think he'd have kept a record of the amounts somewhere.
Conceivably, of course, he could have had another safe-deposit
box at another bank, but if so where the hell was the key?

He called Marcia Coleman and asked about the mail. "Well, I
thought of it, of course," she told him. "I told the post office to
put a hold on it. Stop delivery. They wouldn't have gotten much
mail, mostly ads—a couple of Mama's old friends wrote to her occasionally. Why do you want to know?"

"I've just discovered he probably had some other bank accounts. The monthly statements ought to be drifting in, and it's the only way we're going to find out where and what."

"Do you want me to come and pick up what's there? Right now?"

"It's a long drive," said Jesse. "I apologize, but you couldn't authorize me to do it over the phone. Uncle's so persnickety about custody of the mails."

"I'll come up right away and bring it to your office," she said at once. "I can authorize you to get it from now on while I'm there, can't I?"

She must have gotten right on the ball; she came into the office at eleven o'clock and handed over a little package of mail. "I've got to get back—pick up Bobby at nursery school, and Marion's got a music lesson. But you can get the mail from now on."

Jesse was grateful and told her so. And when he went through the pile—catalogs, ads, no personal letters at all—there were two bank statements. One on the account they knew about, at Security-Pacific. And a statement from a Bank of America on Western Avenue. He ripped that open and looked at it and said, "Well, there we are. Good God. A mind like a corkscrew." The statement showed a checking account in the amount of twenty thousand even. No checks written on it in the last month—or probably ever.

Jesse lit a cigarette and thought about it. Why a checking account? In a savings account, he'd be earning the little interest at least—yes, but the withholding tax automatically abstracted to offset that—and the other way, the money immediately available.

He called Dobson and told him about it. "Probably some more will show up. I'll let you know."

"What a character," said Dobson. "Just keep me informed."

Jesse was just starting out for lunch when William DeWitt came in without being announced, as a privileged person, and said, "I forgot all about our ledger, Jesse. Miss Duffy just ordered some new letterhead stationery, and you know how fussy she is about keeping records. She reminded me to pick it up." He sat down in one of the clients' chairs, briefcase on his knee for once. "I've got a rather interesting transcript with me, a session with Wanda and a new sitter last night—some rather evidential material. I'll take you out to lunch and you can look it over."

"Fair enough," said Jesse. "And what's the latest on your ambiguous seeker after truth?" DeWitt looked blank. "The lady who thinks the medium's reading her mind."

"Oh, the Finch woman," said DeWitt. "My God, it makes you wonder about people, Jesse. If she's open-minded enough to go to a psychic, she ought to be willing to accept what she gets and evaluate it logically, good, bad, or indifferent. But that damn fool of a woman—worse than the other damn fools who are ready to swallow anything and everything a psychic says as gospel truth—she wants to believe it, but there's a lifetime of agnosticism, no conviction of survival, and when she comes out of the emotional jag she's got to hunt for the rational explanation. Telepathy!" said DeWitt, as if it were a four-letter word.

"Oh, yes," said Jesse. "Survival. It'll be interesting to find out what happens next, William. To what we take with us when we leave. I do just wonder what's happening to a late client of mine. Don't think anything very pleasant, William. Trust not, anyway. Where are we going for lunch?"

CHAPTER 6

Athelstane's friend or not, Nell knew that dog, and if he found anything edible around he wasn't going to leave it for anyone else. She spotted the cat about the middle of the afternoon, coming out from under the trees at the back of the yard and sliding under the shrubbery by the fence. She wondered, hunting for mice, gophers? She called Athelstane in and, as she had done yesterday, took out a paper plate heaped with fresh hamburger. She was careful not to go too near to where she'd seen the cat vanish, but she talked to the cat coaxingly, put the plate down on the edge of the lawn, and came back to watch at the kitchen window.

After about five minutes, the cat cautiously came out onto the lawn; it had waited longer yesterday. It approached the plate warily, and took its time about sniffing carefully at the contents. But then it hastily bolted down the hamburger, not in the normal leisurely way of a cat confident of routine meals, but seizing a windfall before it should vanish. The cat was certainly very thin, and its fur rough-looking, but now Nell had a good look, it was a once-handsome seal point Siamese.

"I wonder," she said aloud to Athelstane, "where on earth you came from and what happened to you."

Jesse descended on the precinct station in midafternoon and interrupted Clock typing a report on a burglary. Clock was the sole occupant of the detective office, and he told Jesse he was busy. "I need somebody to talk at," said Jesse, dragging up Petrovsky's desk chair and sitting down across from Clock's desk. "Discuss what's showed up. I think you were all a little hasty about sending the reports down to the D.A.'s office on this one, Andrew."

"Oh, hell," said Clock, "I guess I'm due for a coffee break."

They brought paper cups of coffee and napkins from the machine down the hall. "What's on your mind now?"

"Dammit," said Jesse, "I suppose we'll uncover all the loot eventually. It's more important to me right now to think about this trial. How the hell to handle it. There are other possibilities here than the single-minded theory you relayed to the D.A. And especially, when I got to thinking about it, this Worth female." He told Clock about that: Clock was safe, and wouldn't pass it on; at the moment there was nothing to warrant any more police work on the case. "Think about it. She had, God knows, a motive. Vanderveer was in the phone book, she'd know where to find him. She could have done a little rudimentary snooping around, found out that Dulcie was out all day, even when that visiting nurse was there. Dammit, I wouldn't like to throw her to the wolves, but— And Vanderveer would have let her in."

"And just how could she have managed to set up that funny situation?" asked Clock.

"Well, I can think of ways," said Jesse uneasily. "She could have pretended to come to ask him, oh, to take one big lump sum once and for all and leave her alone. Maybe she brought a gun along intending to shoot him, for all we know. He was in the habit of ordering his wife around, he could have told her to stay in the bedroom while he and Gloria talked."

"And before she got around to shooting him, she asked to use the bathroom and just by chance opened the medicine cabinet and happened to notice the codeine capsules," said Clock. "So she offered to make him a cup of coffee in his own kitchen. And why kill the old lady too?"

"Well, if she'd seen her— And dammit all to hell, Andrew, there's an even likelier possibility. As I said before, the coincidences do happen—not everything in life is reasonable. The old fellow was getting shakier, feeling his age, missing his lifelong pal, and realizing whether he admitted it or not that his wife was getting worse. I don't think he cared much about her, but at the least she was going to start costing him a lot more money. It is just possible that he's the one arranged the overdose that morning—thinking they'd both be better out of it—and Gloria Worth walked in on him just afterward. She may not have planned to kill him—just plead with him—and there was an argument, and she lost her wits and grabbed up the poker when he got abusive. The autopsy report said it was just as likely that Myra Vanderveer fell out of her walker—hurrying to see what the noise was all about—and knocked herself out."

Clock sat back and scratched his big jaw. "Well, it's a little forced, but you've got an imagination."

"The back door," said Jesse. "Somebody went out that door after the old man was incapable of rehooking the chain." He was silent, and then he said, "Hell and damnation, I wish I had some vague idea of how to handle the case in court. What with Eberhart— Eberhart so sure and certain of his story—" And then he stood up and said loudly, "But, *Eberhart!*" He dropped his cup on Clock's desk. "Eberhart! Eberhart—suppose—"

Clock leaped up and snatched papers off the desk, began to mop up spilled coffee with a paper napkin. "For God's sake, what bit you? Look at this mess—"

"But suppose—" said Jesse. He sat down again. "I've been taking it for granted that Eberhart remembered seeing Dulcie come home for her keys on Tuesday morning, two days before—but suppose he was absolutely right and it was Thursday? My God, Andrew, don't you see it? It just suddenly struck me—it could have been the other one he saw—they're alike—and Marcia drives a tan two-door Chevy."

"For the love of Christ," said Clock, and stared at him. He dropped the sopping napkin into the wastepaper basket and lowered himself into the chair. "From out in left field. But—"

"And now I see it, it makes a hell of a lot more sense," Jesse said.

"Why?" asked Clock.

"Let me go on thinking, get it straight in my mind." Jesse stared into space for three minutes and then uttered a deep sigh, sat up, and lit a cigarette. "And it fits like a glove. I like it—it makes sense. What did everybody say? Marcia was the rebellious one, who got away, out from under his thumb. She has her own life, busy wife and mother, fond husband. But she's fond of her sister too, and feels guilty she couldn't help her more, as the situation got worse— Yes, and she wouldn't have gotten up to Hollywood often—once a month, less than that?—talked on the phone with Dulcie, that's all. But Griffin died at the end of July, and when she saw Dulcie at the funeral she realized just how exhausted she was, almost at the end of her rope. And she felt guiltier. Didn't know what to do about it, went on worrying about it. And then we get that family row after the visiting nurse talked to Dulcie, when they tried to persuade the old man to put his wife in a rest home and he refused to listen—that must have brought matters to a head. The girls were both fond of their mother, but Marcia had nothing but dislike for the old man—and Dulcie would have told her how Mama kept saying she just wanted to die and be at rest. And the more she thought about it, the more she saw it as a solution. She'd escaped, but Dulcie had sacrificed her life to the old people, and the mother's life was only a misery to her, the pain and helplessness. It would be a kindness to put her at rest, same as we have the decency to do for an animal we're fond of who's suffering. And how easy it all falls into place from there, Andrew."

"I see it," said Clock slowly. "It's possible."

"Yes, the busy wife and mother, children at school—even Bobby at nursery school—and Charles at his English classes at the college. She'd always have errands to do, out every day in her own car. Ask where she was? At the market—busy supermart where nobody'd remember if she was there or not. And the times fit so nicely too—she'd have gotten up to Hollywood about eleven, surprise visit to Mama and Papa. And of course she had the freedom of the house. She knew all about the codeine capsules. And they were both used to being waited on, the old man because that's what women were for, the old woman because she couldn't do much for herself. And another thing you said, that other story sounds forced—yes, the reason I don't halfway like it. Because Vanderveer wasn't at all the kind to think of suicide. He was too passionately interested in the affairs of this world, in the material possessions."

"Yes," said Clock. "But when it went wrong—how did it, do you think?"

"The same way you said it went wrong for Dulcie. She thought the old man was already unconscious, brought out the suicide note too soon—and he realized what she was up to and lashed out at her. He was old and shaky, but he'd been a powerful man in his prime—if he had the poker—and she grabbed it and got in a lucky hit. The old lady, coming to investigate, fell out of the walker."

"What I was going to say," said Clock, "when she saw the fake suicide wasn't going to stand up, why didn't she fake a break-in? It'd have been easy enough, make it look as if some casual thief had pried open the kitchen door. Wouldn't she have realized that Dulcie might be blamed?"

"I don't think," said Jesse, "that she would have been thinking very clearly right then. She'd had to nerve herself up to do the thing at all—the physical struggle would have finished her for any straight thinking. She just ran." He got up and stood looking out the window, to the parking lot below. "It wasn't until later she realized what the police thought. What she'd inadvertently let Dulcie in for. And she'd be feeling a hell of a lot guiltier now. I think if I tackled her on the stand she'd come right apart and admit it. Think even if I tackled her right now—or if you did—she'd admit it." After a silence, he added, "And I can imagine how Dulcie would feel about that."

"Oh, so can I," said Clock heavily.

Jesse got back to the office at four o'clock. There was paper work to do. The girls were turning down appointments for this week and next; he had to have time to think about all this.

Ten minutes after Jesse came in, Jimmy announced that Mr. Renaldo wanted to see him. A Roberto Renaldo. Jesse put down his pen.

He was a handsome young fellow in his early twenties, dark and romantic-looking like the hero in a young-adult novel. He was tall, and he had brooding dark eyes, arched thick brows, a mobile mouth. He was neatly dressed in casual sports clothes. He greeted Jesse with formal courtesy.

"There is a notice in the mail, that this is where the rent is to be paid? You are a lawyer who processes the will of the old man, his property?— Ah, I thought this when I see the door outside, attorney at law. I have come to give you notice that we leave the house."

"Oh," said Jesse.

"The atmosphere of the house, it disturbs my wife, Lucia. Since the old man is murdered. He was a very wicked old man, and since he first upset Lucia we have thought of moving anyway. Now he is murdered she is more upset, naturally, to think of a murderer about, and so we will move. It is expensive and a great trouble, but there is no choice."

Jesse asked, "How did Vanderveer upset your wife?"

Remembered fury came into the dark eyes. "Ah, it was an outrage! Imagine, this ancient, this old *padre caballo lascivo,* he has made the dirty advances when he came to collect the rent—imagine, a man as old as that, it was an outrage! He thought because we have not much money, we are not born Americans, he can take the liberty with a respectable girl! Lucia is upset and frightened—perhaps he has another key to the house, she says—I went to see this creature, and I am calm, I do not shout or swear at him, I merely tell him if he comes again to do this I will have the police arrest him, and if they will not I will kill him myself with a knife."

"Fine," said Jesse. "Did you scare him?"

"Oh, he sneers and swears, but I do not think he will come again, and he did not," said Renaldo. "And I put the chain on the door to calm Lucia. But the atmosphere—like all women she is a little superstitious, and says the spirit of a man murdered will still be about. Myself, I do not believe this. But we will move." He fixed Jesse with a royally fierce stare. "We will not always be poor, you understand. Now I drive a taxi, but I study the accounting in night school and someday will have my own business."

"Well, good luck to it," said Jesse.

Renaldo gave him a correct little nod. "I thank you, sir." He added casually as he went to the door, "It is devoutly to be hoped that the old man has now found his home with the devil, as no doubt he has." He marched out stiffly.

And Jesse thought, dammit, he wasn't a real estate agent. Another empty house. Better turn it over to an agent and let somebody else worry about it.

On Tuesday morning he faced Dulcie in one of the bare little rooms at the women's jail. "I just think we'd better lay a few things on the line, Miss Vanderveer. I don't want to sound pessimistic, but facts are facts and as your lawyer it's my job to tell you the truth."

"I should hope so," she said. She looked plain and washed out in the ugly tan uniform dress, without much makeup, her brown hair flat and uncurled.

"You'd better realize," he said expressionlessly, "the cumulative effect of all the evidence. First of all, of Eberhart's evidence. He's so very positive that he saw you drive in that morning, and he apparently has good reason for being positive."

"He's wrong, that's all."

"Well, he says he has a plausible reason for being sure. But beyond that, there's the entire background—the family situation. Your parents had very few close friends, very few visitors. There weren't many people who would have had the automatic freedom of that house, to locate those codeine capsules, to arrange that fake suicide setup so easily—to prepare the eggnog, the coffee, type that note, and so on. It would, as anyone can see, have been very easy for you. You didn't know any of the neighbors, or they you—most people on that block are out at work all day. The chances were good that nobody would notice you coming home that morning. You knew that Klein would be out, wouldn't miss you at the office. You see how it builds up—to anyone who doesn't know you."

"Yes," she said. "Do you think I haven't thought all that out for myself?"

"Let's just think," said Jesse, "who else might have been able to do it. Who would be automatically admitted, could wander around the house without causing any surprise. Now there's Mrs. Griffin. She's known you all your life, and she felt sorry for you just lately. She always disliked your father, felt sorry for your mother. She might, let's say, have decided to do a good deed and rescue you from a difficult situation. But it seems a pretty big responsibility for her to have taken—a double murder—and as you told me, you'd never really been close with the Griffins, though you called them aunt and uncle."

"No, that's ridiculous," said Dulcie with a faint smile. "She'd never have thought of such a thing, of course."

"Well, now, who else is there? There was a woman who had a great fear and hatred of your father—I needn't go into details—and he'd have let her into the house. But she wouldn't have known about the codeine capsules, and if she'd gone prying around he'd have objected, been suspicious, wouldn't he?"

"I don't want to know anything about her, Mr. Falkenstein. Yes, of course he would have been."

"The same thing holds true for a few other people—people he'd had arguments with lately. But there's a much better possibility we can think about. There's a fellow owed him some money, and he's a much better bet—he's the pharmacist where you got your mother's prescription."

She looked astonished. "Mr. Schultz?"

"That's right. Now, he could have come right in, and said there'd been some mistake in filling that last prescription, so he could get hold of the capsules. It's possible, say, that your father had already fixed the eggnog and coffee, and Schultz managed to slip the capsules into both. But it's a little hard to see how. It wouldn't be just one or two, but quite a lot. It wouldn't be easy to do, without being observed. Of course, he'd probably heard your father use that phrase—better out of it—he'd know enough to prepare that note."

"Oh, I don't think it could have happened like that," said Dulcie. She was looking at him calmly. "Papa often warmed up a cup of coffee for himself, I left a pot on the stove after breakfast. But he never bothered to get anything for Mama. On her good days she could get out to the kitchen, warm up coffee, or make a cup of tea. I left her a sandwich for her lunch. But that day she wasn't feeling well at all, I'd been worried about her all day. I don't think she'd have been able to fix herself that eggnog."

"Well, you can see how all this is going to sound in court," said Jesse briskly.

"You mean you think I'll be convicted?" She considered. "I've been thinking, Mr. Falkenstein, and I wonder if it was all just a terrible coincidence. Papa was always saying that, better out of it, if we never thought he meant anything by it. But he might have. He might have noticed Mama was so much worse, even if he wouldn't admit it, and decided to do that. Take her with him. And just afterward, some one of those people he'd had fights with came, and—there was another fight."

"Oh, yes, I thought of that too."

She said seriously, "But there's a good reason that that might have happened. When the doctor prescribed those capsules for Mama I wanted to know all about them, and I looked it up at the library in the P.D.R—the *Physician's Desk Reference*—where all prescriptive medicine is described. And one thing it said is that an overdose causes excitability at first."

"Oh, really," said Jesse, taken off base.

She nodded. "If somebody Papa'd had trouble with came in just after he'd taken that overdose, Papa might have been mad enough and excited—by the overdose—to grab up the poker and attack them. Him. It sort of makes sense, don't you think?"

Jesse said quietly, "Now, you might just have handed me the line to follow in court, Miss Vanderveer. But there's another possibility, you know. We said Eberhart confused the days. Suppose he didn't?"

There was a long silence. Faintly through the closed window they could hear the hum of traffic outside. Dulcie turned a little paler, but met his eyes, and the small square jaw looked squarer. "You mean Marcia," she said quietly. "I was hoping you wouldn't think of that, Mr. Falkenstein."

"So you thought it out too."

"Oh, yes. Our cars look alike, don't they? And we're generally alike in size and coloring. And she'd been calling me oftener, she said it wasn't until she saw me at Uncle Howie's funeral that she realized how run-down I was, and she was feeling guilty at not being able to help me more. Oh, of course I thought of it."

"And when it all went wrong and this happened, she'd be feeling guiltier, wouldn't she? She'd probably admit to the truth, if I taxed her with it now. Or got her on the witness stand and browbeat her a little."

"No!" said Dulcie sharply. "No, Mr. Falkenstein, you mustn't do that. I'm not going to say—if I think—she did it or not. But there's Charles, and the children. It doesn't matter so much about me. You said it would probably be two or three years—well, that's not so long really. It doesn't bear thinking about, what it would do to the family—if she was in jail instead. Please promise me—you won't even ask her—please, Mr. Falkenstein! You can try—the other story—at the trial, can't you? About the excitability—because it's quite true—and it would have been somebody just defending themselves, really. If they believe you, all right—and if they don't believe you, that's all right too—because it doesn't matter much about me."

Jesse said gently, "Don't you think you've sacrificed enough of your life, Miss Vanderveer?"

She gave him that faint ghost of a smile. "It's been this much, this long—what's a little longer?"

And he had unexpectedly gotten a very cogent lead from those old fellows at the rest home, and another stray idea had occurred to him. Vanderveer had gone to the public library—to read *The Wall Street Journal,* she had said. Jesse wondered if he'd got talking to other men there, if it was worth asking about. The old man hadn't been much of a reader—there wasn't a book in that house except in Dulcie's room where a little shelf held a modest stack of light romances and some modern poetry. It was doubtful if he'd had a library card, or really had spent much time there. But Jesse drove out to that branch on Santa Monica Boulevard just on the chance.

The woman at the desk didn't recognize the name, and Jesse gave her a description—a tall thin old man with a prominent nose, in shabby clothes—he probably sat in the periodical section. Her expression lightened doubtfully.

"Oh, if that's the one you mean, yes, I think I remember him. He came in nearly every Saturday to read the newspapers, but he never checked out any books."

"Ever notice him talking to anyone here? Another regular patron?"

She shook her head. "I couldn't say. But I remember he asked to see the head librarian once. Only he just said, the boss here."

"Oh, really," said Jesse. "And where would I find her?"

"It's Mr. Underhill," she said disapprovingly. "His office is through that door, next to the children's section."

Underhill looked more like a pro football player than a librarian. He was a youngish sandy fellow, with an amiable expression. He listened to Jesse's description, grinned, and said, "That one. People do constantly surprise you, what they get up to. Yes, I remember that old chap all right—it was about six months ago. He came in here to ask me about dirty books."

Momentarily confused, Jesse repeated, "Dirty books?"

"The porn," said Underhill. "You know. He asked if we didn't have some stuff like that under the counter. An old fellow that age! I just laughed at him. I told him all the blue stuff was on locked shelves at the main branch, available to serious research students on request, and he just gave me a disappointed look and shuffled out."

"That damned old goat!" said Jesse. "All right, as long as I'm here, I'd better take a look at something called the P.D.R."

"Sure. The girl out front will find it for you."

It was an unwieldy tome, but once he got onto the system it was easy to find what he was looking for, and he scanned the description swiftly. Good material for the trial. *Ban Cap Codeine Capsules*—and a technical list of contents—*Warning May Be Habit Forming . . . provide effective analgesia in a wide variety of conditions.* . . . And on down through a long paragraph, until he finally came to *Dosage in excess of two Ban Cap codeine capsules may cause excitability.*

And dammit, no, Vanderveer hardly the suicidal type, but was there one? And it made a story—it was just possible he had decided to take the quick way out. And take her with him. Missing Griffin, and all that had happened to him lately, little things, but it was often little things that triggered suicide. The typing—what were six words?—with a little care he could have produced that note.

And that damned house—holding any more secrets?

On the way, he stopped at the local post office and collected the recent mail. There was another bank statement, from a United California Bank on Western, showing a checking account with a balance of ten thousand dollars, no checks drawn on it. Catalogs and ads, no personal letters, and then something different. An ordinary plain postcard, with its printed stamp, a Los Angeles postmark, and the address hastily scrawled on the front. On the back was another scrawl. *Couldn't reach on phone, thought as price down you might be interested in another deal. Won't last!* It was signed *K.A.* Jesse regarded this anonymous message with some exasperation, and proceeded on to Kingsley Drive.

They hadn't looked at the garage. Dammit, he and Clock had covered this place—there wasn't anywhere else to look. He looked at it now, but not long: it was just an old single-car garage, with

Dulcie's old tan Ford sitting in it. There was a workbench built across the back, and everything was very neat, out in plain sight. A metal box full of different bits for an electric drill. The drill itself in a box. Boxes of nails, a few tools hung tidily on the wall, a ladder against one wall. There were open rafters, but nothing on them. Both electrical outlets were genuine.

Jesse went on into the house for no good reason. Dammit, they had looked everywhere there was to look. And eventually the different bank accounts would be turned up via the statements. He wondered academically whether anybody would have found out about those accounts if he hadn't talked to the old fellows at the rest home; Marcia might have thrown the whole lot of mail straight out, knowing there was seldom anything personal, and would it have occurred to him to ask about it? Probably not. But— but— There wasn't anything else to look for here, was there?

But he still had the uneasy little conviction that somewhere here there could still be a secret hidey-hole, larger than the little ones they had found, large enough to hold a real wad of cash. . . . What indeed did get into the ones like Vanderveer? Flo Griffin was quite right; men of completely different temperaments could be good friends; but Griffin by all accounts had been a civilized human being, while Vanderveer— Well, they had probably split the profits down the middle: but look at their lives. Both of them shrewd investors, building up the capital. But while the Griffins had enjoyed it—the nice house, the cars, trips, theaters, clothes—as it came in, Vanderveer had squatted in this sad little house like an old toad, avidly putting the profits back to work, squirreling them away in sterile banks, living on the mean edge of nothing. . . . Dulcie, adding part of her salary to buy the little treats Mama liked. . . .

He wandered down to that cramped squalid den and looked at the stuffing coming out of the old chair. And what for? What did it all come to? *For unto a malicious soul wisdom will not enter . . . and in the death of a man there is no remedy.* "Ephemeral" was the word. A flash—eighty-one years; and what had he taken with him when he left? What of any value in the eternal importances? And he had been calling Vanderveer an old bastard, but just now, looking into the room where the old man had spent so many hours, he saw him as not so much evil as merely stunted. Perhaps evil was never the mighty wrathful force it pretended to be, but a whining, deformed, ignorant child without understanding of itself or anything else.

Getting philosophical in his old age, he thought. He didn't know what the hell he was doing here.

He reached into his jacket pocket for his keys, and suddenly said, "Oh, for God's sake! For *God's*— how stupid can two grown men be?" Tapping the walls and closet shelves, my God, and it had never occurred to either of them— He went across to the wardrobe and started to examine all those clothes, feeling in all the pockets. The simple, elementary thing, simply not occurring to them before.

The old man had run true to character about his clothes, of course. These had all been worn threadbare, and none of them had been expensive to start with. Most of the suits were styles years out of date, with shiny patches and missing buttons. There was only one fairly new one, a navy wool; he wondered if Vanderveer had worn that to Griffin's funeral. And there weren't many clothes—he had moved in here when Dulcie had to be up so much with her mother—his shirts, socks, ties, underwear would be in drawers in the front bedroom.

For the moment Jesse wasn't interested in those. He went through every pocket, even felt in the turn-ups of trousers; and he was rewarded with exactly one find.

It was crumpled into the side pocket of an old herringbone suit jacket, and it was a sales slip. At the top was a logo produced by a rubber stamp: The Red Knight, an address on Santa Monica Boulevard. Below was scrawled in ballpoint pen, *Rcvd. 2.10.*

The Red Knight. It sounded like a restaurant or a nightclub, but the amount didn't match that.

It was rather far out on Santa Monica Boulevard, on his left as he passed it, and a glance showed a rather tattered red and white awning bearing the name, fancy scarlet letters above on the face of the building. He found a public lot and walked back. As he walked, he realized that these blocks up here were rapidly running to seed, sidewalks cracked, buildings in need of paint, stores empty. When he came to The Red Knight, it was sandwiched between a defunct cleaner's and a dark old independent drugstore.

There were scarlet curtains across the store window. He opened the door and went in.

Immediately beyond the door was a table littered with books; it was a bookstore. He took one look and said, "Oh, my God," disgustedly. More waste of time.

"Just take your time, look around, buddy," said a friendly voice. "We gotta lot of interesting stuff here, cater to all tastes like they say."

There was a partition halfway up the length of the store; over to the left was a table with a cash box on it, and a hairy young fellow was sitting behind it.

"Why," asked Jesse, "The Red Knight? For a porno book-store?"

"Hah? Oh, see, the name was on it. A restaurant or something folded. And I started with hardly any bread, see, I figured just leave it. Could I help you find something?"

"No, thanks," said Jesse. "Do you remember an old man coming in here—tall, thin, with a hooked sort of nose, shabby clothes? A fellow about eighty years old—"

"What the hell you got to do with him?" asked the hairy one.

"Do you remember him? He did come in here?"

"You're not a cop—I can smell fuzz. I don't know what you want that one for, but you can stop lookin' for him here. Do I remember him? I should live so long to forget him! In the first place, it's not natural, a guy that old, one foot in the grave, inter-ested in what I got here—it sort of turned my stomach, if you un-derstand me. I didn't like to see him come in. Well, it was about a year back, just after I opened the place. And he never spent much, just a little bit now and then. Did a lot of looking, and I make no bread on that. Well, we show movies in the back room on Satur-day afternoon, and he showed up for that a couple of times. Just once he took me, see—the movie, it's no big deal, five bucks per, but five is five. He showed up one day with the rest of the crowd, I'm taking the money at the door, he says he'll pay in a minute, wants to use the john—it's just back of the partition—and like a damn fool I let him in. I forgot about it till after the show, but when he comes out I say, hey, you owe me five, and he says he forgot his wallet, he'll pay me next time he's in. If there is one thing I hate it's a cheapskate welsher. What could I do at the time, but next time he comes in I remind him, he makes with the excuses and I say that's all, buddy, you get out and don't come back. I never saw the creep again and I don't want to. An old guy about ninety—turned my stomach."

Dobson called on Wednesday morning. "I tried to reach you yesterday but you were out. I just thought I'd check with that Bank of America, and Vanderveer has a safe-deposit box there."

"The hell you say," said Jesse.

"That's right. One of their medium-sized boxes, sixteen dollars a year. Number five-thirty-nine."

"But where the hell is his key? That damned old lunatic, it could be hidden anywhere and it wouldn't take up much space—"

"Have you been all through the house?"

"Have I been all through the *house?*" said Jesse. "I'm beginning to feel like a burglar. I seem to have spent most of my time lately going through that old devil's house. But anything as small as a key, for God's sake— Would you like to help look?"

"We're not paid to do jobs like that."

"Just," said Jesse bitterly, "to abstract their own money from the citizens and call it a service. For *God's* sake—"

He sat thinking, which wasn't productive of anything; finally, grumbling to himself, he went out to the car and drove down to Kingsley Drive. He'd be having nightmares about this house before he was much older. He didn't know where else he could look, dammit. It was bad enough hunting the possible hidey-holes big enough to hold a wad of cash, but a damned key—the long narrow steel key, with its number stamped on it—of a bank vault's safe-deposit box—

Hopelessly, he started the hunt all over again. The den: they had really exhausted the den, he and Clock. They had even moved the studio couch. This again was a case where the old man wouldn't have put it where the women might come across it. He went into the living room and looked around. The TV, he thought. Dulcie and her mother didn't watch it much, but he did. Jesse looked it over, lifted it from the metal stand with a little effort; there was nothing underneath. He put it on the floor and turned the stand upside down. Nothing. His gaze wandered around the room and lit on the mantel. There was a brass match box hanging on one side of it; he picked the matches out and felt in the bottom. Nothing. He felt along the underside of the mantel without result. But a *key*—you could fasten it with tape almost anywhere— Suddenly inspired, he began feeling the undersides of windowsills. He went through the entire house on that inspiration, and came up empty.

He sat down in the living room to rest and have a cigarette, fetching a saucer from the kitchen to use as an ashtray—of course Vanderveer had never used tobacco or liquor, they cost too much —and suddenly noticed that the old-fashioned breakfront in the dining end of the room had an ornamental ledge running around its middle. He leaped up to feel under that. Nothing.

When he had finished the cigarette, he stared into space for three minutes, and a hazy recollection came to him of a detective novel he'd once read where a key was hidden in a jar of cold cream. The bathroom—

It was typical of its period, a square room with linoleum on the floor, painted walls; tub on one side, commode behind it; a built-in washstand with a medicine cabinet above the bowl, two drawers and a cupboard below. He looked into the medicine cabinet. Three glass shelves: aspirin, antacid, half-used tube of toothpaste, a patent cream to hold false teeth, one lone toothbrush on a metal rack inside the door. Dulcie's. Both the old people had false teeth, he deduced.

The left-hand drawer held a package of razor blades, Band-Aids, a styptic pencil; the old man's things. He yanked it right out and emptied it: old razor blades, tubes of shaving cream, more Band-Aids, a dime-store comb, a cheap and probably useless gadget supposed to sharpen old blades. He took the old newspaper out of the bottom and discovered another rusty blade and a dead silverfish. Dulcie would be mortified; she hadn't had time for thorough cleaning lately.

The other drawer would be hers, but he went through it to be thorough. Cosmetics, comb, brush, a packet of Kleenex, hairpins, a hand mirror with a magnifying second side.

He felt under the overhanging edge of the counter. He took the top of the toilet tank off and peered inside.

Frustrated, he went back to the den, making a detour to pick up his ashtray on the way, and sat down to rest again.

He was about ninety percent convinced now that Marcia had done that murder. He thought Dulcie was a hundred percent convinced. He felt abstractly very sorry for both of them. He could see exactly how the whole sorry thing had happened—human nature— Well, that was something both lawyers and cops saw a lot of. If it weren't for the husband and family, Marcia would probably have confessed as soon as Dulcie was arrested. And it was a question— She was a nervous, emotional, at the moment highly tense woman; would she on impulse, during the trial, break down and shout, I did it so let her go? Don't even ask her, said Dulcie. He wouldn't need to call her as a witness, but the other side would: and under the urbane handling of one of those slick assistant D.A.s—Mrs. Coleman, you were aware that your sister had been under a good deal of physical and emotional strain lately, were you not?—

He sighed and put out his cigarette. The trial was some way ahead. He was supposed to be thinking about something else right now. Pull yourself together, boy, he thought, and use some common sense on it. This safe-deposit key. Well, depending on what you kept in a safe-deposit box, it wasn't a thing you visited every day, every week, even every month; but if you went to it fairly often you'd want the key handy. Ordinary people without corkscrew minds kept keys on key rings, but if you didn't you'd want it somewhere fairly accessible.

The idiot boy and the lost horse, he thought. If you were a horse— If you were a queer secretive old man with a yen to hide things, where would you hide a key? He looked around vaguely.

At least the weather had cleared up. The sun had come out today, and it was slightly warmer. There was more rain predicted for the weekend.

He looked over the contents of the room again. Furniture: all examined. Carpet nailed down. Wardrobe examined. One window, nothing taped to underside of sill; heavy brown drapes at window, an old-fashioned double-hung window with a wooden box valance hiding the curtain rod—that was a thought— He went over and examined the hems of the drapes. They were intact, and he could feel nothing sewn into them.

"Hell!" he said. He straightened and collided with the straight chair beside the studio couch; it fell on its side and he picked it

up. It was a humble old pine chair with a dark finish, and as he sat
it upright the light from the window fell full on it and he noticed
how scarred the unpadded seat was, with raw wood showing. An
old chair, but it couldn't have had much use in here, the old man
sitting in the desk chair—

He looked from the chair to the window. "By God!" he said.
He set the chair under the window and tried the left side first,
standing on the chair and feeling along the valance top. Nothing.
He moved the chair to the right side and his groping fingers encountered what he was hunting—the loose key resting on top of
the valance.

It was the right key: the long slender key of a safe-deposit box,
and it was stamped 539.

He met Dobson after lunch at that Bank of America and got
the IRS authorization to open the box. The short fat woman who
presided over the vault said of course she had known Mr. Vanderveer. "He used to take his box out and stay for quite a long time,
I suppose going over his investments."

They took the box into a cubicle and opened it. Inside there
was five thousand dollars in cash, the bankbooks for the extra account, half a dozen pornographic books, and a receipt for fifty
dollars from a *James Toomey, Private Investigations,* an address
on Melrose. It was dated six weeks ago.

CHAPTER 7

James Toomey looked at the receipt and said, "Yeah, that's mine. What about it?" He looked again at Jesse's card.

"The man you gave it to is dead," said Jesse, "and I'm the lawyer settling the estate. I'd like to know what you did for him."

Toomey sighed. Some private investigators were ex-cops, or, even if they weren't, smooth and experienced operators, on the ball. Toomey didn't look like one of those. This was a cheap little office in a run-down old building far out on Melrose past Highland. There wasn't even a typist doubling as receptionist out in front: just Toomey; and he didn't look very prepossessing. He was a discouraged-looking middle-aged man with a bald head, prominent ears, and an habitual nervous tic in his left eyelid.

He said mournfully, "Oh, well. He was quite an elderly man, wasn't he?"

"What did he come to you for?" asked Jesse.

Toomey smoothed a hand over his bald head. "Well, he wanted me to look up records for him. The record of a divorce, a long time back. A divorce from his wife. She'd got it, and he'd lost the papers, and he wanted a record of it. It was 1936, a hell of a time back, but of course if she'd gotten it here the record would be on file at the courthouse, and he said he thought she'd gotten it here. So I went and looked, but I couldn't find any trace of it. So of course the next place I thought of was Reno, and I got a contact up there to look, and it wasn't there either. So then I got somebody to look in Vegas, and that was N.G. Well, I called and told him if I didn't know where to look, it was a waste of time. She could have gotten it anywhere, after all."

"Well, this is something new," said Jesse. "I wonder what's behind it—talk about ancient history. Did he say why he was anxious for this record? He wasn't a man who enjoyed handing out money, Mr. Toomey."

"Oh, I gathered that, he bitched like hell about the bill—that," said Toomey, nodding at the receipt, "was just a first retainer. I had to pay the operators in Nevada. I charged him a hundred and fifty all told. Well, he said he'd lost the papers on it and wanted a legal record. But like I say, and like I told him, she could have gotten it anywhere and when he didn't remember where—" Toomey shrugged sadly.

"I'll be damned," said Jesse. "That was it?"

"That was it. I reported to him last over a month ago."

"So, thanks very much."

"No trouble," said Toomey dispiritedly.

Jesse got back to his office about three o'clock, and as he came in Jean said, "Mrs. Gorman called for an appointment. She wants—"

"Oh, no," said Jesse. "To make a new will." Mrs. Gorman made a hobby of making wills; this would be at least the tenth he had made for her.

"What else?" said Jean. "She's worried about her dogs now, wants to make a definite provision for them. I gave her an appointment next Monday afternoon, if that's all right."

"Yes, yes," said Jesse. He went into his office and sat down, thought for a couple of minutes, and called Florence Griffin. She sounded surprised to hear from him, and even more surprised at his question.

"Aline?" she said. "Johnny's first wife? Why, yes, it was her that divorced him. Why? I told you—"

"Do you have any idea where she got the divorce, and when?"

"Why, I suppose right here. I should think. She was a local girl, I think her family lived in Santa Monica. That's funny, that you should be asking about her, Mr. Falkenstein, because after we were talking the other day I got to thinking about Aline—she was quite a nice girl, I liked her the little while I knew her—and all of a sudden I remembered that I did see her once after she divorced Johnny. It must have been three or four years afterward, the nearest I can pin it down, it was just before the war anyway. I remembered that I ran into her unexpectedly in the public waiting room at Bullock's, on the seventh floor just outside the ladies'

room, you know. We were both shopping—I remember we had lunch together, and that was the last time I ever saw her."

"Remember anything she said about herself then? Did she mention the divorce?"

"Why, yes. She'd just gotten married again, she told me. She was looking quite smart—she was a pretty girl, with a lot of curly black hair—and she looked happy. She told me her new name, but do you think I can remember it now? It was an ordinary name, but not as ordinary as Smith or Brown, of course I hadn't any reason to remember it, and all those years ago—but why do you want to know about Aline?"

"Well, it doesn't matter, but they were definitely divorced then, if she was married again."

"Oh, yes, of course. Aline was rather straitlaced, I know Johnny's swearing bothered her, and off-color jokes and things like that."

"Do you know if there was any alimony, a settlement?"

"Oh, there wasn't anything like that, or Johnny would have mentioned it to Howie. They'd only been married about a year, and none of us had any money then—Johnny and Howie had just started the business about that time. What's this all about, Mr. Falkenstein?"

"Were they married here?"

"Yes, of course. What—"

"Well, it's just a little something that came up," said Jesse vaguely. "Thanks very much."

He put the phone down and ruminated about this. Why all these years later had Vanderveer been concerned about that? There wasn't anything funny about the divorce, when the first wife had remarried—evidently a respectable conventional girl. It didn't seem to make much sense, laying out money to get the record of that— Well, suppose for once that he'd been telling the plain truth? He had told Toomey he'd lost the papers. He would have been served divorce papers, of course. And it was a long time ago —in all the years of piling up the capital, of using different bank accounts for the partnership and business, of shuffling accounts around and possibly changing safe-deposit boxes, he could have misplaced the papers. An uneducated man, he might have thought them necessary to make the will valid, something like that. But it was a little funny all the same.

Still, in connection with another line of thought—could the old man have been going a little senile? Or beginning to go that way— Evidently he'd been something of a chaser in his young virile days, and here he was just lately developing a prurient interest in pornography, patronizing a place like The Red Knight. Well, that retired teacher at the rest home saying, a very quick mind—but it might have started to go just along that one line.

The phone buzzed at him and Jean said tersely, "It's Sergeant Clock."

"I did predict it," said Clock. "That house on Kingsley's been broken into—the man on the beat just discovered it. I thought you'd want to know about it. Pete and I are just going over to have a look."

Jesse swore and said he'd meet them there.

It was the usual unholy mess, which Clock and Petrovsky were more used to looking at. It was adding insult to injury to leave the wanton mess behind, on top of theft. In fact there probably wasn't much gone; there hadn't been much here of any small portable value. The one item like that, the TV, was missing. But every drawer had been yanked out and dumped on the floor, the carpet slashed in every room, the pictures smashed, in the kitchen dishes from the cupboards thrown onto the floor. The drawers of the old rolltop desk were on the floor in the den—Jesse had been through those, of course, and there'd been nothing of any value there. Not much here in the way of loot, but the old woman might have had some jewelry—"I'd better ask Marcia Coleman," said Jesse on that thought.

There were clothes from all the wardrobes underfoot, and in Dulcie's room the mirror over the dressing table was smashed.

The uniformed man, Ramirez, who had noticed the open front door and gone in to check, said, "Juveniles. What it smells like."

The back door had been forced with something like a jimmy.

"Oh, every time," said Clock. "Well, we have to work it like any burglary. The lab will be out. Not a chance in hell they'll give us anything, but we have to go through the motions."

"And somebody will eventually have to clean up the mess,"

said Jesse. He went back to the office and called Marcia Coleman.

She was distressed and angry. "Oh, I was coming up tomorrow to pack all Dulcie's clothes. This is all we needed! Yes, Mama had a few things, her wedding ring was buried with her, but there was her mother's big cameo pin, and a couple of garnet rings, and one of those old-fashioned wide gold bracelets, she hadn't worn them in years, but they were there in a box on the chest of drawers."

"Could you identify any of them?"

"I could the rings, one has three triangular stones and one, just a big one, they're set in yellow gold— Oh, Lord, I'd better come and salvage what I can, I suppose. Tomorrow morning—"

"The police are there now anyway."

"Fee—kitt'ns," murmured Davy drowsily, and slept. Nell looked fondly at him and tiptoed out of the nursery. It was just after one o'clock. She slipped lightly downstairs to the kitchen and looked out the window. Athelstane was out there at the rear of the lawn where the grove of trees ended, and the cat was sitting composedly beside him; they looked as if they were meditating together.

This was the fourth day she had been feeding the cat, and yesterday it had emerged from the bushes as soon as she got into the house, to clean up the plate. She would try an experiment today.

She called Athelstane in and prepared the plate of canned cat food. Athelstane had a water bowl outside as well as on the service porch; she had wondered if that was what had attracted the cat in the first place—where would an animal find water in California's long dry summer?—and she had left dry cat food out each night. She remembered that most Siamese didn't like milk. Now she went out quietly, talking soothingly to the cat, and put the plate down at the edge of the lawn, but this time she didn't go back in the house. She went into the garage by the side door and watched.

The cat came out to the plate at once; it was now taking more time to eat, not as frightened of possible interruption. When the plate was half empty, Nell slipped out the side door and knelt down in the flower bed there as if she was weeding; she could see the cat out of the corner of her eye. It froze, but stayed crouched over the plate; when she came no nearer it went on to finish the meal, and then retreated to the edge of the lawn and began to wash its face. It was a good-sized cat for a Siamese; by the size and shape of its head she thought it was a tom. Nell talked to it from where she was, softly and coaxingly, and the cat looked up several times as if it was listening. She felt sure by now that the cat had at some time lived with people who cared for it, had been used to human voices and stroking hands. She wondered how long it had been on its own—and why.

Jesse left the office early and got home just before dark. As he came in and bent to kiss Nell, she said, "You know, I think that cat had a good home once, it's a lot tamer already."

"Good," said Jesse absently, and then Davy ran up to be greeted, and Athelstane. He went upstairs to the bedroom to take off his jacket, and as he emptied his pockets on the tray on the chest, out with a handful of loose change and his cigarettes came the little old address book. And the third time around a bell rang in his head about it, and it struck him forcibly just how queer it was that the old man had been carrying it. He picked it up and looked at it. The thing was years out of date—he could see how it might still have been lying around at the back of a drawer some-where—but an old man at home on a rainy day, as he had thought before, wouldn't be carrying much on him. His billfold had been on the desk; all he'd had on him had been keys, a handkerchief—and this thing.

He took it downstairs with him and went carefully over it again. Nell was busy in the kitchen, and Davy was playing a game of his own on the floor, Athelstane patient about being crawled over.

The only other queer thing about the address book was that set of cryptic notes: A—Archer—1459. BC—Brown—480. C—Canning —1240. He pored over them and still couldn't make head or tail of them. But could you deduce that they were the important thing about the address book, the reason it had been preserved, the reason the old man was carrying it? That there was something significant about those letters and numbers? It really seemed to be the only logical conclusion.

Nell came to take the baby upstairs; usually he didn't raise a fuss, but he did tonight and it took her a little while to get him set-tled down. Jesse built himself a drink while he waited for her, and went on staring at his little puzzle. She came back presently and got herself a glass of sherry while he renewed his drink, and he told her about the burglary.

"And you're pretty good at crossword puzzles, are you any good at cryptograms?" He went into the study for a sheet off his memo pad and wrote down the three mysterious lines and handed it over. "What does this say to you?"

"B.C., Before Christ," said Nell. "It doesn't say anything else to me. What is it?"

He explained, and Nell was intrigued. "It's funny. That old man, all you've said about him, a real character."

"Oh, in spades," said Jesse.

"All that occurs to me offhand is that whatever it means, it has something to do with money."

"Now that I would lay a bet on."

But the thing wouldn't go out of his mind. What in hell could those lines mean? The innocent-looking combinations were so meager and yet so mysterious. They couldn't refer to the combination to a safe. They weren't long enough to constitute a real cryptogram. They ran through his head monotonously, insistently. A for Archer 1459. BC for Brown 480. C for Canning 1240. It made a weird pattern of a sort, A B C. But what were the figures meant for?

After dinner he went to his desk and played around with it a little. He tried adding up the figures, which gave him 3179, which didn't seem to mean anything either. He tried turning that back to its component parts, as in numerology, and got 20 or 2, which didn't mean any more. Finally he stacked some Bach on the stereo and tried to forget it, but the three little lines kept running through his head.

On Thursday morning as he came into the office there was a *Times* on Jimmy's desk, and she said, "There's a little in the paper about it, maybe they're short of news, impossible as it seems."

It was one paragraph on an inside page, about the burglary at the house, residence of the Vanderveers, murdered October twentieth, and one line about the daughter accused and awaiting indictment. Jesse grunted at it. He hadn't any appointments today or tomorrow. He wrote out the three lines on Jean's memo pad and thrust it at her. "What do you think this means?"

"B.C., Before Christ," she said. "I can't make anything of the rest of it. What's it supposed to mean?" Jimmy just shook her head at it.

"Dammit, it's got to mean something," said Jesse morosely. He went into his office and sat down at his empty desk, swiveling around to stare out the window.

Twenty minutes later Jean buzzed him and said he had a call. It was somebody from the Mexican Consulate. "What?" said Jesse. "What now? All right, put it through. . . . Yes. Yes, this is Mr. Falkenstein. What can I do for you?"

"Ah, Mr. Falkenstein. This is Eduardo Rivera, of the staff of the Mexican Consulate here." It was a pleasant masculine voice with scarcely any accent. "Over breakfast this morning I was reading the paper, and I noticed a small article which interested me. I thought perhaps the police would be interested, as it is a criminal case, and so I called headquarters—I am told I must call the Hollywood Precinct—I call there, and talked with one Sergeant Clock. And he tells me that you will be interested, and so I call you."

"Yes? What's it about?"

"This little article in the paper, about a burglary—a husband and wife murdered, their daughter accused—such terrible things that happen these days—the name, as you put it, rings a bell in my head. A Dutch name, Vanderveer. Mr. Falkenstein, that gentleman had an appointment, to come to our office here, to consult one of the staff, myself or whoever should be available. It was for the date of October twenty-fourth."

"The hell you—" Jesse caught himself and said, "That's very interesting, Mr. Rivera. And also very surprising. Why did he want to see somebody there?"

"Now that I'm afraid I could not tell you, Mr. Falkenstein. He telephoned, I remember, and asked to speak to the consul. Of course"— Rivera coughed gently—"that was not possible, the consul is provided with a staff to take care of the casual visitors, those who may simply want travel information or such. I happened to take the call. I asked him if I might answer any questions on the telephone, what were the nature of his inquiries, and he simply said that he must speak to someone who could give him special information. Well!" Jesse could nearly see Rivera's massive shrug over the phone. "What to do? I gave him an appointment at three o'clock on the twenty-fourth. Naturally he did not keep it. You find this interesting?"

"Very much so," said Jesse. "I'm very obliged to you for telling me. But what the hell it could mean I'd like to know. He didn't give you any hint at all?"

"None," said Rivera. "It may not mean anything, of course. We have people calling here for the most trivial reasons, you understand—asking all sorts of questions. We hand them the standard little brochures and are very polite, and they go away satisfied."

"Somehow I don't think he wanted to ask about rare orchids or the best nightclub in Mexico City," said Jesse. "But thanks very much."

And now what was that all about? Something new to think about. Why in hell should Vanderveer have been interested in Mexico? The wild thought crossed Jesse's mind that he had gotten fed up paying United States income taxes and was thinking of becoming a Mexican citizen, but, for God's sake, that was ridiculous. He swiveled around to the window again, and again the three little lines arranged themselves before his mind's eye, teasingly. Once in a while they seemed to be just on the verge of meaning something, and then the meaning slid away into mystery.

For want of anything better to do, he went out about eleven o'clock and drove down to the local post office to collect the Vanderveers' mail. The postal clerk behind the counter was a consciously efficient young man with an infectious grin. Jesse took the package of mail and handed him the slip of paper from his breast pocket. "What does this mean to you?"

The clerk took it and read it. "B.C., Before Christ. Is it a puzzle? Hey, it's a sort of catch, isn't it? Ross MacDonald."

"Come again," said Jesse.

"Guy writes detective stories about a detective named Archer. And come to think, there's a Somebody Canning who's a writer too, adventure stuff. And then there's Father Brown. You know, the priest who's a detective. Not that I ever went for those much, that Chesterton guy's quite a one for preaching at you."

"Yes," said Jesse, regarding him with some fascination. "Yes, he is, isn't he? I'd forgotten that Archer. That's very funny. Coincidences."

"What about 'em?"

"Just that they exist," said Jesse. He took back the slip.

There were no bank statements in the mail, and no personal letters. He looked at it, a few catalogs and throw-away ads, and tossed it into the back of the car. But he sat for a while thinking about the coincidences.

It didn't, in one sense, mean a damned thing, of course, but it was very funny because old Vanderveer had probably never read a book of fiction in his life. Lew Archer and Father Brown. Jesse laughed. But on the other hand, the fact that a queer, tenuous connection of sorts could emerge from such a meaningless set of figures and numbers—

Coincidences did happen. And with that idle little thought in his mind, he reached to turn the ignition key and started back for the office. At the next intersection he caught the light, and as he sat waiting for it to change, a delivery truck crossing in front of him stopped to wait for oncoming traffic before making a left turn. He never knew then or later what it was carrying or advertising, but it bore a large panel sign in red and blue letters, and the sign said, DON'T LET YOUR WIFE KILL HERSELF!

It made the left, the light changed, and the car behind him blew its horn angrily. Jesse took his foot off the brake automatically. "But my God, my God," he said aloud, "why not?"

Coincidences!

Yes, that had been a forced story—the old man deciding in earnest that they were better out of it, and lacing the midmorning drinks. Vanderveer all his life had been too materially concerned with life in this plane—the very conception of self-destruction would have been unthinkable to him. The earthy, greedy old man with his mind still running on sex and money— And he had never had any love for his wife; her illness and misery were nothing to him. He wouldn't have cared if she lived or died, and on the whole he would probably have preferred her to die and save him all the money it cost to care for her—and was going to cost in the future.

But, the wife! But, Mama! She had been a nonentity to Jesse all along—the passive invalid creature in the background. Now his mind raced busily, building her up as a person; and he thought, why not? Why not, indeed? It made a great deal more sense, in any terms of human nature.

He had never laid eyes on her, didn't know whether she'd been pretty, or homely, or in-between in her youth; he didn't know anything (except her maiden name on that marriage certificate) about her background. But from the meager mentionings that he had heard, from Dulcie, from Marcia, from Flo Griffin, he thought about her.

A nonentity. She would already have been labeled a spinster, nearly forty when Jan Vanderveer married her. Just to have a cook and housekeeper. He could buy the sex—but would prefer it free, from the willing good-time girls. But Myra—Myra putting up with that, with his grouches and penny-pinching all those years, bearing him two daughters in her middle life, living that mean restricted life in that poor little house (while the Griffins enjoyed the fruits of success)—and at the end, crippled with arthritis, fast becoming helpless, knowing what a burden she was to her home-staying daughter— Mama! They had all discounted Mama, just a name in the case, but she could be the important figure.

If anyone had a good motive for suicide, it was Mama. She had said she wanted to die and be at rest. And nonentity though she might have been, wasn't it all too likely that over those long years she had come to hate Jan Vanderveer deeply, for what he had been and had not been to her?

Not feeling well that day, said Dulcie. But there was a strength born of desperation. She could have done what was done. The old man used to her hobbling about the house; she could have gotten that cup of coffee for him. She had once worked in an office; she could have typed those six words. And then—and then—even as he had planned to build the story in court, someone coming, and the old man excitable under the overdose—someone like the gardener, or Renaldo, or the evicted tenant—almost anybody—

Back at the office, he paced, seeing that happen in his mind's eye. In terms of human nature—

It could indeed have happened that way.

He forgot to go out for lunch, and he was again brooding over the slip of paper when Marcia Coleman called. "All I needed was to see that house. My God. Of course there wasn't much of any value there, but what a mess. Mama's jewelry is gone, and the TV, that's all I can tell is missing. I saw the police and gave them a description of the jewelry."

"I don't suppose there was a record of the serial number of the TV? Well, never mind."

He did remember lunch then, and went down to the coffee shop on the ground floor of the building. The front tables were all occupied and he had to go to one at the back, near the door to the kitchen; instead of his usual waitress, the pert blond May, he got a thin-faced girl with glasses. He ordered at random, and was sitting staring at the hieroglyphics on the slip of paper when she came up and twitched it away and set his plate before him.

"Hey," said Jesse.

She handed it back. "Afraid you'd drop it in your gravy."

"What does it look like to you?" he asked curiously.

She took it again and studied it. "Doesn't look like anything. A, B, C. I'll bet it's one of those crypt things. A secret message, like. Where some naval plans are hidden or something like that. Or it could be a clue to buried treasure."

"You're a romantic."

"You bet. Nothing I like better than a good story about buried treasure, with duels and a sinister villain trying to seduce the heroine. What is this thing, anyway?"

"I wish I knew."

The only diversion he had in the early afternoon was a telephone conversation with Lenhoff's attorney, who was now in a storm of activity getting out legal evaluations of the property. It didn't look as if Lenhoff was going to miss the settlement for his wife.

At three-thirty Jean put through a call from Clock. "One of the reasons," said Clock, "that this job can be boring is that the punks are so damn stupid. The patrolman on the beat just spotted a couple of juveniles on the front porch of the Vanderveer house, and when they tried to get away he grabbed them, and found the loot in the back of their car. One TV, a handful of jewelry the Coleman woman described. They hadn't gotten around to pawning it yet."

"Congratulations," said Jesse. "Why did they go back there?"

"You never know what the stupid punks will do," said Clock.

But forty minutes later he called back. "I think you'd better come up here and listen to a story. It's an interesting one."

Jesse rather doubted that, but he was tired of sitting in the office. He drove up to the Hollywood Precinct station, parked, and went down past the desk sergeant into the big communal detective office. Clock was leaning back at his desk, Petrovsky lounging at the window. Planted on two straight chairs before the desk were a couple of sullen-looking teen-age boys.

"Not enough space in an interrogation room," said Clock. "Meet Marco Ruiz and Pedro Sanchez. Pedro has something interesting to tell you. Go on, Pedro. Let's have it all over again, just the way you told it before."

They would both conform to roughly the same description: sixteen or seventeen, dark, thin, shabbily dressed. "Both of them have little records," said Petrovsky dispassionately to Jesse. "Petty theft, purse-snatching."

"I said he was crazy—it was Pedro's idea," said Ruiz. "I didn't think there'd be nothing there, and there wasn't. Why the hell should anybody got a million bucks live in such a crummy neighborhood? Hell, I heard all the talk, but that's just what it was—I was crazy to tag along—and then him saying we must've missed something—"

"I got eyes, ain't I?" said the other one angrily. They both spoke unaccented English. He looked at Jesse. "Why we got to tell it to every cop in the precinct? Think we'd robbed a bank or something. Look, like I told you, all my life I heard how rich that old guy is—we lived there since I was a kid, everybody on that block heard that! He's got money hid all over the house maybe. I was always hearin' that. And I don't give no damn what you say, Marco, I know it's so, see? After they got murdered, I thought we'd prob'ly get in the house easy, it bein' empty like that, and we did. So O.K., we took a couple things—"

"All there was to take," said Ruiz. "What a big deal. Maybe twenty bucks at a hock shop, if we hadn't got picked up."

"All I said is, there's got to be more loot hid away! I saw it myself, only nobody believed me—me and Bill saw it."

"What did you see, and when?" Jesse pulled up a chair from an empty dsk.

"It was when I was just a kid, maybe four-five years back," said Pedro. "Me and Bill Perez saw it, only nobody believed us when we told about it. We was playing in Bill's yard, his house sorta backs up to old Vanderveer's, it's on the next street, see, and we was at the back end of the yard and we see old Vanderveer diggin' behind his garage. We was under the bushes at the back on account we'd been playin' jungle fightin', I said we was just kids then, and Bill called him a name because he's their landlord and always raisin' the rent—and he said, I bet he's buryin' money in his yard, Ma says he's a miser—so we watched. But he wasn't buryin' no money, he was diggin' some up! We saw it. He puts down the spade, and kneels down—he never reached into his pocket or nothin', but when he gets up he turns around with a great big hunk of folding money in his hands—we saw it! So he did have money buried—I wanted to go look there, Marco said it was crazy and besides there was a guy out in the next yard—"

Clock grinned at Jesse. "By bits and pieces you seem to be finding this estate you're supposed to be settling, Jesse."

Petrovsky tapped Ruiz on the shoulder. "Come on, *hermanos,* we've just got time to book you into jail before they serve supper." He led them out. Of course they'd only stay in overnight, and get probation from a judge.

"How in hell did I get into this?" asked Jesse plaintively. "Now I have to go digging up his whole backyard? Nobody buries money in the backyard. And I'm not a manual laborer—supposed to be a brain worker." He laid his slip on Clock's desk. "What does that say to you?"

"B.C., Before Christ," said Clock. "What's it supposed to mean? My grandmother's maiden name was Archer, and I went to the academy with a fellow named Canning."

"More coincidences," said Jesse. "Very funny. You wouldn't be inclined to come and help me dig, would you?"

"My part of the case is over," Clock pointed out. "The estate is your business."

"Oh, hell," said Jesse. "And it's nearly dark now. It'll have to wait until morning. Why your officious patrolman had to spot that pair—"

The only thing in his favor was that the weather wasn't hot. And after this, he was sure to have nightmares about this house.

He found a spade in the tidy garage, and went around behind it. Postponing work, he walked down to the end of the yard to see where the boys might have been when they saw Vanderveer. He hadn't realized that the house on Winona backed up to this one.

There was a picket fence at the end of this lot, and some tall hibiscus bushes at the rear of the adjoining yard. Here, there had once been a patch of lawn, as there still was in front, but it had died from lack of water, and there wasn't any attempt at shrubs or flowers. It looked as mean and shabby as the house itself.

Behind the garage, Pedro said. Jesse was thankful that it was a small garage; but it must be at least twelve feet wide, and just where behind the garage did X mark the spot? He had put on an old pair of slacks and a sports shirt; he eyed the spade with dislike, and drove it into the ground a foot behind the garage in the middle of the wall.

Luckily the ground was not packed hard, but already loosened with those two early rains, and it could have been harder digging; but as he had said, he was no manual laborer, and after half an hour he was grateful that Nell had made him take her loose gardening gloves. Without them, he'd already have had a fine crop of blisters. He dug a trench straight along the garage wall, going down about a foot and a half, out to the driveway, and of course turned up nothing at all but a few earthworms. Breathing hard, he went into the garage and sat in Dulcie's car to smoke a cigarette.

Next he started in the other direction, and muttered to himself, "Out of condition, sitting in an office all day." He felt as if he had dug out half a ton of dirt; it looked like a young trench, and he was drenched with sweat.

When he thrust the spade down and put his heel on it for about the seven thousandth time, it wouldn't go. It hit something solid—more solid than earth, about a foot down. He tilted it at a sharper angle and scraped earth away.

What he uncovered looked like a lid: a solid wooden lid with a handle on it. He uncovered it quickly, at the last kneeling to use his hands. "I will be damned—even that fanatical old fool—burying it in the backyard, for God's sake—" When it was clear of earth he tugged at the handle, and the lid came off in one piece; it wasn't fastened down. It revealed a little vault cemented on all sides; the lid had fit solidly over it. The man had been a carpenter, after all.

And it was absolutely empty.

Jesse sat back and used a number of regrettable words. All that damned work for nothing! Well, the workout probably hadn't done him any harm, but it was a damned nuisance, and he was filthy. Looking at the vault, the lid, he judged that it had been built years ago, and the old man had had second thoughts about its vulnerability. Or maybe when it got to be a little difficult for him to use the spade—

Jesse was dripping sweat, his hands were filthy even under the gloves; he was hot, dirty, and very tired. Even in that wreck of a house there would be hot water, and he had the keys on him. He went in, and among the tumbled mess in the hall found a clean towel, one of those pulled out of the linen closet. When he had taken off his shirt and washed the worst of the sweat and grime off, he felt better. Still wiping his face, he went down to the den, where he had left his saucer-ashtray, to rest awhile before he went home to change into civilized clothes.

There was litter all over the floor where the punks had ransacked the place, and he had forgotten about the slashed carpet. Halfway across the room his toe caught in a tear and, being off balance, he took a header, nearly knocked himself out against the opposite wall, and sprawled his length on the floor.

Before he picked himself up to feel for any broken bones he relieved his feelings with a few more regrettable words. "Not my day," he said bitterly, bracing himself on his hands; and then he just stayed there, frozen, looking at the piece of carpet under his nose there in the corner.

Carpeting all snugly wall-to-wall, fastened down, solid, so of course nobody had looked at it. But this piece in the corner wasn't. It was turned back in a V, and the inside edges didn't have the little tape that held fitted carpet flat. It had a few tiny tacks, that was all.

He bent closer and peered. Tiny holes in the hardwood floor where this corner of carpet had been tacked down; and now he could see where the carpet tape had been cut away. He got up to his knees and pulled the corner of carpet back with a mighty tug, and about two feet of it obediently folded over and revealed, against the dark-varnish finish of the old hardwood floor, a square of raw new wood. It was completely level with the rest of the floor, there was only a sliver of crack around all four edges to reveal that it was a separate piece. The man had started out as a carpenter.

"No fool like an old fool!" said Jesse savagely. He stood up and looked around for the steel letter opener, found it in the corner by the door, inserted it into one crack and pushed down. A little reluctantly the square of unfinished wood tilted and he got it up far enough to get two fingers in and a grip on it. It slid out without much trouble.

Underneath it were two steel cash boxes resting on the studs of the low foundation.

"Oh, my dear God," said Jesse wearily. He lifted them out and carried them over to the studio couch. Both of them had a stack of folding money inside. The first held twenty thousand dollars in fifties and hundreds; the second, twenty-five thousand, mostly in hundreds.

What in the name of all that was holy that ancient lunatic had thought he was doing— Nobody knowing. Nobody having even a hint.

He looked helplessly at all the money. He really didn't want to put it into the office safe, and in fact, of course, he was bound by law to deposit any loose funds which would be transferred by a will into an interest-bearing account, pending the end of probate. When they had come across that cash in the other safe-deposit box on Wednesday, he had opened an account at that Security-Pacific branch, a savings account labeled J. W. Vanderveer Estate. That was where this had to go.

He said a few more things. He was starving, it was after noon, and a respectable lawyer didn't go around in dirty slacks and sweat-stained shirt on a weekday; but he didn't feel much like driving all the way home with forty-five thousand dollars of some-body else's money on him. The crime rate was up, even in broad daylight.

He took the cash boxes out to the car and drove up to the bank —the one where Vanderveer's working account was lodged. He was going to cause some stir, walking in with all this cash, and he made for the New Accounts desk, recognizing the efficient gray-haired woman who had filled out forms for him on Wednesday. He groped for her name—Mrs. Lorenzo.

He planked the cash boxes down and explained frankly. "Good heavens," she said, amused, "the things people do. Well, we'll have to get a mutual count on it—several of us checking it, you know—the chief teller's out to lunch but he should be back shortly. Meanwhile you can make out a deposit slip." She slid one across to him.

He had just written the date and *J. W. Vanderveer Estate* when a pretty dark girl came up to the desk with a check in her hand. "Oh, excuse me, Mrs. Lorenzo, but it's this new account, the one just transferred from UCB—is it still on hold? I couldn't make out the date—"

Jesse started violently and dropped the pen. "Bank of California!" he said loudly. "Bank of California!"

They stared at him. "Why, yes, that's what it used to be before," said Mrs. Lorenzo.

He rushed into the precinct station at ten past one, found Clock just going out on a new call, and said frenziedly, "Battle stations! I need your official help, the damn banks won't give out information over the phone to me—we'll have to get the IRS on it too, that'll help—" He thrust the paper under Clock's nose. "Don't you *see* it? It's plain as the nose on your face! But it only hit me when that teller used the abbreviation—UCB, United California Bank—it used to be the Bank of California before it amalgamated with some others—B.C., Bank of California, so you can see what this has got to mean, can't you? Oh, my sweet God in heaven, that crafty old twister—didn't he get one hell of a kick out of planning all the secrets, and no good goddamned reason for it at all— You see what this has got to be?"

"No," said Clock. "I'm busy, I've got work to do. What are you talking about?"

Jesse was shaking the old address book at him. "This was a reminder, so he wouldn't forget names and numbers! And he must have had one of them at least since before that merger—he wouldn't notice the name change. BC Brown 480. It says he's got a safe-deposit box under the name of Brown at a California bank, box 480. And another one at a Bank of America under the name of Archer, box 1459. And another one at a Crocker bank under the name of Canning, box 1240. It just came to me when that teller said—"

Clock began to laugh. "And none of them any banks where he was known as Vanderveer," said Jesse, "and how the hell to pin them down—we'll need official help, and Dobson— Uncle so powerful these days—"

"I can't help thinking," said Clock, "what beautiful legal fun you'll have with Uncle!"

CHAPTER 8

Dobson came up at once—Uncle was always so quick on the trail of anybody suspected of trying to hide untaxed money away. He pointed out the major difficulty fretfully. "Dammit, the man's dead!" he said. "If this is true, Falkenstein, how the hell are we going to connect him legally with these safe-deposit boxes? I'll have to look up the ruling—these are all common names, and if he didn't visit the boxes frequently it may pose an identification problem. But we'll certainly look into it—"

"And the damn banks closing for the weekend in four hours," said Jesse.

"Well, of course the only place to start is to locate the individual banks, and our office can do that by phone—there's really no need to bring the police into it," said Dobson, looking disdainfully around the detective office. "It isn't very likely that he'd have used branches at a great distance, as he didn't drive—"

"But we don't know how long he'd had these boxes, dammit, that one at the California bank for nine or ten years at least! And the keys!" said Jesse in something like a wail of agony. "Where in the name of holy Almighty God are the keys? There's no crevice in that house where they could be—I know that goddamned house better than my own, and I swear those keys aren't there!"

"Nonsense," said Dobson coldly. "They've got to be somewhere. You simply haven't come across them—he probably had some rudimentary hiding place, taped to the inside of a drawer or somewhere like that." Jesse groaned. "But the identification has to be definite, it would be extremely awkward if any mistake were made."

Yes, indeed, if by chance there should be an honest citizen named Archer who rented safe-deposit box 1459 at a Bank of America branch, and found out that Uncle Busybody had unwarrantably examined the contents, there would be a howl: there might be a lawsuit. The citizen still had rights, if fewer every day, and sometimes even Uncle had to walk like Agag.

In the end, Dobson went back to his office to start hunting for the right banks, and Jesse called Marcia on Clock's phone. "Do you have any photographs of your father? Recent ones?"

"For heaven's sake, there wouldn't be many anywhere, we never went in for snapshots much. But Dulcie has a camera, she got it in high school, she used to take snapshots sometimes. Oh, I remember she took one of Mama and Papa on their fortieth anniversary, that was nearly two years ago— I've got a copy of it somewhere, and Dulcie would have too. You do ask for the queerest things, Mr. Falkenstein—why do you want that?"

He explained, and she said angrily, "Oh, just like him, of course—*just* like him! I suppose this lets us in for a fine from the government, and if I know the government it'll be a whopping big one."

"Well, we'll have to sort that out later. Right now we need this picture."

"All right, I'll look for it and bring it to you on Monday morning, if that's all right."

"Fine," said Jesse, remembering that Dulcie was due to be indicted on Tuesday; he'd had the official notice from the D.A.'s office in the morning mail yesterday.

He went up to his office, still in the dirty old clothes, and the Gordons were astonished. "What on earth have you been doing, Mr. Falkenstein?" asked Jean.

"Digging," said Jesse, and went on into the inner office and hauled out everything he had taken from Vanderveer's desk and file cabinet. He sorted through it. He gathered together a lot of canceled checks for specimen signatures, all the writing he could find. The account book would be useful if there was any question of identity.

He called Dobson before he left the office. "No, we haven't pinned one down yet, they could only let me have one man, but we're working on it. It's a pity the weekend has to intervene, of course, but it can't be helped. I'll be in touch with you on Monday, then."

*   *   *

Nell thought the whole thing was hilarious—except for the family, of course. "But really, Jesse, don't these people realize that they're going to die sometime? And whatever they leave will have to be sorted out?"

"They don't have that much imagination," he said bitterly. "In fact, if they can't take it with them they'd just as soon keep anyone else from laying their paws on it." He sounded annoyed.

Nell realized that he was upset about the situation, and she knew he was worried about that poor woman in jail—wondering how to handle the case. Occasionally he got involved with clients he liked.

Wisely she left him alone, and after dinner he went into the den and stacked some Bach on the stereo.

That afternoon the cat had let her come within ten feet of him and gone on placidly eating, though keeping an eye on her.

On Saturday morning the predicted rain didn't materialize; it was overcast, but in midmorning a watery sun came out. The dry cat food she had left on the back porch was gone, and that Athelstane wouldn't touch. After lunch, with Davy bedded down for his nap, she went out with a plate of food and put it down at the side of the lawn where the cat often sat these days crouched under the bushes. She thought it was spending most of the time in their yard now. She sat down on the grass six feet away from the plate and waited hopefully. In a few minutes the cat came out from under the bushes, approached slowly, sniffed the plate over fastidiously, and began to eat. She talked to the cat in a soft voice. Now, with a close look, she could see that it was a neutered tom, and normally would be a big cat for a Siamese. He looked a little fatter already. This time, after cleaning the plate, he didn't go away; he sat looking at her thoughtfully, and his eyes were a vivid brilliant blue in the thin sunlight.

"You're a very handsome boy," Nell told him. "You have gorgeous eyes, do you know that?" The cat answered her conversationally, in a raucous bass voice. "Will you let me pat you? Do you remember when people used to stroke you and tell you what a lovely pussin you are?" She began to edge nearer, cautiously, and the cat didn't move. He spoke again questioningly, and didn't stir when she laid a hand on his head. She moved the hand down his back, and felt the automatic arching of his spine to her stroke. His coat looked smoother, and his back felt warm in the sun. She went on stroking him, and presently was aware of another feeling under her hand, a slow throbbing just beginning. The cat was purring. It was a rusty purr at first, as if long unused, but it grew louder.

On Sunday morning, when she looked out the kitchen window after breakfast, the cat was drinking daintily from Athelstane's water bowl on the back porch. Nell went out—she could load the dishwasher anytime—and he didn't move away, just looked up at her. She sat down on the back step and talked to him, stroked him again. Athelstane, observing this, was delighted. He came up and pushed his large wet black nose at the cat, who patted it with a black velvet paw and uttered a comment in the raucous bass. Nell laughed at the pair of them, and the cat gave her a long deliberate stare and climbed into her lap.

"Well, aren't you a one," said Nell, highly pleased. "You were just waiting for a lap to be offered? You're a beautiful boy. What happened to you, pussin, and how did you get up here?" The cat gave a little contented sigh as she went on stroking him, and she felt his drowsy purrs coming up under her hand. Athelstane gave a huge noisy yawn and flopped down at her feet. Fifteen minutes later Jesse came looking for her.

"I wondered where you'd got to—oh, I see." He eyed the cat amusedly. The cat sat up and looked at him consideringly.

Nell said, "I think we've got a cat. Isn't he a beauty?"

"Very handsome," said Jesse. The cat got up and stretched in slow dignity, jumped off the side of the porch, and stalked across the lawn.

On Monday morning Dobson called ten minutes after Jesse got to the office. "Well, we've just located the United California Bank where a Brown has a safe-deposit box, and it's the right number. It's a branch on Sunset. What have you got in the way of identification?"

"I should have a photograph this morning, and I've got handwriting samples if we need them."

"That should do," said Dobson. "What we have to do, and it's a damned nuisance but it all has to be according to Hoyle, when we're sure that this is the right man, we have to get notarized affidavits from the bank personnel, from the family in regard to the photograph, and then we can proceed with the usual IRS authorization to examine the box."

"I see," said Jesse. "I never ran into this situation before, but I can see the reason for that. But how in hell, will you tell me, are we going to get into the boxes without keys? I swear there's not a place in that damned house I haven't looked—"

"Well, you'll simply have to find them," said Dobson. "They must be somewhere, after all. I should think you'd have been through the personal effects by now."

Jesse said bitterly, "If I have to search that damned house again, I'll put a match to it afterward."

"It's imperative that you locate them," said Dobson, sounding impatient. "I'll let you know when we've identified the other banks."

Jesse hung up and looked at the phone. If Dobson only knew, he thought. And for all they did know, these safe-deposit boxes might have been permanent caches, he might not have gone near any of them in a blue moon, and those damned keys could be somewhere quite inaccessible. But, for God's sake, where?

Marcia Coleman came in at eleven-thirty. She was looking drawn and tired; she would, of course, be worrying about Dulcie. "I had a hunt for it, but here it is," and she handed him the picture. Jesse studied it with interest. It was a five-by-seven enlargement from a colored snapshot, in a cardboard folder. It had been taken inside by flash, and the old couple was sitting at the dining table with plates in front of them. He remembered Vanderveer from the time he had seen him over six years ago—tall and gaunt, with thinning gray hair and a longish nose with a little hook at the end; he looked older here, and thinner. And she—it was impossible to say whether she'd ever been an attractive young woman or not. She was just an old lady, a rather plump old lady, with a round wrinkled face and gray hair worn in an outmoded style, curls around her face and little bangs. She was wearing a black dress with a big cameo pin at the neckline. But she had the same square little chin as Dulcie. It was a gentle face in a way, he thought, but not without character. Mama could indeed have been the X factor.

He told Marcia about the affidavit. "Well, I've got plenty of time, I asked Mrs. Burke to pick up Bobby. I'm going on to see Dulcie. What do I have to do?"

He dictated the affidavit to Jean, a short paragraph testifying that Marcia identified the accompanying photograph as that of Jan Willem Vanderveer, made at such and such a date. Jean typed it up, Marcia signed it, and Jimmy as an accredited notary public signed and sealed it. "So far so good," said Jesse.

She left at twelve-thirty, and Jesse looked at his Gordons and said, "All right, come on, we're going to close the office for the day. I'll buy us all lunch, and then you two can have the fun of searching that damned house again. I've run out of energy and imagination."

They were pleased at a little adventure, a change in routine. And he looked at them rather fondly across the table in the coffee shop downstairs. Quite a credit to be seen with, the Gordons: brown-eyed blondes and identically pretty.

When they got to the house on Kingsley, he said as he unlocked the front door, "Maybe female intuition will lead you straight to those keys, but I'd better tell you all the places I've already looked, hunting other things, so you won't waste time." They went in.

Both the Gordons said simultaneously, "What a mess!" and Jean added, "I'd hate to be the one who had to clean it up. But, Mr. Falkenstein, are you absolutely sure the keys are here somewhere?"

"They've got to be," said Jesse. "It's the only place they could be—the only place he had to keep them. Unless he buried them in the backyard, in which case we'll never find them—I refuse to do any more digging."

They began to poke around the living room, and he went to sit on the couch in the den. "Take your time," he called to them. "Just remember the old adage—if you were a horse—"

Jean said from the hall, "Uncle Foster used to hide things in shoes. He nearly lost a diamond ring once when Aunt Betty gave some stuff to the salvage."

"I've already looked there," said Jesse.

But, he suddenly remembered, he hadn't looked among the old man's underwear and so forth— He went into the front bedroom. Everything out of the old double dresser had been dumped onto the floor; it was impossible to say which drawer had held what. Her clothes and his were mixed up: shabby brassieres, panties, cotton stockings, worn little handkerchiefs, along with his under-wear, socks, ties. There was nothing but the clothes among that heap. There was nothing taped to the bottoms of drawers, or any sign that anything had been. The window in the den was the only one in the house with a box valance; all the others had curtains on plain rods.

The girls presently progressed to the kitchen. He finished his fifth cigarette and strolled out there. Jimmy was on top of a fold-ing step stool with her head inside a top cupboard; Jean was emp-tying the stove drawer.

He said doubtfully, "I don't think he'd have hidden anything here—the women coming and going. No luck yet, I see. No bright ideas?"

"This was an impossible house even before the burglary," said Jean. "What do you *do* with only a single sink?" She took the last iron skillet out of the drawer and began to feel inside.

"Well, as I said, take your time—it's only two-thirty," said Jesse idly.

"And no light over the stove," said Jimmy, descending from the stool and moving it under the middle cupboard.

Jean let out a loud scream. They both swung on her eagerly, ex-pecting revelation. "Oh, how perfectly terrible!" she exclaimed. "Oh, Mr. Falkenstein, I never did such an awful thing before—I can't imagine how we came to forget—"

Twins often communicated without speech, and Jimmy said, "Oh! Oh, Jeanie, how *could* we? Supposed to be top-notch legal secretaries—it's perfectly terrible, Mr. Falkenstein—"

"What are you talking about?"

"Mrs. G-G-Gorman," wailed Jean. "She had an appointment at two o'clock—we'd never get back in time to catch her with all the traffic—"

Jesse leaned on the doorjamb and laughed. "Well, that makes three of us—I forgot all about her too. Let's be philosophical about it, girls—either she'll be so annoyed she'll find another law-yer, or she'll forgive us—and it's past praying for now, she'll have been there and left. I really don't think he'd have hidden the keys here."

"If you're going to do something, do it right," said Jimmy. "Oh,

I do feel awful about Mrs. Gorman, but of course you're right—spilled milk."

They spent another twenty minutes in the kitchen, and of course found nothing. The refrigerator, he noticed, had been cleaned out and unplugged; that would be the efficient Marcia.

"I wonder—" said Jean suddenly. "You know those little magnetic boxes to hide keys in—some people have them to hide a house key, or an extra ignition key, in case of getting locked out—"

Galvanized by this inspiration, they examined everything made of metal in the house, and Jesse pulled the stove and refrigerator out to examine the backs; Jimmy ran an arm behind the washer. Nothing.

"They can't be here, Mr. Falkenstein," said Jean at last. "We've simply looked everywhere, even places you'd looked before. Do you suppose they could have been in something the burglars took?"

"But they got the loot back—it hadn't been pawned yet."

"Well, unless it's like *The Purloined Letter,* I give up," said Jimmy. "And if those keys are out in plain sight, we're all going blind."

"*The Purloined Letter,*" said Jesse thoughtfully.

"Yes, you know, the Poe story. Everybody was looking for it up the chimney, and it was in the letter rack all the—"

Jesse clapped a hand to his head. "Misdirection! Have I been just a little bit too clever? Oh, glory be—I wonder—" He plunged out the back door and made for the garage. They trailed him interestedly. At the neat workbench, he seized the box of drill bits and upended it: nothing but drill bits. He wrenched the lid off a tin box that had once held chocolate mints, and a collection of used washers fell out. The next box held screws of all shapes and sizes, and that was all. But when he turned the third box of sixpenny nails upside down over the bench, together with all the nails there fell out three keys, the long slender steel keys for safe-deposit boxes; and they were respectively stamped 1459, 480, and 1240.

"Eureka," said Jesse feebly.

"But I really feel awful about Mrs. Gorman," said Jean.

They went back to the office and Jesse called Dobson. "Dammit, the banks are all closed now," said Dobson, annoyed. "Well, I'll meet you there at ten."

"No, you won't," said Jesse. "I've got a client being indicted. It'll be more like eleven."

"Oh, hell," said Dobson. "No, we haven't located the other two yet. There are a lot of banks in this town, you know."

Jesse said he was aware of it, and called Mrs. Gorman to apologize. "Well, I was a little surprised," she said in her amiable woolly voice. "But if it was an emergency—oh, I quite understand —things do come up, I know—it's just that I'm rather anxious to include these provisions in my will, I mean we never know, do we, in the midst of life as they say, and while I'm only sixty-one, well, who knows?"

"Who indeed?" said Jesse. "Suppose you come in at two o'clock tomorrow."

"Oh, that'll be fine."

On Tuesday morning Nell went out and sat on the back porch; in about five minutes the cat appeared from the grove of trees, and Athelstane went to meet him happily. They touched noses. Nell called to the cat, and he came to her directly and pushed his head under her hand. "Now what happened to you, boy? You're used to people, you like people—somebody took good care of you once, didn't they?" They would never know where he'd come from. Could he have gotten loose from a car, she wondered. Some Siamese liked to ride in cars. Somewhere, perhaps, someone had been frantic, missing him. She wondered how he had gotten all the way up here.

Presently she said, "If you're going to be our cat, you'd better explore your new home," and she got up and opened the back door. "Come on—do you want to come in?"

The cat's vivid blue eyes fixed hers, and he uttered a long Siamese comment; and then he walked in ahead of her, tail straight up in the air. Nell left him to his own devices and hurried into the living room to pick Davy out of his playpen.

"Now we're going to have our own kitten, darling, but we've got to be nice to him, and not hurt him or scare him, see? We—"

"Kitt'n!"

"That's right, but we mustn't ever grab his tail—" He was really too little to understand yet, but he was a good baby; and if she knew cats, the cat would simply elude those fat reaching fingers and ignore him.

The cat came right into the living room and made for the corner of the hearth where the log box was. He looked from the logs to Nell and made a loud bass comment. Then he turned and started for the stairs.

"Just make yourself at home," said Nell, and Davy squirmed in her arms.

The indictment didn't take long: automatic legal process. Dulcie was dressed up for it, in one of her plain shirtmaker dresses; she had bright lipstick on, and looked a little more sophisticated. He talked to her for ten minutes afterward, the wardress waiting stolidly in the background.

"Mr. Falkenstein," she said worriedly, "Marcia was telling me— all the trouble about the money. He was always so queer about money. But if there's going to be trouble with the government—if there isn't going to be much left—there'll be your fee, and—"

"Needn't worry about that. There'll be more than enough left," he said, thinking about those fat packets of blue-chip stock. "There's just a lot of red tape. Don't fuss about it." And he wished he could formulate clearly in his mind just what tale he was going to spin to a judge and jury.

She sighed. "Mr. Klein's been to see me. He said if there wasn't enough money he'd see you got paid."

"I know. He's a nice fellow."

"He's been awfully good to me. I didn't know much when I first went to work for him. You wouldn't think so, he's always cheerful and telling jokes, but he's had a lot of sadness in his life. His wife died of cancer when she was only forty, and they never had any children."

He would probably never mention Dan Wolfe to her. He said lightly, "You just sit tight. I want to have a talk with you soon— plan exactly what we're going to say at the trial. You've got everything you need?"

"Oh, yes, I'm fine. Marcia's been coming every day."

"I'll see you soon."

He got up to the bank on Sunset at eleven-thirty. Dobson was waiting for him, pointedly under the clock at the entrance. "Sorry," said Jesse. "The judge was a little late."

"You did find the keys, I trust."

"Finally."

"I said it would just take a little looking. Well, I've seen the manager here, and there's a public stenographer and notary available."

They proceeded downstairs to the vault. There was a man and a woman in attendance. Dobson produced his credentials and said, "Someone called you from my office yesterday morning, about a Mr. Brown who had—has—a safe-deposit box here."

"Oh, yes," said the man. "Yes, that's right."

Jesse produced the photograph. "Is that Brown?"

They both looked at it. "That's him," said the man. They were looking at Dobson with disfavor, but curiously. "What's this all about?" Jesse launched into an explanation. "Well, I'm damned," said the man. "We never had such a thing happen before. He's dead, you say? Well, he didn't come in just so often, I think the last time we saw him would be about five, six weeks ago or more— but that's him all right, isn't it, Marion?"

The woman nodded. "All right," said Dobson. "Now I want you to compare some handwriting—may we see the card, please, with Brown's specimen signature—"

But both of them were positive, and of course when they'd seen him so recently— Dobson got hold of the public stenographer and had her type up the affidavits, got the two upstairs one by one to sign them before the notary. By then Jesse was starving, and Dobson probably was too, but he had blood in his eye and was anxious to get on with the job. They went back to the vault and he laid out his IRS authorization. The woman led them past the massive steel doors, Jesse handed over the key, and she slid out a medium-sized steel box and handed it over. They took it into one of the cubicles.

"*Just* as we suspected," said Dobson in quiet satisfaction. There was a small stack of cash in the box, and lying on top of it a ragged slip of paper with something written on it. Jesse picked that up and Dobson sat down and began to count the money. It amounted to five thousand dollars in twenties. "I'll give you a receipt for this, of course. There'll certainly be a full audit, I can promise you that. And I'll let you know when we spot the other banks."

"You do that." Jesse was looking at the paper. The scrawl across it wasn't Vanderveer's writing: a bolder hand. *Ray Holst,* and a telephone number, and an address on Lomita Street in Glendale.

He very nearly missed another appointment with Mrs. Gorman, but he had to snatch a sandwich before going back to the office. And she took up time as usual, burbling gently away about her garden, her dogs. The new will was on account of the dogs; she had realized she ought to make provision for their care if she should die suddenly, they were only three years old and you never knew. "I don't know if you're fond of animals, Mr. Falkenstein, but those of us who are get so attached—they're like my children really, Chico's a Chihuahua, you know, such a darling, and Beau's a miniature poodle, I've always adored—"

"We have a mastiff," said Jesse.

"A mastiff! In town!"

"And we've now got a Siamese cat. But we can take care of all this without a new will, you know, we can just make a codicil." He got rid of her finally, and thought she was still a little bemused by the mastiff as she went out.

It was four o'clock. He considered the slip of paper, pulled the phone nearer, and dialed. It rang four times at the other end before a woman answered. "Mr. Ray Holst?" asked Jesse.

"Oh, he's not here, he's at work." It was a neutral kind of voice, but sounded amiable. "Could I take a message?"

"When do you expect him in?"

"Oh, he'll be home after work, about ten-fifteen."

"If I call him at ten-thirty, you're sure he'll be in?"

"Oh, he'll be home then, yes. The last show starts about nine-forty and he gets away then."

"Thanks very much." He put the phone down. He wondered what he was going to hear from Ray Holst. This was all the damndest rigmarole he'd ever run into. And Dulcie—

He was thinking so hard and deep about that forthcoming trial that Jean had to prod him to show it was time to go home. "And it's started to rain again."

"Going to be a wet winter all right." It was coming down in earnest; he turned up his collar and made a sprint for the Mercedes in the lot. It was a slow drive home, up the twisting canyon road; but once he turned into their street, the twin gate lamps were faithfully beckoning him, and the gate was open. He got wetter getting out to shut it; but once he was in the house, the steady roar of the rain on the roof was rather pleasant, and Nell said she'd built a fire. There was a welcoming smell of pot roast in the kitchen.

Too lazy to go upstairs, he shed his jacket and made himself a drink, carried it into the living room, while Nell finished setting the table. Athelstane's huge brindle bulk was stretched out in front of the fire, with his stomach blissfully exposed to the heat. The cat was lying on the mantel beside the clock, paws well tucked in.

"Well," said Jesse, "you've decided we're satisfactory people to live with, have you?" The cat gave him a thoughtful blue stare. Davy had gone sound asleep in his playpen across the room.

Nell came trotting in with a glass of sherry. "Davy's worn himself out trying to get at that cat all day, but he'll calm down when the novelty wears off. Yes, it was the funniest thing, Jesse—it was just as if he'd been waiting for an invitation—first he came in here, and then he went right up to our room and smelled all around for ages, and got up on the bed and talked a blue streak to me. I wish I understood Siamese."

"We ought to think of a name for him. He looks like royalty on a throne up there. Caesar—Pharaoh—Sophocles."

"I don't like any of those. We'll live with him awhile and something will come to us. He's obviously been a house cat. I got him a litter pan—lucky you don't have to housebreak cats—and he'll have to be fed on the kitchen table, I suppose, or Athelstane would steal everything. He is a beauty, isn't he? Oh, Fran called, and she's feeling fine. Whatever it was went away and the doctor's pleased with her."

"Good. Wonder how little sister'll do at being a mother."

"Oh, Fran's good at anything she does," said Nell confidently.

She had already gone upstairs to read in bed when Jesse tried that number again at ten-thirty. This time a man answered.

"Mr. Ray Holst?"

"Yeah, that's me."

"I think," said Jesse cautiously, "you know the name of Van-derveer?"

"Yeah, that's right, who is this?"

"I'm Mr. Venderveer's lawyer—"

"Well, you took your time getting back to me," said Holst roughly. "Oh, excuse me, I know these things take a hell of a time, all the red tape—what have you found out?"

"I think," said Jesse, "I'd rather talk to you personally, Mr. Holst. I really don't have too much information, but—"

"Well, O.K.," said Holst. "I could come to see you in the morning, I don't go to work till one. Where do I come?"

Jesse told him. Cross questions and crooked answers, he thought. Well, see what Holst looked like. At least he seemed willing to talk. Whatever he had to talk about.

He showed up at the office at ten-thirty on Wednesday morning, and he turned out to be a rather rugged-looking young man in his early thirties; he was medium height, stocky, with dark curly hair. He wasn't exactly handsome, with a slightly pug nose and a large mouth, but he had a frank, ingenuous expression and very blue eyes.

"Well, I'm pleased to meet you, Mr. Falkenstein," he said. He sat down beside the desk and got out a cigarette. "Haven't you found out anything?"

Jesse said, "Suppose you tell me your end of this first, Mr. Holst. I'm not really too clear on the whole—" He let that trail off.

"Oh," said Holst. "Well, for God's sake, I thought he'd tell you about that, but I guess he's a pretty close-mouthed old geezer, maybe not quite all there, his age and all. Haven't you—well, excuse me, don't mean to tell you your business." He shrugged. "But Ma's kind of curious, and"—he laughed—"so am I! See, it was funny—I knew Ma had been married before, she'd said this and that about her first husband, but it wasn't till after Dad died that she told me *that*. She said it was a long time ago, and she guessed once she'd have felt terrible about it, but now it didn't seem to matter much—anyway, she wasn't sure if they were really divorced. Legally, see. It was in the Depression, she didn't have a job or much money, so she went down to Mexico to get a divorce because it was cheaper, and it wasn't till years later she heard that wasn't always legal. Well, she was married to Dad by then, she just didn't say anything about it—well, I tell you, it shook me a little, think I might be a bastard!" He laughed easily. "But hell, it is a long time ago—they were married nearly ten years before I came along—it sort of seemed like water under the bridge."

Jesse said, "But later on it got more important to you?"

"Well, it did," said Holst, very frank and earnest. "When I heard about the money. Ma always said her first husband had the makings of a miser, saved every penny, but I never thought much about it, why should I, until the house next door got put up for sale. See, some real estate guys came to look it over, this was back like maybe August sometime, and they were out in the side yard there, and I was in our yard because Ma'd asked me to weed the rose bed. I couldn't help hearing them talk, and pretty soon one of them said you'll never believe who I ran into the other day, old Johnny Vanderveer, and the other one said my God, I thought he was dead, and the first one said no, he looked about a hundred but he was still shuffling around, and he says, I'll bet he's got a pile laid away, very warm man as the British say, and the other one said yeah, he and Griffin had made a fortune apiece, real bundle of loot, in that building boom. Well—" Holst gestured graphically. "Maybe you can see that sort of made me think. It isn't an ordinary sort of name—so I asked Ma again and she said that'd be him, he was in construction work. I looked up the address— See, I'm a projectionist at the Glendale Theater, I don't make the hell of a lot of money, and Dad didn't leave much, he was a bus driver for the city. If Ma never was really divorced from this guy—why, they were still legally married and—well, hell, all she's got is the Social Security. We own the house, but it's tough to get along these days. You can see what I'm driving at."

"Clearly," said Jesse. "You're not married, Mr. Holst?"

"Who, me? No, Ma and I get along just fine, I never met a girl I felt like settling down with. Well, frankly, Mr. Falkenstein, I thought Vanderveer ought to know about this situation, see, I thought he might be interested to know about it—we didn't know if he'd ever got married again or not, but see, if he had and there were any kids—well, maybe he'd want to do something about it."

A little blackmail on the side, thought Jesse, whether the mother knew about that or not. Thinking Vanderveer would slip them a little something to keep quiet about the possibility. But pieces were falling into place. "So what did you do?" he asked. And at the back of his mind he was thinking what an unholy mess this was going to be if there hadn't been a legal divorce. God in heaven. All that money—whatever and wherever it was, however it had come—the second marriage invalid, the girls illegitimate, that will worth absolutely nothing. It would, of course, be a very simple matter, legally speaking. The legitimate widow would get a third, and the state would probably get the rest, when there wasn't a valid will. God.

"Well, I went to see him, on my day off. That house sure as hell didn't look like money, but what those guys said—well, you never know till you try. So I rang the bell, and he answered the door—I mean, it had to be him, way Ma had described him—and I'd just said my piece about the divorce when he lost his hair and threw me out—I mean, for real, gave me the bum's rush and calling me a goddamn liar and don't dare ever come back—"

So that was what that had been all about. And of course the old man would have realized the legal aspect of the thing— With a flash of insight Jesse saw that the old man hadn't been so much concerned about the effect on his will as the possibility that the first wife would have some claim on him here and now. And so first he had gone to Toomey, to check on the divorce. He'd never had any divorce papers; possibly she'd just told him she was going to get one. And then, when Toomey couldn't turn up any records, he'd intended to try to check with Mexico, hence the call to the consulate. And his third thought, of course, had been legitimate legal advice, and he had made the appointment with Jesse. It all followed as the night the day.

"So?" he said.

"Well, hell, I had to make him listen to me—get at him about maybe owing something to Ma, make things easier for her. She's never had much," said Holst emotionally. "If they were still married—I figured he'd stand still to read a letter from her, and I got her to write one. I went back there one morning, I was trying to think of some way to calm him down until I could hand him the letter, I was just going up the walk when I saw him come out the back door with a wastebasket—he was going to the garage to empty it, see, and when he got in there I nipped up the drive and got in the door quick before he could see— I figured—"

"Oh, you did? Suppose there was somebody else in the house?"

"Why, I thought he lives alone," said Holst. "I didn't see anybody else there the first time—" Holst's eyes narrowed on Jesse. "Anyway, I just waited on the service porch and he came back in a minute, he started to yell when he saw me, but I just handed over the letter—and he *did* read it. He read it right there. He just sort of grunted at it, and then he said we'd have to find out for sure about the divorce, if it was legal or not. He said even if it wasn't he didn't figure he owed Ma anything, and I said I thought he did, and he said to get the hell out, he'd let Ma know about it when he found out one way or the other. And that was that. We've been waiting to hear, see?"

"Do you remember what day that was?"

"Hell, I don't know. Five, six, seven weeks back. So when you called, I naturally thought—"

And Jesse, looking at him coldly, thought—possibilities here? The careful old man, going out to empty the wastebasket, the back door unlocked for two minutes. If Holst got in once he could get in twice. Yes? Or anybody else?

Holst the type for petty blackmail. Who could say whether the old man had slipped him fifty or a hundred to keep quiet, and then when he thought about it—and then decided to go the legitimate route, disappointing Holst?

The coincidences. He could be quite right that it was Mama who had arranged the overdose—and it could very well have been Holst who walked in on Vanderveer ten minutes or half an hour later.

He put out his cigarette. Holst was looking at his watch and saying he had to get going, pick up lunch and get to work. "You don't seem to be aware," said Jesse very gently, "that Mr. Vanderveer is dead, Mr. Holst."

Holst subsided back into the desk chair as if he'd been shot. "Dead?" he said. "Dead!" He licked his lips. He looked at Jesse in silence. Then he said slowly, "He was a damned old man. But— you'll have to find out about the divorce, won't you? If he had anything to leave—and they weren't divorced—will Ma get anything? Maybe?"

Jesse was just leaving the office when Jean said, "Mr. Dobson's on the phone—they've found the other banks."

"I've just left, have him call me back."

The house on Lomita Street in Glendale, oddly enough, was almost a replica of the house on Kingsley Drive, an old California bungalow painted white with green trim, on a shabby residential street in an old part of town. Aline Holst welcomed him in amiably. Again, it was impossible to say if she'd been pretty as a young woman, all those years ago. She was a little dumpy now, dowdy in a printed cotton housedress, low-heeled slippers. She had gentle, vague blue eyes and a soft girlish voice.

"Well," she said, "I always thought Johnny'd be one to end up with some money. But it never occurred to me I might be due any from him, till Ray said—and then it came to both of us, if that wasn't a real legal divorce—I was sort of a green girl back then, I just knew I wanted to get shut of Johnny Vanderveer, and a girl friend of mine said it was quick and cheap over the border, so that's where I went."

"Where exactly?" he asked. Tijuana, and the divorce was almost certainly not legal. God.

"Oh, Mexicali," she said. "It was only nine dollars on the bus, I remember."

He breathed a little easier. A fairly big town even then—quite a big town now—a better chance that records would be straight, crooked lawyers at a minimum. "What was the date?"

"Oh, I couldn't say exactly, it being so long ago. It was the spring of 1936, about then. When I got back I just phoned Johnny and told him we were divorced. But when Ray found out just a while ago that Johnny probably had some money, he said we ought to go into it, find out, and maybe I'd be due something. Ray's pretty smart, now that Chuck's gone I usually take Ray's advice about things."

CHAPTER 9

Twenty minutes after Jesse got back to the office Dobson called. "I thought you were supposed to keep regular office hours, Falkenstein," he said coldly. "Really I would think you'd be concerned to get on with this matter, as it's a question of settling the estate—of course I realize that can't be resolved finally until after the trial, but that's your side of the business. As far as my own office is concerned, we're anxious to find out all we can about this as soon as possible, and after all your cooperation—"

Jesse apologized. "Things come up," he said vaguely. "Where have we gotten to now?"

"We know the other two banks. A Bank of America in Atwater, a Crocker bank on Third Street. It's too late today to get into them, but I'd be obliged if you'll meet me at the Crocker bank at ten tomorrow morning, if that's not too much trouble." Jesse hastily agreed that he'd be there.

The client with the four o'clock appointment was a woman who had a divorce in mind. Taking notes on that, listening to her ramblings about her delinquent husband's drinking and playing around, he was abstracted. He left a little early; Fran and Clock were coming for dinner.

He looked at his little sister across the table—Fran looking quite herself again, despite the bulge in the middle—a very pretty girl, Fran, with her pert gamine face and smartly cut black hair—and Clock said amusedly from beside him, "I hope to God it looks like her."

Athelstane, of course, came around the table begging for handouts, and Fran said disapprovingly that they ought to cure him of that, it was an obnoxious bad habit. "Sally never does, she's good as gold, never comes near the table."

"That hairy floor mop," said Jesse.

They heard about the cat, and Fran said how funny for Athelstane to make friends with him, it showed that the big bumble-headed idiot had some finer instincts after all. The cat made a studied regal entrance after dinner, coming down the stairs; he now condescended to let Jesse stroke him, but obviously preferred women. After making a token visit to each of them in turn he leaped lightly up to the mantel from the log box and settled down with paws well tucked in.

"He really is a beauty," said Fran. "You'll have to think of a special name for him."

But, with the girls talking babies at the other end of the room, Jesse brought Clock up to date on Vanderveer. "This is the damndest rigmarole I ever came across."

"Well, I'm bound to say," said Clock, "if you're right that the girl didn't do it, I think you may have something about the old lady. She really did have some reason for suicide, and with all you've turned up, she'd probably hated that old devil for years, the life he led her."

"Yes, what belatedly occurred to me too. But you know, Andrew, he'd never have remotely realized it—realized why most people didn't like him—he didn't know they didn't—he didn't miss the social contacts, the affection—he just didn't know any better. I can see him as a rather pathetic character really, not an ogre—the narrow, selfish, greedy old man completely ignorant of the realities of life, the real importances."

"Yes, in a way," said Clock doubtfully. "How are you going to play it at the trial?"

Jesse tossed his cigarette stub into the low fire. "Dulcie won't like it, or Marcia, but it is the likeliest answer, isn't it? Mama. Mama arranged the overdose, and somebody walked in on the old man. There are possibilities to suggest—I'd better look up those evicted tenants—there were plenty of people who had reason to have a row with him—and it mightn't have taken much to provoke him into a physical attack."

"That's very funny, about the initial effect of the overdose—there wasn't anything in the autopsy report about that."

"Technically speaking, it might have been no more than self-defense," said Jesse. "There's Schultz, and now Holst—there are, when you think, quite a few people—it could have been anyone."

"What about the divorce?"

Jesse groaned. "Oh, my God, that's another thing. Write the courthouse in Mexicali, see if there's any record on it. At least there she was more likely to pick up a legitimate attorney, instead of some fly-by-night who'd take her money and assure her the divorce was legal. Yes. Even in 1936. When Vanderveer went to Toomey he hadn't received her letter, he probably thought she'd gotten the divorce here and Holst was just trying to slip something over on him for the little payoff—and then he found out it was a Mexican divorce from her letter. And at the last, he'd evidently intended to hand the whole thing over to me. Hell, I don't know, Andrew. About the trial. Dulcie will put up a good appearance in court, and if I play on the sympathy of the jury, emphasize the home situation, even if they think she did it they might let her off."

"I suppose so," said Clock, massaging his jaw. "There but for the grace of God."

"And I don't know that I'd worry about any circumvention of justice," said Jesse morosely. "The old man had had a longer share of life than a lot of people, to grab what he could on this physical plane, toil and moil away piling up the money. And the old woman's life was no pleasure to her, God knows."

He met Dobson at the Crocker bank on Third Street on Thursday morning, and here again they hadn't much difficulty. The supposed James Canning hadn't come in often to visit his safety box; the latest time had been eight months ago; but Vanderveer was a distinctive old fellow, and all three vault attendants identified the photograph without hesitation. They swore to the affidavits, so Dobson and Jesse didn't have to consider the handwriting samples. By eleven-thirty they had the box handed over and were opening it in one of the cubicles.

There was a little stack of cash in it, a folded sheet of typewriter-size paper, and a business card. Dobson sat down and before he began to count the cash he said, "Why in God's name do people do such ridiculous things, Falkenstein? If you hadn't figured out what those jottings meant, all this would never have come to light—when the rent was up on these boxes they'd have been opened and examined and the money turned over to the state as untraceable. What the hell did the old boy think he was doing, not telling a soul about where this was? He'd have known that too."

Jesse said absently, "He was just following a pattern. The habit of secrecy had grown on him." He had unfolded the sheet of paper and was reading what was on it.

It purported to be a partnership agreement, and it had been composed by someone who had very hazy ideas about legal terms. It was amateurishly typed on an old machine with elite type and several letters out of alignment.

This is to certify that an agreement is made this day—it was a date about a year in the past—*between Richard Bugotti and J. W. Vanderveer in partnership with J. W. Vanderveer to put up whole cost of establishing a business at the below address in return for 50% of all gross profits.* It was an address on Hollywood Boulevard. *Richard Bugotti contracts to take all responsibility to establish the business and operate.* There were signatures and witnesses to signatures: Henry Dudenhoff and Antonio Vasquez.

The business card simply said *Kevin Anderson, Investment Specialties,* and bore an address and phone number in San Marino. The bits and pieces the old man had left behind— He wondered what that agreement was all about.

Dobson gave him a receipt for another five thousand dollars, and they stopped for a sandwich before proceeding on to the Bank of America in Atwater. Here they ran into trouble: nobody there had any vague recollection of Robert Archer, or recognized the photograph. Dobson said resignedly that he'd see the manager, follow it up, and see what showed; Jesse had an appointment at four o'clock and left him to it.

But he had some time on hand, and instead of going upstairs he got into the Mercedes and drove up to Hollywood Boulevard. The address on that peculiar agreement was spang in the central part of town, and it had a sign on the double glass doors, The Blue Room. He parked a block up and walked back. It was a fairly big and classy porn shop: books, pictures, and no doubt other things under the counter; as the fellow at that other place had said, catering to all tastes. With the relaxed laws, there wasn't much the police could do about these places. At this hour, there was quite a little crowd in, all young men. There was a counter with a cash register on it at the rear of the store, and a man lounging behind it. The atmosphere was strangely quiet and peaceful; the men stood around browsing at the tables as if they were in trances.

Jesse went up to the counter. "I'm looking for a Richard Bugotti."

The man looked him over. "That's me. What can I do for you?" He was about twenty-six, with a widow's peak of black hair and handsome sharp features; his eyes were dark and cynical.

Jesse handed him a card. He looked at it and said, "A lawyer. That's sinister, man. What do you want with me?"

Jesse produced the funny little typed agreement and said, "Did you know that Vanderveer's dead? I'm responsible for getting his estate settled."

Bugotti looked at the paper, looked back at him, and said expressionlessly, "Yeah, I read it in the paper. So you found that stashed away." He was silent a moment, and then went to a door leading into the rear of the store. "Hey, Henry, come out and take over awhile, will you?"

A sandy beefy-shouldered young man about the same age appeared. "Sure, Rick."

"Come back here," said Bugotti, and led Jesse into a cluttered tiny office with a scarred old desk and a couple of straight chairs crowded together. He flung himself into the chair behind the desk. "That thing!" he said. "I've been worrying about that damn thing so bad I can't sleep. I guess it's true, you sure got to learn by experience. I was the biggest goddamn fool on the face of the earth to sign that thing. What I'd like to know is—you a lawyer, you can tell me—what position am I in now the old bastard is dead? Do I still have to go on paying, like to his heirs?" He looked angry and anxious.

"Suppose you tell me how you came to sign it," said Jesse. "It's an odd enough little document, Mr. Bugotti."

"Is it? I don't know much about the law, but I tried to make it sound, you know, businesslike—he told me what I should put down more or less. Hell, I even typed it, on that old thing." There was an ancient Olivetti on the desk. "Talk about goddamned fools! I'll tell you how it was, Mr."—he glanced at the card—"Mr. Falkenstain. I had a hole-in-the-wall porn store way out Vermont, making peanuts because I hadn't any capital to buy really good stock, rent a bigger place in a better location. Look, I don't happen to go for this crap myself, but there's a big demand, there's a market for it, and you supply what the public wants, you build up business and make money, no? It's simple. But you got to have capital. This old buzzard used to come in sometimes, bought a couple of things—surprised the hell out of me, see a guy his age still interested, you know? Well, about the third time he came in, Henry out there had dropped by to see me, and I was bitching about the way things were going, said if I just had the capital to stock a bigger store some place better, I could make some real money—and the old guy sort of pricked up his ears, know what I mean, and right out of the blue he said, sounds like an interesting proposition, what do you say if I put up the capital? I was flabbergasted, I nearly laughed in his face—he looked like an old bum, ragged old clothes. But then I saw he was serious. He asked all sorts of questions, how much it'd cost to rent a place and stock it, and in the end he offered me twenty thousand to get started. I didn't believe the luck—then! I was the original eager beaver, rarin' to go and make a million— I started to look around, I found this place at a pretty good price, up for lease. Well, I expected I'd sign a note for the bread at so much interest, but the old man says he's interested to keep an eye on the business, we make it like a silent partnership, and he suggested what we should put in that agreement. Hell, I can add and subtract, but I'd never been in big business before, and being a damn fool it sounded O.K. to me, I typed it up and we signed it. Then he gave me a cashier's check and I went to the bank—signed the lease that day. This place was a mess, needed painting and cleaning, and I got a couple of pals, the same ones witnessed that thing, to help—we really did a job, slicked it up good, and I ordered a lot of stock and we opened with a bang."

"How's business?" asked Jesse. "This was about a year ago, by this date."

"For God's sake!" said Bugotti. "You should ask? I just hadn't thought the thing through! We started to do business hand over fist—right on the boulevard, all the walk-by traffic, it was great! I went on thinking of that old bastard as a kind of fairy godfather for a few months, and then I woke up. With another bang."

"Yes," said Jesse. "You were doing all the work, and he was taking half the gross profit as the silent partner."

"You're goddamned right. Hell, I knew about net and gross, it was him said to put that in, but it wasn't until I was keeping the books it hit me between the eyes. Here I was paying the rent, paying the utilities, paying Henry to help wait on trade, and that old s.o.b. is taking fifty percent of all the profits! He'd taken me like some hick in from the country the first time, and the more I thought about it the madder I got. I told him so next time I saw him—he used to come in the first of the month to get his cut—and he just grinned like an old snake and said I could put it down to getting business experience, there was our agreement all nice and legal. I couldn't weasel out of it, he said, and I'd know better next time. I told him what I thought, but he didn't give a damn if I called him every name in the book. When I'd run out of things to say, he just said, how much did we make this month?"

Jesse asked curiously, "And how much have you been making, if you don't mind telling me?"

"It's been running about ten thousand a month gross—"

"Oh, ouch," said Jesse.

"Yeah, you see what I mean! And another thing, God, how could I be so innocent? Me! I mean, I knew what he was doing, but I was so grateful to the old bastard then I agreed to it—he wanted to be paid in cash—he wasn't reporting that to Uncle Sam. Along last April, I woke up to the trouble I could get into there, and I told him that was a no-no from now on. He bitched about it, but I wouldn't play. After that I gave him cashier's checks."

"Very wise of you," said Jesse dryly.

"My God, when I saw in the paper he was dead—I'm not surprised somebody murdered him—I was never so thankful in my life! But listen, what's the legal position? Do I have to go on paying his heirs?" Bugotti ran a nervous hand through his black hair.

"This contract or whatever it's supposed to be isn't legal, you know—and it was just between the two of you, and he's dead. You'd paid him back his capital plus whatever interest he'd have gotten on a loan."

"That I had."

"Why don't you just tear this up and forget it?" said Jesse casually, and laid the sheet on the desk.

"Do you mean it?" asked Bugotti incredulously. "Well, thank God! But I guess the old bastard taught me something, at that—and maybe he was right, the business experience was worth it."

Jesse just made his appointment, with a new client who wanted a legal separation from his wife, but as he took notes and answered questions, at the back of his mind he was thinking, another one with cause to hate the old man—another possible enemy who could have dropped in on Vanderveer to argue about money that rainy morning. When the client had left, he folded his notes together and sat staring out the window, thinking about it.

Whoever might have come by ending up committing a homicide, all too likely in self-defense. The picture was taking clearer shape for him, what might have happened that morning. He could see the old woman—not feeling well that morning, said Dulcie—lying in her bed wishing she could be rid of life and at rest. Thinking of the crabbed, unloving old husband, and how they were a burden on Dulcie—why shouldn't he be removed too? And painfully getting herself out of bed, onto the walker, hobbling into the kitchen—warming up the coffee, making the eggnog. Such a dark gloomy morning it had been, raining and cold, just the day for suicide and murder. He could see her getting the codeine capsules from the bathroom, adding them to the drinks, putting the bottle back. Taking the coffee to the old man sitting in the living room, or calling him to come and get it. Getting herself back to the bedroom, to lie and wait for the blessed unconsciousness— And then? Who had come to the door and played a part in the final scene?

Marcia—no, she belonged to another story. If Marcia was guilty, she had done all of it. But he could see Holst, coming back to argue that Aline was owed money—saying they knew the divorce wasn't legal, he didn't have to investigate, and he'd better pay to keep them quiet. Or Schultz, coming to beg for more time on that IOU. Or the evicted tenants to argue about the damages. Or Bugotti, swearing about how he'd been conned. Or even Bill Perez, learning of the indignities the landlord inflicted on his mother. Or—or Gloria Worth, futilely pleading to be let off the blackmail?

What a grubbing, grasping, mean-minded old bastard he had

been. And the one or the other of them losing his temper, reaching for the poker.

He could suggest all that to judge and jury. There were enough witnesses to testify to his character. And it was an academic question—they'd never know who had last handled that poker and struck the old man down.

The cat was already choosing his own places in the house, his own routines. Like all animals who tended to be creatures of habit, and turning into a properly respected house cat again, he was developing new habits for the new house. He spent the mornings outside with Athelstane, unless it was raining; about eleven o'clock he came in and went immediately to the log box to curl up for a nap there. In the afternoon he would be folded neatly together on Jesse's desk in the study, and the evenings he spent largely on Nell's lap; but promptly at ten he went upstairs to the master bedroom, where he spent the night at the foot of the bed.

"I wish I could think of an appropriate name for you," Nell told him as she got out his lunch. "You're quite an addition to the household."

The cat answered her at length in Siamese.

, Before he drove down to Sybil Brand Institute on Friday morning, Jesse dialed the phone number on that business card. An obviously efficient secretary answered the phone: "Investment Specialties, good morning." Jesse asked for Mr. Anderson. "I'm sorry, Mr. Anderson is in Phoenix on business. He's not expected back until Monday. Could someone else on our staff help you?"

"No, I'd like to speak to Anderson."

"Whom shall I say called? Is there a message?"

"Never mind, I'll call back."

When the wardress brought Dulcie into the bare little room, and stationed herself outside, Jesse said, "Now I'm going to say a few things you're not going to like hearing, Miss Vanderveer, but they've got to be said." He began to sketch the story to her, watching to see how she took it.

"No!" she said in distress. "No—not Mama! Mama was brought up to believe that suicide's a sin."

"Well, you know," said Jesse quietly, "sometimes people get to thinking different about things as they get older—and in different situations. She'd said to you that she wanted to die and be at rest, hadn't she?"

"Yes, but she didn't mean it—like that."

"She'd been suffering a good deal of physical pain, hadn't she? And she was getting more helpless."

"Yes," whispered Dulcie.

"And she knew what a burden she was being, and was sorry about that, sorry for the trouble she was to you—"

"She was a good woman, Mr. Falkenstein," said Dulcie unsteadily. "Every time I did something for her she always thanked me. She was so sorry she had to get me up so much at night—she couldn't help it."

"No," said Jesse. "And it's not a very kind or nice thing to say to you, but—looking back—do you think she'd really had a very happy life with your father? Even if she'd loved him when they were married, or even just liked and respected him—even if she'd just married him to have a husband—do you think she could still have had any positive feeling for him now, all those years later?"

Dulcie's mouth set in a firm line. "I don't know—if anybody could judge that." And she was silent, and then suddenly she sat up straight and met his eyes, and her little jaw was set and her voice harder than he had ever heard it. "I never knew him to speak an affectionate word to any of us. He was a mean, cantankerous, selfish, horrible old man, and he couldn't have been much different when he was young. I hope I didn't hate him, because hating just comes back on you, it's hurting yourself really—but I don't think anybody could ever have felt the least affection for him anytime. Oh, I know what you'll say—Uncle Howie—but it's different with men, and he didn't see Papa at home—just in business—he didn't realize how he was to us. Aunt Flo did, of course. Oh, I can remember things—the things Mama wanted and never had—that cheap little house, when Uncle Howie bought that beautiful, beautiful place—I was just fourteen, and I thought it was the loveliest house I'd ever seen, and all the beautiful new furniture— and I couldn't understand—if they were partners, why didn't Papa have enough for a house like that—and Mama just saying, your father thinks it's extravagant— Extravagant! She liked the movies

when they used to make good ones, but he always grudged the
money—gave her twenty dollars a week for the groceries, he always had to see the bills—a little more later on but—oh, I remember so much, when I was starting to grow up and realize
things—understand things." Her hands were twisting together convulsively. "Just ordinary things!" she said a little wildly. "Permanent waves—it sounds silly, but it's important to a woman to look
right—and Mama liked nice things, liked to look right—it wasn't as
if they cost much back then, you could get a permanent for ten
dollars, but he—but he— And shoes, she had trouble getting fitted,
and the only ones really comfortable for her were those Enna Jet-
ticks, and they cost more than most shoes and he said the ones at
Sears were just as good, she could go there— Dishes!" said Dulcie
incoherently. "It wasn't as if she wanted Haviland. They hadn't a
thing when they got married, she'd been living in a furnished
apartment—and I know it was still the Depression then, and not
much money—but later on, when I was noticing, all we had were
odds and ends of things that didn't match, and she wanted nice
dishes to look nice on the table, the set she wanted was forty dollars at Ward's, and he wouldn't let her—she saved it up from the
housekeeping money, it took her ages. After I was working—he
never gave Marcia and me any money at all, like an allowance,
you know—I tried to get her things she wanted, take her places—
oh, you mustn't think Marcia didn't care, but she was living away
from home, and then she was married— Catalina!" said Dulcie,
and began to cry bitterly.

"Catalina," said Jesse cautiously.

She cried for just a minute, and sat up and groped for a handkerchief. "I'm sorry. It was just—about the first time I noticed—
how things were—I guess I was about seven or eight. Her friend
Mrs. Wayland wanted her to go to Catalina with her for the weekend, just a little vacation, it would only cost about thirty dollars—
and he was furious, he wouldn't let her go. I'm sorry, it was just
that it all—sort of came back at once. How everything was. She
was a good, kind woman, Mr. Falkenstein—and of course she was
miserable with him, how could she help being miserable? Oh, I
hope not hating him— But what could she do? She wasn't young—
when Marcia and I were born—she couldn't get away, because of
us. And he never gave anybody anything, not even a kind word—

he just took and took, all her work and all her youth and all her happiness—and forty-two years—*forty-two years*—the meanest kind of living, that old-fashioned house in an old street, never any money for decent clothes, never going out anywhere, never any fun, never having *anything*—"

"You should have let all that out before," said Jesse.

"Oh, don't you think Marcia and I have said it a thousand times? Haven't thought about it?" She was silent, still mopping her eyes, and then she said very quietly, "I've got to say—I think it's possible, Mr. Falkenstein. It's clever of you to see that—it never entered my mind—it could have been Mama. But it could have been."

"We'd never prove it, you know. But I think I can make a good case to put to the jury. It's not going to be pleasant for you and your sister to hear all this in court, about your father and mother— but you're more important than two people who are—out of it."

"That's one way to look at it," said Dulcie. "You're the one to say. You know what ought to be done at the trial. You do what you think is right." She looked exhausted now, and went off down the corridor with the wardress, walking slowly.

Dobson called at three-thirty on Friday afternoon. "I don't know how we're going to get over this one," he said grimly. "That box at the Bank of America—I was chasing all around that damn bank yesterday, and then over hell's half acre trying to get current addresses. He rented that box sometime in 1960, and he'd never been near it since as far as we can make out."

"Oh, for the love of—"

"Yes," said Dobson. "I know. Nearly twenty-two years, and practically all the bank personnel has changed. Also, they had a fire that destroyed some records in 1965, and there's no record of who rented him the box. There were four people who worked in the vault—that is, three regulars and one posting clerk who substituted during lunch hours, and any one of them might have waited on Vanderveer that day. One of them is now dead."

"Fine," said Jesse. "But they must have had an address, to send him the yearly bill?"

"That's right. General Delivery, the Hollywood post office. He paid in cashier's checks."

"Very helpful. What do we do about it?"

"Well, we'll have to try. If you'll meet me at my office in the morning, we can use my car." He didn't sound hopeful.

Still, a picture was supposed to be worth a thousand words.

Jesse went home to find Nell poring over a dictionary of names. "Oh, I didn't realize it was that late," she said, looking up in surprise as he came in. "I'm sorry, darling, I forgot the gate."

"I know you did, it's all right. What are you doing, naming the baby?"

"Now, Jesse—you know that's been decided months ago. It's Amanda Elaine for a girl and Geoffrey Andrew for a boy. No, I'm looking for an appropriate name for the new member of the family, and I can't find one. Nothing seems really to fit him." Davy was prattling to himself in his playpen, Athelstane was sound asleep in front of the fireplace, and the cat was curled up on the mantel watching them with his brilliant blue eyes. He looked much fatter and sleeker now.

"Have you thought," asked Jesse, "of doing anything about dinner?"

"Heavens, the meat loaf!" Nell dropped the book and fled.

But over drinks before dinner, she reverted to the topic. "Nothing seems to fit him, but there's something queer about it too."

"Always something queer about cats. The ultimate independent entities," said Jesse lazily. "Reason some simian human beings don't like them—they just can't understand anybody who's completely indifferent to somebody else's opinion."

Nell laughed. "Quite true, but there is something funny about it." She sipped sherry. "I very nearly christened him Solomon this morning—he looks so wise, after all—and when he came in with Athelstane for lunch I asked him if he'd like to be called Solomon, and he stopped short and looked at me, and honestly, Jesse, I could nearly hear him saying, no, that's not my name."

"Imagination."

"It was not. And I thought of a few others, like Graymalkin and Chang and Domino and Thibault. And Tobermory, only he didn't speak Siamese. And Webster."

"That's a new one on me."

"The cat in the Wodehouse story."

"Oh. Yes."

"But they don't fit."

"Something will occur to you."

"Well, I hope so. We can't go on calling him Puss. He's going to the vet for immunization shots on Monday, I hope he won't mind. And how are you coming with your little puzzle? Found any more wads of cash stuffed into old chairs?"

"Don't remind me. We seem," said Jesse, "to have run into a little snag."

"I don't expect," said Dobson, "that we'll get a single reaction, but of course we have to try." They had started out at the bank in Atwater.

It had been there a long time, and it was a big bank. Only three of the personnel who had been there in 1960 were still there: the manager, the chief teller, and a security guard. None of them, of course, had anything to do with the vault, but Jesse showed them the photograph and they all looked and shook their heads at it.

"I couldn't say I never had seen him," said the chief teller, "maybe coming in once—but nobody'd remember just once. And that long ago—"

At least the manager had been able to supply Dobson with the names of the employees who were on duty at the vault then. "How do you know it was 1960 if the records were destroyed, by the way?" asked Jesse.

"They were only partly destroyed. Up to 1959 that box was rented by somebody else, there's a listing on that, and it's never been on the free list since. I had a hell of a time tracing down addresses for these people, they'd all moved since leaving the bank. These post office people are getting more inefficient every day."

"Look who's talking."

"Two of these people retired—Mrs. Willey and John Partridge—and another one was fired, James Lukens. In 1970."

"What did he do, try to embezzle funds?"

"He was found drunk on the job. Mrs. Willey went to live with her sister when her husband died, the people next door gave me that. It's Altadena."

Mrs. Willey, who was small and neat and obviously consci-

entious, pored over the photograph for some time before she said,
"Oh, dear, I wish I could help you, but I don't recall ever seeing
this man in my life. You say he rented a box? Well, you know, the
vault's open the same hours as the bank, and it could have been
any one of us who waited on him. I might have been out to lunch
when he came in, or waiting on someone else so I didn't notice
him. And of course Mr. Lukens came down from upstairs on
different lunch hours, or if we were busy. And Mr. Brandon—oh,
dear, that was such a dreadful thing—he had the heart attack right
in the bank, you know, he dropped dead right in front of the New
Accounts desk—he was only fifty-nine and such a nice man—" She
handed back the photograph. "I wish I could help you, but I can't
say I'd seen him when I never did."

Mr. John Partridge lived in Hawthorne. He had moved in with
his daughter's family when his wife died. And it was obviously a
nice family: the daughter, Mrs. Pickering, was friendly and attractive, and there was an enticing smell of fresh-baked bread in the
house. "Something about the bank? Well, Daddy's out in back
planting bulbs—he always was a gardener, he's made a difference
to this place, I don't have the time and my husband can't abide
yard work." She showed them out the kitchen door into a green
and pleasant backyard.

Partridge was a perky thin little man in his seventies, with a
thin halo of white hair around a large bald spot. He sat back on
his heels and dropped his trowel and said, "I was late getting the
new ones in this fall, but looks as though we'll have a wet winter,
I hope they'll do well. You from the bank, you say? What can I
do for you?"

"IRS," said Dobson curtly, and Partridge's smile faded. Jesse
hastened into the conversation and explained what they were
after.

"Well, now, isn't that a thing," said Partridge. "False name,
hah? On a lockbox? I don't know that I ever ran into a thing like
that before. We better go in, I've got to wash my hands before I
look at your picture." They went in and sat in a comfortable,
homey living room while Partridge washed his hands.

He came back and sat down and Jesse handed him the photograph. He studied it carefully. "I've never laid eyes on him," he
said regretfully. "I've got a good memory for faces—dealing with

the public, it makes a difference if you take the trouble to remember people, call them by name. In a bank, of course, it's not
the same thing as your own business—people have to deal with
banks—but it makes things more friendly. I knew all our regulars,
of course. But this"—he tapped the photograph—"I think I'd have
remembered him, if I'd ever seen him. He's not just ordinary-look-
ing. But I never did. Rented a box from us, did he? Well, it could
have been Mary Willey or Bill Brandon or even Lukens rented it
to him. When I was out to lunch or busy with somebody else. You
know that Brandon's dead? Died of a heart attack, right at the
bank."

"We heard," said Dobson sourly.

"Well, I'm sorry I can't help you," said Partridge. "Renting a
box in a fake name—you know, come to think, people might be
doing that all the time, all we ask is a name and address and the
rent."

James Lukens, Dobson had located in Huntington Park. On the
way, Jesse said, "The handwriting analysts can come up with
some hard facts these days. Think I might get Sergeant Clock to
turn Questioned Documents onto it."

"Onto what?" asked Dobson briefly. "We've got plenty of samples of Vanderveer's writing, but the form he filled out, renting the
box, is gone. They've got nothing to show us but cashier's checks—
that is, the latest one."

"Oh, Lord, of course."

The address in Huntington Park was one side of an old frame
duplex. The woman who opened the door was about forty, with
hennaed hair and a bad-tempered mouth. Inside the living room,
immediately inside the door, a TV was on loudly.

She went over and turned it off with a snap. "Somebody to see
you. I didn't get who, you run that damn thing so loud."

"From the bank," said Jesse. "That is, going back to your job
at the bank, Mr. Lukens—"

"If you only had that bank job back," said the woman bitterly.
"Good steady money—but you had to get drunk on the job—"

"Shut up," he said. He was a middle-aged man, too fat and
pasty-faced, in slacks and a T-shirt. "I got a job, haven't I?"

"Oh, you got a job! A lousy part-time job at a liquor store, not enough to pay the rent, I got to wait on tables at that Mex restaurant to put groceries on the table—"

"Knock it off. What are you guys after?"

Dobson told him. He said, "Dammit, that's a hell of a long time ago. I couldn't tell you." He looked at the photograph again. "He doesn't look like anybody I ever saw before."

"You wouldn't recognize him if he was your best pal," she said. "You half drunk alla time—"

"Shut up, you bitch," he said tersely.

Dobson turned the ignition key in expressive silence. On the way back to Hollywood, he said, "So there's absolutely no way we can prove any connection! We know Archer had to be Vanderveer, but there's no way to prove it legally. The box rent is paid up to January. All we can do is wait until then to get a look at it—our office has the authorization, but of course you haven't anything legally to connect it with the estate—"

"Not one damned thing," said Jesse. Maybe just because he couldn't get at it, he was damned curious about what was in that safe-deposit box.

CHAPTER 10

It occurred to Jesse that he should at least get the names of those evicted tenants to add to the list of people with reason to dislike Vanderveer, and on Sunday morning he went up to that apartment on Fountain. It was the kind of place called, for some unfathomable reason, a garden apartment, built the long way of the lot with some landscaping and open carports at the side; the building was two-storied. He started with the ground-floor front; the name slot beside the door held a slip with a typed name: R. RYAN. The woman who opened the door was a young, fairly good-looking blonde. She listened to his self-introduction and question and said, oh, the Sidneys. They had moved out a couple of months ago.

"I understand," said Jesse, "that there was some trouble with Mr. Vanderveer—the landlord."

"That's right," said Mrs. Ryan, "but a lot of people in this place had trouble with him. You're the lawyer seeing about the will and so on? I wonder if we could get that money back—it was only forty dollars but it was the principle of the thing—come in and I'll tell you about it." She introduced him to her husband, who looked like a sub-junior executive type; they were both in their mid-twenties. "It's the lawyer arranging all that old man's affairs, Rex. It's awful about his daughter, we didn't know he had one, but she probably had a reason. Sit down, Mr. what did you say?—oh, Falkenstein." The little apartment was bright and neat, built on an open plan and furnished in Danish modern. "Listen," she said, "this is the kind of thing he'd do. He always came the first of the month to get the rent checks—if it was a weekday he'd come in the evening. He was a real old creep, like a mummy come to life. But after all, he owned the place, he was supposed to keep it up. And the dishwasher went on the fritz—"

Rex Ryan said mildly, "Not a plumber. Like Vera says, he was supposed to keep up the place." He had pale blue eyes and a prominent Adam's apple, and was wearing a red plaid robe over pajamas. "The old man came and worked on it, said it was fixed. It wasn't. Finally, after he'd fooled around with it a couple of times, I had to call a plumber, and the bill was forty bucks. I sent it to him, and he hit the ceiling. I had a hell of a row with him, he wouldn't pay, and of course I was the one who got dunned. I paid it—didn't have any choice—and never got him to fork over."

"Well," said Jesse. "Did you know the Sidneys?"

"Now there," said Vera Ryan judicially, "I have to admit he had a case. You're not supposed to have children or pets here, but she had her sister's two little boys this summer, the sister was sick, and they were real brats, threw stuff down the toilet and ruined the plumbing and crayoned all over the walls and carved up the kitchen counter—I saw the place when they moved out."

"Do you know where they moved?" Neither of them did.

"They were riffraff anyway," he said.

"Who's going to own this place now?" she asked. "We had notice to pay rent to some other address—"

"There's some question about that, it may not be settled for a while." And that was just more grist to the mill.

On Monday morning Marcia Coleman came into the office about eleven o'clock. She was looking rather fine-drawn and haggard. "I don't want to take up your time, Mr. Falkenstein—I know I haven't got an appointment, and you're probably busy—but Dulcie told me on Saturday—what you think. What—well, what line you'll take at the trial. I just wanted to put in my opinion—for what it's worth."

"As I said to your sister, not very pleasant hearing in court—for either of you. But—"

She made an impatient gesture. She sat down in the chair beside his desk, accepted a cigarette and a light. "It doesn't matter. It's queer, but it never remotely occurred to either of us that *that* was the answer, Mama was always so gentle, never complaining, putting up with things and making do—never any arguments, everything just the way he ordered it—but now you bring up the possibility, both of us can *see* it. There must have been just one last straw. After forty-two years. I wonder if it was the washing machine."

"What about the washing machine?" asked Jesse.

"Well, there was the usual fit about that when we got it—and when was that?—Charles and I have been married fifteen years, and it was about three years before that, so it must have been 1962 or 1963. Mama had an old wringer washer, and it finally gave out—of course she should have had an automatic years before. But equally of course he said they cost too much. But Dulcie stood up to him for once and kept after him until he finally went to Sears and bought one. It was fine for quite a long time, but they don't last forever and the last couple of years it needed repairs and parts a few times, and of course he kicked about that. And the week before—before they died, it went out again and the repairman said it couldn't be fixed, they'd need a new one. And Papa said no, Dulcie could take everything to the Laundromat. On top of everything else she had to do. You wouldn't wonder but what it was the last straw. For Mama. She knew what a lot of work she made for Dulcie, and that was going to be too much. And maybe, after forty-two years, she finally hit back at him." Marcia was silent, smoking, and then said with a little laugh, "I nearly didn't marry Charles—on account of Mama and Papa. Kids —they take their attitudes to life, and to marriage, from their parents. It's an irrational thing, by then I was an adult, and I'd had some experience with people, different kinds of people. But when I thought about marriage, all I could see was Mama, forever shortchanged and going without and making do, putting up with that damned old tyrant—my God, Charles as different from Papa as night from day—but you see what I mean."

"I do indeed," said Jesse thoughtfully.

"And I knew I wasn't like Mama either—if I'd been in that situation, hard as it was, not young and with two kids to raise, I'd have spit in his eye and gotten out, if I had to scrub other people's floors or whatever to support myself. I never could see why Dulcie didn't get out long ago. After Mama had the arthritis and strokes, of course she was stuck, and she was over thirty then, knew she'd probably never marry. I couldn't have stood it—but Dulcie's a pretty strong character in her own way. Well—" She stood up. "I just wanted to let you know that I'm quite willing to cooperate, whatever you want me to do at the trial, whatever you want me to say. No, it's not a very nice story, is it? But if it's the way to get Dulcie off, we'll have to play it that way. Just tell me what you want me to say—the unpalatable truth as it were."

"Thanks very much, Mrs. Coleman. I'm glad to know that, and I appreciate your coming in."

As he ushered her out past the Gordons' desks, Roberto Renaldo was sitting in the outer office, handsome and phlegmatic. He stood up and gave Jesse a correct little bow. "I have come to give you the key of the house, sir. We have found another house, near to Lucia's sister, and have moved yesterday. You understand, we want a house because we hope to have sons and daughters, and in all these apartments it is forbidden to have the children. It is very strange—American landlords would perhaps like to see the race of man die out entirely?"

Jesse grinned. "I can see it might look like that."

"So, we have moved. The rent is paid to the end of the month, but Lucia was impatient to move, she says she can see the terrible old man in every corner as if spying on her—women have fancies, but I love her, what am I to do?" He shrugged cheerfully and went out. Jean reminded Jesse that Mr. Hausman was due to come in to sign his will, and there was a new client at two o'clock.

The new client turned out to be a Mrs. Ringrose, breathing vengeance at the Griffith Park Observatory, on whose too-polished floor she had broken an ankle and sustained other injuries. Jesse listened to her, soothed her by saying they'd get her medical expenses with no difficulty: a routine claim against the city. She went away mollified, and he suddenly remembered Kevin Anderson.

He sat back and lit a cigarette and got out that business card from the second safe-deposit box and dialed the San Marino number. On the second ring the phone was lifted at the other end, "Investment Specialties, may I help you?"

"I'd like to speak to Mr. Anderson."

"Thank you." And a moment later a deep masculine voice said, "Anderson here."

"I think," said Jesse, "that you knew a Mr. Jan Vanderveer."

"Knew? Is he gone? Well—who is this?"

Jesse introduced himself. "Oh, I see," said Anderson. "Well, he was getting up in years, of course. I hadn't seen him in some time, as a matter of fact."

"Do you mind telling me the nature of your, er, connection with him, Mr. Anderson?"

"Why, no," said Anderson, sounding a little puzzled, "but since you knew my name I assumed— He'd been buying gold from me for about fifteen years. That's what we deal in—silver, gold, investment diamonds."

Jesse said gently, "Mr. Anderson, will you please stay right in your office and I'll be with you in half an hour. I think we've got things to talk about."

It was a small office building on a secondary main street in that exclusive community. There were several smartly groomed secretaries flitting about a communal office. Individual executive offices were along a side corridor; Anderson's was at the front. Everything was very top quality and quietly elegant. Anderson was no exception; a stocky fair man in an expensively tailored silver-gray suit. He looked at Jesse across his wide oak desk, smiling. "He was a very shrewd man, Mr. Falkenstein, as you probably know. He saw which way the economy is headed. When a government is operating on fiat money, the unbacked paper, it's in deep trouble—there's bound to be a crash of some magnitude sooner or later. And at a time like that, the only assets of any immediate value are the actual specie, gold and silver. Vanderveer had been in the stock market all his life, and he was holding a lot of top-grade paper. He thought—and I won't say whether I agree with him—he thought that the biggies would be shored up, some value still there, and after some bank failures some of those would come back too, but in the meantime he was sinking some large investments into the hard stuff."

"My God, my God, I might have known!" said Jesse. "Why didn't I guess it? But what the hell was he doing with it? Where did he keep it?"

Anderson's confident smile vanished. "You don't mean to tell me you haven't *found*— Well, he took it away with him, of course. You buy gold, you make your own arrangements to store it. You don't mean you didn't know about it? That nobody—"

"Oh, no, no, no," said Jesse, "do I have to get a bulldozer to dig up his whole damned backyard? There is no place left to look for anything in that damned house—"

"He didn't leave any record of where he stored it?" Anderson was appalled. "Good God—at current prices he must have been holding half a million in double eagles and Krugerrands—"

"Oh, my God, that safe-deposit box!" said Jesse. "There's one we haven't been able to get into—" He explained, and Anderson just shut his eyes in brief comment.

"These secretive souls—how big is it?"

"One of the medium-sized ones, why?"

"Then you can forget it," said Anderson. "It wouldn't be big enough to hold it all. I thought the old man had better sense—my God."

"He didn't even give you a hint as to where he was keeping it?"

Anderson gave him a wintry smile. "You don't ask clients loaded questions, Mr. Falkenstein. It's people's own business. Good God, this is a hell of a situation. I can give you a list of exactly what he held, and I can tell you that he told me he was sitting tight on it, the gold he'd never sell. He got a lot at bottom prices before it started up so fast a few years back, and of course there's been fluctuation—he hadn't been buying for a couple of years, but I had a standing order to let him know if it went below a certain price. I—"

"You sent him a postcard the other day." Jesse had just remembered it.

"Right. Gold took a little dive, but I knew it wouldn't stay down long. I couldn't get him on the phone—of course I had no idea he was dead."

"My God, would he have kept it in the house? That's impossible, for God's sake, I've been through everything—"

"People do," said Anderson. "In safes. He never would have a safe in the house, he said somebody always knew and it was just advertising that you had valuables in the place."

"Oh, my dear God," said Jesse, "not another lockbox in the name of Fred Zilch, no, please God—there's no record of another one, of course—"

"I had just mentioned to him that he might find it practical to rent one of these private storage boxes—it's rather a new firm, but the idea is catching on. There are branches all over the county and up the Coast. You can rent boxes of any size, and unlike the ones at the bank, you get the only key."

Jesse uttered a heartfelt groan. "Don't ask me to believe there is another key hidden in that house! Besides, there'd be some record— Oh, God, would there? We'd better ask at those places— can you give me the company's address?"

Anderson nodded wordlessly. "I don't know what else to tell you. He didn't inform anybody?—he didn't leave any—my God. And I thought he was a shrewd man."

"How did he take delivery?"

"Well, the actual gold comes in here, he'd come to pick it up and hand over payment—he'd know the exact figure from phone confirmation, and he always used cashier's checks. The last few times I saw him, the D.M.V. had stopped him driving, and he came in a cab—he was in a hurry to pick up his gold and leave."

"How's it packaged?"

"In plastic tubes the diameter of the coins. Oh, my God, when I think what he was holding!" said Anderson almost in agony. "I can make you an exact list—but at least three quarters of it is in double eagles—uncirculated twenty-dollar gold coins—and a good many rolls of Krugerrands and British sovereigns—at the current price, sweet Jesus, when I think—"

"How much space might it take up?"

Anderson was holding his head. "Call it two feet by one, stacked close. That's another reason to hold gold, you know. This is a hell of a situation for you—my good God, I hope you can locate it. I really thought the old man had better sense—these damned secretive lunatics—well, let me know, will you?"

"Just make me up that list, as soon as you can."

"I'll get right on it."

Jesse sat outside the elegant office, behind the wheel of the Mercedes, and considered this new problem. That forever-foxy old man playing both ends against the middle!—and he should have expected this, he really should. But what in the name of God and all the angels had he done with the lovely shiny gold?

On Tuesday morning Nell was just about to leave for the market when the doorbell rang. She went to answer it, and on the front porch was a nice-looking elderly woman in a rather old-fashioned navy-blue tailored suit. She wore rimless glasses and her white hair was done up in an untidy bun very unlike Nell's own neat fat chignon. She began talking as soon as the door opened.

"This is a quite unwarrantable intrusion and I do apologize. But I've just got home, you see, oh, dear, I should introduce myself, I'm Mrs. Frances Lucas. I just got back to California. I've been worried about it for months, ever since I knew she had died, and I just had to come and ask. And I don't even know your name, I'm sorry—"

Nell told her. "But what—"

"You see, I'd gone back to Indianapolis to spend Christmas with my daughter, and I fell on the ice and broke my hip," said Mrs. Lucas earnestly. "I was in the hospital quite a long time, they couldn't get that pin to stay in, you see, and then I had pneumonia, and altogether it was nearly April before I was sitting up and taking notice again—"

"Yes, but what—well, won't you come in?" said Nell with reluctant hospitality.

Mrs. Lucas followed her into the living room, and got out a minute handkerchief to dab her eyes. "Oh, dear, it all looks so *different*—oh, excuse me, it's all very nice, of course, but all Bertha's things gone—you see, Bertha Spicer was one of my oldest friends—"

"Oh, I see," said Nell, enlightened.

"And I never knew when she died! My daughter was worried about me, I'd really been very low, and when Bertha died—it was very sudden, a heart attack, just after Christmas—a mutual friend wrote my daughter, but she was afraid to tell me, that it would be too great a shock. Oh, it was April before she told me Bertha was gone—and I was just heartsick. Well, about Bertha *too,* of course— And that friend, Mary Thompson, can't drive and she lives in Long Beach, so there was no way—and nobody knew the lawyer's name or I'd have written to him—I knew I had it written down somewhere at home, Bertha had told me in case—she was quite alone, you see, no relatives here— And my daughter said I wasn't to come home and live by myself again until I was perfectly well— I've been there all summer—and I just got back on Saturday. And I found the lawyer's name and called him, and he said the estate was settled and the house had been sold—"

"Yes, we bought it in June."

"Oh, Mrs. Falkenstein—" Her faded blue eyes filled with tears. "I just had to come and ask—if anybody had seen—oh, dear, it's Bertha's cat! He was only two years old and just like her child, he ruled the household—his little bed just at the right of the hearth, and—and the house was shut up right away, and the lawyer didn't know about him so he never looked—"

"What kind of a cat, Mrs. Lucas?"

"Oh, he was a beautiful big seal point Siamese with the bluest eyes—"

Nell smiled at her. "Come here and look." She shepherded Mrs. Lucas out to the service porch and opened the back door. On the back porch Athelstane's huge bulk was stretched out comfortably in the pale sun, and the cat was curled between his front paws.

"Why, *there he is!*" cried Mrs. Lucas joyfully. "Oh, and he looks fine! Oh, how could he have—"

"He's been here all the time," said Nell, with awe in her voice. "Only we didn't know. She went away and left him, but he stayed —because it's his house. He must have nearly starved, living on what he could hunt up here—I don't know how he survived. Mrs. Lucas—what's his name?"

"Why, his name is Murteza—it means the lion of God in Arabic —some of the pictures Bertha was painting just before she got him were for a children's book about Sinbad—oh, Mrs. Falkenstein, I'm so thankful to know he's all right! I'm so thankful! You know, I put up a prayer to St. Francis for him every single night."

"And maybe that helped," said Nell. "Maybe it did, Mrs. Lucas. I'm thankful too."

"But he always hated dogs—and that enormous creature out there—"

"Well, it was really Athelstane who found him," said Nell. "Let's have some coffee and I'll tell you all about it."

On Tuesday, Wednesday, and Thursday, Jesse spent all the spare time he had chasing down all the branches of that private storage firm. He had called Dobson to tell him about this latest development, and Dobson said viciously that he was sorry he'd ever heard the name of Vanderveer. It was, of course, necessary to visit all the various depositories, armed with the photograph, in case Vanderveer had used another alias.

But at three o'clock on Thursday afternoon Jesse knew definitely that he hadn't rented space in any of these places; all the various attendants had denied the photograph. There weren't that many of these private depositories, and he wasn't known at any of them.

What the hell had he done with it? What the hell? Jesse would take seven Bible oaths that that gold was nowhere in the house. The backyard—impossible. Even Vanderveer—even if he had been losing his wits, and the experience of Rick Bugotti gave no evidence of that—

He sat in the Mercedes outside the last place he had checked, which was in South Pasadena, and wondered just where to go on this now. And suddenly he thought, I'll bet Howie knew—I'll bet he told Howie. Howard Griffin must have been the one man Vanderveer had trusted absolutely. But—Howie enough like him that he wouldn't trust a woman with a secret? Not his own secret—no reason to tell her, every reason not to. She didn't know anything, obviously, or she'd have spoken up. But she might, just possibly, hold some sort of tenuous clue.

He got to the house in West Hollywood forty minutes later, and Flo Griffin was surprised to see him. "I was just going to have a cup of coffee in front of the fire—such a cold dreary day—it'll be nice to have some company."

And when he told her about this latest hunt, she said incredulously, *"Gold?* My good heavens. My good *heavens.* Could that have been what— Was it something real, then? I thought it might be just cash—Johnny was always a miser—if there was anything to it at all— Could that have been what Howie was talking about?"

"Did he tell you something?" asked Jesse. "About what?"

"Yes—no—I really don't know, Mr. Falkenstein." She stirred dairy creamer into her coffee. "Of course Johnny told him things—and usually he'd never have dreamed of telling me—confidential things between partners, you know the sort of thing. But you see, Howie wasn't really himself—that last couple of weeks. He'd ramble on about something that happened years ago, and then in a minute he'd be talking quite sensibly. You just didn't know. But—I remember now—just a few days before he died, I was with him one afternoon, in his room, and he was going on, just rambling talk, about how Johnny always said, the only safe place for whatever valuables you had was right under your own hand—and how he had a pretty cute hiding place in the house, a place nobody would ever think to look. He said Johnny had fixed it himself years ago, and he was the only one who knew about it. All the same, he was worried, he said, because there were smart burglars around, he'd told Johnny he ought to move it, didn't know if he had—"

"Well," said Jesse.

"But, Mr. Falkenstein, I never thought it really meant anything —I just didn't mention it, because the way Howie was—he could have been talking about something that happened years back, you see? And to tell the truth, even if that were so, I thought Johnny might have been spinning him a tale, Johnny always liked to boast about how clever he was."

"Yes, I see," said Jesse thoughtfully. That house. Again. A pretty cute hiding place. His imagination had deserted him. He simply didn't see how there could be another hiding place in that house. Well, they hadn't taken all the floors up, of course. Or looked up the chimney. Or there was the crawl space above the ceiling. Or—

He yawned and apologized. He'd been doing a lot of driving in the last three days and he was tired. And he was very tired of the house on Kingsley Drive. In any case he couldn't do anything about it tomorrow; he'd be in court most of the day, and there was paper work at the office.

On Saturday night there was a movie being rerun on TV that Nell wanted to see. It began at nine-thirty; but the newest member of the family did not approve late hours and could tell time as well as anybody. Promptly at ten o'clock Murteza proceeded up to bed. When they came up at eleven-thirty he was asleep on the foot of the bed.

"The lion of God—I do like that," said Nell. "Murteza just fits him, of course, because it's his name. I'll bet Miss Spicer always went to bed at ten o'clock every night. I do hope she knows he's all right and happy again."

"I can only say it's lucky we decided to get a king-size bed," said Jesse. "Being aware that any cat always runs the house." He scratched Murteza's ears in passing and the lion of God uttered a sound of disapproval at being wakened. Athelstane had followed them up, and now subsided onto his rug at Nell's side of the bed with a noisy yawn.

"I'll just go check on Davy."

But they were all wakened by the shrill summons of the telephone an unspecified time later. Jesse sat up sleepily and peered at the bedside clock. It was three-thirty. "What the hell?" he muttered, thrusting the covers back. The phone in here was across the room. He staggered over there in the dark and got it on the seventh ring. "Yes?"

"I thought you'd want to know," said Clock tersely. "Pete went on night watch on Monday, and he called me ten minutes ago—the beat man suspected arson right away and called in. That house on Kingsley—there are two companies out now, and it looks as if the whole thing's going to go up."

"Oh, my God."

"It evidently got a good hold inside before anything showed, and in the middle of the night—I needn't have waked you up, I suppose, but I thought you'd want to know. You thought there might still be something there that you missed, didn't you?"

"I don't know," said Jesse. "I really don't know. But if there was—"

"Past praying for now. I thought you'd be interested."

At 8 A.M., when Jesse parked in front of the place, Clock's Pontiac was parked just ahead, and Clock was standing in what had been the drive of the old house. The house was gone, and the garage; there was nothing but a blackened waterlogged mass of crumbled charred wood fallen in on itself. All Dulcie's and Marcia's bitter memories, the few possessions Dulcie had had here, the portable typewriter and the cheap furniture, the old rolltop desk with its secret drawer, the dishes Mama had saved up for—it was all gone. He walked up to where Clock was standing. There were a few people out from the apartment house next door; he saw Eberhart at the rear of the drive, peering over at the black rubble.

"Probably juveniles out for a Saturday night kick," said Clock sadly.

"Kind of thing they'd do. I wonder if there was any insurance. I don't think so—I haven't come across any policies."

The nearest door up the apartment-house driveway opened and a man came out, came over to look next door. That would be the kitchen door of the downstairs apartment there; those people, Jesse remembered, had been away somewhere. Somebody had said the name—Lutz.

The man turned and looked at them. He was a nondescript medium-sized man in his forties, with horn-rimmed glasses. "That's quite a mess," he said. They agreed. "You know there was a murder in that place the other day."

"Yes," said Clock, and Jesse introduced himself.

"I was around here asking questions—I was Vanderveer's lawyer. I understand you'd left the day before on a trip."

"No, it was that same day," said Lutz. "Of course we never heard about it till we got back. Is that so? Don't think I ever heard those people's name. Hell of a thing, we got back at five o'clock yesterday, and then get hauled out in the middle of the night, but thank God there wasn't any wind, and it didn't spread. Yeah, we were sure interested to hear that—imagine, right next door. But any city these days—" He left the thought there. "We've been in Florida visiting the wife's mother." After a minute he went on, "Funny sort of people lived there, I guess. The place was usually quiet, you hardly ever saw any comings or goings. This drive right across from our back door, we noticed. Yeah, we left that morning about ten, the plane didn't leave till noon but the wife always likes to be early. It was raining like hell that morning, you know. Reason I happened to notice, somebody came next door then to see those people."

"Oh?" said Jesse.

"That's right. I just happened to notice. The cab came into the drive, easier to load the suitcases from the back door, and I was helping the driver get them into the trunk when this car drove in next door."

"Have you heard much about the murder?" asked Clock.

He shrugged. "Heard the daughter put poison in the coffee at dinner, wasn't it? Just from the lady upstairs—like I say, we just got back yesterday."

"But you saw a car drive in here that morning? On October twentieth?"

"Yeah, and the reason I remember is that I happened to notice the tag—it was funny—one of these vanity license plates, and it was the same name as our best friends—vanity plate with a name on it, you know."

Jesse asked gently, "And what was it?"

"Why, it was Seager. Spelled the same way as Bob and Emmy spell it, too, and I—"

Clock and Jesse looked at each other. "But who the hell—" said Clock.

"Oh, Howie knew," said Jesse. "Howie the only one who did know—and there's a possible witness, and what the hell was the name—Dickey, Adam Dickey."

Clock could ask for a search warrant, because they had an exact description of what they expected to find—Anderson had sent Jesse a list of all those uncirculated coins. But it was Sunday, and it took a while to rout out a judge. It was three-thirty when Clock, Jesse, and Petrovsky—who said he wanted to see the finish of the thing—stood waiting outside an apartment door. It was an old apartment building on Romaine Street, and well-built; the hall was very quiet.

She opened the door, and Clock and Petrovsky held out their badges. She looked at them, the rather tall thin woman with too-golden tinted curls, and her expression didn't change at all. Her skin had a grayish tinge in the harsh cold light of the hall window; it was dark and raining again today.

"Mrs. Patricia Seager?" said Clock formally. "We have a search warrant which allows us to search this apartment. I think you know what we're looking for."

Her eyes moved over his rough-hewn face incuriously, and passed on to Jesse with no sign of recognition. After a long dragging moment she said, "But how could you possibly know? How did you?"

"There was an unexpected witness next door, Mrs. Seager," said Jesse, "who noticed your license plate. He only mentioned it this morning."

She threw her head back and laughed, high and sharp. "The

millionth chance!" she said. "That's funny. That's really very funny. But it's all funny. A comedy of errors."

"And there may be another witness—Mr. Dickey, the temporary patient sharing Mr. Griffin's room just before he died. He might be able to tell us that you spent a lot of time with Mr. Griffin, talking to him—and listening to him."

She looked at him with complete indifference. "Oh, I'll tell you all about it," she said casually. She turned to Clock. "It's all at the back of the wardrobe in the bedroom. I was going to sell it but I thought I'd better wait awhile. It doesn't matter now. Now that I won't get to enjoy it. I was just diagnosed yesterday, the final results came back from the lab—terminal cancer of the liver. So I suppose I can do a last good deed and let that other woman off. Yes, Griffin told me about it. He was getting a little childish, and the effect of so much analgesic medication—after he'd first mentioned something about Johnny's gold, and a secret hiding place, it didn't take much persuasion to get it all out of him when he was half under. All that gold. And the hiding place—a very good hiding place, too. It was a false wall at the back of the shelf in the front hall closet. Just a piece of plyboard cut the right size and wedged in, painted the same color as the wall—about six inches out from the real wall. With things stacked against it, you'd never notice."

"Oh, by God," said Jesse. "Yes, I see—so very simple."

"It wasn't any trouble—I knew it wouldn't be. It just went wrong at the end." She sat down on the couch and lit a cigarette. "I've never had much," she said dreamily. "Worked hard all my life, and nursing can be damned hard work. I had a husband and a boy once, but they were both drowned—on a camping vacation up north, a freak accident. That was ten years ago. And I thought, that old man, with all that gold—what good was he ever going to get out of it? I thought—I'd have something—while I could still enjoy it. That old man had had his life, and I'd heard from Mrs. Griffin that his wife was a hopeless invalid. In my job, you know, death isn't that important. It's a great relief and a release sometimes." A little spasm passed over her face: other deaths than mine, she meant.

"No trouble?" said Clock. He sat down beside her.

"No. I knew what medication his wife was on because once

when I brought Mr. Griffin his capsule, Vanderveer said that was the stuff his wife took. I brought an extra supply along in case there wasn't enough there, but the bottle was nearly full. And of course Vanderveer was always saying that, you're better out of it when you get to be old—not that he meant it—so I thought that would do for the note." She put out her cigarette. "I just called the house and said I was checking on their visiting nurse, I knew there was one coming in because Mrs. Griffin had asked Vanderveer about it once when I was in the room. I know all about that service, of course, and how it works. So I knew what days the woman was coming. I just drove in that morning, thought I'd better leave the car in the garage, and it looked natural because of the rain. I went to the door and explained that I was their new visiting nurse, the schedule had been changed, and I'd come today instead of tomorrow. I was in uniform, and I'd gotten a black wig and used a black pencil on my eyebrows. Vanderveer didn't look twice at me."

Jesse didn't interrupt her to ask what car she drove; it would be a medium-sized tan car like Dulcie's, like Marcia's.

"Neither of them paid any attention to what I was doing, of course. I was just the nurse, coming and going in the house. I warmed up the coffee and made the eggnog—the old woman was pleased at that, a little extra attention—I went to the bathroom for the codeine capsules and dissolved them in the drinks and took them in. The old lady was in bed, I helped her to sit up to drink it. I had a cup of coffee myself, waiting. For them to settle down, pass out. It might take half an hour, forty minutes, before they were unconscious. But I didn't wait quite long enough—that was what made it go wrong. I found the typewriter—I was going to do the note by hand and I was looking for some paper—you see," she explained. "I thought nobody would look into it very thoroughly, they were just two useless old people nobody cared about. But I thought the typewriter would be better, just in case. And I did the note, and brought it out to the living room—too soon. I didn't realize the old man was still conscious—he saw me put it on the mantel, and he managed to stagger up and look at it, and he called me a bitch and grabbed the poker, hit out at me—and before I thought about it I got it away and hit him. I had to stop him then."

"What about the old woman?" asked Jesse.

"Oh, I suppose she heard the noise, I couldn't bother with her—I wanted to finish it and get out, then. Seeing the suicide plan wouldn't work, I threw the note in the fire. I found where the false wall was wedged in, and I got all that gold—it took three trips with my nurse's bag to get it out to the car. I took the piece of plywood too so nobody would find it and know there'd been anything there —and I put all the boxes back on the shelf, so it all looked ordinary. The old woman had knocked herself out falling. I just left her. And that's all, isn't it?" She looked at Clock, and there was an attempt at cool cynicism in her eyes. "It doesn't matter now, I don't suppose you'll have time to bring me to trial. I've got about three months. But it doesn't seem fair—when I nearly got away with it."

And Petrovsky came in from the bedroom with his hands full of round plastic tubes and began to arrange them on the coffee table; through the clear plastic the deep yellow shining color of the heavy gold coins drew all their eyes automatically.

And Jesse said in a remote voice, "Old Jeshu ben Sirah said it a while ago, Mrs. Seager—*Gold hath destroyed many, and perverted the hearts of kings.*"

"Well, at least," said Nell, "that poor woman is out of jail. She sounds like rather a nice woman. Andrew should have listened to you in the first place."

Jesse laughed. They were relaxed in front of the fire, Athelstane asleep at their feet and Murteza dozing on the mantel. "You know, I had a little thought about it. It would be funny if she and Klein got married. I think it'd be a damned good idea. Think they'd get along just fine. As old Jeshu says, *Forsake not a wise and good woman, for her grace is above gold.*"

The lion of God sat up and yawned, leaped lightly down to the arm of the couch, and made for the stairs. "There, it's ten o'clock exactly," said Nell. "I'm going up to read in bed."

Jesse, getting up to follow her, yawned too and thought, but it would be funny—and somehow he had the little hunch that that was exactly what was going to happen.

DeWitt came into the office on the first day of the month with the account book. "And how is your latest client doing—the one who's hung up on telepathy?" asked Jesse idly.

"Who? Oh, the Finch woman. Oh, she's abandoned us—we're all a bunch of frauds. But we got some very evidential material through her, at that. It's funny how things work out," said DeWitt.

And one day in early December, with another rainstorm predicted, and the baby imminently due, Fran and Clock came to dinner. Afterward, with the girls talking obstetrics, Clock said to Jesse, "That indictment got postponed again. The Seager woman. I gather they don't expect her to last long, and the D.A.'s going to save the county the expense of a trial."

"Oh, really. Simplest thing to do in the long run."

"That was a very damned funny business," said Clock. "A complicated business."

"Oh, no, it wasn't so complicated, Andrew," said Jesse soberly. "Not complicated at all when you sort it out. Matter of the workings of human nature. And it had a very simple moral for us, too. *Every man shall be put to his death for his own sins.*"

Lesley Egan is a pseudonym for a popular, very prolific author of mysteries. Her most recent novels are A CHOICE OF CRIMES, MOTIVE IN SHADOW, and LOOK BACK ON DEATH.

"Hello, Mrs. Caylor."

Lauren stepped over to the table, where a picture of a colorful hot-air balloon was taking shape.

"Hey, that's pretty," Lauren said.

"I put that one in," Emily said proudly, touching a piece with her finger.

"Good for you."

"Well, I put *that* one in," the other girl told Lauren.

"Oh yeah?" the boy said, and all three children began giggling and pointing to each and every piece, some of them not even in the puzzle yet, saying, "I put *that* one."

"Didn't you help?" Lauren asked Miss Wilson.

"Apparently not."

After Emily said good-bye to her teacher and friends, Lauren walked her outside, opened the car door for her, and helped her fasten her seat belt. During the twenty-minute drive home she talked with Emily about her day in school and learned that the most notable event had been the appearance of a puppy.

"A first-grade teacher brought it to our room," Emily said. "She let us pet it. It was white and it had black spots and it was so soft. It went pee on Johnny Baskin's shoe."

Lauren tried not to smile. "Poor Johnny."

"Yeah. He cried. But it was sort of funny. That puppy was so cute. And I got to hold it."

Lauren waited, knowing what was coming.

"Mommy?"

"What, hon?"

"Can we have a puppy?"

"We already have Amos."

"But he's a *big* dog. Can't we have a puppy?"

"Gee, honey, I don't know." Lauren was thinking of soiled carpets, chewed furniture, and the pee on Johnny Baskin's shoe. "I don't think so right now," she said. "Maybe after we move."

"Are we going to move?"

"Well, maybe. You know that Richard and I have talked about it."

"*Then* can we have a puppy?"

"Why don't we discuss it with Richard."

Lauren turned onto Larkdale Way. Palm trees stood at attention along both sides of the gently curving street, and the houses were separated by manicured lawns and flowering bushes. Halfway down the block Lauren turned into their driveway. She clicked the remote control, waited for the double garage door to open, then slowly steered the Honda inside. After she helped Emily out, she reached for the switch to close the garage door.

She hesitated.

A dark blue car slowly passed the house.

Lauren frowned and stepped toward the yawning opening of the garage. She watched the car disappear around the curve in the street.

"Mommy, what are you doing?"

"Nothing, honey."

Lauren flipped a switch and the big door slid down and clicked shut. She opened the side door of the garage and found Amos standing there waiting for them, his long tail swinging slowly from side to side. He was a brindled greyhound, an old dog, big and gentle, a racer in his youth. Richard had saved him from being destroyed—the fate of most greyhounds too old for racing. He'd acquired the dog three years ago, about a year after he'd moved to San Miguel and before he and Lauren had met. When Lauren had first seen Amos, she'd resisted having him around. He was scary-looking, like a stretch-model, tiger-striped Doberman. She'd soon realized her fear was unfounded—Amos was as laid back as they come. And although he would never bite anyone, Lauren felt he afforded protection: His very size would scare away a potential thief or mugger.

"Hi, Amos." Emily put her arm around the dog's neck, her shoulder not much higher than his.

Lauren crossed the small concrete patio and unlocked the back door of the house. Without waiting to be let in, Amos pushed through his dog door, a rectangle cut in the bottom part of the door and covered with a heavy rubber flap.

When Lauren opened the door, Amos was there to greet them again in the service porch. Lauren scratched his ears and led the way past the washer and dryer and the laundry sink to the kitchen, an airy room with oak counters and wide windows overlooking the backyard. There were hanging copper pots, leafy plants in terra-cotta pots, and a skylight in the ceiling, which added to the sense of openness. Lauren dropped her purse and keys on the counter.

"Shall we take Amos for a walk before dinner?"

Before Emily could answer, Amos began prancing like a yearling, recognizing the word "walk." He turned to Emily and licked her face.

"Hey, Amos, watch out!"

Lauren grinned. "Why don't you put him on his leash while I change clothes?"

Lauren passed from the kitchen through the family room and down the hallway to the master bedroom. It felt stuffy, so she slid open a window. After she'd slipped off her low-heeled shoes and skirt and put them away, she took off her blouse and bra and pantyhose and dropped them on the bed. Laundry, she thought. Then she laid out a pair of panties, blue warm-up pants, scruffy white running shoes, and a white cotton T-shirt with *LA Dodgers* printed in blue across the chest.

She padded barefoot into the adjoining bathroom and washed off her light makeup, patted her face with a fluffy towel, then quickly brushed out her shoulder-length hair. With courage and resolve she stepped onto the bathroom scale.

A hundred and *fifteen,* she read. What happened to a hundred and *ten?*

She gave herself a cursory once-over in the long mirror.

Everything still looks pretty firm, she thought, for a thirty-year-old broad anyway. Then she patted herself on the thigh and decided that she and Emily should take a *long* walk.

After Lauren dressed, she carried her keys through the house to the front door, where she found Emily and Amos waiting in the entryway. The big dog wouldn't stand still.

"All set?" Lauren asked.

"Amos is being *goofy.*"

Lauren laughed. "He's just anxious to go."

Amos barked once in confirmation.

Lauren pulled the door closed behind her, making sure it was locked, then followed Emily and Amos down the front walk.

"Which way, Mommy?"

"Let's go right."

Emily and Amos stepped lively, heading south on the sidewalk that paralleled Larkdale Way. Lauren trailed behind them.

Then she stopped dead in her tracks and stared across the street.

2

THE HOUSE across the street had been vacant for eight months.

It was owned by Madge Grey, whose husband, Cecil, had died last fall after a long illness. Madge had moved to Tucson to live with her sister, and she'd put her house up for sale. It had remained vacant all these months, Lauren believed, because it was priced too high for the present housing market.

And regrettably, the property had deteriorated under the none-too-watchful eye of the property management company employed by Madge Grey. The single-story white stucco home still looked to be in good condition, but the yard had been neglected. The management company occasionally sent someone to mow and water the lawn, but they didn't do it often enough. And as far as Lauren could tell, no one had fertilized the grass, sprayed for weeds, or trimmed the trees and bushes since Madge moved out.

What had surprised Lauren—and pleased her as well—was the missing For Sale sign. And there was a car parked in the carport beside the house.

"Finally," she said under her breath, "new neighbors to clean up the place."

As Lauren turned to follow Emily and Amos, she saw movement in the front window across the street. Overgrown bushes obscured much of the window, but Lauren could see that the living room drapes were slightly parted and someone was peeking out. She had a partial view of a face, but she couldn't tell whether it was a man or a woman.

Then the drapes fell back into place—nearly: There remained a thin, dark line down the middle, an opening of no more than a finger's width. Lauren had the uneasy feeling that whoever was in the Greys' house was watching her.

Terrific, she thought, catching up with Emily and Amos. Our new neighbors are weirdos.

Lauren enjoyed walking through their neighborhood. All the yards were well tended and lush with vegetation. And the neighbors were friendly, always ready with a wave and a hello. Lauren knew many of them by name, even those living several blocks away—after all, she'd been strolling these streets ever since she moved here from Los Angeles.

That was six years ago.

She and Paul Webb had been married just over a year at the time, both working for a large engineering and architectural firm in L.A., he as an architect, she as a landscape architect—similar titles but with a world of difference between them. As Paul liked to say, "To be an architect you need a big ego. You're designing structures that will be out there for the world to see for the rest of your life." Of course, a landscape architect also had to be creative, but there were other constraints, mostly the site itself, which often dictated what could or could not be done. Another difference, more evident to Lauren than to Paul, was that landscape architects were more concerned with preserving the environment than with increasing a developer's profits.

Differences aside, both Lauren and Paul were career-minded. They agreed that children could wait, perhaps five years, perhaps longer.

However, one romantic weekend in San Francisco, she'd mistakenly left behind her birth control pills and Paul had decided a condom would put him "out of the mood." So they'd taken a chance. Two months later she learned she was pregnant.

Paul had shrugged it off. "So you'll have an abortion. I'll call the doctor myself. It's no big deal."

But it *was* a big deal to Lauren.

Not that she objected morally to abortions. She'd always reasoned that so long as the fetus was symbiotic, incapable of living outside the womb, then it was a part of the woman, not a separate life. Not a person. And so if a woman wanted to have an abortion, it was entirely up to her.

But when she discovered she was pregnant, she'd immediately sensed the fetus inside her as a living thing. A human being. Her child. There was no way she would destroy it.

Paul had argued: "What about your career? And all the things we planned to do and the places we planned to visit?"

"We can still travel, Paul."

"Not with a small child. And how far can we go with just one of us working?"

They'd fought. For a time Lauren wondered if Paul might leave her. She worried that he wasn't the person she'd thought he was when they married. But he eventually came around to her point of view.

He'd insisted—and she'd agreed—that they move out of L.A., too congested and polluted a place to raise a child. So they'd bought the house in San Miguel, and Paul had begun the daily forty-minute commute north to his office in downtown L.A.

When Emily was born, Paul acted like the proudest man alive, happier than he'd ever been.

But being a father was a novelty with him, and it soon wore thin. Lauren sensed resentment. At first she thought perhaps she'd been showing him too little affection, giving so much attention to Emily. However, she came to realize that the most important thing to Paul was his career, followed closely by his freedom. The latter, in his opinion, was smothered by a wife and child waiting at home. And as much as he professed to love Emily, he still blamed Lauren for getting pregnant in the first place, forever altering their future, altering it in a way he'd never wanted.

Soon after Emily's first birthday Paul began harping at Lauren to get out of the house, to resume her career.

Lauren refused.

It wasn't that she liked the idea of Paul paying all the bills— particularly since there were now more bills and less money coming in. It was Emily. Lauren believed that the first two years of life were the most important in a child's development. She wanted to be with Emily as much as possible during that time. Of course, she knew that eventually she would go back to work and trust her daughter's care to strangers—day-care workers and teachers. But not yet.

It had driven another wedge between her and Paul.

When Emily was two years old, Lauren began to look for a job. Paul could've gotten her rehired at his firm, but there was a tension at home that they both sensed might become unbearable if they were together twenty-four hours a day. So Lauren looked elsewhere for work.

She soon received two job offers.

One was with another architectural firm. The job was nearly identical to the one she'd had before, and she knew it would be a charged environment filled with soaring egos, continual deadlines, and constant competition—the latter coming not only from other firms but also from within, as employees fought to rise within the company.

Naturally, Paul thought she should take the job. It's what he would've done in her place.

Lauren chose the other position, the one with the city of San Miguel. The salary was comparable, but the job itself seemed more secure. And the atmosphere was definitely more relaxed. Also, she had a good feeling about the people she'd met during the application process. She was assigned to the planning department, where her tasks were varied: preparing landscape designs for the park planner, producing graphic presentations for the planning department, and in general helping out where needed.

Paul was completely against her decision.

"Jesus, a civil servant," he'd said sarcastically. "Feeding from the public trough."

Lauren said nothing. She'd had her fill of arguing.

A year later they divorced.

They'd made it clean and simple. Lauren and Emily kept the house, and Paul moved back to L.A. Paul could have Emily every other weekend, one week each summer, and every other Christmas.

As it turned out, though, he rarely exercised his weekend rights more than once a month. Lauren guessed that he enjoyed his new-found freedom more than the presence of his daughter. She regretted this for Emily's sake. But she couldn't help feeling, perhaps selfishly, that the more time she spent with Emily the better.

And being with Emily helped Lauren fight the depression brought on by her failed marriage.

She helped herself further by staying busy at work. And she received a lot of moral support. First from her mother, who came out "just to visit" for a few weeks, and then from her friends. Some tried to fix her up with men. It was a while, though, before she began dating.

Soon thereafter she met Richard. They'd gone together for a year before they were married.

That had been six months ago.

Now she and Emily and Amos were half a mile from home. They turned north and headed back. The sun was low to their left, a hazy, warm orange ball floating above the red-tile rooftops and palm trees of San Miguel.

Lauren followed Emily and Amos back up their front walk. Before she went inside, she paused to look at the house across the street.

The front of the house was painted red orange by the setting sun. The carport and driveway were empty. Lauren tried to remember the type of car that had been parked there earlier. It had been fairly new, she thought. A two-door or a sedan? She couldn't even remember clearly what color it was. Brown?

Lauren peered at the front window, partially obscured by overgrown bushes. The drapes were closed, but there remained a narrow opening down the middle, just enough for someone to peek out. Whether or not anyone actually *was* peeking out, Lauren couldn't tell.

She unlocked their front door, and Emily unfastened Amos's leash. The big dog stood with his mouth open, his tongue hanging out, and his sides heaving from the walk. When he was racing, his name had been Xpress Male and he'd even won a few races, but those days were long gone. Now he was a tired old hound, looking up at Lauren with sad eyes and waiting to be told what to do.

She smiled and rubbed his head. "Come on, Amos, let's get you some water."

After she filled his nearly empty water dish on the kitchen floor, she went to the bedroom, undressed, and took a long shower. Then she put on jeans and a rugby shirt and went back to the kitchen to fix dinner.

Lauren prepared sliced turkey breast with gravy and a salad of lettuce, tomatoes, chopped celery, and carrots. She and Emily ate without waiting for Richard. This was Thursday, the one night when the hardware store stayed open until nine.

Emily set down her half-full glass of milk, leaving a thin white mustache.

"Mommy, are we really going to move?"

Lauren reached over with her napkin and dabbed at the corners of Emily's mouth.

"I don't know yet, baby, but if we do, it will be someplace close. Maybe even in this neighborhood."

"Why?"

"Because we like this neighborhood."

"Then why are we moving?"

Good question, Lauren thought, but the answer is a little difficult to explain.

24

"So we can live in a better house."

"But I like our house."

"I know. But maybe we can get a *better* house."

"Will it have a swimming pool?"

"Maybe."

"Hey, neat," Emily said.

The truth was, Lauren liked this house too. Loved it, in fact. After all, it had been her home for six years. It *felt* like home. At least it did to her and Emily.

She wasn't so certain about Richard.

Lauren could understand his feelings. The house had originally belonged to her and Paul Webb, and even though she and Richard had the deed transferred to their name, it would always carry memories of Paul. *Vague* memories, as far as Lauren was concerned. However, if Richard didn't feel comfortable living in "Paul's former house" and he wanted to move, she wouldn't protest.

It would be difficult for her to give up this house, but what mattered was her and Richard's happiness. And of course, Emily's. So far, though, she and Richard had only talked casually of moving. And in fact, it had been a while since they'd done even that.

Perhaps, she thought hopefully, he'll forget that Paul ever lived here. God knows *I* have.

After Lauren cleared the table and washed the dishes, she sat with her daughter in the family room and played cards. Eventually Emily matched up the last pair.

"You're the old maid!" she cried.

Lauren made a funny face, and Emily giggled.

"The old maid doesn't *like* little girls to laugh at her," Lauren said with a cackle. She reached out for Emily, her fingers hooked like claws. Emily let out a scream of delight and scrambled to her feet. Lauren chased her around the love seats and the coffee table and into the hallway, being careful not to catch her until they had both reached Emily's bed, where they flopped down, laughing and out of breath.

"You're not *really* an old maid, Mommy."

"Hey, thanks."

"I'm glad you're not."

"Well, so am I."

"Because you *were* sort of scary-looking."

"What?" Lauren tickled her.

Later, after Lauren had read along with Emily from Dr. Seuss, she tucked her in bed and kissed her good night. Amos curled up in his usual place on the floor on the far side of Emily's bed. Lauren turned off the light but left the bedroom door open so the room wouldn't be totally dark for Emily—and in case Amos wanted out.

In the kitchen she poured Chablis from a jug in the refrigerator and carried her glass to the living room. She sat on the couch, tucked her feet under her, and opened this week's issue of *Time*.

She waited for Richard to come home.

Only once did she part the drapes in hopes of catching sight of the new neighbors. But she saw no one.

3

LAUREN HEARD Richard's car turn into the driveway.

She set aside the magazine and carried her empty wineglass to the kitchen just as he came in the back door.

Lauren still felt a thrill whenever she saw him. In her opinion, he was a very handsome man. He was a few years older and half a head taller than she, just over five feet nine, with wavy black hair and an athletic build. His eyes, though, were his sexiest feature, she thought. They were so dark they were nearly black.

He went to Lauren, smiling. "Hi, babe."

They hugged and then kissed.

"I missed you," she said in his ear.

"Me too."

"Did you eat?"

"I snacked."

She leaned back and looked up at him, her arms still around his waist. "Can I fix you something?"

"I'm really not hungry."

"How about a glass of wine?"

"Sounds good. Is Emily asleep?"

"Yes, I put her to bed about an hour ago." She opened the refrigerator and took out the jug of wine.

"I'm going to peek in on her."

Lauren smiled to herself. She had always been touched by Richard's love for Emily. In fact, that was one of the reasons she'd married him.

She remembered the dozen or so dates she'd had as a single parent before she and Richard found each other. Most of the men she'd met had been interested in her only until they learned she had a small child at home. And the two or three who stayed around for more than one date had been awkward and uncomfortable with Emily. Lauren thought she knew why. A child meant commitment, something for which those men weren't prepared.

It had been quite different with Richard. He'd been delighted to learn that Lauren had a daughter, and he and Emily had gotten along right from the start. A lot of love was being shared by the three of them, Lauren knew, and she felt that things could only get better.

Richard returned to the kitchen.

"She looks like a little doll when she's sleeping," he said, smiling. Then he looked around. "Where's Amos?"

"The last I saw him he was curled up beside Emily's bed."

Richard shook his head. "You know, when I was living in my apartment, that dog could hardly wait till I got home from work. Man's best friend."

Lauren laughed and handed him his wine. "He still likes you, but his attention is divided."

They touched glasses, drank a toast to each other, then moved to the family room.

Lauren settled into one of the love seats. Richard drew the drapes over the sliding glass doors leading to the deck and the enclosed backyard, hidden now in darkness. When he sat beside her on the love seat, she leaned her head on his shoulder.

"Nice."

"Yes, it is." He put his hand on her leg.

"How was your day?" she asked.

"Long."

Now it was her turn to pat his leg.

"Isn't there some way you can get out of working late *every* Thursday?"

"Somebody's got to be there besides the clerks, and Arthur won't do it anymore. I don't blame him. The man is in his sixties." Richard sipped his wine.

"Well, when he retires and lets *you* run the business, you can hire an assistant to work Thursdays."

"It'll be a few years before that happens."

"I guess we'll have to tough it out until then."

Richard smiled. "Where do you get 'we'?"

"It's rough on me, too, you know," she said in mock seriousness. "Every Thursday night I have to be here alone—sprawled on the couch, reading magazines, drinking wine . . ."

He laughed. "Speaking of which, do you want some more?"

"I'm fine," she said. "I'll pour you a refill, though."

"No, you just sit here and rest." He kissed her on top of the head, then stood. "You've had enough exertion for one night."

"Very funny."

She watched him walk through the doorway to the kitchen. As she'd done many times before, she inwardly thanked Arthur Mc-Fadden for having hired Richard. If he hadn't, she and Richard might never have met. Someone else would have waited on her and Emily that morning a year and a half ago, and they would have gone home with only a new pair of rose clippers and not a luncheon date for that same day.

Lauren thought of how far Richard had come in the three years he'd worked for Arthur—from just one of a dozen clerks to Arthur's chief assistant. In fact, he was now in line to become an equal partner and manage the store when Arthur retired.

Some people might have considered Arthur rash for bringing Richard to his side so quickly, but not Lauren. She'd come to know Arthur as a kind and gentle man, but also as a levelheaded business-man. After all, he'd built McFadden's from a one-man operation into the largest independent hardware store in the region, and he wasn't about to turn things over to anyone with less business sense. And if nothing else, Richard was a keen businessman.

Of course, Lauren had to admit, part of Arthur's decision con-cerning Richard had been made with his heart. He and his wife, Betty, were childless, and Richard seemed to represent the son they'd never had. Or at least the nephew. In fact, she and Richard both thought of Arthur as their adopted uncle.

When Arthur did retire and Richard ran the store, it really wouldn't change their lives that much, Lauren decided. Except, of course, they'd have more money. And Thursday evenings together.

Richard returned with his glass of wine.

"So," he said, sitting, putting his arm around her, "did I ask how *your* day was?"

"No, but actually it was pretty good. I've been assigned to design the new park under—"

"Hey, that's great."

"—under, of course, the watchful eye of the park planner."

"Still . . ."

"I know. I'm really happy about it."

"Well then, here's to you."

They clinked glasses.

"By the way," she said brightly, "we've got new neighbors."

"We do?"

"Someone moved into Madge Grey's house."

"You're kidding. I never saw a Sold sign."

"Me neither, but someone's in there."

Richard nodded. "That's good. Maybe now the yard will get tended. Have you seen them?"

"Well, partially."

Richard smiled. "Partially?"

She nodded and smiled back. "When I took Emily and Amos out for a walk, I noticed the For Sale sign was gone and a car was parked in the carport. Then I saw someone in the front window peeking out, real sneaky, as if he were *spying* or something."

"What?" Richard's smile began to fade.

"I say 'he,' " Lauren said, her voice light, "but I couldn't really tell if it was a man or a woman—all I saw was part of a face, you know, sort of hiding behind the drapes. Then whoever it was closed the drapes, but not completely. There was still a little opening, and I think he or she watched me walk all the way down the block."

Richard set down his wineglass.

"It was kind of creepy and—"

He stood.

"What's wrong?"

"Probably nothing." He walked from the room.

Lauren stared for a moment at the empty doorway, then she went after him. She found him standing in the living room by the front drapes, holding them open just enough to peer through.

"Richard, what is it?"

"Turn off the light," he said, still looking out the window.

"What?"

"Please," he said. "Turn it off. Just for a minute."

He continued to stare through the part in the drapes. Lauren hesitated, then moved to the end table and switched off the lamp. The room fell into semidarkness, illuminated only by the pale light spilling from the family room. She joined Richard at the window, feeling uneasy.

"What is it?" she asked.

"You said you didn't see who was over there?" His eye was still fixed to the opening in the drapes.

"No, not their faces. What—"

"So you didn't actually see them move in—I mean furniture and so on."

"Come on, Richard, I was at *work* all day."

He nodded absently. "I see a light at the side of the house. And there's a car under the carport." He let the drapes fall back into place and turned to Lauren.

"Is something wrong?" she asked.

"No, of course not."

She could barely make out his facial expression in the dim light, but she could tell that his smile was forced.

"You act as if there is."

"I'm sorry." He put his arm around her waist and led her toward the family room. "You just got me worried, is all, talking about weird people spying on you. I thought perhaps someone had broken into the Greys' house."

Lauren stopped short. "That never occurred to me. Do you think—"

"No, I think someone probably *did* move in." He walked with her to the love seat. "But maybe I'll phone the property management company tomorrow, just to make sure. Didn't Madge give us their number?"

Lauren nodded yes, frowning, picking up her wineglass.

"Hey," Richard said, reaching for her hand. "I'm sure everything is fine. I didn't mean to overreact."

"Okay." She smiled.

"It's just that I love you and Emily so much, and, well, I worry about you both when I'm not with you. There are too many nutcases out there."

"What, Mommy?"

"Nothing, honey." She reached out and stroked her hair, then turned to Richard. "So you were too shy to even get a date for the museum."

"That's right, babe, there was no one before you. My life began when we met."

Lauren rolled her eyes. "Oh, brother."

He leaned over and they kissed.

Then he glanced at his watch. "I've got to go." He stood and touched Emily gently on top of the head. "Good-bye, honey."

" 'Bye, Richard."

After he left, Lauren washed the breakfast dishes, smiling to herself and remembering Richard's words: "I was just a shy guy." She had to admit, though, there was a grain of truth in that—at least if she were to judge by the scarcity of his friends. In fact, other than Arthur and her old friends and the people they'd met since being together, Richard had no friends in San Miguel. Of course, she knew he'd probably left behind lots of people when he moved here from Philadelphia.

On the plus side, she thought, now he's got me.

Lauren packed her lunch in a paper sack—a container of lemon yogurt, a granola bar, and an apple—then went through the house making sure all the lights were off, all the windows closed, and the front door locked. She checked herself one last time in the mirror, spotted a renegade thread on the hem of her skirt, and carefully pulled it off.

Lauren found Emily in her room lining up a host of dolls on her bed for an apparent conference.

"Time to go, honey."

Before leaving by the back door, Lauren checked Amos's water bowl. He watched her with mournful brown eyes, mustering some enthusiasm when she gave him a beef-flavored strip of rawhide.

In the car Lauren buckled Emily into her seat, then backed out of the garage. She stopped near the street, checking for traffic. Her gaze drifted to Madge Grey's house.

The front windows were covered by curtains. But the living room drapes were still parted a few inches, leaving a dark slit. Lauren imagined someone watching her, although she saw no sign of anyone. She was about to pull into the street when Connie Pickering came out of her house, lifted the morning paper from the lawn, and waved at Lauren.

Lauren raised her hand in greeting; then on impulse she shut off the engine and set the emergency brake.

"I'll just be a minute," she told Emily.

She climbed out of the car and called to Connie, who had started back toward her house.

Constance Pickering was a big woman. Her feet were bare and brown, and her black hair was pulled back behind her ears. She wore a pink and orange muumuu that flowed about her, giving her the look of a Hawaiian queen. In fact, her grandmother had been Polynesian. Lauren had known Connie for six years, ever since she'd moved next door to her and Benjamin and their three children.

" 'Marry a doctor,' my mother told me," Connie had said to Lauren soon after they met. "She told me they make big bucks and never run out of work. I came as close as I could." Benjamin was a dentist.

Connie didn't work—that is, she didn't have a job—however, she was active in community affairs. She'd even appeared on local TV stations, petitioning for better street lighting or stricter noise control or freezing the salaries of elected officials or—her current crusade— registering all firearms owned by residents of San Miguel.

"When the NRA starts to fight me," she'd told Lauren not long ago, "I'll know I'm making progress."

Now she met Lauren on the grass between their driveways.

"Good morning." Connie's dark eyes sparkled above high, round cheeks.

"Hi. I've only got a minute—I just wanted to ask you about the new people across the street."

"I haven't met them yet."

"Have you seen them?"

"Briefly, when they were moving in yesterday."

"So they really did move in?"

Connie grinned, pushing her cheeks even higher, making her eyes squint nearly closed. "Yes, they *really* did. They had a U-Haul truck and everything." She searched Lauren's face, still smiling.

"It sounds silly now," Lauren said, feeling a bit foolish, "but yesterday I saw someone peeking out of the front window over there as if they were hiding behind the drapes. Richard and I wondered if somebody had broken into the house."

Connie shook her head. She was a few inches taller than Lauren and seemed to look down on her now like an older sister.

"Nope," she said, "nothing so exciting. They're a nice-looking couple, your age or younger. Some men in a truck helped them carry in furniture and boxes." Her eyebrows moved together. "You know, now that I think about it . . ."

"What?"

"They didn't have much furniture. In fact, they didn't have much of anything."

"Really?"

Connie shrugged. "Maybe they belong to an obscure religious sect that finds sofas blasphemous."

Lauren smiled. "Funny."

"Hey, it could happen. Anyway, you'd better get to work or you'll be late."

"Right away, Mother."

Connie swatted her lightly on the arm with the newspaper.

"I'm not *that* much older than you."

"I'll talk to you later."

"Okay," Connie called after her, "and I'll keep my eye on Mr. and Mrs. Mysterious across the street."

By the time Lauren took Emily to school and drove to the San Miguel municipal building, it was two minutes to eight. Usually she arrived early enough to park near the building. Today, though, she was forced to leave the Honda near the edge of the lot and walk past a dozen rows of cars to the main entrance.

Once inside, she let her gaze soar to the atrium roof three stories above her. She walked past the information desk (where the receptionist was chatting with a pair of uniformed policemen), past the hallway leading to the city courtrooms (where traffic offenders were already lined up, ready to plead their innocence), past the elevators (where a clutch of citizens waited to be carried up to the zoning and licensing section), to the curving, open stairway that climbed the north wall.

As Lauren went up the stairs, she was afforded a fine view of the adjacent park through the towering glass wall of the building. A man and woman in T-shirts and shorts were jogging along the path that snaked between grassy hummocks, flowering bushes, and an occasional gazebo.

On the second floor Lauren exchanged good mornings with fellow workers making their way through the vast room, which was sectioned into cubicles by head-high, sound-dampening dividers. In addition to these work areas there were a few separate offices occupied by the city engineer, the director of planning, and the director of public works.

Lauren's cubicle was eight by ten feet, with a drafting table in the left-hand corner and a layout table along the opposite wall. A cabinet filled with files and supplies and crowned with a spider plant in a yellow pot stood at one end of the table. Lauren pulled open the bottom drawer at the side of her drafting table and put her purse inside.

"Good morning."

A tall, bearded man wearing white duck pants and a lavender shirt with a pale tie stood in the entryway. He held a file folder in one hand and a steaming coffee mug in the other.

"Oh, hi, Geoffrey."

Geoffrey Leiderhaus was San Miguel's park planner. Lauren had worked with him before and knew he was talented and fair in his dealings with subordinates. However, he fancied himself a ladies' man, and sometimes that was a problem.

"Have you got a minute?" he asked.

"Sure."

"I hate to drop this on you so early in the morning, but I've got a meeting in ten minutes and I'll be out of the office for the rest of the day."

He set his mug on the layout table, pulled up the only chair, and sat down. Lauren's drafting stool was too high for the table, so she remained standing beside Geoffrey. He opened the folder and began spreading out sheets of paper: a legal description and sketch of a piece of property once owned by a Mr. Will, some handwritten notes from a meeting of neighbors likely to be impacted by the new park, recommendations from the recreation staff, letters from city council members, a demographic study, a drainage study, a soil analysis, and so on. Altogether they represented the initial stages of the new park project.

"I'd like you to get started on this today," Geoffrey said. "Familiarize yourself with everything here, mostly this shopping list from the neighborhood meeting. As you'll see, they're big on tennis courts. Also, you can pull our survey of the park site and start sketching out some conceptuals."

"Okay." Lauren was eager to begin.

"We'll get together Monday afternoon and look over your sketches."

"Sounds good."

He looked up at her from his chair. The smile on his face, Lauren assumed, was meaningful.

"I'm glad we'll be working together," he said with feeling.

"Me too."

"I mean it." Geoffrey stood.

Lauren smiled and met his gaze. "So do I. In fact, I was just telling Richard about you this morning."

"Oh." Geoffrey suddenly looked sheepish. "How is Richard?"

"He's great. I'll tell him you said hello."

"Do that. Well." He checked his watch with a flourish. "Got to run. Have a nice weekend."

"You too."

Lauren smiled to herself as she watched the back of his head move down the aisle between cubicles. There were a number of ways she could have established the ground rules with Geoffrey, but mentioning Richard was probably the quickest. And with Geoffrey, Lauren knew, it was best to let him know where you stood without delay. Beyond that, he wasn't such a bad guy.

She opened the top drawer in her drafting table, searched the two trays of colored marking pens until she found a hot pink one, then drew a stylized flower on her lunch bag. She carried the paper sack and her coffee mug to the supply room. There was a refrigerator in the corner under the coffee machine, away from the metal shelves and cabinets and the Xerox copier. Lauren wedged her sack inside among the others, its pink flower standing out on a field of brown. Then she filled her mug with coffee and carried it carefully to her cubicle.

Lauren spent the rest of the morning going through the information Geoffrey had left her and gathering together a few things he'd left out: plats of subdivisions surrounding the park site, a topographical map of the area, and construction drawings of bordering streets showing rights of way, easements, and underground utilities. She also carried the 24- by 36-inch Mylar drawing of the existing park site to the copy room and made a blueline copy to work on, wrinkling her nose from the faint ammonia smell that emanated from the machine.

At noon she met Susan Aikens, and they took their lunches downstairs and out the rear entrance to the park. The sun was warm, and there was a gentle breeze from the west, bringing with it the smell of the sea. Lauren and Susan walked a hundred yards along the bike path until they found an unoccupied gazebo.

Susan was a petite woman with pale blond hair and faint blue eyes. She was Lauren's closest friend at work. In fact, next to Connie Pickering, she was Lauren's closest friend, period.

Lauren had been temporarily assigned to Susan soon after being hired by the city. Susan was a civil engineer, and she'd been working on a presentation for the city council: Proposed Community Improvement Districts. She was putting together a booklet, each page displaying a map of a neighborhood and the proposed improvement. The job was simple enough—cutting and pasting and drawing North arrows. But there was a lot of it to do, and no available drafters to do it. Susan was grateful for the help.

She and Lauren had hit it off right away, possibly because of all they had in common. They'd both come from the Midwest (Lauren from Nebraska, Susan from Kansas), both had begun college as art majors before following different courses, and both had a small child in day care. Also, Susan was a single parent, and although they didn't know it at the time, Lauren was soon to become one.

Eventually, of course, Lauren would remarry. Susan was still single.

"What are you guys doing this weekend?" Susan asked between bites of her sandwich.

"Tomorrow we're driving down to San Diego and Sea World. Emily's never been."

"I hope she likes it."

Lauren paused with her spoonful of yogurt in midair. "Why do you say that?"

Susan shrugged. "When I took Timmy, he got scared and had nightmares for a week. Big fish trying to get him."

"Oh, great. I never even *thought* of that."

"Hey, I'm not trying to talk you out of it. Timmy's just sensitive, that's all." She took a bite of her sandwich and shook her head. "Jesus, I hope I'm not turning that kid into a wimp."

"Su*san*."

"I'm serious. I think maybe a boy needs a father. A girl, you know, like Emily, can get by with just a mom."

"Somehow that sounds sexist," Lauren said.

Susan looked at her with a serious expression. "You want to trade?"

Lauren smiled. "You mean Emily for Timmy?"

"No. I mean my little black book of single guys for your husband."

Lauren laughed. "I'll check with Richard. On second thought, I'd better not. He might go for it."

"Fat chance."

After lunch Lauren returned to her cubicle. She used her drafting machine to square up the blueline drawing on her worktable, then brushed the paper to flatten it and fixed the corners with masking tape. The drawing, a bluish-white background with dark blue lines, showed an eighteen-acre site that was nearly a perfect rectangle, bordered on four sides by city streets, featureless except for a few small squares and scallop-edged circles that indicated structures and prominent vegetation.

Lauren had driven past the site numerous times, and she was familiar with its history. The structures were decrepit outbuildings and a ranch house built a hundred years ago by Mr. Will's grandfather. There'd been a spring on the property, since gone dry, just large enough to nourish a small family and a few horses. In recent years the city of San Miguel had grown around the Will family's property, and developers had tried without success to purchase it.

A few years ago Mr. Will had died without heirs and willed his land to the city, with the stipulation that they "plant some trees and grass and not any more damn buildings." The city eventually put before the voters a bond issue that included money to turn the land into a park. The bond had passed overwhelmingly.

Probably, Lauren thought now, because everyone was as sick as she was of driving past an eighteen-acre eyesore.

She taped a sheet of white flimsy paper over the blueline drawing, then began sketching her first conceptual of the new park. She was aware that the engineering department used a CAD system for their designs, and she wondered how long it would be before the planning department asked her to put away her drafting machine and pencil and learn to design with a computer.

The longer the better, she thought, and drew in a softball field.

Later in the afternoon, after she'd produced several ideas of how the park might look, she phoned Richard at the hardware store. She'd meant to call him that morning but had become preoccupied with her new assignment. She wanted to tell him about the new neighbors—that they definitely *were* neighbors, not burglars. But while she waited for him to come to the phone, she realized how silly that would sound.

In fact, she guessed he'd probably forgotten all about them.

"Hi, honey," he said.

"Hi. Are you busy?"

"A bit. What's up?"

"I just wanted to tell you that I talked to Connie this morning. She watched our new neighbors move in. They're a young couple."

"I know."

"You do?"

"I called the property management company this morning and asked," Richard said. "They were reluctant to give out any information on the phone, so I drove up to their main office in L.A. and made a nuisance of myself until they told me that the Greys' house had been rented, not sold, to Mr. and Mrs. Ipswich. Hal and Monica. He's a writer and she's a housewife. So I guess you were worried about nothing."

"I guess."

"I've got to go, honey. I'll see you tonight."

He hung up.

Lauren sat for a moment, staring at the phone. As far as she knew, Richard never left the store during his work hours unless there was an emergency. He was too involved with the store's operation to simply walk away.

But today he'd driven forty miles to Los Angeles, battling freeway traffic there and back, certainly missing at least two hours of work, to say nothing of causing a scene at the office of the management company. "Made a nuisance of myself," he'd said.

To check on the new neighbors.

Why?

5

THAT EVENING Lauren put pasta in boiling water, then opened a jar of gourmet spaghetti sauce, extra thick with mushrooms. Richard laid out place mats and silverware on the dining room table.

"What time do you want to leave tomorrow?" he asked from the doorway.

"What?" Her mind was on something else.

"For Sea World."

"Oh, sometime before noon, I guess."

Richard looked at her, his head cocked to one side. "What's wrong? You don't sound too enthusiastic."

She shook her head and smiled weakly. "It's nothing."

"It's *something*. Come on, tell me."

It's your trip to L.A., she thought, and the two hours you were away from the store to check up on the new neighbors. "It's what Susan told me today," she said.

"Yes?"

"It's no big deal. Just that when she took Timmy to Sea World, he got scared of all the big fish. He had nightmares."

"**Do you think Emily . . ?"

"I don't know. She'll probably be okay."

Emily chose that moment to enter the kitchen.

"I'm hungry, Mommy."

"Well, dinner's almost ready."

"Why don't you stand over here," Richard said, "and you can watch me make the salad."

"Okay."

Emily stood at the counter, and Richard began slicing a tomato.

"You know we're going to Sea World tomorrow," he said.

"Yeah! And we get to see Shamu and Baby Shamu!"

"The whales," Richard said.

"The *killer* whales," Emily added.

"Right." Richard glanced at Lauren, then looked down at Emily. "What do you think Shamu will be like?"

"I'll bet he's *neat.*"

"He's really big, you know. Probably as big as . . ." Richard looked around. "Well, he's probably longer than the whole kitchen."

"Wow!"

Richard turned to Lauren. "Wow," he said.

When Lauren spoke, it was to Emily. "And he can jump way out of the water."

"I know. I saw it on TV. Can we eat pretty soon?"

Lauren smiled. "Pretty soon."

After dinner they all sat in the family room and watched a movie on The Disney Channel. Later Lauren tucked Emily in bed. Richard came into the bedroom behind her, reached down, and gently touched Emily on the head.

"Good night, sweetheart."

"Night, Richard."

"Sweet dreams," he said, then left them alone in the room.

"See you in the morning," Lauren said. She bent down and kissed Emily's cheek.

"Night, Mommy. Mommy?"

"**What, baby?"

"Will Richard ever be my real daddy?"

"Richard is your stepdaddy. Remember, we talked about this before?"

"I know."

"Paul is your natural father. He'll always be that. But Richard loves you just as much as if *he* were your natural father. He loves you as much as I do."

"I know. I just . . ."

"What?"

"Sometimes I want to call Richard 'Daddy.' Would it be okay if I did that?"

Lauren sat on the edge of the bed. She put her hand on the blanket over Emily's shoulder.

"Yes, baby, I'm sure it would be okay."

42

"Would Richard get mad?"

"Mad?" Lauren gave her a smile. "Not at all. In fact, I think it would make him very happy."

"Would Daddy, I mean *real* Daddy, would he get mad?"

"No," Lauren said firmly, then more gently: "No, honey, I'm sure he wouldn't mind. But if you like, I'll ask him."

"Okay." Emily reached out and gave her mother a hug around the neck.

Lauren was enormously touched by Emily's request and thankful for the matter-of-fact way in which she considered these things. She knew that divorce and remarriage could be complicated for a child.

Child, nothing, she thought. For an adult.

She remembered trying to explain to Emily why Paul was moving out of the house. Emily had been three years old—old enough to understand that her father was leaving. She'd cried, thinking her daddy was going away because he didn't love her anymore. Lauren had taken great care to explain to her that Paul had left because of his wife, not because of his daughter.

Of course, the truth wasn't quite that simple. Lauren knew it now and she'd known it then. Paul had felt stifled by a family. He'd never come right out and admitted it, but his attitude had been admission enough.

That's *his* problem, Lauren thought.

The trouble was, it had been a problem for her and Emily as well. But they'd gotten over it, survived the divorce. They'd adapted well to living together as two, and when Richard came along, he'd fit in perfectly. However, after the marriage Emily had been confused and upset: Their last names were different. Lauren Webb had become Lauren Caylor, but Emily Webb was still Emily Webb.

Lauren had tried to explain: "When I married your daddy, I changed my last name to his: Webb. And when you were born, that was your name. Now that I'm married to Richard, I've changed my last name to Caylor, but your name is still Webb. They're only last names. We're still the same people and I'm still your mommy."

"But why isn't my name Caylor?"

"Because Richard is your stepfather. Daddy, er, Paul is still your daddy. Your last name will be Webb until *you* get married."

Sexist but true, she'd nearly added. She wished Paul would step aside and let Richard adopt Emily. It would simplify things. But even though Paul spent little time with Emily, he remained adamant about her last name, as if it were a point of honor. "She's my daughter," he'd state, "and she'll carry my name."

Lauren wondered whether Paul would change his mind if he heard Emily call Richard "Daddy."

She turned out the light in Emily's room, stood in the doorway for a moment, then went to the family room. Richard had already put on a tape of quiet jazz, and now he leaned in from the kitchen.

"Do you want a glass of wine?"

"No, thanks."

He came in carrying one glass and sat beside her on the love seat. He put his arm around her shoulder and kissed her on the cheek, then pulled back slightly when she didn't respond.

"Richard, I . . ."

"What, hon?"

"I wanted to ask you about today."

"Today? What do you mean?"

She took a breath and let it out before she spoke.

"Why did you drive all the way to L.A.?"

"Why?" He smiled. "I told you. To check on the people across the street."

"I know. But *why*?"

"For you."

Lauren shook her head slowly from side to side. "No."

Richard removed his arm from her shoulder and turned in the seat to face her. Her eyes met his, then she looked away.

"Lauren," he said gently. "You're the reason I drove up there. You and Emily. Look at me." He touched her shoulder. "I mean it. Yesterday you seemed genuinely concerned about the people across the street. Well, the more I thought about it, the more concerned *I* became. I mean, you and Emily are everything to me, and I wasn't about to take any chances with your safety. I wanted to find out for sure if those people were legitimate."

"Legitimate?"

"You know, if they'd purchased or rented the house or if they were, I don't know . . . squatters."

"But leaving the store . . ."

"Arthur was there, and I explained the situation to him. He agreed that I should check on them. In fact, he encouraged me to go."

44

"He did?"

Richard smiled. "Yes. What did you think, that I ran off in a paranoid frenzy?"

Now it was Lauren's turn to smile. "Well . . ."

"Hey, come on," he said, setting aside his wineglass. He put his arm around her shoulder and gave her a squeeze. "Give me a *little* credit."

"I'm sorry. I guess I thought you were overreacting, and I couldn't imagine why."

"I understand," he said. "Maybe I should have called you first to let you know what I was doing. Then it wouldn't have seemed so mysterious." He kissed her. "Next time I will."

"Let's hope there won't *be* a next time."

"I'm sure there won't," he said.

Later that night Lauren awoke from a troubled sleep. She lay staring at the dark ceiling, trying to reconstruct her dream. Richard snored softly beside her. She raised up on one elbow and looked over him at the alarm clock: 3:29.

Careful not to wake Richard, she got out of bed, padded across the room to the bathroom, and drank a glass of water in the dark.

She started to get back in bed. Then she changed her mind and walked down the hallway to the guest bedroom at the southeast corner of the house. One of its windows faced the street.

Lauren pulled aside the curtain.

There was a streetlamp down the block that cast sickly yellow light and shadows onto the yard across the street. The Greys' house was dark and still. Something seemed different about the front window, although Lauren couldn't be sure what it was. One thing for certain, the drapes were still slightly parted, leaving a narrow, black space between them.

Now Lauren noticed that the house was not entirely dark. A light was on near the back. She pictured the inside of the Greys' house and decided that the light was coming from the kitchen.

She shivered in her thin nightgown.

Odd that someone's in the kitchen this early in the morning, she thought. Why are they even up?

Then she smiled to herself and let the curtain fall back in place.

Why am *I* up, for God's sake?

She went back to bed.

45

. . .

On Saturday morning they drove to San Diego.

Richard steered his Chevrolet Corsica south on the San Diego Freeway, then west on Sea World Drive. When he turned into the oceanarium's huge parking lot, it was already nearly full.

Lauren had been to Sea World once, before Emily was born. She'd enjoyed it then, but she feared she might be a bit bored the second time around, so she carried the camera and declared herself to be the official snapshooter. She soon found, though, that the park had too many attractions to be boring. Besides, it was all new for Emily and Richard, and Lauren quickly became caught up in their excitement.

The first thing they did was sit with a few thousand people in an outdoor stadium and watch the killer whales perform. Lauren thought it was incredible that creatures so large could maneuver so precisely. When one of the sleek, black and white mammals shot high out of the water with a female trainer perched on its snout, Emily squealed with delight.

"Amazing," Richard said above the applause of the crowd.

Lauren nodded, smiling, hoping she'd snapped the picture at the right moment.

After the show they visited the Marine Aquarium. There were a few dozen display tanks, each with an astounding array of fish and other sea life. Lauren let Richard and Emily walk ahead of her in order to photograph them. She got what she hoped was a good picture of Emily pointing, her finger pressed against the glass, and Richard leaning over her, peering into the tank.

They ate lunch at an outdoor table: hamburgers and sodas.

"How do you like it so far?" Lauren asked Emily.

"It's *neat!*"

"I want to get some shots of you and Emily," Richard said.

"How about all of us together?"

Richard turned to a young couple getting up from the next table and asked if the man would take their picture.

By late afternoon they were all tired and ready to go home. They agreed that the highlight of the day had been the petting pool, where they'd actually touched a dolphin. Lauren thought its skin had felt like wet suede, smooth and soft.

In the parking lot they became temporarily lost, until Richard got

his bearings and led them to the car. Lauren checked her camera—
one more frame left.

"Stand by the car," she said, "and I can get you two with the main
entrance in the background."

"What do you think, Emily? Should we let her take *another* picture
of us?"

Emily giggled. "I guess so."

"Come on," Lauren said, moving away from them, "you know
you love it."

She arranged them in the viewfinder so that the Sea World sign
was over Richard's right shoulder. There were also dozens of parked
cars and a few other people in the background, but that couldn't be
helped. She snapped the picture.

When she lowered the camera, she noticed a man standing near a
car not far behind Richard. He seemed to be staring at her, and not
too kindly. Then he ducked down, as if he were in a hurry to get in
his car.

Lauren walked to Richard and Emily.

"Did you get it?" Richard asked.

"Yes, but I think I also got some grouch in the background who
didn't want his picture taken. He was staring at me."

"Where?" Richard looked concerned.

"Over that way."

Lauren pointed, but the man was gone.

Richard scanned the lot, his expression troubled. "What did he
look like?"

"I don't know, just some guy." Lauren studied Richard's face.
"Does it matter?"

He forced a smile. "No, of course not."

As they drove back to San Miguel, Lauren noticed that Richard
checked the rearview mirror more frequently than usual.

6

IT WAS Saturday evening in Albuquerque, and Albert Novek was deciding how to kill Gus.

If he had a gun, he'd shoot him. But he didn't have a gun. He'd briefly considered a knife, but knives were messy, which was why Novek had never liked to use a knife.

He'd even thought about crushing Gus to death with the front-end loader. In fact, he'd thought about *that* at least once a week for the past three years, five months, and twelve days, which was exactly how long he'd worked at Gus's Hauling and Salvage. He could even make it look like an accident, although now it didn't matter if it looked like an accident or not. Anyway, the loader was no good because he'd have to wait until Monday when they went back to work to catch Gus unawares in the yard. And Novek wanted to kill Gus tonight. Tomorrow he had places to go and people to see.

So Novek figured he was down to two choices: beating Gus's brains out with the pry bar or choking him to death with his bare hands.

Each choice had something in its favor. The pry bar would be quicker and easier. Less fuss. But choking would be more satisfying. He'd be able to actually feel that fat slob die.

Gus was a big man, though, and he wouldn't just sit there and let Novek strangle him. He'd fight like hell. Not that Novek couldn't beat Gus in a fight. He was as big as Gus and in better shape, stronger and quicker—certainly more experienced. Still, Gus might get lucky and poke a finger into one of Novek's eyes.

That settled it. The pry bar.

The more Novek thought about it, the more he liked the idea of killing big Gus with a tool of the trade. It would be poetic. For years he'd taken orders from Gus, and one of Gus's favorite orders was: "Take the pry bar and pull all the nails outta them boards. I gotta guy who'll pay me two cents apiece for 'em."

48

I've got your two cents, Novek thought.

The ancient refrigerator chugged to life. Novek got up from the kitchen table, pulled open the door, and took out a can of beer. He went to the living room, crossed the ratty carpet, and stood at the window. It was open, but there was no breeze. The May evening was warm and still.

Novek opened the beer and took a swig, then pressed the cold can to his right temple and gazed out the window.

His apartment was on the fifth floor, and there was a parking lot across the street, so he had a good view. He stared across the night lights of Albuquerque and tried to picture where Gus lived. The house was a few miles away, in a neighborhood of green lawns and flowering bushes. Novek had been invited there only once. That had been over a year ago, when Gus needed help moving a coffin-size freezer from one end of the finished basement to the other.

Novek smiled to himself. He remembered how he'd thought about killing Gus then and shoving him into his own freezer. But of course, that would have blown his cover.

He drank some more beer, then checked his watch. It was six-thirty. He'd better move it if he wanted to get to the office before Gus.

One thing about Gus, he was reliable. Every Saturday night after work he'd go home, clean up, and have dinner with his wife. Then at seven he'd drive back to the office and work on the books for an hour or so. Sometimes he'd stay longer, fooling around in the garage, trying to find something to criticize Novek about on Monday.

Novek finished his beer in the bedroom and set the empty can on the dresser. He looked at himself in the cracked mirror.

He was in good shape, maybe the best shape of his adult life. The work he did for Gus had hardened his muscles. His weight was down to one ninety, which was about right for his height. He was very dark from the sun. Novek ran a hand through his hair. He kept it short, and to change his appearance even more, he plucked it back with tweezers, giving him a high forehead.

He tried to picture what he'd looked like before. He *remembered* what he'd looked like, but he had trouble seeing himself that way now. Pale skin, big belly, long hair and sideburns, low hairline. He'd been heavier in the old days, the *good* old days, before the operation had been turned upside down and he'd been forced to go underground.

It had been difficult at first, living under a cover name, pretending to be another person—so many lies to keep straight. Of course, with time it had gotten easier, although it had never been easy taking orders and verbal abuse from Gus. But that was over with now—he'd received his *real* orders and it was time to move.

Killing Gus had nothing to do with business. It was personal.

Novek pulled on a blue sport shirt and gray slacks. He laced up his black shoes, which were out of style but well shined. He took his wallet from the top dresser drawer and thumbed through his cash. Just over two grand, all he'd managed to save during his three years of low pay. But it would be enough to get him back to the real world.

He removed his jacket from the closet, then went through the small apartment, turning off lights. After he stepped into the hallway, he pulled the door shut behind him and locked it for the last time.

As he walked the four blocks to the salvage yard, he went over his plan once more.

He'd dump Gus's body in the trunk of his own car, drive it to the airport, and take the first flight out, no matter where it was going. He'd pay cash. When he got there, Denver or Atlanta or wherever the flight carried him, he'd book a seat on the next flight to L.A. From there it would be an easy drive to San Miguel.

Novek wondered if his chief had sent anyone else to San Miguel or if he was the only one involved.

No use worrying about that now, he thought. I'll find out when I get there.

The important thing now was to do Gus and get out of Albuquerque as quickly as possible. Novek knew he'd have some leeway, but not much. Gus's wife would expect him home by eight, nine at the latest. After that she'd call the office and then probably Novek's apartment. When no one answered, she might figure they'd gone out for a beer. Later, though, she'd drive down to the yard. No Gus and no car. She'd call the cops.

Eventually, Novek knew, they'd find Gus's car and Gus, and they'd start looking for him.

Let them look, he thought. They don't know my name or where I'm going.

Novek crossed the deserted street and walked directly toward the chain-link, razor-wire-topped gate. He unlocked the padlock, pulled out the chain, and swung open the gate. He decided to leave it open for Gus. Sometimes he did that, came back and worked late. Gus wouldn't think anything of it—in fact, it would make him happy. Novek strode across the hard-packed dirt yard and unlocked the garage where they parked the truck and the front-end loader and stored the tools. He switched on the lights and started looking around for the pry bar. He noticed that he was getting his hands dirty, so he wiped them off with a rag.

He heard Gus's car out front.

Then he found the pry bar on the worktable beside a toolbox. He picked it up. It was forged steel, two and a half feet long and an inch in diameter.

Novek heard Gus unlock the front office door.

He moved to the side door that separated the garage from the office. When he opened it, Gus was already seated behind his battered wooden desk. The fat man put on his half-spectacles, opened his ledger book, and looked up at Novek.

"You gonna change the oil in the truck tonight?" Gus asked. Then he showed surprise. "Hey, you're all dressed up."

"I'm going on a trip," Novek said, coming through the door.

"A trip?"

"That's right. And I just wanted to say good-bye."

He walked toward Gus, the pry bar low at his side.

7

ON SUNDAY while Richard mowed the lawn in the backyard under casual observation from the deck by Emily and Amos—one putting together an imaginative structure with interlocking plastic pieces, the other lying in the shade—Lauren did the laundry. She smiled, remembering the exchange that morning at the breakfast table.

They'd nearly finished eating their French toast, when Emily said, "I had a dream last night about Shamu." Lauren had glanced at

Richard, whose coffee cup was motionless midway between the table and his lips, then looked at Emily.

"Shamu?"

Emily nodded seriously. "Uh huh."

"What happened in the dream, honey?"

"Well, first I fell in the big tank with him and—"

Richard put down his cup, a worried look on his face.

"—and then he swam over and started talking to me. It was some kind of fish talk, but I knew what he wanted."

Lauren waited, fearing Emily would say the whale had wanted her for lunch.

"He wanted out."

"Out?"

"Out of the tank. So I swam over and unlocked the gate and Shamu pushed it open and swam into the ocean with his family. They were all real happy."

Richard looked relieved, but Emily seemed sad. Lauren put her hand on her daughter's arm.

"What's wrong, honey?"

"I don't know how to unlock the gate and let Shamu out."

Lauren smiled. "That's okay. Shamu doesn't really want to get out. That was just your dream." Although he'd be freer in the open sea, she thought.

"He doesn't?"

"No," Richard said gently. "He's happy there. He gets to play all day with his family and they have lots to eat. Plus he gets to entertain people like us. Wasn't it fun yesterday watching him?"

"Uh huh."

"Well, Shamu was having fun too," Richard had told Emily.

Lauren stopped daydreaming when she heard the phone over the sounds of the washer and dryer. It was Connie Pickering.

"We're having a few people over this afternoon for a barbecue. You want to come, or are you busy?"

"No, it sounds good. I'll check with Richard and call you back."

"Don't bother," Connie said. "You know how much he loves my cooking."

Lauren laughed. "That's true. What can we bring?"

"Your appetites. And your swimming suits, too, if you want to take a dip. Come over anytime after one."

"Great," Lauren said, and hung up.

She went outside to tell Richard.

He turned off the mower when he saw her coming. He'd nearly finished the job, and the air was fresh with the scent of newly mown grass.

Lauren loved that smell. It reminded her of the house where she'd grown up in Lincoln, Nebraska. It had a huge backyard, larger even than this one, and there had been a swing set near the back fence. Lauren had had the swings mostly to herself, since her brother and sister had nearly outgrown them by the time she'd come along—a "mistake." Or a "happy surprise," as her parents had put it.

When she and Paul looked for a house in San Miguel, one of the things Lauren liked about this one was the yard. The previous owner had done a good job of landscaping; there were large trees along the back, lush bushes, and well-tended flower beds. And there was a beautiful expanse of green grass.

Paul hadn't thought too much of it.

"We'll have the only house in Southern California without a pool," he'd complained.

After they moved in, Paul called a contractor for an estimate. Lauren had objected, not only because the cost of building a pool seemed prohibitive, but also because they'd be giving up most of their beautiful, green backyard. After a prolonged argument Paul had gone along with her wishes. Of course, he'd never missed an opportunity to use it against her: "First the pool and now this."

"You look like you're having fun," she said, crossing the lawn to Richard.

He wore a T-shirt, shorts, and running shoes without socks. Fine grass clippings freckled his ankles. He wiped his hands on his T-shirt and smiled.

"You bet I am," he said. "Especially with this magnificent mower from McFadden's Hardware. Of course, if I wasn't so liberal with the terrific lawn feed, also from McFadden's Hardware, I wouldn't be having nearly so much fun now."

She put her arms around his waist, tipped her head up, and kissed him.

"You'll get sweaty," he said.

"That's the idea."

"What's the idea?"

"We send Emily next door and do it right here."

He leaned back to look at her with mock horror on his face.

"Do you know how bad that is for the lawn?"

She laughed and gave him a playful punch in the stomach, feeling hard muscles there.

"Connie invited us to a barbecue this afternoon."

"Great."

"I don't know who else will be there."

"Does it matter?"

It used to, she thought. "No." She kissed him. "I'll let you get back to your precious lawn."

As she turned to walk away, he gave her a light slap on the back-side.

"Hey!"

"You love it," he said.

"You could be right."

Back in the laundry room Lauren realized how thankful she was that Richard had changed. There'd been a time not too long ago, before they were married, when he was reluctant to go to Connie's parties, or any place where he'd be forced to get acquainted with new people—not necessarily Lauren's friends, but friends of friends. He seemed painfully shy, and when she finally was able to drag him to an occasional party, he'd stay by her side, not mingling, not being open and relaxed the way he was when they were alone or with a few of her close friends. When innocent questions were directed to him, particularly about his past, he'd answer as briefly as possible, volunteering nothing:

"Are you from California?"

"No."

Pause. "Oh. Where are you from?"

"Philadelphia."

"What did you do back there?"

"I worked for a company involved in government projects."

"Interesting. What sort of projects?"

"They were classified. Excuse me, I need a refill." End of discussion.

But that was then and this is now, Lauren thought with some relief, pulling clothes from the dryer and piling them on top.

Even Richard acknowledged it. "Before I met you, I was a shy guy," he'd say. "You changed me."

• • •

At one o'clock they locked up and went next door. Lauren's gaze swept over the house across the street. On Friday night she'd thought something was different about the house's front window. Now she knew what it was. The bushes near the house had been trimmed and no longer obstructed the window. Lauren scanned the rest of the yard, still an ill-tended mess. Apparently, only the bushes by the front window had been clipped.

Richard rang Connie's bell, even though the front door stood wide open. They heard her yell from somewhere in the house, "Come on in!"

Connie and Benjamin Pickering's living room had a hardwood floor adorned with several large handwoven rugs from their last trip to Santa Fe. The walls were white and hung with southwestern prints in chrome frames. The couch, long and low and covered with soft white leather, faced an empty fireplace. A man-size cactus stood in one corner of the room in a terra-cotta pot.

"Hi, guys!"

Connie came into the room, her colorful muumuu flowing behind her. She gave Richard and Lauren each a kiss on the cheek. Then she squatted down before Emily.

"Give your Aunt Connie a big hug. Mmm, yeah."

She held Emily's hand and led them all through the house. Lauren peeked in the kitchen as they walked past, spied an enormous wooden bowl filled with a green salad, and guessed Connie had invited more than "a few people."

"You're the first ones here," Connie said, taking them out to the covered patio.

Two redwood picnic tables had been pushed together and covered with a blue and white checkered tablecloth. At one end were a stack of white plastic plates, a tray filled with silverware, and a pile of napkins. A barbecue grill—large enough, Lauren thought, to roast a boar—stood near the edge of the patio.

Lauren saw Benjamin leaning over the swimming pool, holding a long aluminum pole with a screen attached to the end. He skimmed a tiny leaf from the water's surface, and now the kidney-shaped pool that dominated the backyard was perfect, pristine, gleaming aqua blue under the hazy blue sky.

When Benjamin saw them, he set his pole aside and crossed the twenty feet of pebbled concrete that separated the pool from the patio.

55

"Hi, Lauren, Richard, glad you could come."

Benjamin wore a loud, flowery shirt, light blue cotton pants, and sandals. He was middle-aged, a bit taller than Richard, and slightly stooped over—probably, Lauren believed, from years of leaning down to drill and fill teeth. Also, she thought he was too pale for a man who owned a swimming pool. Of course, that could come from raising three kids.

Lauren gave him a hug. "Your pool looks beautiful."

"Thanks. Jump in when you're ready."

"Maybe later."

"Can I, Mommy?"

Emily tugged on Lauren's shoulder bag, which held their swimming suits and towels.

"Right now?" Since there was a proliferation of pools in San Miguel—alluring, but potentially deadly—Lauren had insisted that her daughter learn to swim. Emily took swimming classes at school, and Lauren was confident in her ability, but she preferred to be nearby whenever Emily went in the water. "Um, first I have to help Connie in the kitchen, and then . . ."

"I'll watch her," Richard volunteered.

"I can *swim*." Emily was indignant.

"I know, hon." Richard turned to her, putting his hand on her head. "But don't you want me to watch?"

"Sure!"

As Lauren and Connie went into the house, they met Connie's two sons at the door—Ryan, six, and Christopher, nine—both wearing baggy, neon-colored swimming trunks. Christopher had a skin diver's mask strapped to his head like a hat.

" 'Lo, Mrs. Caylor," they said in unison, and ran for the pool.

"Don't run!" Connie yelled after them.

"Where's Michelle?"

"Probably in her room leafing through beauty magazines."

"Already?" Michelle was eleven.

Connie's kitchen was nearly twice as large as hers, Lauren estimated, with spacious tile countertops and a butcher block that could seat four. Connie already had the feast well in hand, with few things left undone.

"You can slice the kiwis," she told Lauren, then called through the window for Benjamin to answer the doorbell.

During the next half hour guests began passing by the kitchen to the patio, stopping to greet their hostess. Lauren looked out the back window and saw Emily wading in the shallow end of the pool with Ryan, while Christopher paddled around, facedown, a snorkel tube protruding behind his head. Richard stood near the pool talking with two men and a woman, none of whom Lauren recognized.

The oven timer chimed, and Lauren helped Connie take out loaves of bread, filling the kitchen with a wonderful aroma.

"How many people do you expect to feed?"

"About twenty," Connie said, "if everyone shows up. I even asked the new people across the street."

"You did?"

"It seemed like the neighborly thing to do."

"Did you talk to them?"

"Just the husband."

"Hal Ipswich."

"Yes, and—say, how did you know his name?"

"Oh, ah, I guess Richard told me." Lauren hoped Connie wouldn't ask her more. She would rather not mention Richard's impromptu trip to L.A. "Are they coming?"

Connie shook her head. "No, and it's probably for the best. The guy's kind of weird."

"How so?"

"Well, I rang the bell a few times, and when no one answered, I thought they weren't home. Then I wondered if they hadn't heard the bell, because it sounded pretty faint to me. So I started knocking real loud, in case they were in the rear of the house. All of a sudden Hal Ipswich yanked open the door. It scared the hell out of me, because I'd been listening for footsteps or any other movement inside and I'd heard nothing. It was as if he'd been standing right there the whole time, two feet away from me. Anyway, he held the door open about halfway and stood in the opening, as if he were trying to block me from even *looking* inside."

Lauren frowned. "That *is* weird."

Connie shrugged. "Maybe they're just loners. Anyway, Hal thanked me for inviting them and said he was sorry they couldn't make it, very polite and all. But he seemed anxious for me to leave."

Lauren studied Connie's face, waiting for more.

Connie shrugged again. "Help me carry these out, will you?"

Outside, Lauren noted that a number of partygoers were crowded around the pool, in imminent danger of stepping backward and falling in. She was acquainted with a few of the guests, but most were strangers to her and Richard. She estimated that at least half of them were involved with Connie in her current crusade to register firearms. Lauren heard her tell one woman, who she believed was an attorney, that she'd already received an anonymous phone call.

"Not exactly threatening," Connie said. "But he was pretty pissed off."

Lauren moved away, looking for Richard. She wasn't interested in talking about guns—she already knew all she wanted to know about them. They repulsed her. Her father had owned a number of rifles and shotguns, and she was frightened by their very purpose: to hurl lead projectiles into a target, sometimes a living target. He'd sold his collection not long after his only son, Lauren's older brother, was killed in Vietnam by a sniper.

Lauren saw Emily, Ryan, and another little girl tossing around a ball in the corner of the yard by the fence. Then she found Richard near the liquor cart talking to a man and woman about lawn care. The woman was very attractive, Lauren thought. She wore the top half of a two-piece swimsuit and a long skirt that rode low on her hips. She hung on Richard's every word. He looked a bit uncomfortable.

Not uncomfortable enough, Lauren decided, and walked up to him, sliding her arm through his.

"Hi."

"Hi," he said, seemingly relieved, giving her a squeeze.

Much later, after most of the guests had left, Lauren and Richard helped Connie and Benjamin clear the picnic table and scrape food scraps into paper trash bags. Connie kept trying to kick them out, but Lauren refused to leave until most of the mess had been cleaned up.

Before they left, Connie said offhandedly, "I forgot to ask you—how's your TV reception?"

"Fine," Richard told her. "Why?"

"Some guy was up on the pole in the alley yesterday and I went out to ask him what he was doing. You know me, nosiest woman on the block. He said he was from the cable TV company and he—"

"Did you see his truck?" Richard asked suddenly.

"His truck? Yes, I looked out through the back gate."

"Was it a company truck?"

"Sure. Why wouldn't it be?"

Richard looked relieved. "No reason," he said. "So what was he doing?"

"Replacing connections or something . . ."

Richard nodded. "They do that occasionally. Usually when people start complaining about their reception."

"Well, I haven't complained," Connie said. "Have you?"

They hadn't.

When they got home, Lauren went into the backyard.

Their neighborhood was old enough to have an alley, with telephone poles standing at regular intervals. Lauren looked up at the pole near the corner of the yard, rising up behind the tall cedar fence and the leafy trees. Telephone and electric wires ran from the pole in both directions along the alley and from the pole to their house. Lauren knew that when cable TV had been installed in this neighborhood, the cable company had utilized the same poles.

She could see a few metal objects on the pole, but she had no idea of their function. Nor could she tell if any of them had been newly installed.

She tried to imagine a man up there, staring down, with a clear view of their yard and their back windows. She shivered, then turned and went into the house.

8

ON MONDAY MORNING Lauren resumed working on the conceptuals for the new park, juggling the positions of the softball field, tennis courts, playground, picnic area, bicycle paths, and so on. She wanted as many sketches as possible, at least a dozen, for her meeting that afternoon with Geoffrey. Together they would narrow the number to three. These she would draw as finished, color renderings for presentation at the next neighborhood meeting.

"Aren't you going to eat?"

"What?" She looked up from her drawing, surprised to see Susan Aikens standing there. "Is it lunchtime already?"

"You're working too hard, girl," Susan said.

The weather was overcast and cool, so they carried their lunch sacks downstairs to the crowded cafeteria. They found two empty chairs at a table occupied by a young man and woman. Lauren couldn't remember the man's name, but she knew he worked in the personnel department. Perhaps the woman did, too.

"Do you mind if we sit here?" Susan asked.

The man gave them a nod and a wave of the hand without missing a beat in his conversation with the woman. Actually, Lauren noted, it was more of a monologue concerning the weekend he'd just spent in Las Vegas.

"How was your weekend?" Susan asked.

". . . saw Jay Leno at Caesar's Palace and . . ."

"It was fun," Lauren said. She described the Pickerings' barbecue the day before and their trip to Sea World on Saturday. Then she remembered the roll of film—she'd drop it off at the grocery store after work. "What about you?"

". . . won forty-two dollars playing keno, but . . ."

"Oh, the usual," Susan said. "Worked in the yard. Cleaned the house. Went to a Dodgers' game with Timmy and Eric."

Lauren raised her eyebrows. Eric was Susan's ex-husband. "You went out with Eric?"

"It wasn't 'going out.' It was just a ball game."

Lauren smiled. "I see."

"And I fixed him dinner."

"Dinner too? This is getting serious."

Susan poked at her cottage cheese.

"There's more?" Lauren asked.

". . . Wayne Newton getting out of a limo . . ."

"He spent the night."

"This *is* serious," Lauren said, grinning. "So, did you do it?"

"*Lauren.*" Susan's face had colored slightly.

"Hey, I just want the facts, ma'am. What did Timmy think about his daddy staying over?"

"Are you kidding? He thought it was great."

Lauren remembered the first time Richard had spent the night at her house. It had been a Friday night, and they'd both wondered what Emily's reaction would be Saturday morning. Lauren wasn't too worried. After all, her daughter was barely four years old, not exactly sexually aware. Richard, though, was a nervous wreck. He feared that Emily would think he'd defiled her mother—especially when the little girl walked boldly into Lauren's bedroom early Saturday morning.

"Morning, Mommy. Hi, Richard."

"Um, hi." He'd pulled the blanket up to his chin.

"You want to watch cartoons with me, Richard?"

"Um, sure."

Lauren smiled now at the memory.

"What?" Susan asked.

"I was just remembering Richard's first overnighter. So, are you and Eric getting back together?"

"I don't know. Can we change the subject?"

Lauren laughed. "Sure." She munched a celery stick.

". . . stay at the Sands next time because . . ."

Susan glanced at the young man, then at Lauren.

"I haven't been to Vegas in years," she said. "Eric loved it. He was pretty good at blackjack. How about you?"

"Las Vegas? I went once with Paul, before Emily was born." She glanced at the young couple across the table, then lowered her voice and shook her head. "It's too glitzy for me. And depressing, somehow."

"Wait a minute—weren't you and Richard married there?"

"No. Reno."

"Reno? Who the hell gets married in Reno?"

They both laughed at that.

"We flew to Carson City," Lauren said, "rented a car at the airport, and drove the half hour or so to Reno. We were married at the Chapel of the Bells."

"Catchy name."

"Then we drove down to Tahoe and rented a cabin on the lake. A one-night honeymoon. We flew home the next day."

"Where was Emily?"

"She stayed next door with Connie."

"Did she understand what was going on?"

"More or less. The hardest part was telling her that my last name was going to be different from hers."

"Jeez, that must have been tough."

Lauren shrugged. "I think she's used to it."

Susan shook her head and smiled.

"What?"

"Reno, for God's sake."

After lunch Lauren counted her sketches, sixteen, then stacked them with her select ones on top. She carefully rolled up the flimsies and the blueline drawing in a bundle and carried it to the small conference room. Geoffrey walked in as she was unrolling the drawings on the long table.

"It looks like you've been busy." He sat in the chair next to hers. "By the way, I've just learned that the park will be called—are you ready?—*Decker* Park."

"You're kidding." Thomas Decker was in his second term as mayor of San Miguel, and six months ago he'd barely survived a recall election brought on, Lauren remembered, because his top aide had been accused of receiving kickbacks from a construction company. The aide had been indicted by a grand jury, but Decker was exonerated of any wrongdoing. Still, suspicions remained.

"I guess Decker is trying to improve his image," Geoffrey said.

"Even so, Mr. Will gave us the land. It ought to be called Will Park."

"You're not the only one who thinks so. But Decker's in office and poor Will's underground."

For the next hour they went over Lauren's sketches. Geoffrey was most impressed by her first one. He set it aside, untouched, as one of the three alternatives. There was another drawing that he also liked—with a few minor changes, such as relocating the footbridge a bit farther up the drainage swale to keep it away from existing trees. Lauren saw her mistake even before Geoffrey pointed it out: too much construction activity near the trees could damage them.

For the third alternative she and Geoffrey combined the best aspects of two remaining designs into one.

"That should do it," he said. "We need these to look real pretty for the citizens."

"I'll use lots of colored pens and mount them on foam core."

"Great. Let's see, with Memorial Day we've got a three-day weekend coming up, so I won't schedule the second neighborhood meeting until the end of next week. Will that be enough time for you?"

"More than enough. I may even finish these by Friday."

Lauren carried the drawings back to her cubicle. In the copy room she made four more bluelines of the park site—three for her presentation drawings and one to try out her markers and play around with colors. Back at her drafting table she began carefully laying out her first design, initially in pencil. She was distracted, though, recalling Susan's comment about her and Richard's marriage in Reno.

She clearly remembered when Richard had asked her to marry him. Actually, she'd nudged him a bit.

They'd been seeing each other for almost a year, and for the past six months he'd been staying overnight with her four or five times a week. Finally one night, perhaps after she'd had too much wine, she asked him directly, "What are your intentions, sir?"

"Intentions?"

"Precisely. Do you plan to ask for my hand?"

"Your hand, your arm, and everything else," he joked.

"Well, then?"

He smiled sheepishly. Then he actually got down on one knee before her on the couch.

"Will you do me the honor of being my wife?"

"I will indeed."

"My heart soars," he said, and jumped to his feet—a little unsteadily from the wine. "Let's do it now."

"Now? You mean tonight?"

"Why not?"

"Because you're drunk. So am I, I think."

"Okay, then tomorrow."

Lauren remembered feeling flushed, and it wasn't just from the wine. "You're serious."

"I am," he said, smiling.

"You mean fly to Las Vegas?"

His smile faded briefly, and then brightened. "Not Vegas. How about Reno?"

"Reno?"

"Sure. We can catch a flight tomorrow morning."

"Okay. But isn't Las Vegas the traditional place for this sort of thing?"

"So who says we have to be traditional? Besides, Reno is practically next door to Tahoe . . ."

His suggestion had seemed perfectly reasonable at the time. Why did it bother her now? She pulled her thoughts back to her work.

Lauren didn't realize it was past five o'clock until she heard movement in the corridor beside her cubicle. People were going home for the night.

She put away her pencils and triangle and brushed erasure crumbs from the table. She left the drawing taped to the table and covered it with a gray plastic sheet, then turned off her light, picked up her purse and sweater, and headed for the door. By the time she got outside it was five-twenty. The air was misty and cool, and the parking lot was already nearly empty.

Lauren smiled. Mondays, she thought. Everyone can hardly wait to get out of here. Next Monday, though, we won't have to worry about it—Memorial Day.

She put on her sweater and walked toward the Honda.

Then she noticed a solitary, dark blue car parked in one corner of the lot. She felt a rush of adrenaline when she realized that it was the same car she'd seen Thursday, the one she imagined had followed her. The man behind the wheel was, as before, engrossed in a paperback book.

Lauren stood beside the Honda for a moment, staring across the nearly empty expanse of asphalt at the man. She wondered who he was waiting for.

He turned a page and raised the book higher before his face, as if he'd sensed her watching him.

The mist in the air suddenly felt colder to Lauren. She climbed in the Honda, started the engine, then turned on the wipers to clear the light accumulation of moisture from the windshield. At that moment two men and two women came out of the building, waved good-bye to each other, and went off in four different directions. Lauren waited to see which of them would walk to the blue car.

None did. They all drove off in their own vehicles, leaving Lauren and the man in the dark blue car alone in the empty lot.

Lauren felt a strong urge to get out of there as quickly as possible. She shifted into gear and wheeled toward the exit, taking one last look back, expecting—hoping?—to see the man still buried in his book. But he'd set it down and turned on the windshield wipers.

Lauren drove rapidly down the parkway, but had to wait at the intersection for a red light. Behind her the blue car pulled out of the lot at a leisurely pace, seemingly staying back until the light turned green.

When it did, Lauren jerked forward. She took the same route to Emily's school that she'd always taken, but this evening she fought the traffic every inch of the way, changing lanes, dodging in and out, cutting in front of other cars, speeding ahead whenever there was a short break between vehicles. But no matter what she did, the blue car kept pace, staying behind her in traffic—and without apparent effort.

Lauren felt as if she were in a nightmare, running with all her might through molasses, while her pursuer glided easily behind her, amused for the moment, but likely to become bored with the chase and overtake her.

By the time she turned the corner near Emily's school, squealing the tires in the process, her heart was pounding. She slammed on the brakes, sliding to a stop behind a parked school bus. She jumped out of the Honda, ready to run into the building and call the police.

The blue car reached the corner.

Lauren watched it pass through the intersection without turning toward her. It moved out of sight, the driver never once looking in her direction.

9

LAUREN STOOD THERE staring up and down the street, expecting the blue car to reappear at any moment. When it did not, her breathing and heart rate began slowing to normal.

He wasn't following me, she thought, reassuring herself. It was just a coincidence. It *had* to be.

Lauren passed through the main entrance of Oceanside Day School and walked down the hall to Miss Wilson's room. Except for Emily's teacher and the little girl sitting beside her at a low table, the room was deserted. There was a globe on the table, and Miss Wilson was pointing to Africa. Lauren smiled briefly, waiting for Emily to turn around. The girl turned, but she wasn't Emily. Panic stabbed at Lauren.

"Oh, hello, Mrs. Caylor." Miss Wilson wore a puzzled look.

"Emily—where . . ?"

"Your husband picked her up twenty minutes ago."

Lauren's cheeks reddened.

"Of course," she said. "I'd forgotten." This morning she'd told Richard she was going grocery shopping after work, and he'd promised to take Emily home from school.

Lauren drove to the Safeway store, angry at herself for being so distracted by something that obviously had nothing to do with her: the dark blue car.

She dropped off her roll of pictures from Sea World at the film counter, then pulled a shopping cart loose from its train and began her trek up and down the aisles. Half an hour later she pushed the heavily laden cart to the end of a long line at the checkout counter. She didn't get home until six-thirty.

"We were beginning to worry about you," Richard said, greeting her in the kitchen. He kissed her, then stepped aside for Emily—"Hi, Mommy!"—who gave her a hug. Amos was delighted to see her, swinging his tail like a metronome. Richard helped her carry in the groceries.

"The store was a mess," Lauren explained. "Plus, would you believe I drove all the way to Emily's school before I remembered you were picking her up."

"You're joking."

"No."

"What were you thinking about?"

Lauren decided not to mention being "followed" by the blue car. For one thing, she was certain—wasn't she?—that the car hadn't *really* been following her. And for another, she recalled how disconcerted Richard had become when she told him about another oddity: the new neighbors. "I just forgot, I guess. I'll bet you two are starving," she said, changing the subject.

"Not entirely," Richard admitted. "We snacked on crackers and cheese."

"Well, I'm famished."

They unpacked the groceries, putting them away in the refrigerator and cupboards. Richard folded the empty paper sacks and stacked them under the sink.

"I'll help you with dinner. What are you hungry for?"

Lauren leaned back against the counter, crossed her arms, and looked around the kitchen.

"All this food," she said. "And none of it sounds good right now."

Richard smiled and put his hands on her shoulders.

"Haven't we gone through this before?"

"You mean like the last time I bought this many groceries?"

He nodded.

"What did we do then?" she asked with a grin.

He kissed her on the forehead. "We went out to eat."

They drove to the San Miguel pier. The parking area was separated from the street by a wide stretch of grass, which formed a long, narrow park that paralleled the beach.

The sky was still overcast, but the mist had evaporated. A mild breeze brought the smell of the sea to them. As they walked onto the pier, Lauren could hear the cry of gulls, the random clanging of a distant bell, the dull thud of the surf.

This end of the pier was actually a mini shopping mall built on wide, wooden planks. There were clothing boutiques, snack shops, souvenir stores, and arts and crafts galleries, all of which were closed for the evening. A few people were window-shopping and a few others—like Lauren, Richard, and Emily—were headed for Tobey's.

The restaurant was always crowded on weekends, requiring reservations. But this was Monday, and the dining area was only three-quarters full. They spotted an empty table by the window and asked the hostess to seat them there, then followed her between tables and down several steps to the lower level. Their table offered a view of the breakers rolling in beneath them, illuminated by lights on the pier.

A waitress appeared, handing them menus. "Can I start you off with something from the bar?"

Lauren asked Emily if she'd like milk.

"Okay."

"I'll have iced tea, please," Lauren told the waitress.

"And I'd like—"

Richard stopped and stared past the waitress toward the front entrance. Lauren saw a man standing by the hostess's station. He wore khaki pants and a dark green windbreaker, and he seemed to be searching the tables. His eyes fell on them. Richard inhaled sharply.

"What is it?" Lauren asked.

Richard said nothing, staring at the man by the entrance, his hand a fist on the table. Then the man turned and walked out. Richard's eyes remained fixed on the door.

"Honey, what's wrong?"

"What?" He seemed suddenly surprised by her presence. "It's . . . it's nothing." Now he looked embarrassed, tension draining from his face.

"Sir?" The waitress was still standing beside the table.

"Oh, ah, just bring me an iced tea, too, thanks."

She walked away.

"Who was that man?" Lauren asked, concerned.

"Which man?"

"Richard, come on, the guy in the green windbreaker. You acted scared to death of him."

"Scared?" He forced a smile. "He just looked familiar, that's all."

He looked down at his open menu. Lauren reached out and laid her hand across it. "Tell me," she said.

Richard hesitated, then he sighed and looked meekly at her.

"Okay," he said, "I thought he was . . . one of the customers from the store."

"A customer?"

He nodded. "This guy, the one I thought he was, came in the store today and caused a lot of trouble. I don't know his name, but he's been in before and he's always got a complaint. Today he returned a gallon of paint that he said wasn't the right shade. One of the clerks, um, Todd, pointed out that he'd used almost half of it, and the guy got angry. He started yelling at Todd, and by the time I'd walked over to them, they were pushing each other. Todd was so mad I sent him home for the rest of the day, and I told this guy to stay the hell out of my store."

"My God."

Richard shrugged. "The guy called me a few names that I won't repeat here. Then he said he'd settle with *me* later, and he stomped out."

"Maybe you should have called the police," Lauren said.

"No, the guy's just full of hot air. But I thought for a minute that it was him standing by the door. I was afraid he'd come over here and make a scene."

"Thank goodness it wasn't him."

"Right," Richard said, looking away from her.

The waitress returned with their drinks and took their orders: grilled swordfish for Richard, halibut for Lauren, and a children's basket of shrimp for Emily.

The food, as always, was excellent.

When the meal was finished, Richard left enough money on the table to cover the bill and a generous tip, then followed Lauren and Emily to the entrance. He quickly moved past them, pushed open the door, and stood for a moment scanning the pier, blocking their way.

"What's the matter?" Lauren asked.

"Nothing." He put his arm around her and led her and Emily onto the pier.

As they strolled back to the parking area Lauren gazed in the shop windows. One displayed seashells and starfish. Emily pressed her nose against the glass.

"I want that one and that one and that one . . ."

Lauren turned, smiling, to Richard. He was looking over his shoulder, searching the pier behind them.

"Do you think he's still around?"

Richard glanced at her, then stared along the pier. "No," he said. "Come on, let's go home."

By the time they returned to the house, it was past Emily's bedtime, but she was so wide awake that Lauren decided to let her stay up for another half hour or so. She got out Emily's large coloring book and the box of nontoxic colored pens, and then they sat on the floor in the family room and turned through the pages, seeking just the right drawing. Each picture was finely detailed and would require hours of coloring to complete. Most of them had yet to be colored.

"This one," Emily said.

The fine-lined, black-and-white drawing depicted a fairy princess in the foreground. There were flowers and butterflies in her long hair. A castle stood on a hill in the distance, and a unicorn grazed nearby.

MICHAEL ALLEGRETTO

"Good choice," Lauren said.

"Are you going to color too?"

"Sure, why not."

Richard entered the room, and before long all three were hunched over the book, carefully coloring in the picture. When Emily began yawning, Lauren took her to bed and tucked her in. As usual, Amos curled up on the floor beside the bed. Lauren returned to the family room and gathered up the pens and coloring book, leaving them for now at the end of the coffee table.

She found Richard in the living room, standing by the front window, peeking out. When he heard her behind him, he pulled his hand from the drapes and let them fall closed.

"I heard a car," he said, adding quickly, "Do you want some wine? I'm going to have a glass."

She studied his face. "Is something wrong?"

"No." He produced a smile. "No, of course not." He led her back to the family room, then brought them each a glass of white wine. He sat beside her on the love seat, put his arm around her, and kissed her cheek.

"I love you," he said.

"I love you too." Then: "Richard?"

"What, babe?"

"That man in the restaurant . . ."

"What about him?" His voice had an edge to it, slight but enough for Lauren to notice.

"You were looking out the drapes—are you afraid he followed us home?" She had a sudden image of the dark blue car behind her in traffic.

"I . . . no."

"Something's troubling you, though, or—"

"It's the people across the street," he said abruptly, then seemed to regret his words. He sipped his wine, saying no more.

Lauren prompted him: "Connie said she thinks they're loners, perhaps a bit weird."

"Weird?" Richard said, setting down his glass, warming to the subject. "That's putting it mildly. Hal and Monica Ipswich never come out of their house, and I've been watching it since Friday. I've never seen them, have you?" Before Lauren could answer, he continued, "I mean, I've never even seen them get in their car—it's either in the driveway or it's gone. What do they do, wait until we're asleep or at work to drive away? And at night they never turn on any lights except at the side of the house. Don't they use their front rooms?"

Lauren was taken aback by Richard's outburst. She saw a desperate look in his eyes, but it soon faded, possibly with conscious effort. He turned away from her, then fumbled with his glass, picked it up, and drank the rest of his wine. Lauren was concerned, not so much by what Richard had observed about Hal and Monica Ipswich, but that he'd been watching them so closely. She had to admit she'd been a bit uneasy about their neighbors, too, but she'd never felt threatened by them. Apparently, though, Richard did.

She asked, "Is there some connection between the man you saw tonight at Tobey's and Hal and Monica?"

He tried to smile, but the desperation had returned to his eyes. "How could there be?" he asked, as much a plea as a question. He picked up the remote control. "Let's see what's on TV."

Later Lauren lay awake in bed, while Richard twisted and turned in his sleep.

She felt certain that he was keeping something from her. This disturbed her because if he was in trouble or in danger, she wanted to know about it, wanted to help. But she was more disturbed by his very act of concealment.

She remembered all too well the lack of communication between her and Paul. It was one of the reasons they'd drifted apart, perhaps the main reason. The possibility that this might happen with her and Richard . . . It was almost too much to bear.

Lauren knew she could encourage Richard to talk about whatever was bothering him. But she would not force him. She would not risk pressuring him, lest he feel trapped. Paul had felt trapped, and that marriage had ended.

She stared up at the darkness and thought about the man in the restaurant and the new neighbors across the street. Richard had tried to convince her that there was no connection between them, but his attitude had belied his words. Apparently, he believed there *was* a connection. Lauren tried to imagine a scenario that would explain it all. She could conceive of only one: Richard was being truthful about the man in the restaurant—he resembled an unruly customer at the store, one whose name he didn't know—*and* he was afraid the customer was Hal Ipswich and had moved across the street from them. Farfetched, but possible. However, if that's all there was to it, why wouldn't Richard tell her?

Perhaps, Lauren thought fearfully, the customer's threats had been more serious than Richard wanted to admit.

Lauren felt she needed to find out.

Tomorrow, she decided, I'll pay Arthur McFadden a visit.

And then she pictured the man in the restaurant: dark hair, average height and build, certainly not threatening in appearance. She wondered if he and Hal Ipswich were the same person.

Tomorrow, she promised herself, I'll pay *him* a visit too.

10

LATE TUESDAY MORNING Lauren phoned Richard from work.

"How're you doing?"

"Busy," he said.

"Too busy to have lunch with a beautiful woman?"

"Are you kidding? What time should I pick you up?"

"I owe myself a long lunch hour," she said, but there was more to it than that. This was the first time she'd ever hidden her intentions from Richard, planned something behind his back. And although she believed it was for the best, she felt guilty. She sat stiffly at her drawing table, squeezing the receiver. "I'll come to the store."

"Great," Richard said.

"See you at noon."

At eleven-thirty Lauren parked her Honda in one of the parking structures near the mall. Her neck and shoulders were stiff—the start of a headache, she knew, unless she could loosen up. She concentrated on relaxing, on letting her arms swing freely as she walked in the bright sunshine.

I'm not spying, she told herself, I'm trying to help.

She was genuinely concerned about the customer who'd menaced Richard in the store. If she learned that the threats had been serious, she'd insist that they notify the police. Especially since Richard had implied that the man might be vengeful.

Lauren walked through the crowded mall. It would be more crowded later, she knew, when office workers and high school students flocked here for their lunch breaks. Now people were window-shopping, sitting on wrought-iron benches under shade trees, and sunning themselves on the low, curving stone wall that circled the fountain.

She checked her watch: 11:37. Good. Richard wouldn't be expecting her for at least twenty minutes. She was purposely early, hoping he'd be busy with customers. This would give her a chance to chat alone with Arthur without arousing the suspicions of either of them.

McFadden's hardware store was at the end of the block.

Lauren pushed through the door, mentally rehearsing the tone of voice she would use to question Arthur—inconsequential, so that he wouldn't immediately summon Richard. She scanned the aisles, expecting to see Richard involved in a sale, ready to make her way unnoticed to Arthur's office.

Then she saw Richard walking toward her and smiling.

"You're early." He kissed her. "Shall we go?"

They walked to the north end of the mall, where Richard bought them each a chili dog and an Orange Julius. They sat at a small, round metal table under an umbrella. Pigeons waddled nearby, pecking at crumbs.

"How's work?" he asked.

"Okay." Lauren toyed with her straw, making circles in the frothy orange surface of her drink. "I've got one design nearly completed and I need two more for a presentation next week." She sipped her drink. "Have you . . . I mean, has that customer been back?"

He frowned. "No, we can forget about him." Then he smiled—with some effort, Lauren thought. "You're still thinking about last night, aren't you?"

"Well, the way you reacted in the restaurant . . ."

He reached out and put his hand over hers.

"You mean *over*reacted," he said. "I apologize for that. It was just so soon after I'd dealt with the guy in the store that I didn't have the incident in perspective. I do now. It was nothing, really."

"It must have been something or—"

"What I meant to say," he said, showing some impatience, "was that it's nothing to worry about. So let's just forget it, okay?"

Lauren opened her mouth to speak, then changed her mind.

After lunch they walked back through the crowded mall to the hardware store. Richard kissed her at the entrance.

"I'm glad you came," he said.

"Me too."

"I'll see you tonight." He turned and put his hand on the door.

"I'm, ah, I'm going to say hello to Arthur."

Richard glanced at his watch. "Won't you be late for work?"

"I think the city can manage without me for another five minutes," she said, keeping her voice light.

She followed him inside. A dozen customers wandered among the long rows of display shelves, and three or four clerks hustled about. The young woman behind the cash register nodded at Lauren.

"Hello, Mrs. Caylor," she said.

"Hi." Lauren couldn't remember her name, and it added to her discomfort.

"I don't see Arthur, so he's probably in the office," Richard said. "Should I get him for you?"

"No, I'll just go back there."

"Okay, babe." He kissed her on the cheek. "I'd better help out on the floor."

Richard moved away from her toward a young couple gazing at a bewildering display of paint cans. Lauren walked down a row of rakes, clippers, edgers, and trimmers to the counter at the rear of the store. A man stood there waiting for the clerk who was operating the key-duplicating machine. The young clerk turned a screw and removed the new key. He picked up a rag; then he saw Lauren.

"Be with you in a minute," he said. He was a good-looking young man with curly blond hair that fell over his ears.

A surfer, Lauren thought. Probably drives the girls wild.

"I'm looking for Arthur," she said.

He began wiping the key with the rag, then motioned with his head. "He's in the office."

Lauren stepped around the end of the counter and found the office door open. The room was a jumble of overloaded metal shelves, cardboard boxes, and file cabinets. In one corner was crammed a large metal desk strewn with order forms and parts books. Arthur McFadden stopped shuffling through papers and looked up.

"Well, hello."

"Busy?"

He smiled. "Thank God, yes. Come on in and sit down."

Lauren sat in a gray metal folding chair facing the desk.

"When Richard told me you two were having lunch," Arthur said, "I hoped you'd stop in. I haven't seen you in a while."

Lauren had known Arthur for only a year and a half, but she thought of him as a dear, old friend. He was a soft-spoken man with thick white hair and a bright smile. A pair of half-glasses rode low on the end of his nose, and the eyes that shone over them were full of attentiveness and good humor. He wore a long-sleeved shirt with the cuffs rolled up over his forearms. There were liver spots on the backs of his hands, but the hands looked strong.

"I know," Lauren said. "My fault. How have you been?"

"Good."

"And Betty?"

"She's fine. She always asks about Emily."

"That's nice," Lauren said.

Arthur nodded. Lauren fell silent. She felt awkward and foolish, as if she were a little girl who had gained an audience with the school principal under false pretenses and now had nothing to say. Arthur watched her over his glasses.

"Richard, ah, told me he had some trouble with a customer yesterday."

"Trouble?" His eyebrows went up a fraction of an inch.

"Yes, he, ah, he said a customer became very angry about something he'd bought here, paint I think. Richard said the man became abusive with one of the clerks, Todd, and finally Richard asked the man to leave."

"He did?" Arthur's eyebrows went up another notch.

"Didn't you know about that?" Lauren felt a small knot of apprehension in her stomach. Had she spoken out of turn, telling Arthur something that Richard had decided he shouldn't know?

"I wasn't here yesterday," Arthur said offhandedly. "Actually, I haven't been here since last Thursday. Betty and I took a little spur-of-the-moment vacation and stayed with her sister in Palm Springs. She married money, you know. But about what you were saying—

Richard didn't tell me, no one did, so it was probably nothing." He shrugged his shoulders. "We occasionally get kooks in here, just like everyplace else."

"I understand," Lauren said, but a tiny voice nagged from the back of her mind: Why hadn't Richard told Arthur? The incident had certainly upset him, so she doubted that it was "probably nothing," as Arthur believed. And there was something else that troubled her, something she couldn't quite put her finger on.

Arthur cocked his head to one side. "Is anything wrong?"

Lauren forced a smile and looked at her watch. "No, not at all, but I'd better be getting back to work." She stood awkwardly.

"Thanks for stopping in," Arthur said. "And don't be a stranger at our house. Betty loves to see Emily. I think she thinks of her as a grandchild."

Lauren smiled, sincerely this time. "I promise." She paused in the doorway. She hadn't planned on taking this any farther than Arthur. But she still didn't know how serious the customer's threats toward Richard had been. "Is, ah, is Todd here today?" she asked.

"Todd? Yes, I saw him out there a minute ago cutting a key for someone."

Todd was no longer at the key-duplicating machine, so Lauren moved through the store looking for him. She spotted Richard near the far wall, talking to a man in a baseball cap. Then she saw Todd halfway down another aisle, unpacking a box of duct tape and stacking the rolls on a shelf.

"Todd?"

"Yes?" He straightened up.

"I'm Lauren Caylor." She paused, waiting for a response. When she got none, she added, "Richard's wife."

"Oh, Mrs. Caylor, hi, I mean, hello."

Lauren glanced beyond Todd to the far wall where her husband was still occupied with the man in the cap. She tried to think of a way to be circumspect with Todd and still find out what she wanted to know.

"Richard told me about the trouble yesterday," she said. "I'm sorry you had to miss part of a day's work."

"Excuse me?"

"I, ah, I just wanted you to know that I'm going to ask him if he'll pay you for a full day. I mean, for yesterday."

Todd smiled uneasily. "Well, okay, but . . ."

"Yes?"

"I *worked* all day yesterday."

"You did?"

Todd looked around for help, then spread his palms toward Lauren. "Yes," he said, shrugging his shoulders, as if in apology.

"Richard didn't send you home early?"

Todd shook his head, shuffling his feet and glancing around, obviously discomfited by these questions.

"He's right over there if you want to ask him," he offered.

"Maybe I misunderstood him." She'd spoken more to herself than to Todd. "It must have been someone else he sent home."

Again Todd shook his head. "No one got sent home."

"What about the clerk involved in the shoving match with a customer?"

"Shoving match?"

"You don't know about that?"

His eyes were wide with innocence. "No, nothing like that happened."

"You're certain?"

"Yes."

Lauren licked her lips. "Were you here all day?" she asked. She could hear the anxiety in her voice.

"Uh huh."

"What about lunch? Maybe it happened while you were gone."

"I brought my lunch and ate it in the back room. We were too busy for me to even take a whole hour."

Lauren hated this: verifying that Richard had lied. "And you're sure there was no customer in here yesterday who got in a big argument with a clerk or with Richard?"

"No way. But maybe you should ask Richard, I mean, Mr. Caylor."

Lauren felt sick inside. "Thanks, Todd. I'm sorry to have bothered you."

"Hey, no prob*lem*-o."

Lauren had difficulty concentrating on work the rest of the afternoon. She'd gone to the hardware store to find out the seriousness of the incident with the customer. She'd even been prepared to talk

Richard into going to the police if the customer's threats warranted it. But there had been no threats, no unruly customer. Richard had invented the entire incident.

And there was another fabrication, one Lauren hadn't realized until now. Richard had said he left the store in Arthur's care last Friday while he spent two hours in Los Angeles checking on their new neighbors. But Arthur hadn't even been in town—he and Betty had been in Palm Springs.

Lauren's stomach felt like a clenched fist. Why was Richard lying to her?

11

LAUREN AND EMILY arrived home earlier than usual that evening. Purposely. Lauren was determined to find out about the man in the restaurant.

She knew she'd raised a few eyebrows at work by taking a long lunch hour and then leaving for home at four-thirty instead of five. No one had said anything, but that didn't mean they hadn't noticed—city employees were notoriously aware of the clock. Even Emily's teacher had commented that Lauren was early.

Now Lauren checked her watch: Richard was due home in twenty minutes. She put Emily to play in her room, made sure Amos was in the house, then locked the front door on her way out.

She walked to the end of the driveway, peering across the street.

The sun, low behind her, harshly lit the house and yard of Hal and Monica Ipswich. The drapes were closed but slightly parted, as they had been for days. Lauren could see only darkness in the narrow slit. Yet she had the feeling either Hal or Monica was there, watching her.

She hoped it was Hal.

She wanted to see him up close. She wanted to know if he was the man they'd seen in Tobey's restaurant, the man who had so obviously upset Richard. If he was, Lauren already knew what she'd say to him: "Stay away from me and my husband or I'll call the police."

Simple, direct. She'd even pictured herself standing toe-to-toe with Hal Ipswich (who would look exactly like the man in the restaurant) and laying it on with a stern tone, while he blinked and backed off, mumbling apologies.

However, she'd imagined this scenario before she visited the hardware store. Then she'd still believed the man in question was a loudmouth who didn't like the color of his paint. Now she had no idea *who* she'd be confronting. Except that he was someone Richard seemed to fear.

Lauren crossed the street, trying to ignore the weak feeling in her knees.

The front yard looked worse up close than it had from across the street. The lawn had deteriorated into dead brown areas and clumps of sickly green crabgrass. Bordering the driveway were the remnants of flower beds that once had been Madge Grey's pride and joy—now little more than dirt and weeds.

Lauren studied the bushes along the house, certain now that they'd been trimmed in front of the window and nowhere else. Cut branches lay scattered on the ground, drying in the sun.

Lauren walked up the driveway to the side of the house.

The door was in the shade of the carport. The carport was empty, but Lauren had the feeling somebody was home. She hesitated, then pushed the doorbell, hearing faint chimes inside. All at once she had the urge to get away from there, to hurry across the street to the safety of her own house.

Toughen up, she told herself.

She pressed the bell firmly, holding it down, listening to the chimes repeat their faint, four-note tune. Her mouth felt dry as she tried to think of what to say when Hal Ipswich answered the door. Nice to meet you, why are you scaring my husband?

But no one answered.

She leaned her head to the screen door and listened. She thought she heard something—or had it been merely her hair brushing against the screen?

She stepped back and scanned the windows on the side of the house. The drapes were closed tight. To her right, between the house and the brick wall at the end of the carport, a six-foot-high redwood gate blocked the way to the backyard.

Lauren hesitated, glancing around. The neighborhood was quiet except for the tittering of birds and a dog barking in the distance. There were no cars in the street, no pedestrians on the sidewalk. She checked her watch again. Richard would be home in fifteen minutes, perhaps sooner.

Lauren took a deep breath, stepped to the gate, and lifted the latch. She pushed open the gate, having no idea what she was looking for or what she expected to find.

What she did *not* expect was a dark blue car. It was parked on the ruined lawn beyond the swimming pool, and it looked very much like the one she'd imagined was following her.

Tiny hairs rose on the nape of her neck.

It's probably just a coincidence, she told herself. There are thousands of cars like this one.

She closed the gate behind her and quickly scanned the rear of the house. The back door and all the windows were closed tight, the windows shielded by drapes. But it wasn't the house that interested her now—it was the car.

She moved around the swimming pool. It was covered with a green plastic tarp that rested on floats in the water and was speckled with fallen leaves. The surrounding yard was dried out and weedy. Only now did Lauren notice that a portion of the high redwood fence had been removed, apparently so the car could be driven in from the alley.

She bent down to peer through the car's side windows. The inside was empty—no loose articles on the seats or the floorboards. No paperback book like the one hiding the face of the man in the municipal building's parking lot.

Lauren walked around the car. The emblem on the trunk lid identified it as a Plymouth Reliant. She examined the ground. Dried grass and weeds were matted with tire tracks, as if the car had been in and out of the yard a number of times. And the ground on either side showed signs that more than one car had been parked here.

Lauren stepped to the opening in the fence and looked up and down the alley. Like the one that ran behind her house, it was paved with concrete, bordered by privacy fences, and overhung with tree limbs from backyards. The boards that had been removed from the fence were stacked nearby.

Weird, she thought. Why would someone open the fence to park back here when they have a carport?

Suddenly she felt anxious to get out of the yard and away from the house. She hurried past the car and the swimming pool and headed for the gate. She reached for the latch.

A car door slammed.

The sound came from the carport, not ten feet from where Lauren stood, hidden from view by the redwood gate.

She held perfectly still, afraid to make the slightest sound, afraid even to breathe. She prayed that whoever had just driven up would go into the house and close the door, allowing her to slip unseen through the gate and hurry home across the street. Her original plan to confront Hal Ipswich was abandoned. Now she just wanted to get out of there.

She waited for the sound of the side door.

Silence—except for the ticking of the cooling car engine on the other side of the gate. Slowly Lauren leaned forward, putting her eye near the narrow space between the redwood boards. She saw no one, only the brown front fender of the car and a slice of windshield.

And then her view was blocked by someone approaching the gate. Lauren jumped back at the sound of the latch being thrown, and she nearly ran for the alley. The gate swung open.

The man standing before her wore a mixed expression of surprise and anger. His brown hair was curly on top and cut close on the sides. He was about Richard's age, Lauren judged, although taller and more strongly built, athletic-looking even under his yellow golf shirt and tan linen sport coat. One thing was certain, though—he was not the man she and Richard had seen in the restaurant last night.

"What are *you* doing back here?" he demanded.

"I'm terribly sorry," she said, forcing herself to be calm. "I didn't mean to trespass. I thought perhaps someone was back here and couldn't hear me ring the bell."

The man stood unmoving, blocking the gateway.

"My, uh, my name is Lauren. Richard and I live right across the street . . ."

The man watched her closely, saying nothing.

"We, ah, well, we wanted to welcome you to the neighborhood." She winced inwardly, knowing how lame that must have sounded. The man nodded, however, apparently accepting her explanation.

"Thanks," he said, his face neutral.

Then he stepped aside, holding the gate for her. As she went past

81

him, she smelled the faint, sour mixture of sweat and after-shave. She moved between the car and the house, forcing herself not to run. At the door of the house she hesitated. It was open, and a woman stood just inside, staring at Lauren through the screen. She wore baggy shorts and a sweatshirt with the sleeves cut off at the elbows. Her blond hair was pulled back over her ears.

Lauren realized now that the woman had been in the house all along. She should have *known* someone was home when she saw the blue car parked in back.

"It's Lauren Caylor," the man said, making Lauren start, he was so close behind her.

Lauren nodded hello.

The woman smiled, but Lauren sensed her uneasiness.

"I hope Hal didn't frighten you," she said, perhaps reading Lauren's expression. "I'm Monica Ipswich."

"Pleased to meet you. I, that is, my husband and I want to welcome you to the neighborhood."

Monica nodded, her smile fixed in place.

Lauren felt obliged to speak, searched for words, blurting, "Perhaps we can get together sometime for dinner."

Monica lost her smile. "Well . . ."

"Of course," Hal said, still standing close behind her.

Although neither of them had said or done anything to threaten her, Lauren was filled with trepidation. She felt weak beside them, inferior. She sensed that they were stronger than she—and not merely physically stronger.

"Well, ah, I'll see you later," Lauren said, edging away from them, then hurrying down the driveway and across the street to her home.

Richard stood in the front doorway, frowning. Lauren was relieved to see him. She put one arm around his waist.

"Did you just get home?"

He nodded, unsmiling. "What were you doing over there?"

"Boy." She shook her head. "Those people are creepy."

"You talked to them?"

"Briefly. Come on, let's go in."

She took his hand, and half led, half pulled him inside, away from the door. He stopped, still holding her hand—gently but firmly. Lauren turned to face him. His expression made her uneasy.

"What were you doing over there?" he asked again, insistent.

"I wanted to see them face-to-face because . . ." Because you lied to me about the unruly customer, she thought, and I wanted to see if Hal Ipswich was the man in the restaurant. "Because you seemed worried about them," she said. "And I was too. Well, maybe not worried so much as curious. So I went over and . . . introduced myself."

Richard let go of her hand. "What did you tell them about me?"

"What?" She was taken aback. She tried a smile. "Nothing. I just welcomed them to the neighborhood."

Richard's eyes searched her face. "What's *that* supposed to mean?"

"Hey, Richard, come on, lighten up."

"I want to know what you talked about, Lauren, what you told them about us. About me."

There was a tone in Richard's voice that Lauren had not heard before—something between urgency and anger. It frightened her. When she spoke, it was with a forced calm.

"Richard, I went there to find out about them, because they seemed to worry you. I . . . wanted to see if Hal Ipswich was the man we saw in Tobey's."

"Is he?" Richard asked quickly.

Lauren shook her head. "No."

Richard nodded almost imperceptibly, and he seemed to sag, as if the air had gone out of him. Lauren touched his arm.

"Honey, what *are* you worried about?"

He met her eyes briefly. "Nothing." His voice was dull, defeated. He turned away from her.

In the bedroom Lauren began changing clothes, trying hard not to slam drawers. She was frustrated by Richard's reluctance to talk to her. And yet she remained hesitant about pressuring him. She feared a confrontation. She'd had too many confrontations with Paul—before their divorce.

She pulled on sweatpants and thought about Hal and Monica Ipswich.

A strange couple. She remembered feeling weak in their presence, as if they were somehow superior to her. And suddenly she thought she knew why—it was some of the things Hal had said.

For one, when he introduced her to Monica, he hadn't said, "This is Lauren Caylor," he'd said, "It's Lauren Caylor." It was as if he understood that Monica already knew there was someone snooping in the backyard—as if she'd been *watching* her.

For another, Lauren hadn't told them her last name, but they both seemed to know it.

And there was something Hal had said earlier that hadn't sounded right. When he first opened the back gate, he'd said, "What are you doing back here?" His emphasis, though, had been on the wrong word—not on "doing," a more likely response to finding a stranger in his backyard. He'd emphasized "you," as if Lauren weren't a stranger at all, but someone he knew well:

"What are *you* doing back here?"

12

THEY SAT in relative silence.

Lauren had baked a chicken and boiled several ears of corn, while Richard set the table and made a salad. He'd apologized for acting suspicious and angry toward her. She'd accepted, nodding. He'd apologized again just before dinner, this time holding her, letting her look into his eyes so she'd know he really meant it. They'd kissed.

But Lauren was still apprehensive. She was waiting, hoping, for Richard to explain his uneasiness about the man in the restaurant and the new neighbors. And then finally, while they ate, he asked about Hal and Monica.

"What do they look like?"

He spoke in what Lauren assumed was supposed to be an offhand manner. But she could detect a quiet intensity in his voice. Maybe this is it, she hoped. Maybe now we can get it all in the open.

She placed half an ear of corn on Emily's plate next to a drumstick.

"Let's see," she said. "Hal is average-looking, I guess—not handsome, not ugly, with curly brown hair. He wore a sport coat and a yellow shirt. He's in his early thirties, I'd say, close to six feet tall. I'm not sure about his weight, but he's pretty big, husky, as if he works out.

"Monica is his age or younger, blond hair, probably long—it was pinned up in back. She was standing in the doorway, a step higher than I was, so I'm not sure about her height, but I'd guess about average, not short or tall. She's attractive, in a plain sort of way, if you know what I mean, and she's in good physical condition like Hal, so maybe she works out too."

Richard was watching her closely, his hands resting on the table on either side of his plate.

"Do I have to eat *this,* Mommy?" Emily pointed at the handle end of the drumstick.

"No, hon. Do you want another drumstick? Or a breast?"

"Drumstick, please."

Lauren set it on her plate.

"Did they ask about me, about us?"

"No."

"What were they like? I mean, how did they act?"

"Odd." Lauren cut a small piece of chicken breast and chewed it slowly. "It's hard to describe, the way they looked at me, as if they were *examining* me. And they seemed to know who I was before I told them. They knew our last name."

Richard waited. "Anything else?"

Lauren was embarrassed to admit that she'd been snooping in their backyard. But she felt it was important that she tell Richard everything—if she expected him to do likewise. However, she didn't want him to make a scene in front of Emily.

"Yes," she said. She held his eyes for a moment, then looked at Emily, munching her drumstick.

"Go ahead," Richard said quietly, "tell me."

Lauren described the Ipswiches' backyard, the opening in the fence . . . and the dark blue car.

"I think I've seen that car before," she said. "Following me from work."

"*Wha*—?" Richard made a visible effort to control himself. He glanced at Emily, then faced Lauren. "Are you certain?" His voice was low, strained.

"No, I'm not certain." She told him about seeing the dark blue car several times in the past few days. "I'm not even sure it's the same car. And it may not even have been fol—"

"Did you see the driver?"

Lauren shrugged. "A man."

"Hal Ipswich?"

"I couldn't tell. But why would Hal Ipswich want to follow me?"

Richard stood abruptly and walked into the living room.

"Richard?"

"Mommy, I'm finished."

Lauren stared at the empty doorway before turning to Emily. "Okay, honey." She dabbed at her daughter's face with a napkin, then helped her out of her chair.

"Can I play with Amos in the backyard?"

Lauren had a partial view of the yard through the kitchen doorway and window. The sun was below the rooflines, but there was still at least an hour of light.

"Okay, but just for a little while."

Emily hurried off, calling for Amos. Lauren picked up the empty plates, hesitated, then set them down and stepped to the living room doorway. Richard stood by the front window, peeking through the drapes, as if he were a child keeping an eye out for the bogeyman. It would be comical, Lauren thought, if he were someone other than her husband. She watched him a moment longer, then quietly returned to the dining room and began clearing the table.

Lauren rinsed the dishes, set them in the dishwasher, and poured powdered soap into the small receptacle. She swung the door closed and turned on the machine. It came to life with a deep humming noise. Lauren put her hand on the enameled surface, feeling the vibration, faint evidence of the maelstrom within.

Like Richard, she thought.

When she returned to the living room, Richard was still beside the window. He'd pulled over a stuffed chair and was sitting on the arm, holding the drapes open a few inches with his right hand. He didn't notice Lauren standing behind him.

"Richard?" she said quietly.

His head snapped around. His eyes frightened her.

"What's going on?" she asked.

He seemed unwilling to face her, turning back to the split in the drapes.

"Richard."

He mumbled something that she didn't understand. She stood there for a full minute, waiting. Finally he lowered his hand and let the drapes fall back into place. He hung his head, staring down at his shoes, keeping his back to her, as if he wanted her to leave him alone.

She had no intention of leaving.

"What are you afraid of?" she asked him gently.

He straightened up, still seated, still with his back to her, and shook his head. Again he said something too softly for Lauren to understand.

"What did you say?"

Now he turned his head sideways, still not looking at her, and spoke too loudly: "I *said*—" He continued quietly, "I said, 'Nothing.' I'm not afraid of anything."

"Like hell."

He looked at her now, one corner of his mouth turned up in a faint grin, as if her response had surprised him, perhaps even pleased him. But the look was soon gone.

"Truly," he said, as if he meant it this time, "I'm not afraid of anything."

He stood, but made no move to leave the room.

"Talk to me, Richard." She was careful not to demand. And not to beg. "Tell me what's going on."

"Nothing's going on."

He started past her, and when she reached for his arm, he pulled it away. She felt anger well up inside her.

"Dammit, Richard, this isn't fair."

"I'm telling you there's nothing," he said, walking away.

"You lied to me."

She'd almost shouted it, and it stopped him, even at that distance, near the hallway leading to the bedrooms. He turned and faced her, waiting.

"You lied to me about the customer in the hardware store." Her face felt flushed, the blood pounding at her temples.

Suddenly she was struck by a childhood memory. She'd been a little girl, not much older than Emily, and she'd pushed her bicycle to the top of a steep dirt hill, one used by her older brother and some of his friends. A hill forbidden to little girls. No one else was around, and she stood alone for long minutes in the late-afternoon sun gazing down at what appeared to be a straight drop to the bottom, fifty feet below. She'd seen the older boys ride down this hill, whooping and hollering all the way, but she'd never dared take the plunge. Now, though, she was ready. She swallowed hard, climbed on her bike, and then without thinking, without giving herself a chance to change her mind, pushed over the edge. She immediately hit a bump and her feet slipped off the pedals, and all she could do was fight for her life to stay in the seat and hang on to the handlebars as the ground rushed beneath her and the wind whipped her hair. She was heading in the direction she'd intended, but the situation was beyond her control and she had no idea how it would end.

Lauren felt that way now, facing Richard.

"There was no incident in the store," she said. "No unruly customer. You made it all up."

For a moment Richard looked ready to give in. Then he set his jaw and asked her evenly, "What makes you say that?"

"I found out today. I asked Arthur and Todd and they—"

"You did *what*?" he said, raising his voice, coming toward her.

She winced, but held her ground.

"I'm not the one who's wrong here, Richard."

He stopped in front of her, his expression hard, as if ready to defend himself, to firmly maintain his position.

"I want to know what this is all about," Lauren said quietly.

Slowly his look softened. Then he turned from her, walked to the couch, and sat down. He leaned forward, forearms on his knees, hands clasped before him, staring at the floor. Lauren sat beside him, not touching him, waiting for him to speak. When he did not, she raised her hand to place it on his back.

"It has to do with . . . a woman," Richard said.

Lauren's hand stopped in midair. The last thing she'd expected— the last thing she'd *wanted*—was another woman.

"It happened before I met you," he said, still staring at the floor. "I met this woman—her name doesn't matter—in a bar here in San Miguel, a place I sometimes used to go. We began seeing each other, either in bars or my apartment—never her house. She, well, spent the night with me a few times. She was secretive about herself, her personal life. I should have sensed that something was wrong." He paused. "She was married."

He sat back and looked at Lauren, waiting for her to respond. Lauren feared the worst, that he'd resumed seeing this woman. She said nothing.

"Anyway," Richard continued, looking away, "her husband found out about us. He showed up at my apartment one night when she was there. He had a gun."

"My God."

"*That's* when I found out she was married. I thought he was going to kill us both. He threatened us for a while, then broke down and cried. She left with him. That was the last time I ever saw her."

"If you never saw her again, then what—"

"I never saw *her,* but I saw *him* a number of times. He was insanely jealous. He'd hired a private detective to follow his wife. That's how he'd found us in the first place. But he didn't stop there—he followed me around for months. I guess he thought I was still seeing his wife, and from what I learned from other people who knew about her, she probably prodded him into doing it. You see, that's how she got her kicks—doing things to make her husband jealous. That was the only reason she'd come on to me to begin with—to get at him, to *toy* with him. She'd just been playing a game with him *and* with me. The problem was, he didn't know the game was over. In fact, it wasn't a game to him. It was real."

Richard sighed and shook his head.

"He harassed me for months afterward. He'd found out where I lived and worked. He would call me at all hours of the night, threatening to kill me if he ever again caught me with his wife."

"Didn't you tell him it was over between you two?"

"Sure I told him, plenty of times. But either he didn't listen, or he didn't want to listen. Or else he was listening to her, and God only knows what lies she was whispering in his ear." Richard turned to Lauren. "He used to follow me home from work at night, park in front of my apartment. It was . . . insane."

"Did you report him to the police?"

"How could I? What could I say? 'I had an affair with this man's wife and he's not happy about it'? No, I figured the best thing to do was to wait him out. Eventually he'd grow bored and quit. And he did. At least I thought he had until last night."

"The man in the restaurant."

Richard nodded. "I'm pretty sure it was him, and he was looking for someone. Realistically, though, I doubt he was looking for me. It's been several years since I've seen him, and who knows how many other men his wife has played her little game with during that time. But sitting there with you and Emily and suddenly seeing this face from the past . . . well, it was shocking. I wasn't thinking logically. And when you asked me what was wrong . . . I don't know, I guess I just said the first thing that came into my mind. Actually, there *had* been a customer I'd had some trouble with—of course, nothing like I described to you."

He put his hand on hers.

"I should never have lied to you," he said. "But at the time, it seemed like too much to . . . confess. I'm ashamed of what happened back then."

Richard's story was upsetting to her, but it did explain a few things. Not everything, though.

"Why are you concerned about Hal and Monica Ipswich?" she asked. "Are they the couple you're talking about?"

"No, not exactly. I thought . . ." He smiled sheepishly. "I thought they might be private detectives hired by—"

"What?"

"—hired by the husband." He read the skepticism in her face and went on quickly. "You don't know the lengths that man went to to make my life miserable. I'm serious—he'd spare no expense."

"But to have detectives rent a house across the street?"

"I know it sounds crazy and, well, I guess it *is* crazy. I was so afraid the husband might interfere with our lives—yours, mine, and Emily's—that I wasn't thinking straight. Anyway, Lauren," he said, moving his hand gently up her arm, "I'm so sorry I lied to you. I wanted to pretend that portion of my life had never happened. I love you so much, and I don't want *anything* to come between us. Without you and Emily I . . . I don't know what I'd do." He paused, his eyes moist. "I hate that I lied to you."

There was no question in her mind that he meant it. The problem was, she hated it too. A trust had been broken. How long before it could be reestablished? Still, Lauren knew her love for him had not diminished.

He put his arm around her and kissed her. "Will you forgive me?"

What could she say? "Of course."

Later that night Richard tried to make love to her. He was gentle and warm, but she couldn't respond—even if she'd wanted to. Troubling thoughts fluttered at the edge of her mind, demanding her attention.

Finally Richard stopped, kissing her forehead, touching her breast, then rolling over. Soon he was asleep.

Lauren lay awake, replaying Richard's story. Somehow it didn't ring true.

Naturally, she'd been startled, even distressed, by his past involvement with a married woman and a jealous husband. She never could have imagined him in such a situation. Of course, anything was possible. But his explanation of how he'd met the woman, practically picking her up in a bar, didn't seem likely at all.

When Lauren had met Richard, he'd been shy, almost withdrawn. She couldn't picture him hanging out in bars, picking up women.

All right then, she told herself, maybe he's changed, maybe he was different then, more extroverted.

But she didn't believe that, any more than she believed that Hal and Monica Ipswich were private detectives spying on them. She wondered if Richard had ever believed it himself. . . .

This thought filled her with dread. For if Richard was lying about that, then he was probably lying about everything else. And if this was so, how could she *ever* trust him? How could there be a marriage without trust?

Lauren squeezed her eyes shut, trying not to believe that this was happening to her again—another doomed marriage. She even found herself attempting to justify Richard's lies: He's protecting me from something.

But from what?

13

IT WAS Tuesday night in Chicago, and an unseasonably cold wind blew off Lake Michigan. Peter Grummund walked out of his apartment with his double chins tucked into his coat collar and his hands shoved deep in his pockets. He gave a final tug to the brim of the hat that covered his round head and thinning black hair.

He'd just received a call from Novek. The younger man had given him the number of a pay phone in L.A. and then hung up, waiting for Grummund to find a pay phone of his own. They had to be careful. Phones could be tapped.

Grummund walked past the barbershop where he'd used the phone the last time he spoke with Novek. Two blocks later he eased his bulk into a phone booth on the corner in front of a deli. He'd hoped it would be warmer in the booth than it was outside. It wasn't.

At least it's out of the wind, he thought, dropping in a quarter. He gave the number to the operator, then pumped in more quarters, listening to them rattle into the box and clang a dull bell in his ear.

Novek answered by saying, "Yeah?"

"What took you so long?" Grummund asked him. He hadn't heard from him since Friday and this was Tuesday and it didn't take four days to get from Albuquerque, New Mexico, to Los Angeles, California, unless you were riding a bicycle. He smiled at the mental image of Novek trying to balance his weight on the skinny frame and wobbly tires of a ten-speed.

"Hey, Pete, give me a break. I haven't just been sitting around, you know."

No, Grummund thought, I don't know.

In the old days he would've known, but he'd been out of touch with him for four years and people change. He didn't know what Novek was like now. This bothered him greatly because he needed help and Novek was the only person he could use. On the other hand, he knew the man must have retained at least some of his former loyalty, or he never would have called in the first place.

"So, did you find him?" Grummund asked, getting to the point.

"I found him."

"Was he where my informant said he would be?" From the beginning Grummund had been dubious about the source of the information, to say nothing of the information itself. It had seemed almost too good to be true.

"Exactly. Him and his wife and kid, a little girl."

Grummund paused, considering this. "Are you sure it's him?"

"Oh, it's him, all right. He looks a little different, but not too much. I'd recognize that traitor anywhere."

Grummund could hear the murderous undertone in Novek's voice. He was satisfied—and perhaps a bit fearful—that that part of him hadn't changed.

"Get this," Novek said. "He works in a hardware store."

"You're kidding me."

"Swear to God. His wife works, too, for the city of San Miguel, and the kid goes to school at—"

"Wait a minute," Grummund said. "Are you telling me you've been following them?"

"Of course I've been following them. How else would—"

"Goddammit, Novek!" he shouted. "I told you to find him and that was all!"

"Take it easy," Novek said evenly.

Grummund opened his mouth to shout again, then checked himself. He'd sensed the veiled anger in Novek's voice. The man had objected to being reprimanded. Grummund wondered how much of a problem this would be in the future. He hoped things would be different when they were standing face-to-face. But until he got to the West Coast, Grummund knew, he'd have to treat Novek more carefully, as if the man were an overgrown adolescent. Which in some ways he was.

"All I'm saying," Grummund said matter-of-factly, "is that he might have spotted you tagging along behind."

"He didn't."

"But he might have. And if he did, everything would be off. Do you understand?"

"Listen, Pete, even if he saw me, he wouldn't know it was me. *You* wouldn't recognize me now."

Grummund doubted that, but he let it pass. "You stay away from him, though, until I get out there, okay?"

"When is that going to be?" Novek said, not making any promises.

"Not until the weekend, after my meeting with the government flunky. If I miss it, he'll know something's up, and I want as much lead time as possible."

"What am I supposed to do until then?"

Novek thought for a moment. "Have you got a gun?"

"No."

"We'll need two."

"Okay, I'll handle it."

"If it's a problem," Grummund said, "I can get what we need here, but that would mean carrying them in my suitcase, and even if

93

I check it through, the airlines are X-raying everything these days. They're worried about the goddamn terrorists."

"I said I'd handle it."

"All right, just be careful."

"Hey, Pete, you know me."

The problem is, I don't, Grummund thought, not the way I used to. "Just . . . don't take any unnecessary chances," he said. He'd nearly said, "Don't do anything stupid," because that's exactly what he was afraid the man might do—do something stupid and ruin everything. Novek might even try to handle the entire operation on his own. Although Grummund doubted that—he'd told Novek there was a lot of money involved, but he'd given him few other details.

"I'll see you in a few days," Grummund said. "Stay out of San Miguel until then, all right?"

Novek grunted and hung up without saying good-bye.

Grummund pushed out of the phone booth and walked back toward the apartment. He wondered if *he* was the one being stupid, if it might be smarter to just forget about this entire operation and stay in Chicago where he belonged.

And do what? he thought. Grow old and die poor?

He blinked involuntarily against a cold gust of wind and shoved his fists deeper into his pockets. He wondered what the weather was like in San Miguel.

14

THE NEXT MORNING Lauren had difficulty concentrating on her work. She tried to focus on the drawing before her, but her mind kept searching for reasons why Richard might be lying to her. Mentally she pushed around the few facts she had, attempting to fit them together like pieces of a puzzle. Richard's paranoia. The man in the restaurant. Hal and Monica Ipswich. Even the dark blue car she'd seen behind her, and the possibility that it was the same car parked in the Ipswiches' backyard.

She came up with a number of wild theories—including the wildest, that Richard was a foreign spy hiding in San Miguel—but none of them seemed very likely.

Maybe it was as he'd said: The man in the restaurant bore a strong resemblance to a jealous husband Richard had crossed paths with several years ago. And Hal and Monica Ipswich? They were just oddballs who'd happened to move in across the street.

There was something else to consider, though. Hal and Monica had moved in on the *same day* that Lauren had noticed the dark blue car. And a few nights later Richard had spotted the man in Tobey's restaurant. Could all that be a coincidence?

At ten to twelve Susan Aikens stepped into Lauren's cubicle, startling her. She'd been staring unseeing at her drawing, wrestling with her thoughts.

"A bunch of us are going to that new restaurant on Esplanade," Susan said. "Do you want to come along?"

Lauren nearly said no—she wasn't in the mood for socializing. But she wanted to break out of the funk she'd wrapped herself in.

"Sounds good." She grabbed her purse.

She and Susan rode with Jack Malone, a drafter who worked for Susan, and a man and woman from the planning department whom Lauren knew only by name. Another car filled with city employees followed close behind. Lauren sat by the right-side window in the backseat, gazing at the passing streets and buildings, removing herself from the conversation in the car. When Jack Malone steered into a parking lot, Lauren snapped out of her reverie. Outside, Susan asked her, "Are you all right?"

"Yes, sorry, I was just thinking about something."

Casa Grande had only been open for several weeks, but Lauren realized she and Richard had eaten there before, almost a year ago. At that time the place had been called Tico's—something of a dive, with flyspecked windows, rickety chairs, and a scratched wooden floor. The food, though, had been excellent and the prices low. Now the interior had a new look: plenty of fresh stucco, ornate wrought iron, terra-cotta pots with luscious plants, even carpeting. Lauren hoped they hadn't remodeled the menu too.

She and the others waited while busboys pushed together small tables, then made them up with white tablecloths, linen napkins, and silverware. Lauren sat between Susan and Jack.

"I haven't seen you for a while," Jack said. "How have you been?"

Jack was in his fifties, a small black man with a shiny bald spot. He'd been a draftsman on and off for thirty years. "My day job," he'd once told Lauren. On weekends he played bass in a small nightclub in San Diego.

"Just fine. What've you been up to?"

"No good." He smiled, showing yellow-white teeth. "What do the powers that be have you working on?"

"The new park project. Decker Park."

"*Decker* Park?" several people said in unison, heads turning toward Lauren.

"Hey, *I* didn't name it," Lauren said, smiling, and everyone laughed.

This started a lively discussion about Mayor Decker's shady dealings. They all had a favorite story to relate, usually something they'd heard thirdhand.

By the time the food arrived, the conversation had fragmented into small groups. Lauren found herself sitting between two: the discussion on her left concerned the perils of Japanese investments in California real estate; the one on her right dealt with the best way to make green chili.

Lauren took a bite of her cheese enchilada. It hadn't been in the oven long enough, and the sauce tasted as if it had come from a can. She hoped Tico was operating another nice dive somewhere.

She gazed idly across the restaurant. It was very crowded now, with people standing and sitting on padded benches near the front entrance, waiting for tables. More people sat at the bar or stood between stools with drinks in their hands. Lauren let her eyes drift over the faces of strangers.

Then she stopped, suddenly alert.

At the end of the bar sat a man she recognized: dark hair, average height and build, wearing khaki pants and a windbreaker. He was the same man she and Richard had seen in Tobey's Monday night.

Lauren gripped the edge of the table. Although the man was facing in her direction, she couldn't tell if he was actually looking at her—he was too far away. Then he twisted on the barstool, turning his shoulder to her.

"See someone you know?" Susan asked.

Lauren had been leaning slightly forward, staring past Susan. Now she sat back, blocking her view of the man—and her exposure to him.

"I . . . no."

The bill had arrived and was being passed around, everyone trying to determine who owed what, including tax and tip. Lauren was only vaguely aware that she'd left most of her food untouched. She dug some bills from her purse and added them to the communal pile.

She eyed the bar.

The man still sat sideways to her, allowing her to study his face in profile. He appeared to be in his late thirties or early forties. Even at this distance Lauren could see gray at his temple. He picked up his beer glass, took a sip, then set it down—someone on his lunch hour waiting patiently for a vacant table.

No, Lauren thought with conviction, he's here because *I'm* here. Could he be the jealous husband Richard described?

Everyone was standing to leave.

Lauren fell into line as they moved single file, snaking between tables, toward the end of the bar and the front door. She walked behind Susan, keeping her eyes on the man, passing within ten feet of him. He sat squarely at the bar, facing away from her now, seemingly unaware of her presence. Lauren held her breath, as if she were trying to sneak out behind his back.

This is stupid, she thought. It's just a coincidence. I've seen him in two restaurants in the past few days. People do eat out.

As she neared the door, she looked past him to the mirror on the wall, which reflected tiers of liquor bottles and the people at the bar. Lauren found the man in the row of faces.

His eyes were locked on hers.

He immediately looked away, and Lauren felt a jolt of fear. Then Jack Malone nearly ran into her from behind.

"Whoa, now," he said.

Lauren hurried out the door. On the way to the car she kept glancing back, waiting for the man to appear. A number of people walked out of Casa Grande, but not the dark-haired man. Lauren climbed into the car, and as it pulled from the lot, she looked through the rear window toward the restaurant entrance, expecting him to appear, fearing that he would. The car rounded a corner and the restaurant disappeared from sight.

Lauren spent the rest of the afternoon on her second drawing of the proposed park. She carefully laid down lines with her colored pens, but her mind was not on her work. Just before five o'clock she realized that she'd been redrawing the *first* design, the one she'd already completed. Everything she'd done today amounted to no more than a worthless duplication.

She uttered a word under her breath that she was not accustomed to using, then switched off her drafting light and threw the cover over her table.

Lauren made sure that she left the building with a group of co-workers. She felt vulnerable, scrutinized, and she was afraid to be alone. When the people she'd walked out with began to separate, she hurried to her car, got in quickly, and locked the door.

Dammit, she thought, what's happening to me?

She'd never felt this way before—scared, but not knowing exactly what to fear, or even if she *should* be afraid.

No, she corrected herself, I *have* felt this way before.

She thought back to the summer before her eighth grade in Lincoln, Nebraska. Her parents had just sold their home and the three of them had moved across town to a smaller house. Lauren had not wanted to move. Her friends were all back *there*.

Her father had tried to explain: The house was too big for them now that her older sister was married and gone and her brother was . . . gone. But Lauren suspected the reason was money. A developer with plans for an apartment building had offered a substantial sum for several houses on the block. She knew her father was nearing his retirement, and his profit from selling the house would benefit them all.

But Lauren's main concern, her main worry, was starting the eighth grade in a new school.

She didn't know anyone. Worse, everybody else knew *everybody*. She was the new kid, alone in the classroom, in the hallways, in the schoolyard. She could feel their eyes on her, and sometimes (although perhaps her ears were playing tricks on her) she could hear them talking about her behind her back.

It was difficult for her to make friends. She wasn't exactly shy, but she was passive. In the past she'd always waited for people to approach her, and then accepted or, less often, rejected them. But here in the new school, no one approached her. At least not for a while. They were thirteen-year-old boys and girls with all the friends they wanted. That's how it seemed anyway.

During the first few months Lauren thought she'd rather die than go through another day of school. She was in a constant state of tension—so *aware* of herself. Before, at her old school and with her old friends, she'd been relaxed. She'd interacted with other people without even thinking about it. She'd just *done* it. The world had been something out there for her to experience and examine.

Here the world examined her.

She remembered thinking that at the old school *she* had the eyes. At the new school *they* had the eyes.

She became so aware of her actions—the way she walked and talked and carried her books—that she sometimes felt she was doing these things for the first time. She found herself concentrating on every movement, afraid to be spontaneous. As a result, she was continually stumbling over her words and dropping things on the floor.

She'd even begun to wonder who she really was. There was no doubt that she felt different than she had at her old school, but had she become a different person?

Eventually, as the weeks and months passed, she made acquaintances, and then friends. And by the end of the school year she was again comfortable, confident. She'd regained her composure and her assuredness, re-formed herself—but she'd changed. She couldn't precisely define the change, but she knew that this Lauren was not the old Lauren who'd finished the seventh grade at another school one year earlier. She didn't try to figure out whether the change was for better or worse. She just accepted it.

The main thing was, she'd "gotten back her eyes" and she could once again watch the world. However, from that time on she'd always been aware, at least vaguely, that the world was also watching her.

She started the Honda.

On the way to Emily's school and on the way home Lauren constantly checked the side-view and rearview mirrors. There were always cars behind her. And in a sense, she knew, they were all following her, all watching her.

15

LAUREN RAISED the garage door with the remote control and drove in, still feeling exposed, as if someone were scrutinizing her every move. She walked around the car and helped Emily unfasten her seat belt.

Suddenly, out of the corner of her eye, she saw a figure appear in the yawning doorway of the garage. She spun around, shielding Emily, her heart pounding and her body tense, ready to defend herself and her daughter.

"Hello." Connie stood just inside the garage, outlined in her muu-muu by the late-afternoon sun. "Oh, sorry, I didn't mean to startle you."

"Hi, Connie!" Emily cried.

"Hi, pumpkin."

Lauren let out her breath and smiled weakly, her heart still racing. "How are you?"

"Bursting with gossip." She glanced at Emily.

"Um, Emily, why don't you unlock the back door for me, okay?" Lauren handed her the key ring, sorting out the one for the house, then watched her leave through the garage's side door. When she turned toward Connie, she was met by an uncharacteristically wicked grin.

"I've been talking to Alice," Connie said, "and she—"

"Who's Alice?"

"You know Alice. Our mail carrier."

Lauren nodded, picturing a middle-aged woman with unruly black hair. She'd greeted her a few times, always on Saturdays, since she was usually at work when the mail was delivered. Although she knew nothing about the woman other than her first name, she wasn't surprised that Connie was on more intimate terms with her.

"Anyway," Connie continued, "yesterday I asked her about our new neighbors."

"Hal and Monica."

"Who else? I figured Alice had had a chance to see them—as the guy on TV used to say—up close and personal. Plus peeking at their mail."

"She reads people's mail?" Lauren didn't know whether to be amused or outraged.

"Not exactly." Connie folded her arms, then glanced behind her, as if she expected Hal and Monica to be watching from across the street. "Unless it's a postcard. But she's aware of return addresses, who gets bills from where, which catalogs and magazines everyone on her route receives, and so on. Plus, if something's going on inside the house while she's putting the mail in the box, she does it very quietly and very slowly, all the better to hear, my dear." Again she grinned devilishly. "You'd be surprised how much little old Alice knows about everyone in this neighborhood, including us."

"Great."

Connie's smile softened. "Believe me, she has nothing but good things to say about you and Richard."

"Oh, that makes me feel a *lot* better. So what did she say about Hal and Monica?"

"That's what's so strange—she had nothing at all to say about them."

"What do you mean?"

"She's never been near their house. They've yet to receive any mail."

Lauren saw Connie studying her face, waiting for a reaction. A car drove slowly down the street, but Lauren hardly noticed it.

"It's not too unusual, I suppose . . ."

"Are you serious?" Connie raised her eyebrows. "They've been in that house for nearly a week, and not one piece of mail, not even junk. Think about it. I'll bet you've received something every day this week. I have."

Although Lauren didn't quite see Connie's point, she was intrigued. "Perhaps they haven't yet changed their address with the post office."

Connie made a face. "Come on, that's the *first* thing people do when they move. They don't wait a week."

"I suppose . . . but it's possible no one's mailed them anything since they've moved."

"Sure, it's possible. That's why I asked Alice to check with the post office."

"You did what?"

"Yesterday, in fact. And you know what she told me today?"

Connie paused for effect, making Lauren wait.

"She said that officially—that is, according to the post office—no one is living in that house."

"What?"

"Right. On their records the house is listed as vacant. In other words, according to the U.S. Postal Service Hal and Monica Ipswich don't exist."

Lauren felt a tightening in the pit of her stomach. "What else did—"

"Mommy, I can't get it open."

Emily had come into the garage with Amos sauntering behind.

"Okay, baby, I'll be there in a minute." She returned her attention to Connie.

"That's all," Connie said. "I thought you'd be interested. Pretty weird, huh?"

Lauren nodded, saying nothing.

"I'm sure they're harmless," Connie said, "but let's keep an eye on them. Listen, I've got to go. I'll talk to you later."

Lauren led Emily and Amos to the back door, where her keys dangled from the lock. Amos didn't wait for them, but pushed ahead through his rubber dog door. Then he greeted them from the middle of the kitchen, wagging his tail and whining.

"Amos wants to go for a walk," Emily said.

Lauren didn't feel like walking, or even leaving the house. Connie's report had only upset her, and she wanted to be home when Richard arrived from work. They had to talk.

"Why don't you change clothes and play with him in the back-yard. I'll bet he'd like that."

"Okay. Come on, Amos!"

Emily hurried off to her bedroom. Amos stood rooted to the kitchen floor and gave Lauren a look that could only be interpreted as dissatisfaction.

"So make me feel guilty." She gave him a Milk-Bone. He carried it whole from the kitchen, apparently not wanting to display slob-bery gratitude in front of her.

Lauren washed up in the bathroom. She was changing into jeans and a pullover shirt, when she heard Richard arrive home. A few moments later he entered the bedroom.

"Hi." He kissed her. "I, ah, hope you didn't have any plans for us tonight." His grin was sheepish. "Arthur invited us over for dinner and I told him yes."

"Fine," she said, unsmiling.

"I'm sorry, I know I should have checked with you earlier, but he didn't mention it until we were closing the store."

"No, it's okay." Lauren realized that Richard was interpreting her manner as disapproval. This morning at breakfast she'd felt at odds with him. Now, though, she felt close to him, or at least she wanted desperately to. There was something . . . *out there* . . . something as yet undefined against which, she felt instinctively, they needed to be united. "It's just that . . . something happened today."

He put his hand on her shoulder, his face filled with concern. "Tell me."

"I saw that man again, the one who was in Tobey's Monday night."

Richard's mouth fell open. "Where did you see him? Around *here*?"

Lauren shook her head and described what had happened during lunch. She finished by saying, "It could have been a coincidence. I mean, the restaurant was jammed with people, and he—"

"Are you certain it was the same man?" Richard's voice was tight.

"I'm positive."

"Did he follow you out?"

"I don't think so. I watched the entrance until we'd driven out of sight and I didn't see him leave."

Richard was nodding, thinking. "When you were in the restau-rant, did you see him come in? Or could he have been there before you?"

"I didn't notice him until after we'd been seated, but I suppose he could've been in there all along."

Richard paused, calculating. "Maybe it *was* just a coincidence." He sounded as if he was trying to reassure himself.

"And if it wasn't?"

He looked away, refusing to speculate.

"It frightens me, Richard. If it wasn't a coincidence, then who is he and why is he—"

"How should I know?" he asked innocently, but there was fear in his eyes.

"Maybe we should notify the police."

"No," he said quickly. He paused, then continued more calmly, "No, I don't think that's necessary. Besides, what could we tell them? That you saw the same man in two different restaurants?"

"Are you telling me you're not concerned about this?"

"I suppose I am concerned, but—"

"Then why *shouldn't* we call the police?"

"*Because*—" He spoke loudly and then stopped, taking in a breath, lowering his eyes in apology. He reached out and drew Lauren to him. "Because there's nothing the police can do," he said quietly. "They have their limitations, and I don't think they can help us. What I mean is, this whole thing is probably just a coincidence and I don't think we need the police to be involved right now."

"Right now," Lauren repeated.

Richard's jaw tightened. "Yes." He pulled away from her, then made a display of looking at his watch. "I'd better get cleaned up. I told Arthur we'd be there by seven." He stepped past her toward the bathroom.

"There's something else you should know," Lauren said, stopping him. She waited until he turned toward her, his face grim. Then she repeated Connie's story: According to the post office the house across the street was vacant, and Hal and Monica Ipswich did not exist.

Richard licked his lips and shifted his eyes from Lauren to the floor and back again, searching for an explanation. Lauren was surprised at herself for feeling a morbid satisfaction at Richard's obvious discomfort, as if she'd scored a point and finally gotten him as upset as she was.

"You've probably noticed," she continued, "that they've done nothing to their yard since they moved in. It's as if they're not really *living* there, just . . . I don't know what. Oh yes, one of them did *some* trimming—the bushes by the front window. I think it's so they can have a clearer view of our house."

Richard opened his mouth but did not speak.

"They're watching us, aren't they?" Lauren said. She saw by his expression that he agreed, and for a moment she thought he was going to tell her something. Then his look changed.

"That's ridiculous." His voice was small. "I'm . . . going to wash up," he said, and walked away from her.

Lauren had hoped that discussing this with Richard would relieve tensions—within her and between them. But it hadn't. And worse, she sensed that Richard had withdrawn farther into himself.

She called Emily in from outside and helped her change into a rose-colored dress with white lace trim. Then she put on a skirt and blouse. Richard had dressed up—pearl-gray slacks, black loafers with tassels, and a navy-blue blazer—as if they were going to Sunday dinner at their parents' house.

There was a charged silence between them in the car.

Richard drove slowly away from the house. Lauren noticed him staring at the Ipswich residence. As usual, the front drapes were closed, except for a pitch-dark slit in the center.

Arthur and Betty McFadden lived in Royal Palms, a lush suburb that had grown from the southeast corner of San Miguel and now stretched for miles into the surrounding desert. The McFaddens' ranch-style home was fronted by surgically trimmed lawn and shrubbery. The green expanse was broken only by a flagstone walk that led from the driveway to the front door, illuminated by evenly spaced lamps set low to the ground.

Apparently, Arthur had heard their car, because he was holding open the door for them as they stepped onto the porch.

"Come in, come in," he said heartily, giving Richard a pat on the shoulder and Lauren a kiss on the cheek. "It's nice to see you again. And who's this young lady?" He stooped down before Emily, who giggled and blushed. "My goodness, it's Emily. How come you get prettier every time I see you?"

"I wore my newest dress," she explained.

Betty McFadden came into the living room brushing a wisp of gray hair from her forehead with the back of her hand. She wore a green apron over her blue print dress.

"Lauren, Richard, it's so nice to have you here. And hello, Emily, how are you?"

"I'm fine."

"My, don't you look pretty tonight."

"She wore her newest dress," Arthur said, as proudly as if Emily were their own grandchild.

"May I help you with something in the kitchen?" Lauren asked Betty.

"My goodness, no. That's one advantage of being retired. You have all day to prepare dinner. Arthur, why don't you show them where to sit?"

They all moved to the dining room table, which had been laid out with a soft white linen cloth, off-white china, and gleaming silverware that Lauren guessed was Betty's finest. Soon they were dining on veal in lemon sauce, rice, and leeks in butter.

The good food and conversation dissolved the tension between Lauren and Richard—at least temporarily. They both laughed easily when Arthur related his misadventures during his early days in the hardware business. Then Arthur and Richard briefly discussed the store hours for next Monday, Memorial Day. There was no question that they'd be open for business, but how late? Last year they'd stayed open until six, and they'd had to turn customers away. They decided on seven, and if they were busy enough to warrant it, they'd remain open until eight. Lauren only wished they'd close for the entire weekend so the three of them could get away for a while, but she said nothing.

When they finished their fresh fruit charlotte dessert, Arthur poured more coffee. Betty left the room for a moment. Richard smiled at Lauren from across the table and mouthed the words *I love you*. Before she could respond, Betty returned with a present wrapped in colorful paper.

"I know it's not your birthday or Christmas or anything like that," Betty said to Emily, carefully placing the box on the table before her, "but I want you to have this."

Emily's face glowed with excitement as she reached for the box. Then she stopped and looked toward her mother for permission.

Lauren nodded, smiling. "Go ahead."

Emily eagerly peeled off the wrapping paper and the lid, then paused, staring in wonder into the box. She reached in and gently lifted out a doll. Lauren saw that it was different from any of her others—old-fashioned, possibly an antique, but in excellent condition. Emily held the doll to her chest as if it were a long-lost child.

"*Thank* you!"

"My grandmother gave that to me when I was just about your age," Betty said. "She'd had it since she was a little girl."

"Oh, Betty . . ." Lauren started to protest, but Betty shook her head.

"Emily's old enough now to take care of this doll," Betty said. "Besides, it belongs in the arms of a girl, not hidden away in a dusty attic." She turned to Emily. "What do you think? Would you like to take her home with you?"

"Oh, yes!"

During the drive home, Richard and Lauren were quiet, content at least for the moment, his right hand resting on her leg, her hand on his arm. There were still things to be settled between them, Lauren knew, but she was feeling confident that it would happen sooner rather than later.

Emily sat in the backseat and talked to her doll, explaining how she was going to have a new home. Lauren turned and asked, "What's her name?"

"Cathy Ann," Emily said without hesitation.

Lauren thought for a moment. "Don't you already have a doll named Cathy?"

"Sure, but this is Cathy *Ann*."

"I see," she said, turning to Richard, smiling.

Richard wore a panicked expression. It was accentuated by a band of light across his face, a reflection from the rearview mirror. He flicked his eyes from the mirror to the road ahead and back to the mirror. His hands were white-knuckled fists on the steering wheel.

"Richard?"

When he answered her, his voice was low, barely audible.

"Someone's following us."

16

LAUREN TWISTED in her seat and stared out the rear window.

San Miguel Boulevard was well lit, and there was little traffic. The nearest set of headlights was almost a block behind them.

"That car's been behind us since we left Arthur and Betty's house," Richard said, his eyes on the rearview mirror.

"Are you sure?" Lauren turned forward and sat rigidly, staring out the windshield. "Maybe it's just someone driving in the same direction . . ."

"We'll find out."

Richard put on his signal, slowed the car, and turned right onto a residential street.

"Where are we going?"

"Around the block," he said.

"Is this our street?" Emily asked from the backseat.

"No, honey."

They drove along the quiet street. Behind the black foliage on both sides Lauren saw warm yellow lights seeping from the houses. She imagined the people inside, talking, laughing, listening to music.

"Here he comes." Richard's voice was tight, a mixture of fear and anger.

Lauren looked back in time to see a pair of headlights turning off the boulevard onto the street behind them. Richard continued to the end of the block and made a left turn. Before they reached the next intersection, Lauren saw that the car had again turned behind them. As she tried to control her growing fear, she was reminded of a silly joke she'd once heard about a psychiatrist's advice to paranoid patients: All those people who you *think* are following you are Hollywood talent scouts.

But this was no joke—a car really was following them.

Richard turned left again, heading back toward San Miguel Boulevard. He waited at the stop sign, eyes on the rearview mirror. There was a large break in the flow of traffic on the boulevard, ample room for Richard to enter, but he didn't move.

"He's just sitting back there, the son of a bitch."

Lauren was as startled by the vehemence in Richard's voice as by his words. Now she watched him looking to his left, apparently calculating the speed of the oncoming swarm of headlights. Suddenly he jerked the wheel to the right and stomped the gas pedal, burning rubber and eliciting an angry chorus of honking horns from the onrushing cars.

Lauren gasped as she was thrown sideways against the seat restraints and then pressed back into the seat as Richard accelerated down the boulevard.

"Richard, for God's sake!" she cried.

He ignored her, his face set, his hands locked on the steering wheel. There were few cars ahead of them. Richard overtook a small foreign car and then a van, still accelerating. Lauren was afraid even to speak, afraid she might distract him and they would end up in a terrible accident. She looked back at Emily, who sat rigidly, clutching her doll, eyes wide with fear. Through the rear window Lauren saw the receding cluster of headlights. Then she was nearly pulled out of her seat when Richard made a hard right turn and sped along a residential street.

Lauren held her breath, fearing a car might back out of a driveway into their path. At the end of the block Richard slowed and turned right, heading in the general direction from which they'd started this evening—away from their home. He drove now at a moderate speed, constantly checking the rearview mirror. They headed down a curving street lined with houses, took a left, then a right, then went along another street that curved first one way, then the other. Lauren had completely lost her sense of direction.

"Richard, where—"

"I think I lost him," he said, more to himself than to her. He continued to check the rearview mirror, still apprehensive.

Despite her own anger and frustration, Lauren could sense his pain. She put her hand on his arm and asked him: "Richard, what's happening?"

He seemed unable to look at her. When they passed beneath a streetlight, she saw a deep sadness in his face.

"Please," she pleaded. "Tell me. If . . . if you're in some kind of trouble, perhaps I can help."

"There's nothing you can do," he said quietly.

"How do you know, if you won't tell me?" She felt her frustration grow.

His jaw muscles were working, as if he was fighting an internal battle. He said nothing.

"*Will you tell me what's going on?*" she shouted, making him wince.

Her words hung in the air between them. Richard remained silent. Lauren pressed her lips together, trying to quell her anger. She was angrier still that they were subjecting Emily to this.

Now they passed under the freeway, and Lauren realized just how far out of their way they'd gone. Richard turned onto the on-ramp, heading home.

When they reached Larkdale Way, he drove past their house without stopping. He turned at the corner, then steered slowly down the alley, which was lit only by the car's headlights. The tall wooden fences on either side were as stark as military barricades. Richard examined the fence behind their house as they slid by, then he went around the block and pulled into their driveway.

Emily had fallen asleep in the backseat, so Lauren gently lifted her out of the car and carried her inside. While Amos curled up on the floor beside Emily's bed, Lauren undressed her and put her into her pajamas. The little girl frowned and mumbled, but never once opened her eyes. Lauren tucked her in bed, kissed her on the forehead, and turned out the light.

She went into the family room and heard Richard talking on the phone in the kitchen. She watched him from the doorway. His back was to her and his shoulders were hunched. He kept his voice low so Lauren could only catch a few of his words. But she couldn't miss the anger and urgency in his tone.

". . . no, goddammit, *now*. . . . Listen, Jameson . . . twenty minutes . . . know where it is . . . Fine."

Richard hung up the phone, then straightened his shoulders and heaved a sigh, his back still to Lauren. When he turned, he was startled to see her standing there. He looked away, avoiding her eyes.

"I have to leave," he said.

"What? Who was that on the phone?"

"I'll be back in an hour."

He started to turn away from her toward the door. She stepped forward and grabbed his arm.

"Richard, where are you going?"

He touched her hand, then gently lifted it from his arm.

"Keep the doors locked," he said quietly.

"Richard, for God's sake, will you tell me what's going on?"

He hesitated. Then he turned and walked out the door, closing it softly behind him, leaving Lauren alone in the kitchen. The overhead light suddenly seemed too bright to her. She heard Richard's car in the garage. The sound faded away.

Lauren stood unmoving, until she became aware of pain in the palms of her hands. She unclenched her fists and looked at the undersides of her hands. Each palm bore a row of angry, red indentations shaped like tiny half-moons.

Dammit, she thought, he has no right to keep this from me, whatever it is.

She yanked open the refrigerator, feeling as if she needed a drink to calm herself. She stared at the half-full bottle of Chablis, but made no move to retrieve it. Then she slammed the door, rattling jars inside, and walked out to the family room.

She felt confined, suffocated. She flipped open the lock on the sliding glass door and pulled at the handle. The door didn't budge, and for a moment Lauren panicked, feeling trapped inside her own home. She grabbed the handle with both hands, then stopped herself, smiling sardonically at her lack of concentration. She bent down and removed the sawed-off broomstick that lay in the metal grooves along the floor, an effective second lock. Now the door slid open easily. Lauren stepped outside onto the deck.

The only light came from behind her, a wide, wedge-shaped yellow-white patch on the redwood boards. To her right, nearly glowing in the shadows, were four white metal chairs around a white table. The umbrella in the center was closed, a mast with no flag.

Lauren walked to the edge of the deck, leaned against the railing, and stared up at the darkly clouded sky. There were a few black patches where stars shone through, cold and perfect. She hugged herself as the chilly air began to work its way through her blouse.

Lauren heard a rustling sound.

She sucked in her breath and tried to peer through the deep shadows by the back fence. An avocado tree stood near the corner of the yard and a few of its branches touched the fence.

The wind, Lauren thought.

Except there was no wind. Lauren stood motionless, holding her breath, staring at the blackness beyond the tree. The shadows seemed to expand and move, but she knew it was only her eyes playing tricks. Again she heard the rustling sound.

It must be a bird, she thought, or a squirrel.

But she felt exposed standing alone on the deck. Vulnerable. She went back inside, slid the glass door shut, and locked it, replaced the broomstick and closed the curtain. She looked in on Emily, who was sleeping soundly. Then she sat in the family room and began flipping through magazines, waiting for Richard to come home.

It was nearly midnight when she heard him unlock the back door. When he entered the room, he seemed surprised by her presence.

"I thought you'd be in bed," he said.

"Not until we talk."

He hesitated, then nodded his head and sat beside her. She could smell cigarette smoke on his clothes, and when he spoke, there was liquor on his breath.

"I'm sorry I left . . . so suddenly."

"You went to a bar," she said.

"Yes. To meet someone. A friend of mine."

"Jameson."

Richard gave her a surprised look.

"I heard you say his name on the phone," she explained.

"Oh."

"Who is he?"

"A friend . . . a cop."

"He's a policeman?"

"Yes, with . . . the San Miguel Police Department."

"I've never heard you mention any friends who were with the police."

"I don't see him very often, but I've known him for years. He . . . I didn't know who else to talk to."

"There's *me*." When Richard said nothing, she asked, "What did you talk about?"

Richard shrugged. "I explained to him what's been going on. He's going to take care of things."

"What things?"

"The situation. You know."

"No, Richard, I don't know. I'm waiting for you to *tell* me."

Her words had risen in both volume and pitch, upsetting her. The last thing she wanted was for this discussion to deteriorate into a shouting match. It had never happened before, not between her and Richard. But she remembered the last weeks and months that Paul had lived here, the arguments they'd had—always loud, bitter, and pointless.

She reached out for Richard's hand.

"I *want* you to tell me," she said, her voice calm but firm.

"Well." He raised his eyebrows. "It's as I said before. Some years ago I crossed paths with a jealous husband, and now he's back. I don't know what he has in mind, but he's following me around and he's making me very nervous and—"

"Then why didn't you call the police?"

He withdrew his hand from hers. "I did. Jameson is—"

"Someone you had to meet in a bar," she finished for him.

"He was off duty." His voice had an edge. "I didn't want to bother his family by going to his home."

"Why couldn't you talk to someone else at the police department? Why did it have to be him?"

Richard's mouth was pressed into a line. Lauren could tell he was nearing the end of his patience.

So am I, she thought.

"Because," Richard said evenly, "this man hasn't done anything illegal yet. He's broken no laws. Officially the police can do nothing."

"And what can Jameson do?"

"Lauren, for chrissake."

"Well, what *can* he do?"

"He can talk to him, that's what. He can tell him to stay away from us."

"How do you even know for sure he was the man in the car following us? *I* certainly couldn't tell who was driving."

"Who else could it have been?" he said, challenging her.

Lauren was silent for a moment.

"What's this man's name anyway?" she asked suddenly.

"Jameson."

"No, the 'jealous husband.' "

"Oh. J-John. It's Johnson."

Lauren shook her head and gave him a wry smile. "Is that the best you can come up with?"

He looked away and said nothing.

Lauren felt sick inside. When she spoke again, her voice cracked with pain. "You've been lying to me all along, Richard. When are you going to tell me the truth?"

He averted his eyes. "I don't know," he said softly.

Then he stood and walked from the room.

Lauren sat there for a long time. She heard water running in the bathroom, and then nothing. The house was silent.

Richard had finally admitted to her that there existed a larger truth, something more than merely a jealous husband, something he was keeping from her. Of course his reticence—his lying—frustrated and angered her. But she was now aware of another emotion.

Fear.

Whatever Richard was hiding was significant enough, *powerful* enough, to alter his behavior and strike him with panic. The question was, could his secret, this *thing,* pose a threat to her and Emily?

Lauren wanted desperately to believe that it could not. She couldn't imagine Richard putting her and Emily at risk. He *loved* them, and he'd always treated them with respect and . . . sincerity.

Obviously, though, Lauren thought, there's something in his past—in his present—that I know nothing about.

This thought brought another fear, one that had been fluttering in the shadows of her mind for several days. She'd tried to keep it there, hidden in the darkness, but now it could not be ignored.

She might be living and sleeping with a total stranger.

17

On thursday morning Lauren woke up determined to find out about Richard, about what was going on.

She believed she could pressure him into revealing the hidden truth, but she didn't know how much pressure it would take. It might cause so much friction and heated anger that they'd say terrible things to each other, things that would be difficult to retract.

Lauren wanted more than anything to preserve the bond between them. She knew in her heart that no matter what had happened in the past few days, she still loved Richard. She loved him as much as she loved Emily.

What infuriated her was that apparently Richard didn't think she was strong enough to handle the truth.

Well, she thought, there's more than one way to get at the truth.

Richard was already out of bed and in the shower. Lauren went into Emily's room and found her sitting at her table having "breakfast" with her new doll and a couple of old favorites.

"Good morning, honey." She kissed Emily on top of the head.

"Morning. Guess what?"

"What?"

"Sally and Cathy like Cathy Ann very much."

"I'm glad to hear it."

"Me too. I was worried."

Lauren smiled. "You were?"

"Because Sally and Cathy already lived here and had their own room and everything and Cathy Ann was new. I was scared they would tell her to leave."

"You were?" Lauren asked again, her smile fading. "Why?"

"Because they didn't know her. I mean, I introduced them and everything, but they didn't know where she'd been living before or who her other friends were. They didn't *know* her."

The way I may not know Richard, Lauren thought.

She helped Emily get dressed, then went back to her bedroom and got ready for work. When she entered the kitchen, Richard was taking down cups and saucers from the cupboard. Water was heating on the stove.

"Do you, um, want coffee or tea?" This was the first he'd spoken to her this morning, and he looked wary, as if he was afraid she might begin asking him awkward questions.

"Whatever you're having." She hoped her tone of voice was light and relaxed enough to assure him that everything was all right between them. It *will* be all right, she reassured herself.

"Tea then?"

"Fine."

They began making small moves around the kitchen, getting things ready to eat. She brushed against him. He turned to her with a wan smile, then he put his arms around her.

"I love you," he said, and kissed her.

"I know." She wanted to believe it. She *did* believe it. "I love you too."

Amos whined from the doorway as if he'd been neglected all his life. Richard chuckled. "Are you jealous?"

The big dog whined again.

"I think he's just hungry," Lauren said.

Later that morning Lauren went downstairs to talk to the police.

The entire lower level of the municipal building—except for the cafeteria—was occupied by the San Miguel Police Department, several hundred men and women. Lauren pushed through the glass doors that joined the two areas.

She'd only been on this side once before, soon after she was hired. Like all other city employees, she'd been photographed while holding under her chin a small black sign with a number on it. Then she'd had her fingerprints taken. The young man who operated the camera and the ink roller joked with her the entire time, but she still felt as if she were being arrested.

Now she stood in a wide, vacant carpeted area: elevators to her left, three doors to her right—Detectives, Bookings, and Information. Lauren imagined that if she were in Los Angeles, or even San Diego, the first two doors would be admitting a continuous flow of suspects and arresting officers. Thank goodness she lived in San Miguel, where crime existed, to be sure—burglaries, dope dealing, even an occasional murder—but on a much smaller scale.

She stepped through the nearest door and entered a small room dominated by a large metal desk. A young black woman was behind the desk, chatting with a uniformed cop. He was big enough to fill the contoured plastic chair he sat in—one in a row along the near wall.

They both stopped talking to look up at Lauren. She felt completely out of place, as if she'd entered an alien land. It was all she could do to keep from saying, "Excuse me," and walking out. But she had to do this. Richard wouldn't confide in her, but perhaps Jameson would.

"May I help you?" the woman asked pleasantly.

"I'm looking, that is, I'd like to speak to Officer Jameson."

"I'm sorry, who?"

"Jameson. Oh, maybe he's not an officer. I mean, he could be a sergeant or . . ."

The woman looked at the policeman.

"Never heard of him," he said flatly.

"Let me check." The woman turned to the computer console on her desk and began tapping keys. She paused, and Lauren could see lines of print filling the screen. The woman shook her head.

"Is he a new recruit?" the cop asked Lauren.

"I . . ." She swallowed and gave a tiny shrug of her shoulders. Richard had said he'd known Jameson for years, but that didn't preclude him from having recently joined the police department. However, she'd assumed the man was older, and she thought the police only recruited men and women in their twenties. But whatever Jameson's age, he was someone Richard trusted enough to confide in, and she wanted to talk to him. She could almost hear Jameson's response: "What? Your husband hasn't told you all about this? Well, it's time you knew . . ."

"I'm sorry, ma'am," the woman said, turning from her computer screen. "There's no one with the San Miguel Police Department named Jameson. Not even a clerk typist."

Lauren felt her mouth go dry. "Are you certain?"

"Yes, ma'am."

"But someone told me . . ."

"Did this man Jameson represent himself to you as a police officer?" the cop asked her pointedly. His voice was hard, professional. "Because if he did, he's committed a crime."

"No, no, it's nothing like that. It's . . . just been a misunderstanding, that's all. Thank you."

She hurried out, feeling their stares on her back.

So Richard had lied again—Jameson did not work for the San Miguel Police Department.

Back in her cubicle Lauren reconstructed last night's conversation after Richard returned from his meeting with Jameson. He'd told her that Jameson was a cop and that he could help them with "the situation." She tried to recall Richard's face and his tone of voice when he said this. She felt sure he'd been telling the truth. However, he'd hesitated when he said, "San Miguel Police Department." She remembered that. Just as he'd hesitated when he said the man following them was named Johnson.

Both lies. One thing in Richard's favor, though, he was a poor liar. Thank God.

She returned her thoughts to Jameson. If he was a policeman, why would Richard lie about *where* he worked?

Lauren mulled over phoning the police departments of every nearby city and town and asking for "Officer Jameson." And if that didn't work, she could call every county in California asking for "Sheriff Jameson." And then she could start with other states.

Ridiculous, she thought. There must be another way.

Richard had told her he'd known Jameson for years. She couldn't ask Richard's parents about the man; they were both dead. And he had no siblings. The only other person she knew who'd known Richard for a long time was Arthur McFadden. Perhaps he knew Jameson. How could she talk to Arthur about this and be certain he wouldn't tell Richard? If Richard found out she was sneaking behind his back again, there could be a major confrontation—exactly what she wanted to avoid.

Since it was Thursday, Arthur wouldn't be at the store today, so Lauren tried him at home. Betty answered. Lauren thanked her again for last night's dinner and for Emily's doll before she asked to speak to Arthur.

"What can I do for you?" he asked when he came on the line.

Lauren concentrated on keeping her voice relaxed, psyching herself up to lie and make it sound real, hating herself for doing it. "I wanted to talk to you about something last night, but I never got the chance to be with you alone."

"Oh?"

"I'm planning a surprise birthday party for Richard."

"Hey, won't that be fun. Betty and I would love to come."

"Ah, great. I haven't set the exact date yet. I was hoping you could help me find—"

"Wait a minute—isn't Richard's birthday in September? The same month as Betty's, right?"

"Ah, yes, that's right." Lauren had hoped Arthur wasn't aware that Richard's birthday was four months away. "You see, I'm getting an early start on this because I want to invite a lot of Richard's old friends and I don't know how long it will take me to track them down."

Arthur was silent for a moment. Lauren was certain he hadn't believed her, and she thought he was trying to think of a gentle way to tell her so.

"I was hoping you could help me find some of them," she said into the silence.

"Sure," Arthur said at last. "I'll help if I can. But really, I think you know Richard's friends better than I do."

"I'm thinking of people from his past, and you've known him longer than I have. For instance, I've heard him mention someone named Jameson. Do you know him?"

"Jameson?"

"Yes."

There was another silence. Lauren held her breath.

"The name doesn't sound familiar," Arthur said finally.

Her hopes sank. "Are you sure?"

"Well, I'm sure that *I* don't know anyone by that name."

"I see."

"Sorry. But there are plenty of people who'd come to the party," he said cheerfully, apparently sensing her disappointment. "Everyone at the store. Tell you what—I'll make you a list of their names and addresses. Assuming you want to invite them all."

"Yes, of course." She wondered if any of them knew Jameson, although she doubted it. Richard was closer to Arthur than to any of the employees. But she was struck with another idea, something related to Richard's job. "Arthur, when Richard first came to work for you at the store, did he fill out an application?"

"Sure. Everyone does. Although it's more for custom's sake than anything else."

"Complete with past employers, references, and so on?"

"Yes, just like a real job application." Lauren could picture him smiling. Then he said, "Oh, I see what you're getting at. You could contact the people on his application for the party."

"Exactly." She was hoping one of them might lead her to Jameson, might in fact *be* Jameson.

"Could you get it for me?"

"I don't see why not."

"Without Richard knowing, of course."

Arthur laughed. "Of course."

"Can you get it today?"

"Today? Well, I suppose so." The laughter had gone out of his voice. "Perhaps I could stop by the store . . ."

"That would be great," Lauren urged. She sensed Arthur's reluctance—after all, this was his day off. But she was afraid to wait, afraid that if she stopped moving ahead with this, if she took time to dwell on what she was doing, she'd lose her nerve. "Perhaps you could get it this morning," she said, "and I could take you to lunch."

"Well . . . sure, why not."

"I really appreciate this, Arthur. Let's see—there's a nice restaurant on Ocean Boulevard, the Pilot House. It's not too far from—"

"I know the place," he said. "I'll see you there at noon."

Lauren left early for lunch, but she got caught in traffic and didn't arrive at the Pilot House until a quarter after twelve. As she hurried through the jammed parking lot, she saw Arthur standing outside the entrance. He wore slacks and a long-sleeved pullover shirt, and there was a manila folder in his left hand. He smiled when he saw her.

"Sorry I'm late," she said.

"No problem." He put his hand on her arm and led her inside. "I've reserved us a table."

The restaurant was festooned with ship's riggings and fishing nets. The windows on the west side offered a view of the ocean, although their table was on the landward side, tucked in a corner. The tabletop was a half-inch-thick slab of clear polyethylene covering a nautical chart. Thankfully, at least to Lauren, the waitresses were dressed like waitresses, not players in a musical comedy about sailing. Lauren ordered a chef's salad, and Arthur chose grilled tuna.

After the waitress left, Arthur removed a form from the manila folder. He gave it a cursory glance, then handed it to Lauren.

"Richard's job application," he said. "To tell you the truth, I never really study these things. I've always put more faith in my impression of the flesh-and-blood person than in any piece of paper."

Lauren quickly scanned the large, heavy sheet of paper, folded in half to create four pages. It was a standard form, with the usual requests for information: personal data, job history, references. All the lines had been filled in with a blue ballpoint pen in a firm, neat hand that she recognized as Richard's. She wanted to read every word right then, but she forced herself to return the application to the folder and push it aside.

"Richard didn't see you take this, did he?"

"Actually, he did."

"What?"

Arthur grinned and held up his hand. "Not to worry. He walked in and saw me take *something* from the file cabinet. I fibbed and said it was an inventory sheet that I wanted to study."

The waitress brought their food. Lauren poked at her salad.

"You know," Arthur said between bites of tuna, "seeing that application made me remember when I first met Richard." He shook his head and smiled. "He's sure changed since then."

Lauren looked up. "In what way?"

"Well, for one thing, he used to be apprehensive around customers, as if he were wary of them. I remember wondering if I'd made a mistake hiring him. Of course, I didn't. He's a wonderful person."

Lauren nodded. "How *did* you happen to hire him?"

"He just walked in. I'd been running an ad in the paper for a salesman, and a number of people had applied. But most of them seemed more concerned about medical benefits and paid vacations than the business. Richard was different. I could tell he really wanted the job. It was almost as if he *needed* it. Although that seemed unlikely—a man of his intelligence and personality.

"Anyway, he'd never worked in a hardware store, but he'd been a bookkeeper, and he had some business experience, *and* he was willing to learn. I hired him on the spot." Arthur shrugged his shoulders. "Maybe I was too impulsive, but I think sometimes you've got to go with your gut feelings. The main thing was, I liked him. Richard's a very—well, I don't have to tell you that—he's a very likable guy."

"Yes, he is."

"Plus," Arthur said, grinning, "he could do the books. That was one area where he *really* helped me out. No more hassling with accounting firms. He volunteered to do the taxes, too, and he saved the store almost enough money in the first year to cover his salary."

Lauren nodded again. Then her eyes fell to the manila folder, and she frowned.

Arthur said, "I hope you find what you're looking for."

"I . . . do too."

"I really couldn't tell you what's in there—I've only skimmed through it. Like I said, I just have people fill them out because it's what you're *supposed* to do. You know, the man or woman is more important than the document. And I'll tell you something else: Everything in a job application is history. It's the past, over and done with. I want to know what a person's like *now*, what they're interested in *now*. And I can tell more about someone by talking with him than I can by studying a whole stack of papers. Richard's honest and dedicated, plus being a great guy, and that's all that matters. Don't you agree?"

"Y-yes, of course," she said, laying her hand on the folder.

18

WHEN LAUREN GOT BACK to her cubicle, the design of Decker Park was the farthest thing from her mind.

She opened the manila folder and removed Richard's job application. She scanned through the four pages with a sense of anticipation, as if she were about to solve a troubling puzzle.

On the back page was a request for personal references—"not relatives or former employers." Richard had written three names, all men, each labeled as "friend." Jameson was not among them. The phone numbers for each began with area code 215.

Lauren assumed the code was for Philadelphia, Richard's previous home. To be certain, she flipped through the phone book until she found the map of time zones and area codes. Area code 215 covered the southeastern portion of Pennsylvania, including Philadelphia.

Out of state or not, Richard's old friends might be able to help me find Jameson, she thought. Or perhaps one of *them* can tell me what Richard is hiding.

Lauren had the urge to start punching out numbers on her phone.

But she knew that all long-distance calls went through the building's main switchboard and had to be cleared by a supervisor. Geoffrey would probably give her permission to make the calls, but he'd ask for an explanation. She'd have to lie, and she'd had her fill of that. Besides, she reasoned, Richard works till nine tonight. She could make the calls before he got home.

Lauren turned back through the application. The two inside pages were devoted to Richard's educational and employment history, all of which had taken place in Pennsylvania and would probably not help her in finding Jameson. The front page contained personal data: name, Social Security number, address, and so on. Lauren read the page carefully, looking for a clue to the man she sought.

Nothing.

She turned the page to "Employment history." The form requested three previous employers, but Richard had listed only one: Darnell Corporation, Philadelphia. He'd worked there for five years as a bookkeeper. His supervisor was listed as Mr. Fenwick.

The name was vaguely familiar to Lauren, so Richard may have mentioned it, although she couldn't recall anything specific. Actually, she knew little about Darnell Corporation—only that they had worked on contracts for the U.S. Defense Department. "A lot of top-secret projects," Richard had told her. "I hardly knew what they were doing there myself, except that it involved lasers and satellites. Mostly I worked on the payroll."

If Darnell was so security-conscious, Lauren wondered if she'd even be able to get in touch with Mr. Fenwick. And if she did, if he'd tell her where to find Jameson—even if he knew. A lot of ifs.

She thought back to her lunch with Arthur, when she'd found herself agreeing with his philosophy: The present *was* more important than the past. Still . . .

Lauren found the date on which Richard had left Darnell Corporation—November 17, three and a half years ago. She turned back to the first page for the date of the application: April 20. He'd been out of work for five months. Had he been fired or laid off?

Lauren again checked the entry for Darnell Corporation. Under "Reason for leaving" Richard had written: "To seek more rewarding employment."

She chewed on this.

Richard had quit his job of five years and moved several thousand miles to work as a clerk in a hardware store. "To seek more reward-ing employment"? Somehow it didn't sound right. Certainly it was possible for someone to get fed up with his job and just quit, pull up stakes and move across country. But Richard? It didn't sound like him—he was more of a stay-at-home type.

Another question came to mind: Why had Richard moved to San Miguel? Sure, it's a nice place to live. Actually, more than nice, Lauren thought, it's wonderful. But it's not exactly a boomtown. If Richard had moved to Southern California looking for work, he would have found more opportunities in Los Angeles or San Diego. Why had he chosen San Miguel?

She'd once asked him that very question.

"The warm weather and the relaxed atmosphere," he'd answered.

"But why San Miguel?"

"Hey, I've got to be *someplace*," he'd said, and they'd laughed, and she'd let it go at that.

Now she wanted to know. He'd had no job waiting for him here, no relatives, and no wife who'd been transferred by her company. As far as she knew, Richard had never even been to California before his move.

So why had he chosen San Miguel? For that matter, why had he left Philadelphia?

Lauren wondered if his old friends could tell her. She also won-dered if his reason for leaving Darnell Corporation had anything to do with what was going on now.

For the next hour she tried to work on the design of Decker Park, but she couldn't concentrate. Nor could she wait until this evening to phone Richard's friends. She had to do it now. She crossed the hall to Geoffrey's office, where he was studying a set of subdivision plans. Lauren knocked on the doorframe. Geoffrey looked up, then raised his eyebrows.

"Problems?"

"What?" She felt he'd read her mind.

"By the look on your face I'd say you've got a problem with Decker Park."

"No, it's not that. It's . . . I don't feel very well."

"Really? I hope you're not coming down with the flu," he said with genuine concern, making Lauren feel doubly guilty for lying. "Do you need a ride home? Or should I phone Richard?"

"No, no, it's okay, I'm all right to drive home. I . . . just need to lie down, that's all."

He nodded. "Of course. And don't worry about anything here—just take it easy. I hope you feel better tomorrow."

Back in her cubicle Lauren began gathering up her things. She couldn't shake her feeling of guilt. She had work to do here, responsibilities.

But she also had a responsibility to find out about Richard.

She hurried from the building.

She'd driven for several miles before she found herself checking her rearview mirror, making her realize that she almost *expected* to see the dark blue car behind her. But there was no sign of it.

It was a little after three when Lauren arrived home. Since she was rarely here at this time on a workday, the house seemed odd to her, unfamiliar.

She laid her purse and the manila folder on the kitchen counter near the phone, then made a cup of tea, trying to calm herself. There was a tightness in her chest and stomach. The things she'd done up to now—talking to Arthur, questioning the boy at the store, even talking to the San Miguel police—all seemed justified, and in a way innocent. They were local and immediate. But making long-distance calls to people from Richard's past seemed more . . . consequential.

This morning she'd believed she was merely attempting to locate Jameson. But now she realized she wanted more. She believed that the key to the present problem lay in Richard's past, in his life before San Miguel, and when she spoke to the people from his past, she'd ask them more than simply how to locate Jameson.

Lauren felt that once she began these inquiries, she'd be crossing a line. And she didn't know how difficult it would be to cross back over. Perhaps it would be impossible.

She stirred honey into her tea, blew on the steamy surface, and took a sip. It tasted bitter. She emptied the cup in the sink, then filled a glass of water from the tap and drank. Her mouth still felt dry as she sat on a stool by the phone, removed the job application from the folder, and turned to the last page. She hesitated, then picked up the phone and punched 1 and 215 and then the seven-digit number for Richard's first personal reference, Joseph Adderly.

The phone rang in her ear.

It occurred to her that eventually Richard would have a written record of her calls—date, time, and duration. When the phone bill arrived, he'd know what she'd been doing. She wondered how he'd react. On the other hand, she knew, it might not matter. By then things would be settled, one way or another.

The phone was still ringing. Lauren counted ten more rings before she hung up. She called the second number. A woman answered almost immediately, startling her.

"Yes?"

"Hello, may I speak to . . ." Lauren read the name from the page. "Robert Traverner, please?"

"Who?"

"Robert Traverner. I'm not sure if I'm pronouncing the last name correctly. It's spelled—"

"Not here," the woman said, and hung up.

Lauren stared at the phone for a moment, then she redialed the number. Again the woman answered almost at once, as if she were sitting by the phone, waiting for it to ring.

"Yes?"

Lauren tried to picture the woman from her gruff voice. Unsmiling, she thought, with curlers in her hair and an ashtray full of cigarette butts at her elbow.

"I'm sorry to bother you," Lauren said. "I just spoke to you a moment ago. I'm trying to locate Robert Traverner."

"Didn't I tell you he wasn't here?"

"Yes, but—"

"Well?"

Lauren didn't know the first thing about this woman, except that she had a mean voice. She felt fairly certain, though, that given the chance, she could grow to dislike her. She took a deep breath and tried to speak calmly, pleasantly.

"Could you tell me a good time to call him?"

"Missy, I don't know a good time to call him. I don't even know a good *place* to call him."

"Excuse me?"

"Excuse you is right. There's no one *here* by that name. Now get off my phone before the radio jackpot people call me, because I happen to know the exact amount right down to the last dollar."

She hung up.

Okay, Lauren thought, so Robert Traverner has moved, and if he'd been living with *that* woman, I don't blame him one bit.

When Lauren tried the number for the third name, Matthew Harris, she got a recording: "The number you have reached is no longer in service. Please check the number you are dialing." Lauren did and called it again and got the same recording.

Okay, she thought, so Matthew Harris moved too.

She looked through the phone book for instructions on calling long-distance information, then asked the operator for the number of Matthew Harris in Philadelphia.

"One moment, please," the operator said. Then: "What's the address, please?"

"I don't know."

"I have two listings for Matthew Harris."

"Oh. Can you give me both of them?"

Lauren wrote down the numbers and then dialed each of them in turn. She spoke to both men, but neither had ever heard of Richard Caylor.

Perhaps, she reasoned, Richard's Matthew Harris had moved out of Philadelphia.

She called long-distance information again for the number of Robert Traverner, but the operator had no listing in Philadelphia for that name. Lauren also asked for the number of Joseph Adderly, the first reference she'd tried.

The operator had no listing for a Joseph Adderly.

Lauren thanked her and hung up, gazing at the back page of Richard's job application. All the names and numbers for his personal references had been written in a careful, legible hand. And all of them, she now believed, were fictitious.

Why? Lauren wondered. Hadn't Richard left behind anyone in Philadelphia who could vouch for him? She knew there were no close relatives—he'd been an only child and both parents were dead. But there must be *someone*.

She opened the job application to the pages containing Richard's educational and employment history. She wondered if he'd made up all that too. Somehow she doubted it. It would be too easy for someone to check, too likely for a potential employer to call his previous boss.

Although, Lauren remembered, Arthur hadn't done so.

She dialed the number for Darnell Corporation. The phone rang and rang. A business that doesn't answer its telephone at—she checked her watch—four in the afternoon? She counted fifteen rings before she slowly hung up the phone. Then she smiled to herself. It's four here, but it's seven in Philadelphia. Of course they don't answer their phone—they're closed for the day.

I'll check the number tomorrow, she thought.

The problem, though, was tonight. How could she act "normally" around Richard while she was secretly checking up on him?

19

IT WAS THURSDAY AFTERNOON in Los Angeles, and Albert Novek was sitting in the rear of a van with a young Hispanic man named Julio. Between them lay an open suitcase, filled with guns.

Novek had spent most of yesterday and all of last night moving from bar to bar, sipping tap beer and dropping hints to bartenders about his desire to purchase firearms. He'd had a more difficult time than he anticipated, even considering that he was out of his element here and dealing with strangers. It was doubly frustrating to know that John Q. Citizen could walk into a *store* and buy a gun. Of course, Novek couldn't afford the three-week waiting period, nor would his phony driver's license stand up to the background check demanded by the state.

Still, there were more guns in this great nation than people, and he only needed *two,* so what was the big deal?

Finally, though, sometime very early this morning, with his head foggy from beer, he'd found a helpful bartender in a seedy, nearly deserted saloon somewhere east of downtown L.A. The man listened calmly to Novek's request. Then he accepted the folded twenty pressed into his palm, stepped to the pay phone in back, and punched in a number. He conversed for a minute in rapid-fire Spanish.

When the man returned to his post behind the bar, Novek noticed that he'd left the receiver dangling by its cord.

"Telephone for you," he said.

Novek went back to get it. He said "Hello" several times with no reply, and briefly wondered if this was somehow a trick to trap him back here where they could rob him of his bankroll.

Then the phone voice asked, "Are you the guy wants to buy a couple radios?"

"What?"

"Radios, man, radios."

It took a moment for Novek to understand that the man was simply being careful. Nobody trusts anybody.

"That's right," Novek said.

"What kind you want, pocket-size or the big table models?"

"The smaller ones."

"You want the kind you got to tune yourself, or the ones that do it automatically?"

"I don't know," Novek said. "I'll have to see what you've got. I don't want junk."

"Hey, man."

"Where can we meet?"

The man was silent for a few seconds before he said, "You just be where you are tomorrow afternoon around two and I'll let you know."

"Wait a minute, I want—"

Novek realized the guy had hung up. He slammed the phone down hard enough to make a few customers in the bar look his way. Then he stomped out, swearing under his breath.

But the next afternoon he'd returned to the bar. And a few beers later he was again talking to the man on the phone, who gave him an address and told him to drive there, then hung up. Novek had to ask the bartender for directions.

The address turned out to be on a gate in front of a vacant lot a few miles from the bar. Novek sat in his rented car for nearly half an hour before a black van with tinted windows pulled up behind him. A skinny Hispanic wearing a hairnet and a stringy goatee climbed out of the driver's side and walked up to Novek's window. He gave Novek a quick once-over. Then he told him to follow, went back to the van, and drove away.

Novek stayed behind the van as it turned down one side street after another. He was more than a little irritated by the guy's precautions—he just wanted to buy the guns and be done with it.

The van moved slowly along yet another street of abandoned brick buildings sprayed with graffiti, and finally pulled to the curb and stopped, its engine shutting down. Novek walked along the windowless side of the van. When he pulled open the passenger door, he was assailed by the reek of marijuana.

"Get in. I'm Julio."

And now Novek and Julio sat cross-legged on a carpet in the rear of the van.

The suitcase between them was filled with scratched and pitted .22 revolvers and .25 automatics and couple of cheaply built .357 magnums that looked as if they'd blow apart the next time they were fired. Novek supposed Julio was dealing all the choice merchandise to the street gangs. Still, he did manage to sort through the mess and find two decent pieces, a .38 Special Ruger with a four-inch barrel and a .45 Colt automatic.

"I'll take these," he said, unfolding his cramped legs and rising to his knees, "and some shells to go with them."

"Hey, man, I don't sell bullets. You can go to a store for that."

Novek ground his teeth and jammed the guns in his jacket pockets, one on each side.

"How much?" he asked.

Julio closed the suitcase. "Eight bills."

The amount represented more than half of Novek's remaining money. But, he thought, one, you get what you pay for, and two, this was not so much a purchase as an investment.

Still . . .

"Eight bills for these two seems high."

"That's eight bills *each*," Julio said.

Novek looked at him. The smaller man must have seen something in his eyes because he swallowed hard, then pulled open his jacket to show Novek the pearl-handled automatic tucked in the front of his pants.

A pimp's gun, Novek thought with disgust.

"This one *is* loaded, man," Julio said, "and I don't want no trouble. If you want the pieces, fine, pay up and everything's cool. If not, leave them here and it's been nice knowing you."

Novek looked at the man through hooded eyes and nodded, seemingly accepting his situation. He'd even entertained a brief thought of settling for one gun, going to San Miguel without Grummund, and handling the operation by himself. But no, that probably wouldn't be wise. He and Grummund needed each other, at least at this point. And they needed two guns.

"I'm not sure I have sixteen hundred," Novek said.

"Well, how much you got?"

"Closer to fifteen, I think." Novek took out his loose roll of money and dropped it on the suitcase—hundreds and twenties. It left him with nothing but loose change in his pocket. "Go ahead and count it," he said.

Julio's eyes shifted from Novek to the money. "I think that's close eno—"

His word was cut in half by Novek's hand on his throat. And then the big man was on top of him, pinning his gun hand to his side and banging his head against the steel wall of the van.

Julio struggled feebly, then went limp. Novek banged his head again and again before he let him slump to the floor of the van, blood flowing from his nose and ears. Novek picked up the bills, which had been scattered in the brief scuffle, and folded them neatly into his pocket. Then he smoothed his hair with his hand and climbed out.

Julio lay perfectly still, whether dead or simply unconscious, Novek didn't know. He had more important things to worry about. Grummund would be here soon, ready to drive to San Miguel. And Novek still needed bullets for the guns.

20

LATER THAT AFTERNOON Lauren drove to Oceanside Day School. "How was your day today?" she asked Emily as they walked hand in hand from the building.

"It was fun. We got to tell about our favorite places."

In the car Lauren asked her which place she'd picked.

"I couldn't think of one," Emily said.

"You couldn't? What about your home? With your favorite *mother* . . ." She reached over and gave her a squeeze on the knee, making her giggle. ". . . and your favorite *dog* . . ." Another squeeze and a laugh. ". . . and your—and Richard." A final squeeze and a cry of delight.

"Not where you *live*," Emily said, giggling again. "It had to be someplace else."

"And you couldn't think of a favorite place?"

"Not for a while."

"What about later?"

"I told them about Sea World. It was really fun."

"Which reminds me," Lauren said, "our pictures are probably ready."

The Safeway parking lot was crowded with after-work shoppers, but Lauren managed to find an empty slot. She took Emily's hand and led her past rows of parked cars, watching for backup lights and overloaded shopping carts, which rattled headlong toward them.

She and Emily moved through the bustling store to the service counter, where Lauren paid for the prints. She let Emily carry the envelope as they walked back to the Honda.

They'd gone beyond the middle of the lot before Lauren realized they'd missed the car. She stopped and looked around until she saw it in the next row, some fifty feet nearer the store. They walked toward the Honda and started to edge between a pair of parked cars.

Lauren hesitated, then stopped near the rear of the car on her left.

She recognized it. It was the same brown car she'd seen parked in Hal and Monica Ipswich's driveway. She bent down and peered through the rear window on the passenger's side.

Monica was sitting behind the wheel.

Lauren had a partial view of her—the top of her blue, collarless blouse, her blond hair pinned back in a bun, the soft curve of her cheekbone, the firm line of her jaw. Monica stared straight ahead and made no move to get out of the car or start the engine. As Lauren watched, she turned her head toward the store.

Probably waiting for Hal, Lauren thought.

Although somehow that struck Lauren as odd. She'd often seen men sitting in cars waiting for their wives to do the shopping, but she'd rarely seen a woman waiting for her husband. Of course, it was possible that they'd been driving by and Hal needed to run in for cigarettes or whatever, and Monica decided to wait in the car.

Although if it was me, Lauren thought, I'd go in, too, if only to avoid being left behind like the family dog. Besides, I'd need *something*—orange juice, bread, toilet paper . . .

But apparently not Monica.

She merely sat and watched the entrance of the store, unaware that

Lauren stood a few feet from her. Then she turned to look through the windshield—not idly, it seemed to Lauren, but with purpose—cocking her head a bit, as if to see past the car parked nose to nose with hers.

Lauren straightened up and tried to follow Monica's gaze. She found herself looking across an open lane at the rear end of her Honda.

Lauren felt hairs stir on the nape of her neck. Was Monica watching her car?

"Mommy, what are we waiting for?"

Lauren held her breath, afraid that Monica had heard, afraid she might turn around and catch her.

Catch me? Lauren thought. Baloney. If anyone caught anyone, I caught her.

She let her breath out slowly, feeling her heart pounding. Then she purposefully led Emily around the rear of Monica's car to the open driver's-side window and stooped down.

"Well, hello, Monica," she said brightly.

Lauren was barely two feet from Monica's face and had an excellent view of the woman's startled look. It pleased her.

"I thought I saw you sitting here." Lauren kept her voice light, which was easier to do now that she sensed Monica's discomfort.

"Oh . . . hi," Monica said uncertainly, attempting a feeble smile.

"So you found the local hangout."

"Um, yes." Monica's eyes shifted nervously from Lauren to Emily and back again.

"Oh, this is my daughter, Emily. Emily, this is Monica Ipswich. She just moved in across the street from us and she shops at the same store we do. Isn't that nice?"

Emily was confused. "I guess."

"Are you coming or going?" Lauren asked Monica.

"I'm . . . just leaving."

Lauren glanced into the car. There were no grocery sacks on the passenger side or on the backseat. Were there any in the trunk?

"Isn't this Hal's car?" Lauren asked, patting the roof. She felt as if she had Monica on a hook, and she wasn't ready to let her off. Some perverse part of her wanted to make this woman squirm, perhaps because she and Hal had made *her* squirm when they'd caught her in their backyard. "Are you waiting for Hal?"

"No."

"So he makes you do all the shopping, huh?"

Monica frowned briefly. "I do most of the shopping, yes." There was an edge to her voice, letting Lauren know that she wanted this conversation to end.

"I suppose he keeps pretty busy at home, right? What's he working on these days?"

"I beg your pardon?" Monica's tone was devoid of friendliness, one shade away from hostility.

"I mean," Lauren said, smiling broadly, "what's he writing? A book? A magazine article?"

"Oh . . . a book."

"How fascinating. What's it about?"

"I . . . don't know, not exactly. He doesn't like to discuss his work in progress." Monica drummed her fingers on the steering wheel. "I have to go now," she said, and started the engine.

Lauren gave her one last smile. "Let's all get together real soon."

Monica nodded curtly. "Sure."

"Come on, Emily."

Lauren led her daughter between cars and across a wide asphalt lane to their car. Once inside, she checked the rearview mirror.

Monica's car hadn't moved. As Lauren drove slowly from the lot, she kept an eye on the brown car. It remained in its parking slot. Lauren pulled into the street, again checking the mirror, but apparently Monica had stayed put.

When they got home, Lauren laid the photo envelope on the kitchen counter and removed a box of Milk-Bones from the cupboard. Amos was wagging his tail and whining. Lauren scratched behind his ears and handed the box to Emily.

"Why don't you give this hungry boy a couple of treats before dinner."

Lauren walked to the living room and looked out the front window. The house across the street appeared to be deserted. A minute later Monica's brown car came down the street and turned into the driveway. Lauren closed the drapes.

In the bedroom she changed clothes, then went to the kitchen to start dinner. She was startled to see Richard's job application lying in plain sight on the counter. Though he always worked late on Thursdays, what if he'd come home early and found it? How heated would his resentment and anger be?

Emily entered the kitchen as Lauren slipped the application into the manila folder. She needed to find a good hiding place.

"Are we going to eat pretty soon, Mommy?"

"Sure, honey." Lauren temporarily set aside the folder to fix dinner—brown rice and stir-fried vegetables.

After they'd eaten, Emily decided they should work on her coloring book. They took the book and box of colored pens into the family room, and soon they were engrossed in coloring the picture of the fairy princess, the castle, and the unicorn—the one they'd begun with Richard last Monday night.

Lauren thought wistfully about how their lives had seemed so different just a short time ago. The three of them were a loving, secure, close-knit family. Now it seemed that outside influences were threatening to tear them apart. Worse, Richard was deceiving her, hiding something. This pained her greatly. She'd always believed that they were meant for each other, and she refused to consider a future without him.

And yet . . .

Lauren felt driven to dig into his past. She had to know what he was hiding from her. And she believed—or perhaps it was merely hope—that after she uncovered his secret, she would still love him.

We'll get through this, she told herself. Dammit, we *will*.

Emily yawned. Lauren checked her watch, surprised at how time had flown—it was nearly nine. Richard would be home soon.

"Hey, kiddo, it's past your bedtime."

She helped Emily put everything away, then got her into her pajamas and tucked her under the covers. Amos curled up in His usual place beside the bed.

"Goodnight, sweetie." Lauren kissed her on the forehead.

"Night, Mommy."

Lauren turned out the light and stepped into the hall. She heard Richard unlocking the back door. A thought stopped her cold: His job application was still lying on the countertop.

She hurried to the kitchen just as Richard entered from the laundry room. He looked more tired than usual, even haggard, but he managed a smile.

"Hi," he said.

The manila folder was on the counter to Lauren's left, close enough for her to touch. She moved past it, feeling like a sneak, a traitor, met Richard in the center of the kitchen, and put her arms around him. They kissed.

"I'm glad you're home." She positioned herself between Richard and the folder.

"Me too. I could use a glass of—hey, what's this?"

Richard reached behind her. His left arm was still around her waist. Lauren held her breath.

"Are these from Sea World?" he asked, picking up the photo envelope.

"Y-yes." Lauren saw that the folder was partially hidden by the blender.

"How did they come out?"

"I haven't seen them yet. Ah, why don't you get comfortable in the family room, and I'll bring you a glass of wine. We can look at them together."

"Okay, but I'm going to peek in on Emily first."

Richard carried the photo envelope from the kitchen. The moment he was gone Lauren snatched the manila folder from the counter, pulled open a drawer, and tossed the folder on top of boxes of sandwich bags, aluminum foil, and plastic wrap.

Breathing a little easier, she poured two glasses of Chablis, took them into the family room, and sat beside Richard on the love seat. He'd already removed the color photos from the envelope. Now he began to slowly shuffle through them, holding each one so they both could see. Occasionally he'd comment—"Hey, that's a good one," or "God, look at Emily. What a doll."

One of the photos seemed to disturb him, but when she asked him about it, he merely smiled and shook his head and went on to the next one. Lauren looked at the pictures without really seeing them. Her thoughts were on the job application and Richard's phony references. And Monica Ipswich.

Richard slid the stack of photos into the envelope. "Those were fun. You did a good job."

"Thanks." She smiled weakly.

"What's wrong?"

"It's . . . Something happened today." She feared that eventually she'd have to confront Richard about the misinformation on his application. Not now, though. But Monica Ipswich was another matter. Lauren still held faint hope that she could nudge Richard into confiding in her—before she found things out on her own. "I think Monica Ipswich was following me today."

Richard grinned. "You're not serious."

Lauren had expected him to show concern. In fact, considering his previous reactions, she wouldn't have been surprised if he'd rushed to the front room and peered through the drapes. But he just stared at her with a dopey grin.

"I am serious," she said. She described her encounter with Monica in the Safeway parking lot.

Richard shrugged. "Maybe she was just buying groceries."

"There weren't any in her car."

"They could've been in the trunk."

"It's possible," Lauren said, "but I doubt it. There's something very strange about her and Hal—you said so yourself."

"They're just oddballs, that's all."

Richard seemed totally unconcerned. Lauren was confounded by his dramatic change in attitude.

"They're more than just odd, and you know it," Lauren said. "They moved in with hardly any furniture, and the only yard work they've done was to trim the bushes by their front window for a better view of our house."

"So they're sloppy, but—"

"They took down part of their back fence to park cars in the yard, God knows why."

"Well, there's nothing wrong with—"

"And they haven't given the post office their new address."

Richard glanced about the room as if searching for an explanation. "Maybe . . . well, let's see . . ."

Lauren couldn't believe what she was hearing. "Why are you trying to defend them?"

"Am I?"

Lauren rolled her eyes. "Yes, you are. My God, Richard, yesterday you were suspicious as hell about those people. You were spying through the drapes as if you thought they were, I don't know, terrorists or something. Now you're acting as if they're *normal*."

Richard allowed himself a hollow laugh. "Come on, Lauren, I admit they're a bit strange, but—"

"A *bit*?"

"—but seriously, who can say what's normal and what's not. I mean, in their eyes *we're* probably the weird ones."

Lauren shook her head in disbelief. "Are you saying you're no longer concerned about those people? That suddenly everything is okay?"

Richard shrugged, maintaining a casual air.

Lauren felt ready to burst. "Everything is *not* okay, Richard."

"Lauren . . ."

"For one thing, we used to be able to talk about things, about people."

"Lauren, please . . ."

"We used to *communicate,* Richard. We were on the same level or wavelength or whatever you want to call it. We saw things the same way. Or at least we *tried* to see each other's point of view. But now . . ."

She waited for him to speak, to tell her she was wrong, to explain what was going on.

He looked away and said nothing.

"Richard, I'm . . . frightened."

He turned to her, putting his hand on her leg.

"Lauren, please, don't be. I'm here with you. We're together and . . . and I love you. More than anything."

Lauren hesitated, then pulled away from him and rose stiffly. She walked out to the kitchen, and stood staring straight ahead, looking at nothing, not knowing what to do. Richard came up behind her so quietly that when he touched her, she jumped.

"Let's go to bed," he said gently.

"I'm . . . going to stay up for a while."

He removed his hand, but Lauren sensed that he still stood close behind her, waiting for her to acquiesce, to accept him. It seemed to her that now *she* was the one responsible for keeping them apart. A feeling of loneliness entered her heart like a cold blade. She turned to him.

But he was gone.

21

LAUREN STOOD ALONE in the kitchen, feeling depression begin to envelop her.

No, she told herself.

She walked out, passing through the dining area to the darkness of the living room, not really going anywhere, just wanting the sensation of movement. She stared at the south wall, picturing the hallway and the master bedroom beyond, wondering if Richard was already in bed. Then she crossed the room and parted the front drapes just enough to see the house across the street. It was dark except for a light falling from a side window, partially illuminating the carport. Monica's car was gone.

Perhaps Richard is right, she thought. Those two are just harmless oddballs.

Lauren let the drapes fall back into place. It occurred to her that possibly she'd been overstating not only the behavior of Hal and Monica but also Richard's. Of course, there was no denying his reaction last Monday in Tobey's restaurant. But he seemed to have a legitimate explanation: The man in the windbreaker was the jealous husband of an ex-lover. That would also explain his agitation at being followed, no doubt by the same jealous husband, on the ride home from Arthur and Betty's house last night. And it would account for his late-night meeting with Jameson.

Maybe that's all there was to it—a jealous husband nosing around, and now warned off by Richard's policeman friend. And Hal and Monica's involvement?

Chalk it up to my overactive imagination, Lauren thought.

She walked back to the kitchen and turned off the lights, aware that her new theory didn't take into consideration Richard's phony references. As she passed through the family room, she noticed the photo envelope lying on an end table.

She sat on the love seat with her feet curled under her and removed the stack of photos from the envelope.

Earlier with Richard she'd been preoccupied, looking at the pictures but not seeing. Now she examined each one carefully, lovingly, trying to recapture the feeling she'd had when the snapshots were taken, the feeling of closeness, of family.

The first photo showed Emily and Richard walking hand in hand away from the camera. They'd just passed through the gates of Sea World and Emily's left arm was raised, pointing at something out of sight to the left.

Something new and wonderful, Lauren thought, smiling.

With one exception—when Richard had asked a stranger to take the three of them together—all the snapshots featured just Emily and Richard, although sometimes with a crowd of people in the background.

The last photo had been shot in the parking lot just before they left for home. Emily's head was cocked to one side as she grinned at the camera, exhausted but happy. Richard stood beside her, his hand resting protectively on her shoulder. Directly behind them was Richard's Chevrolet, and beyond that a row of parked cars. In the distant background was the sign for Sea World along with several people walking through the lot.

One stranger stared directly at the camera. He stood in the background behind a car, a disapproving look on his face.

Lauren smiled, remembering how he'd seemed angry at having his picture taken. Now she looked at him carefully—mid-thirties, prematurely bald with a wide fringe of black hair, thick black sideburns, pale face. Lauren's smile faded. She'd seen this man before—not actually *him*, but his picture.

She flipped back through the photographs.

There. In the photo of the three of them taken right after lunch— the man with the black fringe of hair was sitting at a table. His back was to them, but Lauren recognized his distinctive hairline.

And here. In a photo she'd taken of Emily and Richard near the dolphin petting pool, the man was nearby in the crowd, looking over his shoulder directly at them.

Lauren laid the three photos side by side, comparing them, feeling herself growing cold. There was no question in her mind—it was the same man in all three. Apparently, he'd followed them to Sea World and watched them all the while they were there. Even more chilling to her, this was not the man she'd seen in Tobey's restaurant and in Casa Grande. This was a new player in the game, whatever the game was.

She remembered now that Richard had seemed upset by one of the photos. Had he noticed the man?

Lauren stood abruptly and went to the master bedroom, intent on showing Richard the photos, wanting him to know that she knew, that she had *evidence,* that something was going on, something more involved than merely a "jealous husband."

She entered the dark room, then stopped, listening to Richard's slow, regular breathing. She considered switching on the light and roughly shaking him awake, confronting him with her photographic proof. But proof of what? She could imagine Richard rubbing his eyes from the light, stumbling over his words, and finally dismissing the pictures as inconsequential.

No, she thought, I don't want his denials, I want facts.

She returned the photos to the envelope, turned off the lights in the house, then made her way to the bathroom. After brushing her teeth, she undressed in the bedroom, having left the bathroom light on to avoid bumping around in the dark. As she slipped into her nightgown, she noticed the pale light falling on the dresser, where Richard had left his wallet in a puddle of loose change.

She glanced at the bed, saw that Richard hadn't moved, then lifted the wallet and stepped into the bathroom, softly closing the door behind her.

She hoped to find a clue to Jameson, perhaps a phone number—anything to gain her more information. Still, she couldn't help feeling guilty as she opened Richard's wallet. She firmly believed she had a right to know everything about him, but her conscience told her this was wrong.

The wallet was brown leather with a long compartment for cash, slots in the sides for cards, and a small bundle of clear plastic envelopes for photographs.

Lauren looked through the photos first. She was aware that Richard carried pictures of them, but she'd forgotten which ones he had. There were two of Emily, one in a dress and one in shorts and a Mickey Mouse T-shirt, shot with Amos in their backyard. Two pictures were of Lauren. One had been taken in their house and the other in a room that Lauren didn't recognize at first; she was sitting in an easy chair, smiling up at the camera. Then she remembered. It was Richard's old apartment. There was a photo of Lauren and Emily in their yard and another one of all three of them, probably taken by Connie.

The last photo caught Lauren by surprise—she in her best dress, Richard in a suit and tie, both flushed with joy. Their wedding picture.

Lauren touched the plastic case, remembering how she'd felt that day—so happy, looking forward to the days and years ahead. And now . . .

She set her jaw, turning her attention to the slots in the side of Richard's wallet, hoping for some lead on Jameson. She found cards for Visa, MasterCard, National Video Rental, and the San Miguel Public Library, plus proof of auto insurance, business cards from Mc-Fadden's hardware store, and a California driver's license. Nothing else.

Lauren flipped off the light and opened the bathroom door. She stood in the doorway until she was certain Richard was still asleep. Then she found the bureau in the darkness and replaced the wallet in its original position. She eased into bed, careful not to wake him. The sheets on her side were cold, and her first inclination was to slide over and snuggle up to him, to put her arm around him and feel his warmth.

But she lay near the edge of the bed, her back to him.

On Friday morning after Lauren had taken Emily to school, she drove home and phoned Geoffrey Leiderhaus. He answered on the second ring.

"Hello, Geoffrey, it's Lauren." She'd made her voice sound weak and sickly. She was both surprised and dismayed at how easy it was becoming for her to lie.

"How're you doing?" he asked with concern.

"Not too well. I mean, I'm sure it's nothing serious, probably just a cold, but I'm going to stay home today. As far as Decker Park, I—"

"Don't give it a thought—we've got plenty of time. You know," he said with a chuckle, "with the Memorial Day weekend coming up, some people might think you're stretching it into a four-day vacation. Just kidding. I'll see you Tuesday. In the meantime, take care of yourself."

"I definitely will."

She hung up, then pulled open the drawer and removed Richard's job application from the manila folder. Her eyes scanned the back page and his references—all phony, made up.

Okay, she thought, knowing she was still giving him every consideration, maybe he invented the names because he didn't have any friends to vouch for him.

Lauren opened the application to the middle pages. According to the record Richard had attended the University of Pennsylvania, where he'd earned first a bachelor's and then a master's degree in business administration. After that he'd worked for Darnell Corporation for five years.

Lauren frowned. She'd known that Richard graduated from college, but he'd never said he held a master's degree. She wondered now why someone with that level of education and business experience would want to be a clerk in a hardware store.

Perhaps Jameson could tell me that, too, she thought, if I could find him.

Then she mentally slapped her forehead for not thinking of something sooner. She turned through the white pages of the San Miguel phone directory, but her brief, faint hope evaporated when she found only James and Jammett and nothing in between.

Her attention returned to Richard. Although he'd never mentioned grandparents, cousins, aunts, or uncles, Lauren thought it possible that he had a relative in Philadelphia who could help her.

On the phone again she learned from the long-distance operator that there were seven Caylors in the Philadelphia directory. Lauren tried them all, connecting with four. None had heard of Richard Caylor. She vowed to try the remaining three later, but she sensed that their response would be the same.

Next she dialed the number for Darnell Corporation. She let it ring a dozen times before hanging up. Again she called long-distance information.

"I'm sorry," the operator said. "I have no listing for Darnell Corporation."

"Try Darnell, Incorporated, or Darnell anything."

She heard the operator tapping keys on her computer terminal, then: "I'm sorry. There's no business listed as Darnell."

Lauren hung up. She wondered if Darnell had moved out of Philadelphia or gone bankrupt. Or if Richard's entire job application had been faked.

She tried the only other reference to Richard's past: the University of Pennsylvania. After talking to the campus operator, she was put through to the registrar's office. The woman who answered sounded young enough to be a student.

"How may I help you?" she asked brightly.

"My name is Mrs. . . . Johnson," Lauren said. "I'm a personnel analyst for the city of San Miguel. We have a job applicant named Richard Caylor who indicates that he received a master's degree from your university. I'm checking to see if—"

"I'm sorry," the woman interrupted. "Student transcripts are available only through written request."

"I don't need to see his transcript. I just want to know whether or not he attended the university."

"You'll still have to mail a written request."

"I don't have *time* to—" Lauren stopped and took a breath, regaining control of herself. "Let me speak to your supervisor, please."

"One moment, please."

Lauren was put on hold for nearly five minutes, enough time to flesh out her lie, before another woman came on the line.

"This is Mrs. Eads. May I help you?" Her tone was businesslike.

Lauren repeated her request.

"I'm sorry, Mrs. Johnson, but our policy is clear. We cannot give out that information without a formal written request."

"I understand," Lauren said, maintaining her calm. "And under normal circumstances I wouldn't be calling you. In fact, right now my secretary is typing my request to you for Richard Caylor's transcript. In this instance, though, we are under a time constraint. You see, the city of San Miguel is about to begin a major project, funded in large part by the federal government. The stipulations in the contract are quite specific and—"

"Excuse me for interrupting, Mrs. Johnson, but I am bound by the university's regulations, no matter what your—"

"I'm asking you to bend the regulations," Lauren said firmly. "Unless specific items on Mr. Caylor's application are verified by noon today, under the federal regulation governing this contract we won't be able to hire him, and we *want* to hire. It's as simple as that. Please understand, he moved here with his family because I mistakenly informed him that the job was definitely his. It was my error, but he and his family are the ones who will suffer for it. We're not talking about a rule or a regulation written on a piece of paper, we're talking about a real person. Now I'm asking you, please."

Lauren held her breath, waiting. She'd once heard that truly effective liars believed their own lies. Until now she'd reasoned that that was impossible, but she'd begun to believe herself, and with very little effort.

I wonder if it's as easy for Richard, she thought grimly.

Finally Mrs. Eads said, "All right, but this will take a while. I'll have to call you back."

"Uh, oh, of course. The number is . . ." Lauren was so much into her role as personnel analyst that she nearly gave out her office number.

Half an hour passed before the phone rang. Lauren had begun to fear that Mrs. Eads would call long-distance information to verify the number for the city offices.

"City of San Miguel Personnel Department," Lauren answered. She prayed that the caller was indeed Mrs. Eads and not someone from work checking to see how she was feeling. "Mrs. Johnson speaking."

"This is Mrs. Eads again. I'm afraid we have no record of Richard Caylor as either an undergraduate or a graduate student. Of course, I say this to you unofficially. For an official statement you will still have to submit—"

"No, wait. Richard, er, Mr. Caylor received his master's degree over nine years ago. Perhaps you didn't check back far enough."

"The only Caylor on record," Mrs. Eads said evenly, "is Samuel Caylor. He graduated in 1906."

Lauren slowly hung up the phone.

She felt sick inside—and frightened. Richard's entire application was phony. Perhaps when he got home tonight, she should shove it in his face and demand to know the truth. No doubt he'd give her answers, but what would they be worth? Could she believe anything he told her?

Lauren closed the job application, unsure whether to keep it, return it to Arthur, or just throw it away. Then she saw something on the front page that made her consider another course of action.

She stuffed the application in her purse, switched off the kitchen light, and went out the back door, locking it behind her.

22

LAUREN DROVE NORTH on Ocean Boulevard. The morning was still cool and overcast, the ocean a mournful shade of gray. There were few people on the beach, relentless joggers, pounding along the hard-packed sand near the water.

As she neared Santa Rosa Avenue, she nearly turned right out of habit, which would have taken her to the municipal building. Then she saw a city truck with two surveyors waiting for the light. She knew the driver, having worked with him on several projects. Quickly she put her hand to her face and hoped neither of the two young men recognized her as she passed in front of them. If they did and happened to mention it to anyone at work, she'd have a hard time explaining what she was doing out when she was supposed to be home sick.

Lauren continued north on Ocean Boulevard for several miles.

Near the city limits she turned right. She hadn't been out this way for some time, but she was familiar with the area. She drove for a few blocks before turning again.

The street was a mixture of houses and apartments, all of them stucco, none of them newer than the 1960s.

Lauren parked the Honda at the curb in front of a two-story apartment building. She didn't need to check Richard's job application to know that this was the correct address—she'd been here often enough when Richard lived here.

The building ran lengthwise away from the street. It was quiet and small, ten units, owned and managed by Mr. and Mrs. Bennett. Lauren had met them while Richard was their tenant, but she wasn't certain they'd remember her.

The door to number one was flanked by shoulder-high poinsettia bushes. Lauren rang the bell.

The man who answered was tall, but hunched over slightly by

age, with short gray hair and a tanned face. There were deep lines at the corners of his eyes and mouth. He wore a crew-neck cotton sweater with no shirt underneath, blue cotton pants, and white canvas shoes.

"Yes?"

"Hi, Mr. Bennett? I don't know if you remember me. I'm Lauren Caylor. Actually, the last time I spoke to you I was Lauren Webb, but now I'm married to Richard Caylor."

She saw a sparkle in his blue eyes.

"Of course. I recognize you. I never forget a pretty face."

Lauren smiled. "Thank you."

"And how is Richard these days? I've been hoping he'd stop by and say hello. He was one of our best tenants."

"He's the reason I'm here," Lauren said. She glanced past him. "Could we . . ?"

"What? Oh, yes, of course. What am I thinking about? Please come in."

He moved aside and held the screen door for her. The living room was so crowded with furniture that they had to move single file between a sofa and an overstuffed chair to reach the center of the room.

"Please sit down," Mr. Bennett said. Then he turned toward an open doorway and hollered, "Mother, come out here a minute!"

A moment later Mrs. Bennett appeared in the doorway, her gray hair pinned back in a bun. She was as tan as her husband and dressed like him: crew-neck sweater, blue cotton pants, and white canvas shoes. Lauren imagined they could pass for brother and sister. She wondered if they'd grown to resemble each other over the years, or if they'd simply been attracted to one another because they looked alike.

"You remember Lauren Webb," Mr. Bennett said to his wife. "She was Richard Caylor's ladyfriend."

Mrs. Bennett edged between a recliner and an end table, then gave Lauren a quick but thorough study before turning to her husband. "Of course I remember her," she said, as if Lauren were not in the room. "She used to visit at least once a week. Divorced, I believe, with a little girl named, let me think . . . Amelia . . . Amanda . . ."

"Emily," Lauren said, wondering if the Bennetts studied all their tenants so closely.

"Emily," Mrs. Bennett said to her husband.

"Well, now she's married to Richard."

"She is?" She turned to Lauren for the first time. "How wonderful."

"Thank you."

"It's so nice to see you again," Mrs. Bennett said, as if Lauren had just now walked in. "Would you like some coffee?"

"Thanks, no. I don't want to take up your time."

"Nonsense—I can fetch it in a minute," she said, but she made no move to leave.

"The, ah, the reason I stopped by is, I'm planning a surprise birthday party for Richard." It was a lie Lauren was familiar with. "I'm putting together a guest list."

"A surprise party." Mr. Bennett grinned. "I love it. Don't you, Mother?"

"Yes indeed. We'd be delighted to come."

"That's great. I'm hoping you can help me add some more names to my list. Which of your tenants was Richard closest to?"

"Well, he lived in ten, so the couple across the landing in nine would be the closest."

"No, Mother," Mr. Bennett said. "I think she means 'closest' as in 'friendliest with.' " He turned to Lauren. "Isn't that right?"

"Yes."

Mr. and Mrs. Bennett faced each other and stared, as if they were performing mental telepathy. Slowly they shook their heads in unison and turned toward Lauren.

"You know," Mr. Bennett said, "I don't believe Richard had any friends while he lived here. He pretty much kept to himself. Aside from you, I don't think anyone even came to visit him."

"Except for that man you thought was a policeman. Remember, dear?"

"He *was* a policeman, of one kind or another."

"But you don't know that for certain, dear."

"I sure do," Mr. Bennett said with feeling. He turned to Lauren. "Maybe not your everyday, run-of-the-mill city cop with a uniform, but a cop just the same."

"Policeman, dear."

"Whatever."

"When was that?" Lauren asked Mr. Bennett.

He pinched his lip with two fingers and gave it a little tug. "Not long after Richard moved in."

"I believe it was the first week," Mrs. Bennett said.

"I believe you're right, Mother. I was out front raking the lawn and—"

"I believe you were trimming the jacaranda trees," Mrs. Bennett said.

"No, Mother, I'm certain I was raking."

"Trimming. Don't you remember, I mentioned the week before how overgrown they were looking."

"I believe you're right," Mr. Bennett said.

"Unless you'd *finished* trimming . . ."

Lauren gritted her teeth and forced a smile.

"That was it," Mr. Bennett said triumphantly. "I'd finished trimming and I'd picked up the branches and I was raking up twigs and leaves. And I looked up to see a car parking out front. Right away I thought: Cop."

"Policeman."

"Yes, Mother. The car was what they like to call 'unmarked,' but it may as well have had a sign on it. Solid color, no chrome, no extras, except for the spotlight on the driver's side and the extra radio antenna in back. The man who climbed out wasn't wearing a uniform, but he may as well have been. I could even see the bulge on his hip where he carried his gun. He walked up to me and asked how to get to number ten, Richard's apartment. I asked him if Richard was in some kind of trouble. He said no, Richard was a friend of his. He said it real pleasantly, but I don't think he meant it, not exactly." Mr. Bennett paused. "You look surprised."

"I'm just amazed at your memory," Lauren said. "All that happened almost four years ago."

"Mr. Bennett has an excellent memory," Mrs. Bennett said.

"Thank you, Mother."

Lauren wondered if the Bennetts ever used their first names.

"Another reason this sticks in my mind," Mr. Bennett said, "is, I'd been afraid at the time that we'd made a big mistake renting to Richard. I mean, he'd *seemed* liked a nice enough man, but what if he was in trouble with the police? Who might his friends be? What goings-on would we be seeing? I tell you, I was holding my breath."

"So was I, dear."

"But then nothing happened," Mr. Bennett continued. "We saw this cop visit—"

"Policeman. If he *was* a policeman."

"Oh, he was. We saw him visit Richard several more times in those first few weeks, and then we never saw him again."

"What did this man look like?" Lauren wondered if he was the man they'd seen in the restaurant or the man at Sea World.

Mr. Bennett pinched his lip and gave it another tug. "Forty to forty-five years old, kind of a big man, as if he'd played sports in college. Short black hair, gray on the sides. A colored man."

"Colored?" His use of the word caught Lauren by surprise.

"A Negro," Mrs. Bennett said.

"Of course." Obviously, this man was someone new to Lauren. "Did you get his name?"

The Bennetts looked at each other and slowly shook their heads.

"Was it Jameson?" Lauren asked.

They shook their heads some more. Then Mr. Bennett turned to Lauren. "I don't believe we ever got his name."

"Did you ask Richard about any of this?"

"Oh my, no," Mrs. Bennett said, aghast. "It really wasn't any of our business."

Right, Lauren thought, anxious now to get out of there. She made a display of looking at her watch. "Well, I really must be going now. Thank you so much for your help."

"Not at all," Mr. Bennett said. "When is it?"

"I beg your pardon?"

"The surprise party."

"Oh, I, uh, haven't set the exact date. In a few months. I'm still trying to track down Richard's old friends."

"How lovely," Mrs. Bennett said.

When Lauren got outside, a fine mist was falling, not enough to call rain, but enough to feel on her face. She crossed the street and sat in her car, wondering if she should talk to the tenants. But she doubted any of them could be more observant or nosier than the Bennetts. She also considered going into apartment ten and searching for anything Richard might have left behind.

Then she frowned, remembering . . .

When Richard moved into the house, he'd brought with him little more than his clothes. He'd been living in a furnished apartment, and he'd added little to it—a few cheap prints on the walls, some inexpensive pots and pans, dishes and silverware, towels, sheets. . . .They'd joked about it and given most of it to Goodwill, along with some of his older cold-weather clothes. However, he had brought with him an old suitcase that he said contained "some familiar junk I'd like to keep."

Lauren had never seen the contents, and until now she hadn't given it a second thought. She was certain that the suitcase was still somewhere in the house. Perhaps it contained a clue to Jameson.

By the time she got home, the mist had cleared, although the sky was still overcast and the air cool. When she parked in the garage, she noticed as if for the first time a stack of cardboard boxes in the corner near the shovels and rakes. They'd been there for so long that they'd become invisible. Lauren guessed the only reason she noticed them now was her frame of mind—seek and find.

The three boxes, one on top of another, were all large enough to hold a suitcase laid flat. Lauren pulled open the flaps of the top box and found it filled with old rags, smelling of paint thinner. She wondered if they posed a fire hazard, and she promised herself to get rid of them—later. She poked her hands down through the rags to the newspapers lining the bottom of the box. No suitcase.

Lauren lifted the box from the stack, set it on the concrete floor, and opened the second box. More rags, plus paint cans, brushes, scrapers, and stirring sticks.

The last box was packed tight with flowerpots—small, medium, and large; plastic and clay; new and used. Lauren shook her head. She had no idea how long the pots had been there, years perhaps, and only last month she'd asked Richard to bring home several from the store.

Lauren restacked the boxes. When she left the garage, she was greeted by Amos, who came bounding toward her from across the backyard.

"I wish you could talk, big boy," she said, rubbing his ears. "You could probably tell me a thing or two about Richard."

In the kitchen she gave him a rawhide stick to chew on. It was nearly noon, but Lauren wasn't hungry enough for lunch. She was eager to find the suitcase. And although she knew it might reveal nothing, it seemed to represent her best, if not her last, hope of locating a key to Richard's past.

First she checked all the closets in the house, pushing aside coats and pants, skirts and dresses, peering into shadowy corners. She carried the step stool with her to search the top shelves.

No suitcase.

Oh, she found *suitcases*, but not *the* suitcase. She was beginning to think that perhaps Richard had donated it along with its contents to Goodwill. And then she remembered where it was.

She went out through the sliding glass doors to the deck, and down three steps to the yard. Near the southwest corner of the house, directly under the west window of Emily's bedroom, there was a wooden cover, about four feet square and painted white, one edge flush with the house. Lauren squatted down and lifted the end of the heavy cover, dragged it toward her, then tipped it back and leaned it against the house.

The square, shallow pit before her had a dirt floor and three concrete sides. The fourth side was a gaping black hole that opened into the crawl space beneath the house. A few wriggly brown insects scuttled out of sight.

Lauren nearly stepped down into the hole, hesitating when she realized she was wearing a skirt and blouse and low-heeled pumps. She went inside and changed into a pair of old jeans, a sweatshirt, and tennis shoes; then she rummaged around in the kitchen drawers until she found a flashlight.

Back outside, Lauren stared uneasily into the pit. There were no bugs crawling around, but she knew they were very near, hiding in cracks and holes, just out of sight. She wasn't exactly *afraid* of creepy, crawly things. She just didn't like them.

She sighed and stepped down into the pit.

23

LAUREN CROUCHED on the floor of the pit and peered into the opening beneath the house. The weak sunlight glistened on spiderwebs and lay in a pale wedge on the dry dirt floor. Beyond the reach of the sun lay semidarkness and pitch-black mounds. Lauren hadn't been down here since before Richard moved in, but she remembered telling him about the crawl space as somewhere to store things "out of the way."

She clicked on the flashlight and aimed it like a spear into the crawl space. The black mounds remained black—plastic trash bags filled with dear junk and tied shut to keep out moisture.

Lauren saw no suitcase, only a dozen or so identical shiny black bags with an aisle through them leading to the furnace. She assumed Richard had stored his old suitcase in one of the bags, and she was disheartened by the thought of having to open every one of them. Still, she hoped for the best: Richard wouldn't have crawled under there any farther than necessary.

She brushed aside a spiderweb, then moved on her hands and knees through the opening, stopping at the nearest bag and untwisting the length of wire that held it shut. When she shone her flashlight inside, she was relieved and delighted to see a suitcase wedged between a pair of thick, folded blankets. Lauren set aside the light, then pulled out the blankets and laid them on the nearest plastic bag. The suitcase was a scuffed-up, dark gray two-suiter that appeared to have come from a secondhand store—useful for storage, but shabby for travel. It wasn't too heavy, but it obviously wasn't empty.

After she returned the blankets to the bag, she retrieved her flashlight and crawled toward the opening, dragging the suitcase behind her. She lifted it onto the lawn and climbed out of the pit, brushing dirt from her hands and knees and wiping a strand of spiderweb from her forehead.

In the family room Lauren laid the suitcase on the carpet between the love seats. She tried the latches. Both locked. Not about to waste time looking for the key, she got a thick-shafted screwdriver from the kitchen.

Lauren straddled the suitcase, sitting just behind the handle with her knees bent, hugging the sides, the way a child would ride a hobby horse. She wedged the end of the screwdriver under the first latch, gripped it with both hands, and yanked upward. The lock snapped open.

Lauren smiled wryly, imagining herself trying to explain this to Richard should he walk in right now.

She forced open the second latch, then laid the suitcase flat on the floor, knelt beside it, and opened it.

Each half of the case was enclosed by a soft, gray cover held in place with twist locks. Lauren undid one cover and swung it back on its hinges. Inside were a couple of books and a carefully folded man's black cashmere overcoat that nearly filled the compartment.

Lauren stood and held the coat before her. It fell well below her knees, a beautiful garment, obviously expensive, but certainly not suitable for Southern California. She could picture how nice Richard would look wearing this, and she understood why he'd be reluctant to part with it. However, it seemed odd that Richard should own such an expensive coat. His wardrobe always had been understated, though tasteful, certainly not opulent enough to include cashmere overcoats. Could he have afforded a coat like this, working as a bookkeeper?

Before Lauren refolded the coat, she checked inside the pockets. The left one was empty, but in the right-hand pocket she found two ticket stubs for the Chicago Symphony Orchestra. The tickets were dated over four years ago.

Lauren wondered idly who Richard had taken to the symphony. Perhaps an ex-girlfriend. Had he been in Chicago visiting friends or conducting business? She remembered his personal references and thought briefly about repeating her telephone search with the Chicago long-distance operator, then decided it would probably be a waste of time.

She set aside the coat and examined the two books, both large-size paperbacks: *California, the Golden State* and *A Traveler's Guide to Southern California*. When Lauren thumbed through the latter book, it fell open to a dog-eared page. She read, "Chapter 7—The Saintly Beaches: San Clemente and San Miguel."

Is this how Richard decided on San Miguel, she thought, by reading travel guides?

But when she turned the book over, she received a mild shock. Stamped on the back cover was the name of the store where the book had been purchased—The Book Bag, 2939 Ocean Boulevard, San Miguel, CA.

Apparently, Richard had bought the book after he'd moved here. The question was, *why* had he moved here?

She returned the books and the overcoat to the suitcase, closed the cloth cover, and opened the other side.

Inside were a small wooden box, about the size used for cigars, and a fine leather attaché case, suitable for a successful lawyer or businessman. She pictured how impressive—and handsome—Richard must have been with his attaché case and cashmere overcoat . . . before he moved to San Miguel to become a clerk in a hardware store. Lauren did not try to guess why he'd made the change. She lifted out the briefcase, flipped the latches, and opened it, hoping to find answers, maybe even a gold mine: an address book. There were a number of leather-lined compartments inside, but they were all empty. Not so much as a pencil or a scrap of paper had been left behind.

Lauren closed the case and set it aside, then raised the lid of the small wooden box. She froze.

The box contained a revolver and a box of cartridges. Lauren stared at the gun as if it were a dead reptile, inert but still dripping venom. It was blue steel with checkered wooden grips and a short, deadly-looking barrel. Lauren wasn't certain of its caliber, but she knew it wasn't a .22.

When she was no more than ten, living in Nebraska, she'd fired a rifle and a pistol, both .22-caliber. Her father and brother had owned shotguns for pheasant hunting and small-bore guns for target practice. Although Lauren abhorred the idea of shooting any living thing, her father had insisted that she at least learn how to use firearms.

He'd driven her to a plowed field in his old pickup truck, and they'd set up several tin cans in front of an earthen mound, then moved back about fifty feet. He showed her how to load the single-shot rifle, how to hold it, how to line up the target with the front and rear sights, how to gently squeeze the trigger.

When she did, there was a sharp cracking sound, and one of the cans jumped into the air. Her father proudly proclaimed her to be a "natural shot," and she was afraid to confess that she'd been aiming at the other can.

After that he loaded the pistol for her, a six-shot revolver with a long barrel. She held it with both hands, the way he showed her, and gently squeezed off all six shots, hitting nothing but dirt. When he asked her to try again, she complained that her ears were hurting from the noise. On the drive home he told her that he would not ask her again to fire a gun, but if she ever wanted to or needed to, at least she'd know how.

She hadn't touched a gun since that day.

And now, staring at the revolver before her, she knew without question that this was not for target practice. This was a weapon designed, sold, and purchased for one purpose: to shoot a human being.

Lauren was shocked that Richard owned a gun, particularly one of this type. He was a sensitive man, certainly not a "gun nut" or even a sportsman. So why did he own a handgun? And perhaps more important, *when* had he acquired it, before or after he moved here? Lauren found herself hoping that the revolver belonged to Richard's distant past, because the thought of him buying it after he came to San Miguel was more frightening, more immediate.

She closed the wooden lid, then noticed something under the box. She'd nearly missed it because it was flat and no wider than the box—a silver picture frame. She held it before her, studying the color photograph inside: a full-length view of a man and woman in a snowy park with barren trees in the background. They wore long coats and scarves and had their arms around each other.

The woman was young and attractive, with delicate features and silky black hair that fell to her shoulders.

The man was a few years older, wearing tinted glasses and a neatly trimmed black beard. Lauren thought he might be related to Richard, cousins perhaps—not brothers, she knew, because Richard was an only child. At least that's what he'd told her.

The photograph had been signed with a felt-tip pen in the lower right-hand corner:

To Donny,
with all my love,
from the future Mrs. Donald Rassitter

The date below the signature was five years old.

Lauren again looked at the faces of the man and woman. They were obviously in love, and according to the inscription they were engaged to be married. She wondered why Richard would keep a photograph of these two, particularly one signed by the bride-to-be for her future husband. In fact, how had he come to have it in the first place?

She started to return the picture frame to the suitcase, hesitated, then laid it on the end table. She put the attaché case in the suitcase, closed it, and managed to get one of the latches to hold. Then she carried it out to the crawl space, where she stowed it in its plastic trash bag and lowered the cover over the pit.

Back in the family room she picked up the silver-framed picture and studied the young couple's faces, especially the man's. It seemed doubtful that he *wasn't* related to Richard, because the resemblance, although slight, was unmistakable.

There's only one way to find out for sure, she thought.

She carried the photo to the master bedroom and put it in one of her bureau drawers.

After dinner Emily went into the family room to watch an animated movie on TV. Richard helped Lauren clear the dining room table, leaving only the cups and saucers.

They'd spoken little since Richard arrived home. When he asked, "How was work today?" she'd lied and said, "Fine." He seemed tired, and he was quiet, almost withdrawn. But that wasn't why Lauren hadn't yet mentioned the suitcase. She expected a confrontation, and she didn't want it to occur in front of Emily.

She filled their cups with coffee, then set the pot on a trivet in the center of the table. She waited until he'd stirred in half a spoonful of sugar and taken a sip before she spoke.

"Why did you move here?"

He smiled, confused. "What?"

"I've been wondering why you left Philadelphia and moved to San Miguel. I don't believe you ever explained it to me." She strained to

157

make her tone conversational, but there was a knot in her stomach.

"You know why," he said, trying to maintain his smile. "To be with you."

"No, really, why did you?"

His eyes narrowed almost imperceptibly, and he answered with a question. "Why do you ask? I mean, why now?"

"I'm curious, that's all."

"Does it matter?"

"Yes, Richard, I think it does."

He looked away, obviously reluctant to say more.

Lauren said, "You didn't have a job waiting for you here, so that wasn't the reason. And you didn't have any friends or relatives on the West Coast. You'd never even been to this part of the country before, right? So what made you choose San Miguel? For that matter, why did you move to California?"

"I needed a change of climate," he said evenly.

"But why San Miguel?"

"I'd heard it was a nice place to live. Lauren, why—"

"From whom?"

"I beg your pardon?"

"Who told you that San Miguel was a nice place to live?" She'd dropped any semblance of a conversational tone. Now she was grilling him.

Richard took a careful sip of coffee, then set his cup on the saucer with a deliberate and precise click. "A friend of mine."

"Who, Jameson?" Faint TV noise drifted in from the family room. Lauren prayed it was enough to block their voices from Emily. She sensed that this conversation had already passed the point of no return.

One corner of Richard's mouth went up in a grin. "Yes, as a matter of fact it *was* Jameson."

"If he's your friend, why haven't I ever met him? I don't even know his first name."

"God," he said, more relaxed, apparently on firmer ground, "you're full of questions this evening."

She waited.

"Okay." He seemed to give in. "The reason I haven't introduced you to him or had him over for dinner is because he's not sociable. In fact, I've invited him here on several occasions, and each time he's declined." Richard paused. "And his first name is Felix. Satisfied?"

"Not really. You told me he was with the San Miguel Police Department. I checked, and he's not."

"You what?" He looked offended.

"They're in my building, you know. I went downstairs and asked for Jameson. They'd never heard of him."

Richard blew air through his nose. "Of course not—he's retired. When I said he worked for the San Miguel police, I meant he *used* to, okay? Now why don't we take our coffee in the other room and watch TV."

Lauren felt he was lying, but she ignored it, pressing on. "One more question."

He set his jaw, ready to fight.

"What is it?" he said tightly.

"Who's Donald Rassitter?"

Richard's face turned white.

24

LAUREN WASN'T SURE what reaction she'd expected from Richard. Perhaps astonishment that she'd discovered a name from his past. Certainly not this: stark fear. He clutched the edge of the table hard enough to make his knuckles shine, and he spoke in a harsh whisper.

"How do you know Donald Rassitter?"

"I don't, I—"

"Then how do you know his name?"

Some of the color had come back into his face. Lauren could tell he was struggling to mask his fear. She'd never seen him this way, and it frightened her. She wondered if it had been a mistake to mention the name.

"How?" Richard asked again, his voice clear and loud.

"I found a photograph . . ."

"What?"

"I'll get it," she said, rising abruptly and hurrying to the bedroom, as if she didn't want Richard to follow, but wanted instead to keep the discussion at the table, over cups of coffee. She returned with the silver-framed photograph and set it before him.

He stared at it for a moment, reached out, not quite touching it, and then withdrew his hand. "Where did you get this?" His voice had softened, and he wore a look of defeat.

Lauren eased back into her chair. "I . . . got off work early today," she lied, "and I was looking for things to give to Goodwill. I found your old suitcase under the house and—"

"Suitcase?" Richard looked at her dully, then lowered his eyes to the photograph of the man and woman in winter.

"Are they friends of yours from Philadelphia? Or are they relatives?"

Richard seemed confused. "What?"

"Is he related to you? I see a certain similarity."

Richard frowned at the photograph and slowly shook his head. "No, we're not related," he said softly.

"But there is a resemblance."

"No," he said, and seemed to relax. "It's only because of Donny's glasses and beard. They hide the differences between us, and without them you wouldn't think for a minute that we resembled each other."

"Who is he?"

"He . . . was a close friend."

"Was?"

Richard glanced at her, and touched the picture for the first time, holding it before him with both hands, as if he were reading a book.

"Donny is dead. He and Francine—that's the woman here—were both killed in a . . . tragic accident. It happened shortly before they were to be married."

There was a deep sadness in Richard's voice that Lauren had never heard before. She waited for him to continue.

"Donny left me a few things in his will, and somehow I ended up with this picture. I'm not sure why I kept it, maybe to keep his memory alive. It's stupid, I know, but . . . sometimes it's hard to let go of the past."

"You two must have been very close."

"We were."

"Did you work together?" Now that Richard appeared to have regained his composure, Lauren was resolved to press on.

"Work together? Y-yes."

"At Darnell Corporation?"

"Darnell? Well, yes."

"And did you also work with Joseph Adderly, Matthew Harris, and Robert Traverner?"

Again Richard looked confused.

"Who?"

"Don't you recognize those names?"

"No, I don't," he said, and his expression began to harden. "Who are they?"

Lauren took a breath, feeling as if she were poised on a high diving board, ready to jump. "You listed them as references on your job application."

"My job . . ."

"The one you filled out when you applied at McFadden's Hardware," she said.

Richard looked astonished.

Lauren rushed ahead, not giving him a chance to respond. "I borrowed it from Arthur by lying, telling him I wanted to locate some of your old friends for a surprise party. I was trying to find someone from your past, *anyone*, who could tell me about Jameson or why you seemed so . . . paranoid." Lauren strained to control her voice, fighting the fear and anger that bubbled inside. "Obviously, something's going on, Richard, and you're not being honest with me. Lately you've seemed . . . different, and I want to know why."

He laid the picture flat on the table and sat back in his chair, folding his arms. His cheeks were flushed, whether from anger or embarrassment Lauren couldn't tell.

"What else did you find on my application?" he asked evenly.

"Only that . . . the long-distance operator in Philadelphia has no record of any of these men."

Richard shrugged. "People move. I guess they've left Philadelphia."

"And what about Darnell Corporation?" Lauren said, unable to keep the sarcasm from her voice. "The operator had no listing for it. Did it move, too?"

"No," he said tightly, "it didn't move. It . . . A few years ago I read that it was bought out by General Electric, something to do with their Star Wars research. Apparently, they dropped the name Darnell. Is that all you found?"

"No, it's not. The University of Pennsylvania has no record of—"

"Records can get lost."

"Goddammit, Richard, will you stop playing games!"

Lauren had shouted without meaning to. Now she listened for Emily, waiting for her to enter the room to see what was going on. But only muted TV sounds drifted in from the family room. Lauren breathed deeply, trying to calm herself.

"I also found a gun in your suitcase," she said. "Do you want to tell me about *that*."

Richard shrugged again, nonchalant, but he couldn't help shifting his eyes, as if he were seeking a way out.

"A lot of people own guns," he said weakly.

"That's no answer, and you know it." Then she paused and her tone became ironic. "And as I recall, you helped Connie with her campaign to register all handguns in San Miguel. I'm sure you remember—it was just before we were married."

Richard said nothing.

"You even volunteered to get signatures by posting a petition at the store," Lauren said. "But I don't recall you telling anyone that *you* owned a gun. You must have felt like a hypocrite." .

"Now wait a minute."

"Were you trying to convince us, to convince *me,* that you were someone you're not?"

"That's not fair, dammit, now you listen to me—"

"No!" she cried, banging the table with her fist, rattling the cups, startling Richard, and surprising herself. She glanced toward the family room, then fixed her gaze on Richard. "Don't you *dare* accuse me of not being fair. *You're* the one who's been unfair, you and your . . . half-truths. I want no more of it, Richard, I want some straight answers from you. And if that's asking too much, then maybe we shouldn't be together."

She'd hadn't meant to say it quite that way, but there it was, hanging in the silence between them.

"Lauren, please . . ."

She gritted her teeth and forced herself to ignore the pleading in his voice. "You can start by telling me about the gun."

Richard seemed unable to hold her gaze. He sighed, staring down at the table. "All right," he said quietly. "I bought it for protection."

"What do you mean?"

"It's . . . complicated."

He paused, gathering his thoughts. Lauren couldn't help wondering if he was fabricating another story.

"It has to do with the couple in this photograph," he said, touching the silver frame with his fingertips. "You see, before Francine was engaged to Donny, she used to go out with a man named Charles Dent. Charles was a friend of mine, too, not as close to me as Donny, but close enough. He was insanely jealous of Francine. Even though they weren't living together or engaged to be married, as far as Charles was concerned Francine was his woman."

Richard kept his eyes on the photograph as he spoke.

"One Saturday afternoon Donny and I were fooling around downtown and we ran into Francine and one of her girlfriends. Donny and Francine had never met, so I made the introductions, and then the four of us decided to have lunch. All perfectly innocent. Except that Donny and Francine had fallen in love at first sight. After that day they started going out, secretly at first, behind Charles's back. Donny told me what was going on, and I said he was playing with fire. Eventually he and Francine broke the news to Charles—she was going to move in with Donny."

Richard looked up at Lauren, as if to gauge whether she believed his story thus far. She was reserving judgment.

"Well, Charles went nuts. He broke into their house, slapped Francine around, got in a fistfight with Donny. It was ugly. Donny had Charles arrested, and a judge placed a restraining order on him, telling him to stay away from Donny and Francine. Not long after that Donny and Francine announced their engagement." Richard paused, drawing in a painful breath. "Two days later they were killed in what appeared to be an automobile accident."

"Killed?" Then, "What do you mean, 'appeared to be' an accident?"

"Their car had crashed into a bridge abutment, and there was some evidence that they'd been forced off the road."

"Are you saying they were *murdered*?"

"I considered that possibility," Richard said, "and so did the police, with Charles the primary suspect. But nothing was ever proven. It might have ended there, but Charles began threatening me."

"You? Why?"

"Because I was the one who had first introduced Donny and Francine. In effect, I was responsible for Francine choosing Donny over Charles."

"That's ridiculous."

"Not to Charles. And more, he blamed their deaths on me."

"What!"

Richard nodded grimly. "He'd always claimed he had nothing to do with the accident. He said Francine had died because of Donny's carelessness and that, in his mind, I had put Francine in that car with Donny." Richard shook his head. "It was insane, of course, and I didn't take Charles's threats seriously—until the night someone fired a gunshot through my living room window."

Lauren inhaled sharply.

"That's when I truly began to fear for my life," Richard went on. "I called in the police, but there wasn't much they could do—watch my house, keep an eye on Charles—and they couldn't do that all the time. So I bought a gun, the one you found. I began carrying it wherever I went, even to work—illegally, of course, because I didn't have a permit. I was frightened and paranoid. One day I saw Charles following me on the street, and I realized with horror that I was actually considering shooting him."

He shook his head again at the memory. "That's how bad I was getting," he said. "I knew that if this continued, we'd both lose—one of us was certain to become a murder victim and the other one would go to prison. The only way I could see to get out was to do just that: get out."

Richard heaved a sigh.

"So I quit my job, left Philadelphia, and moved here without knowing how long I'd stay and without telling anyone where I'd gone. Of course, when I met you I knew I'd never leave." He gave her a weak smile. "As far as the gun goes, I put it away right after I moved here, and to tell you the truth, I haven't thought about it since then." He shrugged. "That's it."

Lauren frowned. "And all this, I mean, everything that's happened these past few days, it all has to do with this man back in Philadelphia, this Charles Dent?"

Richard nodded, his mouth a grim line.

"Is that who you thought you saw in Tobey's restaurant last Monday night?"

"Yes. But it wasn't him, I'm sure of that now. Jameson assured me we're safe—that is, that there's nothing to worry about. He said Charles Dent has forgotten about me, that he's married now and still living in Philadelphia. And maybe he actually had nothing to do with Donny's and Francine's deaths."

Lauren was silent for a few moments, thinking. Finally she said, "Who exactly is Jameson?"

"I told you before, he's an old friend of mine, a cop. Ex-cop. I asked him to check out Charles Dent, and he did."

Richard turned his palms upward, as if to show her that he was hiding nothing.

"What about the references?"

"On my job application? I made them up. I didn't want anyone here calling my friends back there, because I thought Charles might be able to find me that way." Richard forced a laugh. "Silly, huh? I was worried for nothing. That guy couldn't care less about me."

He got up and came around the table, then stood behind her, his hands gently rubbing her shoulders. She tensed beneath his touch.

"I'm sorry about all this, Lauren, about my misleading you. I guess I didn't want to upset you with the truth, and I thought a few harmless lies would be better. I was wrong and I apologize."

He leaned down and kissed her cheek. When she failed to respond, he reached across the table and picked up the silver-framed picture. "I'm going to put this back where you found it."

Lauren watched him pass through the doorway and listened to him saying something to Emily in the family room. A moment later she heard the glass doors sliding open and closed. She stood stiffly, feeling as if she'd been in a fight, not knowing whether she'd won or lost. It was frustrating, wanting to believe everything that Richard had just told her, but—

The phone rang, calling her to the kitchen. She set the cups and saucers in the sink and lifted the receiver, almost hoping it was a telephone solicitor, a total stranger on whom she could vent her feelings by being rude and hanging up.

But it was Paul.

"How are you?" His voice was bright.

"Fine," she answered dully. She briefly considered asking his opinion about Richard, perhaps getting a man's point of view—which made her aware of how desperate she was becoming. Paul Webb was the *last* person she'd confide in. If she opened up to him, he'd find some way to criticize her, to blame her for her predicament. It had been years since she'd talked to him about anything more involved than his health or the weather. There was nothing between them now. Almost nothing.

"I'll drop by tomorrow at ten to pick up Emily," he said.

"What are you talking about?" Lauren had forgotten that this was Paul's weekend to have Emily. Since he often waived his weekend rights, he always phoned Lauren by the middle of the week if he was coming. Lauren felt the anger rise in her throat like a hot bubble, knowing it had as much to do with Richard as Paul.

"Do you think you can just call here the night before," she said irritably, "and expect us to jump at your bidding? My daughter is not an *object* to be tossed around like—"

"Hey, she's *my* daughter too."

"When it's convenient for you," she snapped. Then she squeezed her eyes shut, feeling warm tears under her lashes, her sudden anger dissipated. She heard the sliding door open and close again and Richard's footsteps moving through the family room, away from her. "I'm sorry," she said quietly.

"This *is* my weekend to have Emily, you know."

"Yes, I know." Lauren's voice was strained. "Ten o'clock is fine." She started to hang up, then said, "Wait a minute. This is Memorial Day weekend. Are you planning to keep Emily for three days?"

"Ah, well, no. I've got business to take care of on Monday. I'll have her back Sunday night."

"Fine," Lauren said, and hung up without saying good-bye.

She wiped her eyes with a dish towel, leaving a faint smudge of mascara. Then she wet the towel under the faucet, wrung it out, and pressed it to her face, letting the coolness seep through her skin. She was upset with herself for blowing up at Paul, even if he *was* giving her short notice. At least she'd have all day Monday to spend with Emily.

Still, Saturday and Sunday would find her uneasy. Though she knew Emily was safe with Paul, she never felt entirely relaxed being separated from her. She worried about her daughter. Did Paul remember to put the seat belt on her in the car? Did he feed her something other than junk food? Did he hold her hand in a crowd?

Lauren knew that part of her worry stemmed from selfishness. She was deeply attached to Emily, and she missed her terribly when she was gone.

It had been worse before she met Richard. She'd felt completely alone when Emily was with Paul. She would spend the weekend at home, waiting for the phone to ring, dreading to hear that something terrible had happened to Emily. Later, after she began seeing Richard, it had been different: Her weekends were no longer spent alone. Of course, her daughter's absence had still been on her mind, but the worry had been lessened. She and Richard had done things together, laughed together.

But now . . .

She walked into the family room and found Emily sitting on the floor in front of the TV. The sound was low and the screen was filled with animated mania.

"What are you watching, honey?"

"I don't know."

Lauren sat down in one of the two easy chairs that faced the television console. "Come back here with me and let's see what else is on."

Emily climbed into her mother's lap, and Lauren began clicking through the channels with the remote tuner, searching for something palatable. She stopped at an image that could have been a nature program or a beer commercial—a horse running in slow motion. When the narrator began to explain how the relationship between humans and horses was thousands of years old, Lauren set aside the tuner. She watched the screen, but her thoughts were on Richard.

When they first met, he'd seemed entirely open and honest. Now she knew different. He'd misled her, lied to her about the man in Tobey's, first saying that the man was an irate customer, then a jealous husband, and finally a dangerous man from his past, someone suspected of murdering two people. Was this latest story simply another lie? And if so, was there something even more sinister he was hiding?

Richard had said that Darnell Corporation worked on top-secret projects for the Defense Department. Was it possible that the U.S. government was involved?

She had no way of knowing.

Richard entered from the hallway and passed behind Lauren and Emily.

"What's this?" he asked pleasantly. He touched the top of Emily's head.

"Horses!" Emily said.

Richard sat in the other easy chair. The soft glow from the TV bathed his face.

Lauren knew that she could choose to believe Richard's latest story or not. If she chose not to, she felt she had but one way to get the truth: threaten to throw Richard out of the house unless he told her everything. And if he refused to leave? She and Emily could move out.

Desperate measures.

25

BY THE TIME they went to bed, Lauren found herself ready to believe that Richard's latest explanation of events was the truth. She wanted to believe. She felt in her heart that Richard was a good man, good for her and Emily. She'd watched him with Emily, seen the love in his face. She knew he wasn't faking that. He loved them both. And as for his half-truths? They'd been misguided attempts to shield her from unnecessary worry.

Still, as she climbed under the covers she felt tense, as if this were her first time in bed with Richard and she didn't know what to expect. She lay on her side of the bed with the sheet and blanket pulled over her breasts.

"Good-night, babe," he said quietly, touching her shoulder, then leaving his hand there.

"Good-night, Richard."

He rolled toward her, lying on his side, his head propped on his elbow. His features were soft and blurred in the darkness, and when he spoke his face was close enough for her to feel his breath.

"I'm sorry about what I'm . . . about what I've put you through," he said.

"It's all right, you—"

"No, it's not. It's not fair to you or Emily, and I apologize. If I had it to do over again . . ."

"Let's just forget about it," Lauren said. "It's all behind us now, right?"

Richard was silent for a moment, his body very close to hers, though not touching.

"I love you," he said softly. "More than anything."

"I know." And she did. "I love you too."

He leaned toward her, kissing her cheek, her lips. She returned his kisses, hesitantly at first, then with desire—not simply for sex, but for love, security.

And then her arms were around his neck, pulling him to her, their bodies pressed together, and the touch of his hands was both strong and gentle.

He kissed her passionately, and then he moved down, kissing her neck, and down, nibbling gently at her breasts, and down, brushing over her abdomen, and down . . . She moaned softly and pulled his face up to hers. He lay on top of her now, but lightly, keeping his weight off her, and then she felt him inside and she clung to him. He moved, and she moved with him, and against him and with him, and their passion grew until they could no longer contain it.

Afterward, they held each other in the darkness, saying nothing, beyond words, feeling their heartbeats slowing, pulling the blanket back in place as the room seemed to grow cool, finally falling asleep.

On Saturday morning after breakfast they all went for a walk in the neighborhood—Lauren, Emily, Richard, and Amos. Lauren quickly scanned the house across the street, noting that the brown car was under the carport and the front drapes were barely parted, as usual.

The sun was already warm, burning away the early haze from the sea. The air smelled fresh and clean, and it seemed to imbue them all with energy. Even Amos behaved like a greyhound half his age, stepping lightly, his leg and shoulder muscles rippling under his shiny coat, as if he were on his way to the starting gate.

Back home Richard went outside to work in the yard, while Lauren helped Emily pack her small suitcase.

"Mommy, can I go next door and play with Ryan?"

"No, honey. Your daddy will be here soon."

Emily sat down hard on the edge of her bed. "I don't *want* to go with him."

"Sure you do," Lauren said lightly. "You love your daddy."

"I don't want to go."

Lauren sat beside her and rubbed her back. She didn't want her to go either, but she would never say so to Emily.

"You always have fun when you stay with your daddy, don't you?"

Emily shrugged, staring down at her red tennis shoes.

"He always takes you to fun places, right?" He didn't always, Lauren knew.

"I guess."

"And when you come back, don't we always sit down together and you tell me about all the things you did?"

"Yeah."

"Okay then, tomorrow night we'll do that. Is it a deal?"

She held out her hand. Emily looked up and smiled.

"Deal," Emily said, and shook her mother's hand.

Lauren carried Emily's suitcase to the living room and set it by the front door. Then she dragged the vacuum cleaner from the coat closet and began sweeping the carpets. She was still vacuuming when the doorbell rang.

"Hi." Paul Webb flashed her a smile.

He looked handsomer than ever, Lauren thought, and she could easily forgive herself for once having been infatuated with this man. She wondered, though, how she had ever loved him. He was tall and tanned, wearing a powder-blue polo shirt, white pants, and topsiders. He looked to be in excellent physical condition, and Lauren guessed that he'd been spending time on Nautilus machines and racquetball courts. His hair was different than when she'd seen him a month ago—shorter and lighter, bleached by the sun. Or perhaps by chemicals, she thought wryly.

"Come in," Lauren said, holding the door. When he stepped past her, she smelled his cologne: musk.

"Hi, Daddy."

Emily came in from the next room, smiling shyly. Paul caught her by the waist and swooped her off her feet, holding her above his head. Lauren winced.

"How's my little girl?" He grinned up at her.

"Don't drop me!" she cried, giggling nervously.

Paul laughed. "I'd never drop you in a million years."

He set her down, bouncing her lightly on her feet. Lauren straightened Emily's shirt and tucked it in at the back of her shorts where it had come out.

"I've packed several changes of clothes for her," she told Paul, "because I didn't know what you two were doing this weekend."

"I haven't made plans yet for tomorrow." Paul checked his watch. "But I've got a tennis match in less than two hours in Palos Verdes."

Lauren cocked her head and put a hand on her hip. "You're going to play *tennis*? What's Emily going to do?"

Paul looked around him for help from a nonexistent audience. "Watch me," he said, shrugging, "drink lemonade, you know . . ."

"Whoopee," Lauren said flatly.

"Hey, I'm playing at a country club, and Emily's never been to a country club before. It will expose her to a little class."

"Swell. And what does she get to do while you hop around for a few hours in your little white shorts?"

"Beth will be with her."

"Oh, good," Lauren said pleasantly. "And who's Beth? Someone you met on the way over here?"

Paul showed his canines. "Now, now. Beth's a sweet girl. In fact, she's waiting in the car, so . . ." He reached down and picked up Emily's suitcase. "You ready to go to a country club, sugar?"

"Yeah!" Emily said, then: "What is it?"

Paul looked at Lauren. "You see? The kid needs an education."

"You just make sure that—"

"Hey, Rich, how's it going?" Paul looked over the top of Lauren's head, ignoring her.

Richard stood just behind her, wearing a T-shirt, baggy shorts, and old tennis shoes, one with a broken lace.

"Hello, Paul." Richard's voice was neutral. Lauren knew that he had little regard for her ex-husband, in addition to disliking being called "Rich." He smiled down at Emily. "Are you ready to go?"

"Uh huh." Emily looked uncomfortable standing between her two fathers.

"Hey, that reminds me," Paul said. He reached into his back pocket and withdrew a pair of tickets, curved from having been sat on. "Today's game, Dodgers and the Mets, box seats. A client gave them to me and I can't use them."

"I don't know if we—"

"Go ahead," he said, forcing the tickets into Lauren's hand. "Have some fun for a change. It'll do you good to get out of the house."

Lauren ignored Paul's jibes and squatted down before Emily.

"You be a good girl, and I'll see you tomorrow night." She glanced up at Paul. "Not too late."

"Yes, Mother," he said, grinning.

Lauren kissed Emily on the cheek. "Good-bye, baby."

" 'Bye, mommy. 'Bye, Amos." The big dog had ambled into the room and now wagged his tail in slow, sweeping arcs while Emily hugged his neck. She took Paul's hand and turned toward the door, then stopped and looked back over her shoulder. " 'Bye, Richard."

Richard smiled at her. "Good-bye, honey. See you tomorrow."

Lauren watched them go down the walk to the street, where a white Mustang convertible waited at the curb. Sitting in the passenger seat was a young woman with long blond hair. Lauren could see that she was pretty, even from this distance. The woman got out and held the seat for Emily to climb in the back.

Lauren heard Emily say something, but she couldn't understand her words. Then the woman reached down and pulled Emily's seat belt across her, making Lauren smile in spite of herself. Paul climbed in, started the engine with a roar, and drove away.

Lauren watched the car disappear around the curve in the street. She sensed Richard standing behind her.

"I hate it when she leaves."

"I know," he said gently. "So do I."

She turned and looked into his eyes. At that moment she felt very close to him. She kissed him.

"I'd better get back to my yard work," he said, smiling, "before I get too distracted here."

He patted her on the backside, then went out through the kitchen, followed by Amos. Lauren returned to the hallway to her waiting vacuum cleaner.

It was nearly noon when she finished vacuuming and dusting. She went out to the backyard to see if Richard was ready for lunch.

He was pushing the electric mower along the south fence, dragging the bright orange electrical cord across the fresh-smelling, evenly cut grass. Amos lay in the shade of a tree. Lauren could see that Richard had already weeded the flower garden and half filled a lumpy-looking trash bag. She remembered that when she and Paul were married, she was the one who'd done most of the yard work, in addition to *all* of the housework. She shook her head at the memory. Richard switched off the mower when he saw her, and she walked over to him. "The yard looks good," she said.

"Thanks."

"Hungry?"

"Famished. I'll just finish up here and then come in."

Back in the kitchen Lauren cut slices from two blocks of cheese, Jarlsberg and Muenster, and arranged them on a platter along with sliced ham and turkey breast. She heard the mower shut off, and then she saw Richard taking up the cord in big loops, following it toward the garage. When she heard the garage door open, she imagined he was carrying the cord through to the front yard.

She laid out small slices of rye bread, jars of mustard and mayonnaise, and a jar of pickles. Then she pulled the leafy stems from a dozen or so large strawberries and washed the berries under the faucet. After she placed them in the center of the platter, she set the table, wondering what was keeping Richard.

Lauren stepped through the dining room to the living room and walked toward the front window. She saw Richard, but not in the yard. He was across the street, standing on the sidewalk before the unkempt yard of the Ipswich residence.

He was talking to Monica.

His back was to Lauren, but she could tell that he was not engaged in a simple neighborly chat. Richard was gesturing emphatically, as if he were angry with Monica or else emphasizing a point. As far as Lauren knew, he'd never before spoken to either Monica or Hal. At least he'd never mentioned it. However, this didn't appear to be a first encounter.

Lauren moved to the window for a closer look, careful not to expose herself to view.

She could see Monica's expression: concern. The woman nodded and said something, her lips moving soundlessly.

Lauren reflected on how Richard's attitude toward Hal and Monica had changed. When the two first moved in, he'd been extremely suspicious of them, peering nervously through the drapes at their house, turning pale whenever Lauren mentioned some new oddity about them. Then he'd done a complete turnaround, not only dropping his suspicion but actually coming to their defense when Lauren criticized them. And now he seemed to be on familiar terms with

Monica. Lauren tried to remember when she'd first noticed the shift in his attitude.

Suddenly Richard turned from Monica and started back toward the house, making one final angry gesture.

Lauren walked to the kitchen, determined to get some answers.

26

RICHARD ENTERED the kitchen with a look of disgust on his face. When he saw Lauren, he forced a smile and nodded toward the platter of food on the table.

"That looks great." He moved to the sink to wash his hands.

Amos had followed Richard inside and now sniffed at the table, until Lauren nudged him away and told him to lie down. He did so in the doorway, his head on his paws. But his ears were up and his eyes bright, alert for any scraps that might hit the floor.

"What were you and Monica talking about?" Lauren asked.

Richard's jaw muscles tightened, but when he faced her his eyebrows were raised in innocence.

"Excuse me?"

"I passed by the front window and saw you across the street with her. You looked angry."

"Angry?" His smile was strained. "No, not at all." He turned toward the refrigerator. "I need something to drink. Do we have iced tea?" He pulled open the door without waiting for her to reply, removed a plastic pitcher, and took it to the table, where he poured them each a glass. He sat down, then looked up at Lauren still standing behind her chair. "Lauren, come on, it was nothing. She waved me over and asked me about our . . . lawn mower."

Lauren gave him an incredulous look. "Our mower?"

"Yes. You see, Hal needs to buy a new one—that's why their yard is such a mess—and since I manage McFadden's, he thought I could recommend a good model. So he asked Monica to ask me, that's all." He shrugged his shoulders. "Aren't you going to sit down?"

Lauren hesitated, then sat. "You seemed upset with her."

"Well, I suppose I was. She's difficult to talk to. I mean, she's weird, you know? They're both just . . . weird." He put two slices of bread on his plate and began making a sandwich.

Lauren sipped her iced tea and pictured how Richard had looked when she saw him talking to Monica.

"Have you talked to her before today?"

Richard had raised his sandwich to his mouth. He paused and said, "Who, Monica? No, you know, just to say hi." He took a bite.

"But they knew you worked at McFadden's Hardware."

Richard seemed to ponder this as he chewed, then swallowed. "I guess one of our neighbors told them. Seriously, Lauren, is there a problem here? I mean, what are you driving at?"

"I . . . I don't know. It looked as if you and Monica were having a serious discussion and—"

"We weren't."

"—and I was curious about it. I wondered if you two had, well, already gotten acquainted."

"We hadn't, so if that's the only thing bothering you, then, well . . ." He let the sentence hang, waiting for her.

Lauren shook her head to indicate she had nothing more to add. But then she asked, "So you're not worried about them anymore?"

He gave her a genuine smile and reached for her hand. "No, babe, I'm not worried about them, and you shouldn't be either."

She was, though, perhaps more so now that Richard seemed so nonchalant.

After lunch Richard helped Lauren clear the table and wrap the leftovers for the refrigerator. The pair of tickets Paul had given them lay on the countertop. Richard picked them up, then checked his watch.

"You know," he said, "if we hurry, we can probably get there for the first pitch."

"The ball game? I don't know if I'm in the mood."

"Why not?" He put his arm around her shoulders and gave her a squeeze. "Come on, it'll do us good to 'get out of the house,' remember? Besides, we've got the day to ourselves, and I don't want to just sit around, do you?"

"What about the front yard? I thought you—"

"It'll be there when we get back," he said. "Or tomorrow, for that matter."

MICHAEL ALLEGRETTO

"Well . . ." She felt a vague uneasiness, as if she shouldn't leave home today. On the other hand, getting away from here might be just what she needed—a chance to see things from a different perspective. She managed a smile. "Sure, why not."

While Richard showered, Lauren changed into shorts, sandals, and a short-sleeved shirt. She packed her big straw purse with a jacket, cap, and suntan lotion, ready for either the hot sun or cool breezes. These simple, familiar actions seemed to ease her apprehension, allowing her to feel good about leaving San Miguel, if only for a few hours.

In the kitchen she gave Amos a rawhide bone, sorry about leaving him alone on a Saturday. He carried it to the family room to find a comfortable place to chew, pausing only to let Richard scratch his ears. Richard had put on a light pair of cotton pants and a summer shirt with faded palm trees on a blue background. His hair was combed straight back, still damp from the shower.

"I'm ready if you are," he said.

They took Richard's car. When they backed into the street, Lauren glanced at the Ipswich residence, half expecting to see Monica. Instead she saw Hal, standing in his front yard with a hose in his hand, apparently watering his flower garden. Richard kept his eyes rigidly forward, refusing to look at the man. Meanwhile Hal stared at them with no expression on his face, his hand unmoving, the arc of water falling in a steady stream before him.

Lauren sensed something was wrong, and it took her a moment to realize what it was. She'd seen Hal's garden up close—nothing but dirt and weeds. Lauren turned in her seat and stared out the rear window. Hal Ipswich continued to water his "garden," watching them until they'd gone around the curve in the road.

By the time they'd driven to L.A., parked in a lot at Dodger Stadium, and found their seats, it was the bottom of the first inning and the Mets were already ahead three to nothing. Richard bought a soda for Lauren and a beer for himself, and cheered on the home team. It wasn't long before Lauren joined in, having pushed Hal Ipswich from her mind.

Lauren liked baseball. She didn't follow it daily, didn't know which team led the division, or who was on a hot streak or in a slump. In fact, she didn't recognize more than a few players' names on the program. But she enjoyed the game.

176

She liked the quiet tension on the field, the intense concentration of the infielders watching the batter, the batter watching the pitcher, and the pitcher, cool, in control, taking his time. She liked the sound of a solid hit and the yell of the crowd. She even liked the crunch of peanut shells underfoot.

All of it reminded her of her childhood. There'd been many summer Saturday afternoons when she sat in the stands with her parents and watched her brother play shortstop for his high school team. Lauren had learned many of the finer points of the game from her father. She understood the infield fly rule, a hit and run, a balk. She'd even kept her brother's batting average.

Three forty-seven in his senior year, she thought now, smiling to herself, sitting in the sun with her husband.

By the seventh inning with the Dodgers coming to bat, the game was tied at five.

Richard patted her on the knee.

"I'm going to the rest room," he said. "Be back in a minute."

Lauren watched him move down the row of spectators to the aisle, then she turned her attention to the game.

The eighth man in the lineup led off with a pop fly to short left field that dropped in for a single. Then the pitcher struck out, bringing up the top of the batting order. A single, followed by a walk, loaded the bases.

The crowd was yelling its approval, sensing a Dodger rally. Lauren turned in her seat, looking for Richard, hoping he wouldn't be gone much longer. There were only a few people in the aisle—everyone was sitting, eyes forward, focused on the field—but Richard wasn't among them.

The next batter popped up, and the third baseman caught it in foul territory for the second out. Now the Dodgers' cleanup hitter came to the plate.

Some of the fans were on their feet, shouting encouragement. The first pitch was low and outside, ball one. The next pitch was low but over the plate, and the batter took a full swing, smacking it. The ball sailed in a high arc, easily clearing the left-field fence, but just foul.

Lauren felt her anticipation rise and fall with the flight of the ball, with the roar and groan of the crowd. She didn't want Richard to miss any of this. Again she turned in her seat, searching the aisle for him. It was more difficult to see now because so many people were standing.

Then she spotted him. Suddenly all thoughts of the game vanished.

Richard was standing in the aisle, perhaps twenty rows above her, talking to another man. The man wore a sport shirt and slacks, and he was in his thirties, bald on top with a thick fringe of black hair and thick black sideburns. Lauren had seen him before. He was the man in her photos of Sea World.

Lauren heard the crack of a bat, and Richard and the man disappeared as the crowd rose to its feet and roared. Lauren stood, too, the only person among thousands facing away from the field. By the time she spotted Richard in the mass of grinning faces, he was coming down the aisle. The bald man was gone.

Richard returned to his seat, beaming.

"It was so crowded back there I nearly missed all the action. Did you see how far he hit that ball?"

"Who is he?" she asked, her voice strained with apprehension and fear.

He cocked his head, still smiling. "What?"

"The bald man with the sideburns."

"Who?"

"Goddammit, Richard! The man you were just talking to!"

Several people turned to stare at them. Richard looked bewildered.

"Lauren, what . . . Oh, *him*. Some guy who bumped into me in the aisle and asked for the time."

She searched his face. "Are you saying you don't know him?"

"Of course not. What's the matter anyway? You look as if you've seen a ghost."

"I've seen that man before," she said, shifting in her seat and searching the faces above and behind them. When she turned to Richard, she could see that he was worried.

"Are you certain?" he asked.

"Yes, when we went to Sea World. He was following us, *watching us*."

"What?"

"I didn't realize it until later, when I had the photographs developed. He's in several of them."

"Which photographs?"

"For God's sake, Richard, the ones from *Sea World*."

"The ones you showed me?"

"*Yes.*"

He paused, frowning. "Why didn't you point him out to me then?"

Lauren remembered that at the time she'd been more concerned with Richard's job application than the photographs—the next morning she'd phoned the University of Pennsylvania; after that she'd spoken to Richard's ex-landlords; then she'd found the silver-framed photograph and the gun. . . . The Sea World photos had been forgotten.

Lauren looked behind her again, then faced Richard and took his hand. "Please," she said, "let's get out of here. He's probably still back there somewhere, watching us."

Richard nodded soberly. "Of course. Anything you say."

They left their seats and climbed up the aisle, while the crowd applauded and the Dodgers took the field.

When they got home, Lauren went directly to the family room, pulled the photo envelope from the bookcase where she'd left it. She knelt on the floor beside the end table and began spreading out snapshots. Richard stood behind her.

"Here," she said. "This one first caught my eye. I took it when we were leaving—the last picture, the one in the parking lot, remember? There he is looking at us over the tops of the cars. You see what I mean?"

"I see a man looking at the camera, yes."

"And here. I think this is the dolphin petting pool. See him there? He's looking over his shoulder, watching us."

Richard said nothing.

"And this one," she said, holding up a snapshot. "See him at the table behind us? It was right after we'd eaten lunch."

Richard took the photograph from her and squinted at it.

"How do you know this is the same man? You can't even see his face."

Lauren stood beside him, the two other photos in her hand.

"You can tell by his hairline," she said. "And his shirt. See? It's the same shirt."

Richard shrugged. "It's the same color anyway."

Lauren looked at him. "Richard, this man was following us the entire time we were at Sea World."

"Well, he was certainly there. Along with a few thousand other people. But 'following'?"

"The pictures, Richard," she said heatedly. "He's in the pictures, for God's sake."

"There's no need to get upset."

"I *am* upset. You act as if you're blind. Look, he's right *there,* and *there,* and—"

"All right, all right," he said calmly. "Just take it easy. So there's a strange man who shows up in two of your crowd shots at Sea—"

"*Three.*"

Richard sighed. "All right, three crowd shots. But I'll bet if we scrutinize the rest of these photos, we'd find some other faces that appear more than once. You see what I'm saying? It's just a coincidence."

Lauren glared at him, barely controlling her temper. She'd never felt so frustrated before. She took a breath and let it out slowly before she spoke.

"Was it also a coincidence that this same man was at the game today? Was it just by chance that he picked you out of all those people to stop and ask for the time?"

Richard held her eyes for a moment. Then he looked at the photo in his hand. Slowly he shook his head.

"Actually, Lauren, I don't think this is even the same man."

"What! Look, I saw him, too, you know, and—"

"From a distance. I was standing face-to-face with him. Don't you think I'm better qualified to judge than you are?" Again he looked at the photo and shook his head. "I'm certain this isn't the same man."

Lauren stared at him, appalled that he refused to see the obvious or show the least bit of concern.

Richard laid the photograph on the end table. "I'm going to put away the mower," he said lamely. "It's still in the backyard." He turned from her and walked through the doorway to the kitchen and then out the back door.

Lauren gazed at the empty doorway. "It was the same man," she said through clenched teeth.

She tried to quiet her anger, but her hands shook so badly that she had difficulty getting the photographs into their envelope. Richard was lying to her—again—denying that he recognized the bald-headed man. And she believed it was more than recognition. He knew that man. Just as he knew Monica Ipswich.

Lauren felt she'd given Richard every possible chance to open up to her, and he'd done nothing but pile lie upon lie.

She looked at the photo envelope in her hand—the only physical evidence that anything out of the ordinary was going on. Outside of these pictures, everything boiled down to her word against his. She had a disturbing although unexplainable feeling that she should hide the photos to keep Richard from destroying them.

She took the envelope to the master bedroom and stuffed it into the rear of a drawer filled with slips and panties. She paused for a moment at the bureau, *their* bureau, wondering if Richard would feel safe hiding anything in there. Lauren pulled open one of Richard's drawers and began pawing through his clothes, not certain of what she was searching for—anything that might help her cause. When she found nothing, she slammed the drawer shut and yanked open another.

There, half hidden by rolled-up socks, was the small wooden box she'd first seen in Richard's old suitcase.

She raised the lid.

The revolver and the carton of shells were inside. Lauren hesitated, then reached in and lifted the gun, surprised by its weight, holding it with all four fingers and her thumb wrapped around the butt, leaving the trigger free. She snapped open the cylinder. The gun was loaded. She snapped it closed.

Lauren remembered now how Richard had insisted on returning the silver-framed photograph to the suitcase under the house. Obviously, he'd gone down there to get the gun.

This is where it ends, she thought, stepping into the hallway with the gun at her side. He can move out this afternoon and take his loaded gun with him.

Lauren carried the gun through the family room and the kitchen and out the back door to the garage. She didn't want it in the house. She didn't want *him* in the house, not anymore. She intended to tell him to leave at once, to pack all his things, starting with this . . . this weapon. And he could save his lies and his phony explanations for someone else. She only thanked God that Emily wasn't home to see this.

But Richard wasn't in the garage.

The large door was up. Lauren stepped toward it, looking down the driveway, now in shadow from the late-afternoon sun. She saw Richard walking away from her, crossing the street. She stayed inside the garage, out of sight, and watched him raise his hand in a wave.

Monica Ipswich, wearing slacks, sandals, and a sleeveless cotton shirt, came out of her yard to meet him. Richard seemed to be agitated. They exchanged a few words, then Monica put her hand on his arm and led him up the driveway to her house.

Lauren felt her insides wrench as she watched them disappear around the corner of the house. From where she stood she couldn't see the side door, couldn't tell whether they'd gone inside. But she sensed they had.

Is it sex? she thought. Has all this been about sex?

And now she wondered if Richard had been lying to her from the first moment they met, pretending to care for her, to love her and Emily. And all those nights in bed with her . . . What had he really been thinking while he went through the motions of making love?

Lauren felt physically ill. And angry, angrier than she'd ever been in her life.

Was Monica the married woman Richard had told her about before? Perhaps she was, but there had to be more to it than that. Whatever was going on, though, it seemed certain that Hal and Monica were deeply involved and had been from the beginning.

Lauren stepped out of the garage into the driveway. She was suddenly aware that she was still holding Richard's gun. She hesitated, looking from the gun to the house across the street. Then she moved back into the garage and placed the revolver in the corner on the concrete floor.

Now Lauren strode across the street toward the house of Hal and Monica Ipswich. She was going to confront the truth, however appalling it might be.

27

LAUREN WALKED up the driveway to the Ipswich house, then hesitated, sensing that she was being watched, losing a bit of her bravado.

The front drapes were slightly parted, as usual, but she couldn't see anything in the darkness between them. She gave the yard a cursory glance. It was as barren as ever, unmown and dry, except for one muddy corner of the flower garden where Hal had stood with the hose, watching them leave for the ball game.

Lauren rounded the corner of the house. The brown car sat under the carport. The door of the house was ajar. She raised her hand to knock on the screen door, paused, then swung the screen toward her. Slowly and quietly she pushed open the door and stepped into the house.

She stood in a small, tile-floored vestibule, enclosed on two sides by a temporary wooden screen that rose above her head, nearly to the ceiling. Although her view was blocked, she knew that beyond the screen was the living room and to her right a doorway that led to the kitchen.

Lauren stood still for a moment, listening.

There was a murmur of voices to her right, apparently coming from the kitchen. A man and a woman, Lauren could tell, but she couldn't understand what they were saying.

She examined her alternatives: barge in on Richard and Monica and demand to know what the hell was going on, or creep closer to the kitchen and try to hear what they were talking about. There was a third alternative, and part of her mind strongly advised her to take it—leave this house immediately, go home and lock the doors, perhaps hold Richard's gun for protection.

Protection against what?

Lauren eased quietly around the wooden screen into the living room.

Then she stopped dead, trying to comprehend what lay before her.

The room was mostly a barren expanse of wall-to-wall carpeting, dimly lit—heavy drapes covered all the windows, and the only light bled in from the doorway leading to the kitchen. A long table with folding legs stood against the far wall. It supported four video monitors, each with its own VCR. At the end of the table, near a padded chair on rollers, was a telephone and a reel-to-reel tape recorder.

The only other item in the room rested on a tripod near the front window—a video camera with its lens a few inches from the part in the drapes.

Dazed, Lauren moved into the room.

She glanced toward the kitchen, able to see only one corner of a table and the end of the countertop. Richard and Monica had ceased their muted conversation, or else they'd moved into another part of the house.

Lauren approached the TV monitors, each of which featured a still, black-and-white picture. The first three screens depicted, respectively, a street, an alley, and the rear of a house. There was a brief movement on the first screen as a car drove along the street. At the same time Lauren heard the car go by outside.

Then she realized with a shock that the monitors were displaying her street, her house. The fourth screen confirmed this, showing some familiar furniture before a wall hung with a few prints: her own living room. Obviously, the camera at the window had a telephoto lens and—

"What are you doing in here?"

Lauren spun around. Her heart nearly stopped when she recognized the man glaring at her from the kitchen doorway—the bald man with the thick black sideburns. He wore the same sport shirt and slacks as when he'd talked to Richard at the ball game.

"You're not supposed to be in here, Mrs. Caylor," he said angrily, moving toward her.

Lauren was ready to bolt for the front door. Then she saw Richard and Monica appear behind the bald man. Richard's face turned pale and he pushed past the man.

"My God, Lauren, what are you doing here?"

Lauren edged away from him, eyeing the door to her right. "What am *I* doing here, Richard?" She could hear the panic in her voice.

"What are *you* doing here? What . . . what *is* all this?" She waved her hand at the monitors. *"And who are these people?"*

Richard raised his hands before him, as if he were trying to calm a frightened animal, but Lauren could see that he was scared too.

"Lauren, please, take it easy, everything is all right. We're safe. These people are here to protect us."

"Protect us?" Lauren glanced from Monica to the bald man. Monica looked concerned; the man seemed less angry now, merely mildly irritated. "Protect us from *what*?" Lauren demanded.

"It's . . . a long story," Richard said. He'd moved close enough to reach out and touch her. Now he turned and pointed toward the couple. "This is Agent Howard Zale and Agent Monica Sherwood. They're with the FBI."

Lauren shook her head in disbelief.

"It's true, Mrs. Caylor," Monica said.

She approached Lauren, holding out a thin leather wallet. Lauren glanced at the woman and then at her likeness encased in clear plastic. Below the photograph were the words "Monica Sherwood, Federal Bureau of Investigation."

"You might as well tell her everything now," Zale said offhandedly, looking at the monitors.

"Yes, I . . ." Richard touched Lauren's arm, and she recoiled. He looked pained. "I wanted to tell you before, Lauren. Every day that we've been together I wanted to tell you. But—"

"Tell me *what*?"

Richard licked his lips as if he was unsure of where to begin, as if he was afraid to begin.

"Let's take this into the kitchen," Zale said, not making it a request. He locked the front door, then walked out of the room without looking back.

The kitchen was as barren as the living room, with only a Formica-top table and four chairs. Except for the refrigerator and stove left behind by the Greys, there were no appliances—no microwave oven, no blender, not even a toaster.

"Fix Mrs. Caylor a cup of coffee," Zale said.

Monica filled a kettle at the sink and put it on the stove. Lauren saw half a dozen cups and mugs, no two alike, upended on a damp paper towel at the rear corner of the countertop. Beside them were a large jar of instant coffee, a jar of nondairy creamer, and a box of

185

sugar with a pour spout. There was also a flat brown box filled with plastic spoons. It all reminded Lauren of an office lunchroom. She guessed that the cupboards were empty.

"Please sit down," Richard said, offering her a chair at the table.

Lauren hesitated, then sat, reading defeat in his face. Richard sat beside her, and Zale straddled a chair at the end of the table.

"Your husband has been under our protection for some time, Mrs. Caylor. The reason—"

"Wait a minute," Richard said firmly. "I'll do the explaining."

Zale frowned, then gave him an amused look. "Be my guest," he said with sarcasm.

Richard faced Lauren, taking her right hand in both of his hands. She did not pull away. Her fear had given way to a mind-numbing shock as she struggled to comprehend the situation. Richard cleared his throat, and when he spoke, his voice was quiet and clear.

"My name was not always Richard Caylor," he said. "I changed it when I entered the federal witness protection program."

"Witness protection?"

"Four years ago I testified in court against a man named Peter Grummund. He was involved in . . . illegal activities in Chicago. I, ah, I was his accountant. My testimony sent him to prison. My name then, my real name, was Donald Rassitter."

Lauren blinked. "Rassitter . . . That was *you* in the picture I found. The beard and tinted glasses . . . I should have known it was more than just a resemblance."

"That's how I looked nearly five years ago."

"And the woman in the picture?"

"My fiancée, Francine—Peter Grummund's daughter."

The kettle began whistling, and Monica lifted it from the stove.

"Pour me a cup, too," Zale said.

Monica nodded. "Richard?"

"Ah, yes, please, black. Lauren takes cream and . . ." He let the sentence hang as she stared at him, pain and confusion on her face.

Then Lauren heard a car pull into the backyard. Through the kitchen window she could see three late-model, dark-colored vehicles parked between the covered swimming pool and the open portion of the back fence. The doors of one car swung open and two men climbed out. One of them was Hal Ipswich, and the other was a tall, strongly built, middle-aged black man wearing a short-sleeved white shirt and a striped tie. They walked to the back door and entered the kitchen, then stopped, staring at Lauren.

"You've already met Agent Hal Ipswich," Richard said. He nodded toward the black man. "This is Felix Jameson. He's with the U.S. Marshals Service."

"We're briefing Mrs. Caylor," Zale told the men. "Ipswich, go keep an eye on those monitors."

Hal Ipswich left the room, and Jameson stood beside Monica at the counter. Lauren had a fleeting but disturbing impression that she was a child among adults. Richard sipped his coffee before he spoke.

"I think you should hear this from the beginning," he said.

Donald Rassitter grew up in Chicago as the best friend of James Grummund. They played together and attended the same elementary, middle, and high schools. Donald had heard rumors about James's father, Peter: Mr. Grummund was a member of organized crime; his small grocery store and humble appearance were just a front, and he secretly earned a fortune through criminal deeds. Donald only half believed these stories. To him Peter Grummund was a kind and generous man, the father of his best friend, James, and James's little sister, Francine.

After high school both Donald and James were accepted by the University of Chicago. When Donald's parents found they could not afford the tuition, Peter Grummund gave them the money—not lent, gave. After James graduated with a bachelor's degree, he went to work for his father. Donald stayed at the university for another two years. During that time his parents were killed in an automobile accident. The Grummunds became the closest thing Donald had to family.

On the day Donald received his master's degree in business administration, Peter Grummund offered him a job.

By then Grummund owned a number of businesses and he and his wife lived in a mansion in a Chicago suburb, along with their maid, their gardener, and their chauffeur. During the past year Grummund had been indicted for racketeering by a grand jury. He'd stood trial and been found not guilty. There had been accusations of jury tampering but nothing was ever proved.

Donald knew all this, and he wasn't naive enough to think that Peter Grummund was entirely innocent—not by a long shot. In fact, he was fairly certain that the old man had criminal connections. But this did not discourage him. He wasn't being asked to do anything illegal. And there was another point to consider: Peter Grummund promised to pay him three times as much as he could earn anywhere else.

Donald accepted the job of assistant manager of Lake Construction Company, which was wholly owned by Peter Grummund and managed by his son, James.

Donald did the payroll and kept the books—not very challenging, but Peter Grummund promised him bigger and better things if he would merely follow the rules: "Do your job, keep your nose clean, and don't ask the wrong questions."

During his first months of work Donald was party to Grummund's cheating on state and federal tax statements—padded expense accounts, unreported cash transactions, and so on, all relatively small amounts. Of course, he knew this was against the law, but he could accept it. After all, no one was getting hurt except the IRS, and who could feel sorry for *them*?

It was a game, he told himself, played by every major corporation in the country. The government tries to take your money and you try to keep it.

But six months into the job James asked him to enter false figures in the books totaling several hundred thousand dollars. Donald was told to make a small construction job appear much larger than it really was; a lot of money was coming into Lake Construction, and James wanted it funneled through this job. Donald didn't know the source of the money, but he was smart enough to know it wasn't legal.

He was faced with a crucial decision, and he knew that both James and Peter were watching him closely. Would he remain loyal to the Grummund family or would he oppose them?

Donald made the entries and kept his mouth shut. He wasn't exactly sure why he'd done it, because deep down he knew it was wrong and he felt guilty about it. But really, it was still part of the game. And the alternative, leaving the Grummund family, seemed terrifying—they were all the family he had.

He was in.

Over the next two years Donald became the understudy to Grummund's chief accountant, an old man named Lucci. Donald gained access to the accounting books of all of Grummund's businesses, the real books. He finally became aware that Grummund's "businesses" included extortion, theft, and the sale of stolen property.

Donald felt he had to get away from this, but he was hampered by an underlying loyalty to the Grummund family. He went to James with his dilemma. James reasoned with him: "It's a tough world out there, and to survive, we have to be tough, too, and sometimes that means bending the rules. Besides, how could you think of abandoning us? We're your family. We *need* you, and we need your loyalty." Donald wavered.

And then Francine Grummund returned home from college.

Donald had remembered her only as a cute little girl, and he'd lost track of her after he and James began studying at the university. Now Francine was a beautiful woman. She and Donald fell in love almost immediately, and any thoughts he might have had of leaving the family were overwhelmed by his desire for Francine. Besides, he told himself, *he* wasn't doing anything to harm anyone. He was just the bookkeeper, shuffling numbers.

Donald and Francine were engaged to be married. Soon thereafter Lucci retired and Peter Grummund made Donald his new chief accountant.

Now Donald was privy to all of Peter's secrets, including his fierce competition with other crime lords in the area. There were constant "border disputes" and some violence, of which Donald had previously been unaware. He tried to keep his thoughts on Francine, their upcoming marriage, and their future happy life together, but he could no longer ignore the world around him.

Then events took a sudden turn for the worse.

Peter Grummund's wife suffered a stroke and died. Peter was grief-stricken, and for weeks he refused to even leave the house. A rival crime boss, sensing that Grummund had grown weak, attempted to muscle in on part of his empire. Grummund fought back, sending some of his men against the rival's men, and there were killings. In retaliation, a bomb was planted in the car of James Grummund. When it exploded, it killed not only James but also the only passenger—his sister, Francine.

With the murder of Francine, Donald's world collapsed. More, he was appalled by Peter Grummund's reaction to the horror. The old man was saddened, to be sure, but he'd become hard and bitter, thinking only of revenge. He did not blame himself in any way for the murder of his children. To the contrary, he considered their deaths to be honorable—a sacrifice for the family.

Donald Rassitter could take no more. He believed that Peter Grummund was responsible for the murder of Francine and James. For a brief time he even considered killing Peter Grummund to avenge their deaths. But Donald knew he was no killer. So he did the only thing he could to hurt Grummund. He took his accounting books to the Chicago office of the FBI.

At that point Donald had little regard for his own life. However, the FBI wanted him alive to testify against Peter Grummund, so they placed him in protective custody.

Grummund was arrested, and his lawyers began plea-bargaining, eventually making a deal with the federal prosecutors. Grummund pleaded guilty to income tax evasion, and the other charges against him were dropped. He was sent to a federal prison.

Some of Grummund's hirelings, though, escaped the law, and it was believed that, given the chance, any one of them would kill Donald Rassitter for what he'd done.

Donald willingly entered the federal witness protection program. The Marshals Service got him a California driver's license under his new name, Richard Caylor; gave him a little money to live on; and moved him to his new home, one of *their* choosing—San Miguel, California. He was told that to remain safe, he could never reveal his true identity.

After that he was pretty much on his own.

"And so I became Richard Caylor," he said to Lauren. His voice had grown raspy. "I *am* Richard Caylor. And no matter what has happened in the past or what you may think about me, Lauren, I love you. I love you and Emily more than life itself."

Lauren was numb. She pushed back from the table, her chair screeching on the floor. She stood awkwardly.

"I . . . I don't know you," she said, and fled from the house.

28

LAUREN HURRIED across the street to the safety of her own home. But after she'd fled through the garage and the back door and stood trembling in the kitchen, she realized that she was no safer here than outside. This was Richard's house too.

No—it was *Donald Rassitter's* house.

"My God." The words came out as a moan. She staggered to the family room and slumped in one of the love seats.

Amos ambled into the room and stood before her whining, wanting something, but unable to express exactly what it was. She half-heartedly rubbed his ears and told him to lie down. He curled up beside her chair.

An hour ago she'd been furious with Richard, fed up with his lies, ready to throw him out of the house. Now her anger was gone, replaced by a sickening feeling of fear and betrayal. There hadn't been lies. There had been one lie, all-encompassing. From the first time they met he'd been playing a role, pretending to be someone he was not.

She lowered her face into her hands and fought back tears. Had he also faked each of those thousand separate incidents, those subtle and complex moments shared with her and Emily?

"Goddammit!" she said, standing abruptly, causing Amos's head to jerk up, ears raised, eyes alert.

Lauren took one step forward, then stopped, unsure of where to go or what to do. If Emily were here, Lauren knew, she would have packed them each a suitcase and left immediately, perhaps checking into a motel, or else driving straight to the airport and getting on the first plane to Lincoln, Nebraska, staying away until Richard moved out of the house. But Emily was somewhere in Los Angeles with Paul. She couldn't just leave, not now. What if they came back early? Or what if Emily phoned? She had to stay. She'd just tell Richard to leave, that's all.

But he might refuse.

Lauren moved to the sliding glass doors and stared out at the shadows deepening in the backyard.

Deal with this, she told herself. You can do it.

But she began to feel a growing sense of dread, of helplessness, as if she'd lost control of her own life. People were following her, watching her on TV monitors . . .

Lauren gave a start, remembering the tape recorder by the telephone in the house across the street, realizing the implication: Their phone line was tapped. She tried to recall the phone conversations she'd had in the past few days, wondering what "they" had heard.

The calls to Philadelphia, she thought. Richard must have known then that I'd been checking up on him. But how long before that had they been listening?

Her eyes drifted across the darkening lawn and trees and fence, focusing on the power pole in the alley. She remembered last Sunday at Connie's party—Connie had told her about a workman on the pole. Lauren wondered if that was when they'd installed the video camera that was focused on the rear of the house. Then she realized that someone across the street was watching the monitors at this moment, watching her.

She reached out and yanked the cord, closing the drapes with a whoosh.

"Lauren."

She spun on her heel. Richard stood in the kitchen doorway, his arms at his sides, the gun in one hand. He glanced down at it when he saw the look of terror on Lauren's face.

"I . . . found this on the floor of the garage," he said apologetically.

He reached around the doorway and set the gun on the kitchen counter, then came hesitantly toward Lauren. She held perfectly still, not knowing where to run, or if she *should* run.

"Lauren, I . . ." He reached for her, and when she stepped back, he let his hand fall. "I know how difficult this must be for you."

"Do you?"

His eyes held hers for a moment, then he looked away. "No, I suppose I don't." He turned from her and sat on one of the love seats, forearms across his knees, head bowed. "I can explain ev—"

"You lied to me, Richard. All this time, from the first day we met, you've been lying."

Slowly he shook his head. "No. About my past, yes, but my feelings toward you and Emily, they were true, Lauren. I never lied about that. I love you. I always have."

She stared at him, saying nothing.

"I know I've deceived you, and I wouldn't blame you if you never forgave me. But I am sorry, Lauren, more sorry than you can imagine. And I want you to understand that from the day I left Chicago I've had to lie to everyone, not just to you. I had to lie about my past in order to survive."

He let his hand fall to Amos's head, idly stroked his fur. The big dog groaned his approval.

"You see, after I testified at Grummund's trial, when I was put in the witness security program, I was made to follow strict rules. I wasn't exactly treated like royalty. Of course, most of the people in the program are criminals themselves who have testified against—"

"And you're not?" There was sarcasm in her voice.

"No," Richard said quietly, "I'm not. Yes, back then you could say I was. I knew where the money was coming from—that is, eventually I knew—and I kept my mouth shut. I went along. I juggled figures and cashed my paycheck without blinking. I got into it for the money and perhaps because of a misguided sense of loyalty. I was wrong, and I've regretted it every day since then."

Lauren folded her arms beneath her breasts, still standing where she'd been when he entered the room, her back to the drapes.

Richard said, "I can't change my past, Lauren. I did wrong and I'm sorry. And I've paid my debt to society."

"You went to prison? But I thought . . ."

"No, I wasn't in prison, at least not one with bars. Believe me, though, I paid. They took everything from me, Lauren, everything. They took away my life."

He stared at the floor, shaking his head again. Lauren could sense his pain, and it was an effort for her not to sympathize with him. She moved to the other love seat and sat across from him, no longer afraid. Despite his deception she believed she knew the kind of man he was.

"It was a social death," he said. "In fact, the federal agents told me that my friends should consider me dead, because they'd never hear from me again. You have to understand, if Grummund's people even remotely believed that my friends knew where I was, they'd use them to get to me. They'd threaten them, maybe even kidnap one of them to force me into the open so they could kill me. So I've never called or written to anyone." He sighed, still shaking his head. "As I said, it's a prison without bars. There's no compromise. You're either in the program or not. And if you're in, you're in all the way."

He sat back in his seat, moving his neck, wincing as if his muscles were knotted with tension. If he'd done that last week, or even yesterday, Lauren knew, she would have stood behind him and massaged his neck. Now she merely sat and watched, waiting.

"The first thing the feds did," Richard said, "was take away everything with the name Donald Rassitter on it, anything that could be used to identify me. Of course, it was also everything that I'd used to identify *myself*: birth certificate, driver's license, passport, Social Security card, checking account, insurance certificates, voter registration card—absolutely everything. Even monogrammed luggage and cuff links . . ."

"What about the framed photo I found?"

"That . . . should have been left behind too. I hid it and kept it with me, because, well, I needed *something,* some tie to my past, something to hang on to."

Lauren nodded.

"But it wasn't merely physical objects they took from me," Richard said. "They also effectively wiped out my background—socially speaking, of course, but that's really all that matters, isn't it? I no longer had personal references or a work history or a master's degree. I couldn't even prove that I'd graduated from high school. I was starting over, a blank."

He smiled, but there was no humor in it. "It's like people who believe in reincarnation—first you die, and then you're reborn. And I think my rebirth was at least as traumatic as my real birth. In a way, I was yanked from the womb and forced to leave everything and everyone behind. Then I was dropped down in a place I'd never been before, a place not of my choosing. In fact, I didn't even know I was coming to San Miguel until Jameson met me and another U.S. Marshal at LAX and drove me down here. They had an apartment lined up for me, a little money, a new name. That was it. Basically, I was an alien, alone in a strange land, starting a new life without a traceable past."

Lauren tried to identify with Richard's dilemma. She could not.

"Back in Chicago," Richard continued, "I was a real person, someone with a credit rating, a college degree, a home, a . . . history. Here, I was a nonperson, a man who'd never gone to school, never held a job, with no previous address or phone number. Can you imagine what it's like to get health insurance or even a telephone, or to try to land a job—all with no background? It's practically impossible. People want to know about you. They have a right to know." He shrugged. "So I would lie and hope they wouldn't find out. And I prayed I could remember my lies to keep them straight. I lived in constant fear that I'd slip and give myself away. It was so painful to be around other people, to be alert every minute, to watch every word I said, never able to relax that, well, I practically became a shut-in. The only time I left the apartment was to buy food or go to work."

"At McFadden's?"

"No, the first job I tried was as a junior accountant with a large firm in L. A. I'd had plenty of experience and I could do the work, no problem. I made the commute every day for two weeks, until they had time to check out my phony educational and employment background and fire me. I tried a few more 'decent' jobs, with pretty much the same results, and I ended up driving a cab. Then I saw Arthur's ad in the newspaper. Thank God *he* never checked out my résumé, or I would've been back on the street."

"I doubt it," Lauren said. "Arthur's not like that."

"Maybe not, but nobody wants a liar working for them. Nobody likes a liar, period."

He looked at her and she looked away.

"Anyway, Arthur is a terrific guy, as you know. He let me do the work and learn the business, and he didn't ask me too many questions. I began to find my place as Richard Caylor. Not completely, of course. I was still on edge most of the time, and I kept my guard up around customers and the other employees. But as the months went by, and then the years, 'Richard Caylor' became more than a role. The lie had become reality. When I met you, I *was* Richard Caylor. That's who I am, Lauren. Donald Rassitter is just someone from my past, someone in an old photograph. He doesn't exist anymore. He's dead."

They sat in silence for a few moments. Then Lauren said, "Why didn't you tell me all this before?"

"I couldn't."

"Why not?" Her voice was hard. "I've heard of men being placed under witness protection, and I understood that their wives were told everything."

Richard nodded. "That's true—*if* the man is married before he goes into the program. Then his wife goes in too. If you can imagine us being married back then when—"

"No, I'm afraid I can't."

He sighed. "You know what I mean. If we'd been together then, we would have entered the program together, we would have both moved, changed our names, and so on."

Lauren shook her head slowly. "Still, you could have told me."

"I was afraid to. I was afraid that you'd leave me."

Lauren said nothing.

"After all," Richard said, "who'd want to have a relationship with a fugitive?"

"I . . . I don't know the answer to that. But the point is, it should've been *my* decision. You had no right to misrepresent yourself to me and to drag me into this . . . this . . . whatever it is you're involved in, this danger." Her look became intense. "And there is danger, isn't there? To all of us."

"Not exactly. There's—"

"And what about Emily, Richard? Or doesn't her well-being concern you?"

"Dammit, of course it concerns me," he said loudly, his face suddenly flushed. He stared at her a moment longer, challenging her. Then he looked away. "I'm . . . I'm sorry. But Emily means as much to me as you do. You two are everything to me, my life. Withholding my past from you wasn't fair to either of you, I know. But there's one thing you must believe—I never, *never* would have gotten involved with you and Emily if I'd thought there was the least danger to either of you. Never."

"But how could there *not* be a danger, considering the man you sent to prison?"

Richard shrugged helplessly. "Time," he said. "When I met you, Peter Grummund had been in prison for several years. His empire was gone, and his criminal associates were either on the run or in prison. All of his cash had been confiscated, and even his legitimate businesses had been auctioned off by the IRS. Do you understand?

He had nothing—no power, no one working for him. After a while I realized that the danger was over and I was safe. Of course, by then I'd become Richard Caylor."

She started to speak, then pursed her lips and shook her head. "I . . . I don't know."

"I just wanted us to be together," Richard said. "I knew someday I'd have to tell you the truth about myself. I wanted to tell you, and a thousand different times I nearly did. The more I knew you, the more I felt I couldn't live without you. I was too afraid to take the chance that you might leave. I was . . . afraid."

She, too, was afraid, but she said nothing.

"I was determined to tell you everything if we ever decided to get married," Richard said. "But when we did decide, it all happened so fast . . ." He smiled wanly. "I nearly blurted it out when you suggested we go to Las Vegas for the wedding. You see, I'd been there a few times years before with Grummund and some of his cronies. I was afraid someone might recognize me." His smile did not last. "I'm sorry, Lauren."

"Sorry," she said with bitterness. "At least you could've confided in me when all this began, when FBI agents began popping up all around us, sitting in restaurants, following in cars, *moving in* across the street. You could've told me then."

"I didn't know then, Lauren. I honestly didn't know who those people were, good or bad, or if they were just innocent citizens made mysterious by my paranoia. It wasn't until last Wednesday night, when I first met with Jameson, that I learned what was going on."

"Why did you keep lying to me after that?"

"Because that's what they told me to do. Zale ordered me."

"What?"

Richard heaved a sigh. "Zale didn't want you to panic and run. He told me it would be much more difficult for them to protect you if you packed up and left the house. Especially if you left San Miguel. Zale told me—"

"Wait a minute. Emily is *not* in San Miguel."

"I know. She's in L.A. with Paul, and one of Zale's men is watching her every minute."

Lauren shook her head. "Oh God, Richard." She felt overcome by despair.

"Zale told me to lie to protect you and Emily. He wanted you, us, to continue with our normal lives."

"Normal lives," Lauren repeated, still shaking her head sadly. "I doubt that we can ever have *that* again."

Richard hesitated. "I suppose you're right," he said quietly. "And when this is over, if want me to move out, I will. If you want a divorce, I won't fight you." He got to his feet slowly. "Whatever you decide, whatever happens between us, I want you to know one thing. I love you, Lauren. And I always will." He put his hand flat on his chest. "This is who I am. You didn't fall in love with a name, not Richard Caylor or Donald Rassitter. You fell in love with me."

He walked from the room.

They avoided each other for the rest of the evening.

Richard went out once and walked across the street. Lauren ate cheese and crackers for dinner, standing at the kitchen counter. Then she sat in the living room with the drapes tightly closed, her feet tucked under her on the couch, a magazine open on her lap. Her thoughts were with Emily. Richard stayed in the family room; Lauren could hear the TV.

Much later she was awakened by him lightly shaking her shoulder. She was still on the couch in the living room, and all the lights were on.

"Why don't you go to bed," Richard said gently. "I'll sleep in the guest bedroom."

Before she could respond, he walked out.

She stood awkwardly. There was a cramp in her neck. She turned off all the lights and went to bed. She felt strange lying alone, especially with Richard in the adjacent room. It was the first time they'd slept apart since they were married.

As she lay awake in the darkness, she replayed in her mind everything Richard had told her.

All of it, she felt certain now, was true. She tried to put herself in his position when he was relocated to San Miguel. She could understand why he'd been afraid to reveal his past—not just to her, but to anyone.

Of course, later he should have trusted her. He should have *told* her. . . . How would she have reacted then if he'd told her?

It didn't matter. What mattered was now.

The FBI was watching them. Supposedly, they were her protectors. Then why didn't she feel safe?

She thought she knew.

Their presence implied danger—danger not only to Richard but to her and Emily. Someone . . . out there . . . meant them harm.

29

IT WAS late Saturday night when Peter Grummund's flight arrived at LAX. He took a cab from the airport to the address Novek had given him, a run-down motel on La Cienega Boulevard.

He knocked at number six. When the door opened, he thought he'd made a mistake. The man standing before him in a T-shirt was too dark-complexioned and too physically fit to be Novek. And his head looked larger somehow, his forehead higher.

"Hey, Pete, come on in."

There was no mistaking that voice, though, Grummund thought, like a basso profundo with a sore throat.

He entered the room. Novek closed the door and locked it. They shook hands briefly. Grummund nodded his head and Novek smiled with one corner of his mouth, the only display of emotion.

"Jesus, Novek, I hardly recognized you, you look so different. Good, but different."

"What did I tell you?"

Grummund tossed his coat and flight bag on the plastic-cushioned chair in the corner. He sat on the nearer twin bed, the one that hadn't been slept in.

"I'm beat," he said. "What have you got to drink?"

Novek crossed the threadbare carpet to the dresser. He tore the paper from a plastic glass, fished a few floating ice cubes from the water in the limp cardboard bucket, and poured Scotch from an uncapped bottle. He handed Grummund the glass.

The older man took a sip, and then another, before he asked, "Did you get the guns?"

"In there." Novek nodded toward the nightstand.

Grummund pulled open the drawer and lifted out the revolver and the automatic. He checked to see that they were clean, oiled, and loaded, then put them back. He drank his Scotch.

"Did you have any trouble?"

"Very little," Novek said, recalling his encounter with the gun dealer. "So when do we move?"

"Tomorrow, maybe the next day, I don't know yet. I need to rest. I've been in airports or in the air since six o'clock this morning, changing planes, making sure nobody was following me."

"You think anybody tried?"

"No, but I was just making sure." Yesterday he'd had his weekly meeting with his parole officer, and he knew that the flunky was too buried under paperwork to have time to tag along after him. Still, there was something about finding Rassitter so quickly that made Grummund uneasy—but he said nothing.

Novek sat on the unmade bad, facing his old boss. "I've been thinking how we should do this," he said.

"You have, huh." Grummund sipped his Scotch. He already knew how they'd handle things—his way, the right way—but he let Novek talk.

"We can nail him Monday on his way to work," Novek said. "He always parks in an employees-only lot behind the building and he's the first one there in the morning, no one else around. We can grab him, stuff him in the trunk of my car, and bring him back here. Then we can take our time making him talk. What do you think?"

"I think you've been out in the sun too long."

Novek scowled. Grummund ignored it.

"Let's say we get him out of the parking lot without anyone seeing," Grummund said. "Okay, then the next employee who shows up will see his car, but he'll find that the store is still locked and Rassitter's not around. You know what he'll do then? Call Rassitter's wife, who's going to panic, and in twenty minutes there'll be cops all over the place."

"So what? We'd be here."

" 'We'd be here,' he says. And what if Rassitter tells us the money's at his house? Or in a bank vault somewhere? How are we going to get it with cops around?"

Novek hooded his eyes and looked away. "Yeah, *if* there are cops around."

Grummund snorted and finished his Scotch. Then he undid his laces and slipped off his shoes.

"Okay," Novek said, "so how about we grab the little girl? She'd be the easiest to deal with anyway. We call Rassitter, tell him if he wants his baby back he has to pay up. No sweat."

Grummund shook his head. "Right. So then he calls the FBI. Then we've got phone taps, an ambush waiting for us at the drop site, helicopters, night scopes aimed at us, probably an electronic transmitter hidden in there somewhere, and God knows what else."

"All right, all right," Novek said testily, rising to his feet. "So what's *your* plan?"

"Simplest thing in the world," Grummund said. He propped the pillows against the headboard, swung his feet onto the bed, and leaned back. Then he held out his glass and rattled the thin ice.

Novek poured his boss some more Scotch.

"So?"

"So, we grab the whole family," Grummund told him.

30

WHEN LAUREN AWOKE Sunday morning, she was momentarily disoriented, feeling as if she were alone in a strange bed. She turned toward Richard's side and realized that she *was* alone. Then yesterday's events flooded into her mind.

She sat up, a sudden knot in her stomach.

She washed and dressed quickly in jeans, a pullover shirt, and sandals. Just before she fell asleep last night, she'd developed a plan. Or perhaps she'd dreamt it—she couldn't be certain. The plan was to pack a bag immediately with clothes for her and Emily, drive to Paul's apartment in L.A., and take Emily to LAX. They'd fly to Lincoln and move in with Lauren's parents. She would enroll Emily in a new school and try to land a job in Lincoln, perhaps with the city or county . . .

Lauren pushed those thoughts from her mind. That wasn't a plan, she knew, it was desperation, and she wasn't about to abandon her life in San Miguel. This was her home. If there were problems, she'd resolve them—somehow. Running away would solve nothing.

And what of Richard? Was she prepared to force him out and end their marriage?

At this point Lauren truly didn't know whether she and Richard would remain together. But she knew in her heart that she still loved him. If her love had been shaken yesterday when she saw him cross the street with Monica, it had been reconfirmed last night when he described the past four years of his life. There was no doubt in her mind that he'd spoken the truth, having dropped all pretenses and opened his soul to her. And despite an attempt to harden herself against his words, she'd found herself first sympathizing, then empathizing with him. She could understand why he'd lied in the past. And she could almost forgive him.

Almost.

There was still one important question to be asked, and the answer might determine the fate of their marriage and their future life together.

Lauren found Richard in the kitchen, making coffee. The Sunday paper was lying on the countertop, still wrapped in a thick rubber band.

"Hi." He seemed nervous, unsure of how to act.

"Good morning." She pulled a chair from the table, careful not to bump Amos, who was lying on the floor.

"Would you like breakfast?"

"I'm not really hungry."

"Just toast then? I'm going to have a slice."

She nodded. "Okay." Amos looked up at her and whined until she petted him. "What about this big baby?"

Richard allowed himself a smile. "I fed him first thing." He dropped two slices of bread in the toaster, then went to the cupboard for jam.

Suddenly Lauren remembered the gun. Richard had brought it in here from the garage last night. She turned abruptly in her chair, expecting to see the ugly, deadly thing pointed at her from the countertop. But the revolver was gone.

"I put it under the house this morning." Richard had seen her sudden movement, the look on her face. "You were right," he said with conviction. "There's no place in this house for a loaded gun."

"Are you certain?"

He hesitated. "What do you mean?"

"I mean, exactly how much danger are we in, Richard?"

His eyes held hers and he spoke deliberately. "Very little."

"Then why are FBI agents watching our every move, and—"

"It's because of them that we're safe."

"—and why did you feel the need for a gun?"

"I was wrong about the gun," he said. "**There's no need for it. And if those people *weren't* watching us, then I'd be worried."

The toast popped up. Richard put each slice on a plate and set the plates on the table. Lauren watched him pour two cups of coffee and waited for him to explain. He spread peanut butter and raspberry jam on his toast, took a bite, then sipped his coffee.

"Why is the FBI watching us?"

Richard stared down at his cup. "One month ago Peter Grummund was released from prison on parole."

Lauren's breath caught in her throat. "My God, and now he's coming here to—"

"Whoa, take it easy," Richard said, holding up his hand. "He may try to find me and he may not. And even if he does try, it's doubtful he could succeed. Except for a handful of federal officers, you're the only person who knows my former name." He shrugged his shoulders. "And I've known from the beginning when he'd be eligible for parole."

"You weren't concerned about it?"

"Not too much, no. I knew he'd be spending at least four years in prison, and when he got out he'd be sixty-three, an *old* sixty-three after living behind bars for so long. And I knew he'd be penniless—I'd seen to that myself. I'd pointed the authorities toward all of Grummund's hidden bank accounts, and they'd confiscated everything. Also, I figured that after being out of power for four years, he'd have a hard time gathering any of his former men. However—"

"He *has* gathered them."

"Actually, no. Jameson assured me that all these guys are either in prison, hiding from the law, or involved in petty power struggles. In other words, they have troubles of their own and have neither the time nor the inclination to start taking orders again from Grummund—or to help him hunt for me."

"Then what?" Lauren said, waving her hand to indicate all that had been going on.

Richard fiddled with his cup, turning it in the saucer until the handle pointed squarely at himself.

"When I saw the man in Tobey's last week, I thought he belonged to Grummund. I even thought it possible that Hal and Monica were connected to Grummund. After we were followed from the McFaddens' I went running to Jameson, and that's when I found out what was going on, that they were FBI agents. They had to follow us everywhere, because they had no idea when or where Grummund might show up."

"*That's* when you should have told me everything." Lauren's tone was accusatory.

"Yes," he said quietly. He looked grim. "And that's when Agent Zale told me to continue lying to keep you from running off in a panic. I honestly thought I was doing what was best for you and Emily, keeping you here under the protection of the FBI. But I know now that I was wrong not to tell you. And I'm sorry. I should have allowed you the decision whether to go or stay. And also . . ."

"What?"

"I was hoping all this would end right away and—"

"How could it *end*?"

"That's what I was about to tell you. On the day Grummund got out of prison he moved in with his cousin in Chicago, and the feds immediately put a tap on their phone. It had nothing to do with me—they were hoping he'd be contacted by a man named Albert Novek. He was Grummund's driver and bodyguard." Richard rubbed a hand over his mouth. "Novek is not someone you'd like to meet. He was always at Grummund's side, and so my being around him was unavoidable. It was disturbing just to be in his presence. He's . . . psychopathic. When Grummund was arrested, Novek escaped by shooting down two FBI agents, killing them both. The feds have been looking for him ever since."

Lauren felt a chill.

"They believed Novek might try to contact Grummund after his release from prison," Richard said.

"Did he?"

"Yes. The message was brief, but my name was mentioned—my old name, Donny Rassitter. Grummund dropped out of sight soon afterward, and the feds think he and Novek might have teamed up."

Lauren's mouth was dry. "And now they're looking for you."

"Not necessarily, but the feds aren't taking any chances. That's why they're watching us, for our protection against the slim chance that Grummund and Novek might find me before the FBI finds them."

"*Slim* chance," Lauren said. "I thought there was *no* chance. Isn't that what this witness program is all about? Why you changed your name and wiped out your past? Isn't that what all the . . . the deception was for?"

"Yes, of course, but, well, no system is perfect."

"Are you saying it's possible they could find you?" She already knew the answer. The presence of the FBI confirmed it.

Richard shook his head. "It's remotely possible, but the FBI has taken extreme measures to ensure our safety." He reached over and held her hand. "We're safe here, Lauren," he said with conviction. "In a day or so, a week at the most, Grummund and Novek will show themselves and the feds will drop on them and that'll be the end of it."

The phone rang before she could respond. She got up from the table to answer it.

"I've just made my famous apple strudel," Connie Pickering told her after saying hello. "Why don't the three of you come over and have some?"

"Ah, Connie, I don't know." Lauren covered the mouthpiece, glancing at her cold piece of toast, uneaten on her plate. Richard was pulling the rubber band from the Sunday paper. "Connie is inviting us over," she told him.

"Now?" Richard looked up, wrinkling his forehead.

Lauren felt the need to talk to someone not involved in this situation, someone who could be objective and give her an honest opinion. "You don't have to go," she said to Richard, "but I want to."

He nodded. "Sure."

Lauren told Connie she'd be right over, and hung up.

Richard pushed aside the newspaper and reached for her hand. She let him take it.

"When you come back, maybe we can do something, go somewhere."

"Well, maybe."

"Lauren, I'm . . . I'm sorry about . . ."

"I know." She withdrew her hand, then touched him on the shoulder before she walked out.

The moment Lauren passed through the front door she felt exposed. Her gaze was drawn to the house across the street. As usual, the drapes were slightly parted. She pictured one of them—Hal or Monica or perhaps the man named Zale—watching the monitors, watching her.

It occurred to her that this was an odd way to protect Richard and her and Emily. If there was so little danger, as Richard had suggested, then all this seemed too elaborate. And if they truly were in danger, then why didn't the FBI offer to move them all into hiding? Not that Lauren would necessarily agree to that, but she might if they convinced her the danger was real. Or why not simply post an armed guard on their doorstep? It might upset the neighbors, but it would certainly scare away Grummund and Novek. But federal agents hiding—as if they were waiting in ambush—seemed wrong to Lauren.

She hurried across the yard to Connie's porch and found the front door open. When she knocked on the screen, Connie appeared from within the house, wrapped in a flowing purple muumuu. She unlatched the screen and held it open.

"Where's Richard and Emily?"

"Emily's with her father this weekend, and Richard . . . had some things to do."

Connie led Lauren through the house to the kitchen. "Benjamin and the kids are already out by the pool, so we can talk in peace."

They sat at the kitchen table, where Connie poured them coffee in blue mugs and cut each of them a thick slice of strudel. Through the rear window Lauren saw Ryan and Christopher splashing in the shallow end of the pool, while Michelle sat on the edge near the diving board, idly swinging her ankles in the water. She didn't see Benjamin.

"I haven't talked to you in a few days," Connie said. "So what's new?"

Lauren was struck by the irony of Connie's question. She'd been nearly bursting to tell Connie about Richard's past, Hal and Monica, the surveillance cameras . . .

But she knew now that she couldn't say a word. The reason was simple, and she'd only realized it this moment—telling Connie might endanger Richard.

It wasn't that she didn't trust Connie. In fact, she loved her like a sister. But people talk. And even if she swore Connie to secrecy, anything she told her would probably be passed along to Benjamin, also in secrecy. And he might mention it—in the strictest confidence, of course—to another dentist or a patient, who might very well pass it on. Or Connie's children might overhear their parents, then tell their friends, who'd tell *their* parents . . .

Lauren realized that she could tell no one—not Connie, not Susan at work, not anyone. She began to understand what Richard must have gone through every day for years, every day until he felt comfortable with his new role in life as Richard Caylor, assistant manager at McFadden's Hardware.

And even if Lauren could be certain that Connie would not talk, not even to her husband, she still wouldn't reveal the truth to her, because she cared about Connie too much to burden her with their problem. And Connie *would* be burdened, because she'd be forced to carry this secret with her from now on.

Just as Richard has had to do, Lauren thought. Just as I have to do.

"So," Connie said, waiting. "Anything new and exciting in your life?"

"Not really. You know, the same old thing."

Connie nodded. "Not that I was spying or anything, but yesterday I saw you coming out of Hal and Monica's house."

"Yes?"

Connie was slightly taken aback. "Oh, sorry, I'm not trying to pry. I—"

"No, of course not," Lauren said apologetically.

"I just wondered if you've talked to them. No one in the neighborhood seems to know anything about them."

"I don't know much either."

"They're definitely weird, though, right?"

"I suppose." Lauren wanted to change the subject, but she didn't want to be obvious about it.

"Did you see the inside of their house?" Connie asked.

"I . . . yes. The living room."

Connie leaned forward, grinning wickedly. "What was it like? I've got a bet with Benjamin. I say it's as messy as their yard. *He* thinks they've got plastic covers over everything."

Lauren pictured the camera pointed at her house and the video monitors and the tape recorder near the telephone.

"It was . . . sparse," she said. "Not much furniture."

"Messy or neat?"

"Neat, I guess. How, um, how is your gun registration drive going?"

Connie gave her a brief, odd look. Then her face relaxed. "Things are moving right along," she said. "We're taking our petition before the city council next week, and . . ."

Lauren listened to Connie's voice without hearing what she was saying. She wanted to be home with Richard. It seemed ironic to her now, but he was the only person to whom she could freely talk, with whom she could . . . be herself. After a few minutes she said awkwardly, "I, ah, I'm supposed to help Richard with some things." She stood.

"Is anything wrong?" Connie looked concerned.

"No, not at all. I'll talk to you later, okay? And thanks for the strudel. It was delicious."

Connie followed her to the front door. Lauren felt her friend's eyes on her as she crossed the yard to her own house. It was a relief to pull the door closed behind her, temporarily shutting out the world.

But as she stepped through the entryway into the living room, her sense of relief vanished. Sitting there with Richard was Felix Jameson.

31

FELIX JAMESON STOOD, nodded once, and said, "Mrs. Caylor." He wore a white, short-sleeved shirt and a striped tie similar to the one Lauren had seen him wearing yesterday. Today, though, the knot was loosened and his collar was unbuttoned.

"Hello," Lauren said tentatively. "I'm sorry to interrupt." She started to leave the room.

"No, wait," Richard said, rising from the couch. He held out his hand for Lauren to join him. "Felix wants to talk to you."

"Perhaps you should sit down, Mrs. Caylor." Jameson spoke as gently as he could, Lauren assumed, but his voice was resonant, and his request sounded like a command.

Lauren joined Richard on the couch, and Jameson eased himself into the stuffed chair facing them. The big man smiled briefly, then cleared his throat.

"I can imagine how shocked you must have been yesterday when you walked in the house across the street."

He paused. Lauren said nothing.

"And you must have been doubly shocked when Richard explained everything to you, his past and all."

"Yes." Lauren's voice was tight, apprehensive.

"You see, Mrs. Caylor, when we place someone in the witness protection program and that person is married, we brief the entire family from the beginning—the spouse, and the children, if any. Everyone knows what they're getting into. They know the risks involved and the precautions they must take. And there are definite precautions."

"If you're trying to defend my husband's actions, you can save your breath," Lauren said. "I know why he kept his past from me. I understand."

"Then you must also understand why it is important for you not to tell anyone."

"Of course."

"She knows that, Felix."

Jameson looked at Lauren and asked, "You haven't told anyone, have you?"

"How could I? I just found out yesterday."

"You were next door just now," Jameson said. "Talking with your friend, Connie Pickering . . ."

"Yes, she's my friend. And yes, I was next door talking with her. And no, I didn't tell her a damn thing, all right?"

"I'm sorry, Mrs. Caylor, I didn't mean to imply—"

"You didn't?" Lauren was angry and she didn't try to hide it.

Richard put his hand on her arm, then withdrew it. "It's all right, Lauren. Felix has to be sure, that's all. He's just doing his job."

"And what about you, Richard? Are you sure I won't tell anyone?"

"I think you know the answer to that," he said without hesitation.

Lauren felt her anger begin to subside. "I'm sorry. I didn't mean it that way."

"It's all right."

Now Lauren turned on Jameson. "Are you satisfied now? If so, would you please leave my house, our house, and go back to your . . . your little spy's nest across the street."

Jameson nodded, a thin smile on his lips. "I don't blame you for resenting our presence. And believe me, if there were any other way . . ."

"You could've told us sooner," Lauren said, "instead of driving us crazy with mysterious people following wherever we went."

"It wasn't his fault," Richard said gently.

"Your husband's right, Mrs. Caylor. I wanted you both to know immediately when we learned there might be trouble with Peter Grummund and Albert Novek."

"Then why didn't you tell us?"

"It wasn't my decision to make."

"Whose was it?" Lauren snapped.

Jameson sighed. "Special Agent Howard Zale."

"Zale has been in on this from the beginning," Richard said. "He was one of the agents who questioned me back when I first turned myself in."

"Is Zale your boss?" Lauren asked Jameson.

"More or less. You see, I'm with the U.S. Marshals Service, and we administer the witness protection program. Zale is FBI. We both work for the Department of Justice, but in this case the FBI has authority, at least until Grummund and Novek are apprehended. And Agent Zale has a special interest."

"What do you mean?" Lauren asked.

"When the feds went to arrest Novek, he shot and killed two agents. One of them was Howard Zale's closest friend."

Lauren nodded grimly. "And now this killer is coming here."

"We don't know that for certain."

"But there's a chance, isn't there? Which means that Richard and Emily and I are at risk."

"There's an FBI agent assigned to each of you," Jameson said, "in addition to the command post across the street."

"That's not good enough." Lauren rose from the couch. "I'm going to take Emily away from here."

"Lauren . . ."

"Mrs. Caylor, if you're thinking of leaving the city or—"

"That's exactly what I'm thinking."

"I would advise against it," Jameson said.

"I don't give a damn what you'd advise." She turned to Richard and saw that his expression was pained. "I know *you* understand that Emily's welfare comes first. She and I can fly to Lincoln tomorrow, maybe even tonight. We can stay with my parents until—"

"That would be inadvisable."

"Will you shut up!" Lauren yelled at Jameson.

He stared impassively at her. Richard stood, put his hands on Lauren's shoulders, and turned her gently to him.

"Lauren, you're free to do whatever you think is best, and I'll help you one hundred percent."

"Just a minute," Jameson said.

He started to rise from his chair, but when Richard gave him a hard look, he sighed and sat back down.

"I mean it," Richard said to Lauren. "I'd die before I'd let anything happen to Emily. Or to you."

"Then you agree we should go."

Richard hesitated. "No," he said quietly.

Lauren stepped back, out of Richard's grasp. "Then whose side are you on, Richard? Emily's and mine, or . . . or his?" She jerked a thumb at Jameson.

"It's not a question of sides. It's a question of safety."

"I *know* that."

"And this is the safest place for us," Richard said. "For all three of us."

"But—"

"Please, just listen to me for a moment. If you and Emily go to Lincoln, some of the FBI agents will have to go too."

"Why?"

"Because according to Zale, Grummund might be able to trace you there," Richard said. "Listen, that was the first thing I thought about when Jameson told me what was going on. I wanted you and Emily out of harm's way immediately. But as Zale later explained it to me, it would be more difficult to protect you there than here. His people would be spread out. In addition, they'd have to guard your parents, who'd be involved by your very presence. *They'd* be in danger."

Lauren sensed the truth in his words, but it merely increased her anger and frustration.

"So what are we supposed to do?" she asked, her voice low and tight.

"Carry on as if nothing's wrong," Jameson said, rising from his chair. "We'll do the rest. We—that is, *they,* the FBI—have people watching all of you twenty-four hours a day, and they've got an all-points out on Grummund and Novek. Sooner or later those two will show up—somewhere—and the feds will drop a net over them. Then your lives will be back to normal."

"Normal," Lauren said under her breath.

"If you need us for anything," Jameson said, "just pick up the phone and holler. You don't even have to dial."

He walked out and closed the door solidly behind him.

"Isn't that wonderful." Lauren's tone was sarcastic. "Our phone is tapped, so we don't even have to dial."

Richard said nothing.

Lauren sighed. "I'm sorry. I know it's not your fault, not really."

"Sure it's my fault. Everything that's happening is a direct result of my past life, and if there was any way I could change things, Lauren, I would." He seemed to sag. "But there's nothing I can do about it now. It's their show."

212

Lauren reached for Richard, and then they were in each other's arms. It was as if the outside forces that she'd once feared would pull them apart were now pressing them closer together.

"We'll get through this okay," Richard said quietly.

Lauren was silent for a moment, then she asked, "Do you trust these people, Richard? I mean, do you have faith in them?"

"I trust Jameson implicitly. He's been my friend, off and on, for over four years."

"And the rest of them, Zale and the others, do you trust them?"

Richard paused before he spoke, his lips brushing the top of her head. "We have to."

Paul Webb brought Emily home just after six, earlier than Lauren had expected.

"Hi, Mommy!"

Emily ran into her arms, and Lauren gave her a hug. Her hair was mussed from riding in Paul's convertible.

"I have dinner reservations for a new restaurant in L.A.," Paul explained from the doorstep. "For Beth and me. It's very exclusive. They, well, frown on bringing children."

"Sounds like your kind of place."

"Yes, well . . ." He looked past her to Emily. "Good-bye, honey."

" 'Bye, Daddy."

Lauren gave her ex-husband a brittle smile, then quietly closed the door.

Neither of them felt like cooking, so they sent out for a pizza. Lauren let Richard make the call because she hated the idea of a third party listening in, even to such a banal conversation. She set their places at the kitchen table, then remembered the video camera hidden on a pole in the alley, recording everything that occurred in their backyard. She wondered if it could also peer through the kitchen window. Before they sat down to eat, she pulled shut the curtains.

Richard placed a slice of pizza on Emily's plate and asked her what she'd done all day.

"We rode in the car."

"Where did you ride?"

"I don't know," Emily said. "Someplace."

"What did you do when you got there?" Lauren asked.

"Me and Daddy and Beth walked through a house."

"Whose house?"

"I don't know. It was empty except for the other man there. Daddy said he was a real, um, a realer."

"A realtor?"

"Yeah."

Lauren caught Richard's eye, but said nothing. After Emily finished a slice and a half of pizza, she asked if she could get Cathy Ann.

"Sure, honey." Emily left the kitchen, and Lauren said, "Terrific. Paul entertains her by taking her house hunting and then makes reservations at a restaurant that doesn't serve children."

Richard shrugged. "He's a single man."

"He's a lousy father."

"That's why . . ." Richard smiled meekly.

"What?"

"I was about to say, 'That's why you picked me.' But I guess now it doesn't look like such a good choice, does it?"

"Don't say that."

"If I thought it would help," he said, "I mean, help you and Emily, I'd pack up and leave, change my name again, and hide somewhere."

"No."

"The problem is, it would change nothing, as far as Grummund is concerned. If he tracks me here and I'm gone, he'll assume that you know where I am. He'd threaten you to get to me. So if he does—"

"Richard, please don't talk like this."

"If he does show up, it would be better if I was here. Then he'd go for me and leave you and Emily out of it."

"But he's not going to get to you or anyone, not with the FBI camped out across the street."

"What's FBI?"

They both looked at Emily, standing in the doorway, her doll cradled in one arm.

"It's nothing, honey," Lauren said gently. "Come sit down and we'll have ice cream for dessert."

"Ice cream!"

·　　·　　·

Later that night, after Lauren had tucked Emily in bed, she sat with Richard on a love seat in the family room. He'd already put on a tape of soft music.

Lauren sank back into his arms. It occurred to her that without making a conscious effort, she'd completely forgiven him. It was as if he'd confessed to her that he'd been addicted to alcohol or drugs, but now he was sober and clean, and all his mistakes were behind him. Should she hate him for what was past? Or should she be thankful that there were no more lies and no more secrets between them? She knew the answer.

There were other questions, though.

"How likely is it that Peter Grummund could ever find . . . us?"

Richard held her a little tighter.

"It's a very slim chance."

"Then why is the FBI being so, I don't know the word—scheming, elaborate?"

"Because if Grummund found me, he'd kill me, pure and simple. Or else he'd tell Novek to do it, and Novek is fiercely loyal to him. And ruthless."

"I understand that, but all this . . . subterfuge. It seems odd. And was it merely a coincidence that the house across the street was vacant and available for the FBI to use?"

"Actually, yes. Zale told me they were lucky to be able to rent the Greys' house. Otherwise they would've had to set up a mobile command post with a greater chance of being spotted."

"By Grummund?"

"Or Novek."

"And what would be wrong with that?" Lauren asked. "At the first sign of federal agents those two would run as fast and as far away as they could, and we'd be safe."

"Temporarily. Grummund and Novek might run, but they'd be back, and who knows when? Next week? Next year?"

Although Lauren didn't agree with the FBI's line of reasoning, she understood it—lying in wait would be the surest way to capture Grummund and Novek, assuming of course that they showed up. But something about this strategy troubled her deeply.

"Zale is in charge of all this, isn't he?" she asked.

"I'm afraid so."

Lauren turned to him. "You don't like him either, do you?"

"No, he's a class-A jerk. But he's in command, and there's nothing we can do about it."

"Was he in charge four years ago in Chicago?"

"Well, he was the case agent in charge of that investigation, but he was in line for a permanent supervisory position. Apparently, he made it, and now he's got enough pull to get himself assigned as head of this operation."

"You mean he arranged to come out here from Chicago? He wasn't ordered?"

"According to Jameson he pushed for it."

"That bothers me," Lauren said.

Richard gave her a puzzled look. "Why? What difference does it make who's in charge?"

"When Novek escaped four years ago, he killed two FBI agents, one of them Zale's best friend, right?"

"So?"

"So maybe Zale's interest in this is more than merely professional."

"I suppose you're right, but—"

"How bad do you think Zale wants Novek?"

"Pretty damn bad."

Lauren nodded. "Now the question is, what's more important to Zale, our safety or Novek's capture?"

Richard frowned. "What are you getting at?"

"Maybe Zale is obsessed with avenging his friend's death. If so, he might take steps to protect us, but mainly he'd *want* Novek to show up here, right?"

He stared at her, his brows tightly knit.

"Richard, what if . . . what if Zale is using us for bait?"

32

RICHARD SHOOK his head. "I can't believe it. They're here to protect us, not *use* us."

"Not 'they,' " Lauren said, "Zale. He's the one in charge and the one with a personal stake in getting Novek. I think we're bait for the trap. Think about it. Zale knew weeks ago that Novek and Grummund had teamed up and were probably looking for you, and yet he never warned you. Why not, do you suppose?"

"Jameson said the feds didn't want to upset us. They wanted us to act . . . normal."

He stared at Lauren. She nodded.

"Exactly," she said. "Zale wanted us innocent-looking and out in the open where Novek and Grummund could see us and—"

"Wait a minute." Richard held up his hand. "We're getting carried away here. First of all, Zale has superiors he must answer to. He can't just do anything he wants." He paused, frowning. "Although . . ."

"What is it?"

"When I first went to see Jameson, even *he* didn't know what was going on until he made a few phone calls and was put in touch with Zale. I could tell he was angry that he hadn't been informed, but he chalked it up to bureaucracy." Richard looked away, pressing his knuckles to his lower lip.

"What are you thinking?"

He lowered his hand and faced her. "I'm thinking it's possible that Zale could get away with one or two things by misinforming his superiors or withholding information. I'd never considered this before, because the feds have acted in my best interest from the beginning. And after I talked to Jameson last week and found out what was going on, I, well, I was so concerned you'd find out about me that I didn't think of much else. But now . . ."

"Now you think it's possible Zale is using us?"

"I . . . don't know. Although it would explain something else that's been bothering me—the San Miguel police know nothing about this."

"They don't?"

Richard shook his head. "Zale told me he didn't want any 'small-town cops' getting in his way."

Lauren's mouth was dry. "Maybe we should notify the police ourselves."

"I don't know, Lauren. What could we tell them—federal agents are watching us?"

"But we have to do *something*."

He nodded, staring into the middle distance.

"Maybe we should just pack up and get out," Lauren said.

Richard paused. "Perhaps we should."

"Do you mean it?" Lauren felt her heart quicken. Jameson had told them that leaving might be more dangerous than staying. She'd begun to believe that—but not anymore. The question was, where would they go? And how long would they stay away? Most important, should they tell anyone they were leaving? She expressed these concerns to Richard.

"Before we do anything," he said, "I want to talk to Jameson."

"Can we trust him, Richard?"

"Yes, I think so. Jameson doesn't answer to Zale, doesn't have the same priorities. Mostly, though, I believe he has our best interests at heart. And if we decide to go, he can probably help us."

"What if he tells us to stay?"

Richard looked away, then met her eyes. "If you and I decide to leave here, Lauren, we'll leave. But let me talk to him first. He might still be across the street, so why don't I go over there right now and—"

"Let's bring him here," she said. Richard followed her to the kitchen, where she clicked on the light and lifted the receiver. "We don't even have to dial, remember?" she said to him, then spoke into the phone. "Hello, this is Lauren Caylor. I want to speak with Felix Jameson." She paused, listening to the dial tone. "Hello. I know somebody is monitoring this, so wake up and put Jameson on the phone."

The dial tone clicked off. "What can I do for you, Mrs. Caylor?" It was a man's voice.

"Is this Jameson?" Lauren said.

"This is Agent Zale. What's up?"

Lauren mouthed the name for Richard, then: "Let me talk to Felix Jameson."

"He went home for the evening," Zale said. "What do you want him for?"

"Nothing," Lauren said, and hung up. "He said Jameson went home."

Richard took the phone from her and dialed Jameson's number. "I'll have him meet us here." Then he shook his head and replaced the receiver. "No answer. I'll call him in the morning."

That night they slept together, Lauren insisting that Richard not use the guest bedroom. She couldn't stand the thought of sleeping apart in the same house. And more, she felt close to him now, perhaps closer than ever. She believed that she understood him better, too—not just the incidents in his past, but him, the man.

Yes, he'd lied to her. But his intentions had never been evil. He'd always acted in what he thought was their best interest—to preserve their relationship, to keep them together.

And it was possible, Lauren believed, that the pain of their present trauma might serve to bind them even closer, to strengthen their marriage.

Early Monday morning, Memorial Day, Richard phoned Jameson again. There was still no answer.

"I'll contact him sometime today," Richard said. "In the meantime I think we should go about our business as if nothing's changed. We don't want Zale and the rest of them to think we're planning something. At least not yet."

"Would they try to stop us?"

"I don't know."

"My God, Richard, it's as if everyone is against us."

He held her to him. "We've got each other and that's all that matters. Don't worry, we'll get through this."

After breakfast Lauren kissed Richard good-bye and he left for work. The schools were out and the city offices closed, so she and Emily had the day to themselves. Normally Lauren would have had something planned, but her mind had been on other things. Now she considered taking her daughter to the San Diego Zoo or to Disney-

219

land. The idea of federal agents following them wherever they went was not appealing. But then neither was the thought of staying home all day.

The phone rang—Connie Pickering coming to the rescue, inviting them over for a cookout.

"I assumed Richard would be busy with those mammoth Memorial Day sales, so if you and Emily aren't doing anything . . ."

"That would be great," Lauren said, her spirits starting to rise. "Can I bring anything?"

"Just yourselves. We probably won't eat until three or so, but come over anytime."

Lauren felt like asking if they could come right now, but she resisted the urge, deciding that she could keep busy at home for at least a few hours. "How about noon?"

"Perfect," Connie said. "See you then."

Lauren carried the laundry basket to the bathroom and filled it with clothes from the hamper. Washing clothes was not her favorite thing to do, but now it felt good, normal. As she was transferring the clothes from the basket to the washer, Amos sauntered behind her and passed through the dog door. Emily had been following him, and now she struggled with the back door knob.

"It won't open."

"Let me help you, hon." Lauren turned the knob, then noticed that Richard had locked the dead bolt on his way out, something he never used to do. "Um, why do you want out, honey?"

"To play with Amos."

Lauren didn't want Emily out of her sight, not with even the remotest possibility that Grummund and Novek might show up and snatch her from the backyard. Sure, she'd be under the watchful eye of the video camera, but was anyone watching the monitor across the street? And if they were and saw someone climbing the fence, could they get over here quickly enough to protect Emily?

"Why don't you stay inside with me," Lauren suggested. "We're going to Connie's house pretty soon anyway."

"But I want to play outside."

"And I want you indoors with me."

Emily gave her a sorrowful look, and Lauren realized she'd spoken harshly. She knelt and put her hands on Emily's shoulders. "I'm sorry, honey, but I just want you to be in the house with me, okay?

In a little while we'll go next door and you can play with Ryan and Christopher and Michelle. How does that sound?"

"Okay, I guess." Emily stared at the floor.

"Do you want to watch TV? Or we can pick out a picture in one of your books to color. Or—"

"I guess I'll play with my dolls," Emily said resignedly, "but I'd *rather* go outside."

"I know, baby." Lauren kissed her on the forehead. "But do this as a favor for me, okay? Now give me a hug."

Emily put her arms around Lauren's neck.

"I love you, honey."

"I love you, Mommy."

After Emily went to her room, Lauren added soap to the washer, set the dials, and turned it on. Her mind drifted back to an earlier thought: If someone climbed the fence, could help arrive in time? She had a sudden, disturbing image of two men coming over the fence and sprinting across the backyard toward the house.

She peered out the kitchen window. Then she moved through the house to the living room window.

She could see halfway down the block. Many porches were hung with American flags in celebration of Memorial Day, and a few neighbors were outside doing yard work. Hal Ipswich stood in the yard across the street with a garden hose in his hand, looking for all the world as if he belonged there. However, Lauren could see that his attention was not on his watering, but on the street. His head turned slowly from side to side as he scanned the neighborhood, the hose held firmly before him. Lauren smiled grimly and wondered if there was a large puddle of water at his feet.

He's pretending to be a neighbor, she thought, and we're pretending nothing's wrong. *Everything* is wrong.

She walked back to the kitchen and phoned Richard at the store, stretching the cord through the doorway to the family room to shut out the sound of the washing machine.

"Have you talked to Jameson?" she asked.

"Yes." He paused. "Where are you calling from?"

"From home. Why . . . oh." Now she paused. "I'll, um, I'll call you later, okay?"

"Okay," he said.

They hung up. Lauren had momentarily forgotten that their phone

was tapped, that everything they said was being listened to by someone across the street—and ultimately by Zale. If they were going to
leave San Miguel without Zale's knowledge or interference, they
would have to be careful.

Lauren considered running next door to use Connie's phone, but
it wasn't even ten o'clock yet and she'd told Connie she and Emily
would be there at noon.

Take it easy, she told herself, you can wait a couple of hours.

Lauren tried to pass the time by cleaning the bathrooms, but after she'd scrubbed the tile and porcelain and polished the chrome
and glass, it was only a little after eleven. Unable to wait any
longer, she washed up and changed into a clean blouse and shorts.
She found Emily in her room arranging cups and saucers for several dolls, including the one Betty McFadden had given her—
when? Weeks ago? No, it had been only a few days. But what days
those had been.

"Shall we go now?"

Emily looked up, surprised. "Already?"

As Lauren closed the front door, she remembered the load of
laundry, which would be sitting all day, cold and wet in the bottom
of the washer.

The hell with it, she thought.

Leading Emily by the hand to Connie's front door, Lauren glanced
at Hal Ipswich, who was still pretending to water his lawn across the
street. Benjamin Pickering answered her knock wearing a dirty
T-shirt and blue jeans. He had a screwdriver in his hand.

"We're early," Lauren said.

"No problem." Benjamin held open the screen door. "I think
Connie's in the bathroom doing something with her hair."

"Don't bother her. The reason I came now is, um, our phone is
out of order and I have to make an important call. Would you
mind?"

"Not at all—use the one in the den. The kids are out by the pool,
so if Emily will allow me to show her the way . . ."

"That would be great, Benjamin. Thanks."

Lauren sat at the desk in the den and phoned Richard.

"I'm at Connie's," she told him.

"Good. When you called before, I was afraid you'd forgotten
about the phone tap."

"I did for a minute. God, Richard, *why* is it tapped?"

"Supposedly to put a trace on Grummund if he should call to threaten me. But now I think the real reason was to make it easier for Zale to monitor us and possibly know our movements ahead of time."

Lauren made a sound between a moan and a curse.

"I spoke to Jameson," Richard said, "and told him we were concerned about Zale. He doubts that Zale has ulterior motives or is exceeding his authority. But he was surprised by one thing. Apparently Zale told him he'd explained everything to us and we both felt comfortable staying where we were."

"That son of a—"

"I know—that's what I said too. Jameson was angry that Zale had lied to him, but he told me the bottom line is—and he's felt this way from the beginning—there's really no way that Grummund and Novek can locate us, the witness program is just too thorough. That aside, he's going over Zale's head to make some inquiries. And no matter what, if you and I don't feel safe, he can arrange for us to be moved."

"Thank God."

"That's the good news. The bad news is that after Jameson talks to Zale's superior, there will probably be an investigation. Then they'll have to find a place for us." He paused. "It's going to take some time."

"How *much* time?"

"At least a few days, possibly a week."

"No," she said. "I want to get out of here with Emily now, today if possible. I've got a bad feeling that something's going to happen."

"We can't panic, Lauren. Let me talk to Jameson and—"

"The hell with Jameson!" she shouted, then glanced quickly at the den's open doorway. "I don't care about Jameson," she said quietly. "All I care about is getting Emily out of harm's way."

"But where would you go?"

"To my parents."

"Do you think that's wise, getting them involved?"

Lauren pressed her fingers to her brow, squeezing her eyes shut. "All I know is I can't just sit here and wait for something to happen. I won't."

"Hang on a minute." Lauren heard muffled voices in the background before Richard spoke again. "Look, there's a minor crisis here that I've got to attend to. Let me call Jameson again and then I'll call you back. Will you be at Connie's later?"

"Yes," she said dully.

"Okay, I'll talk to you later. I love you." He hung up.

Lauren stared for a moment at the phone. Then she ground her teeth, pulled the phone book toward her, and looked up the number for United Airlines.

A recording told her to please hold for the next available service representative. Lauren listened to elevator music and reexamined her plan: book the next three seats to Lincoln, Nebraska, and take Emily away from here as soon as she could, this afternoon if possible. Richard could come with them now if he chose to—she *wanted* him to come, wanted the three of them to stay together. But ultimately it would be his choice. And if there was a problem with the store, if he couldn't leave today, then he could change his flight to tonight or tomorrow. The important thing now—the only thing that mattered—was to get Emily to safety, no matter what Zale or Jameson or anyone else said.

Lauren was still on hold when she realized that she hadn't told her parents they were coming. She hung up, then dialed the operator and placed a call to Lincoln, charging it to her phone credit card. She felt a pang of guilt when she heard her mother's voice—it had been too long since last she called.

"Hi, Mom, how are you?"

"We're just fine, dear," Lauren's mother said. "Your ears must be burning, because Dad and I were just talking about you. How's that granddaughter of ours?"

"As good as ever," Lauren said. "Listen, we're flying out there and I wanted to make sure it was all right for us to stay with you for a while."

"Don't be silly, of *course* you can. They're coming for a visit," she said away from the phone, and then to Lauren: "When are you coming?"

"Sometime today. As soon as I can make reservations."

"Today? Well, that's fine, but . . . is everything all right?"

"Yes, Mom, everything's fine." There was no way Lauren could explain the situation to her mother, not over the phone, and perhaps not even when they got to Lincoln. "As soon as I know when our flight arrives, I'll call you back, okay?"

"That will be fine." Lauren could hear concern in her mother's voice and knew she sensed something was wrong.

"I love you, Mom."

"We love you, too, dear."

Lauren phoned the airline again, and again was put on hold. She realized that a lot of people traveled on Memorial Day, and she began to wonder if she could get three seats on the same flight. When the ticket agent came on the line, he confirmed Lauren's fear: most flights were booked solid. He could get them to Denver anytime that afternoon, where they could catch a connecting flight to Lincoln, but the only available connection didn't leave until late in the evening. Lauren hated the idea of her and Emily sitting for hours in an airport. So she made reservations for the next morning, when there were many vacant seats.

She phoned her mother and said they'd be in Lincoln tomorrow afternoon around two. Then she called Richard.

"I've booked the three of us on a plane tomorrow to Lincoln. It leaves LAX at eight-forty A.M. I've already phoned my parents and told them we're coming."

For a moment Richard was silent, and Lauren feared that he disapproved. She would do this alone if she had to, but she knew they were stronger together.

"Okay," he said finally. "But there's no way we can sneak away from the feds and Zale. They'll follow us to the airport tomorrow and find out where we're going."

"True enough, but they can't stop us. And they can't follow us to Lincoln, at least not Zale, not if he wants to get Novek and Grummund. Zale will have to stay in San Miguel and keep watching our house, because if those two men are coming, that's where they'll go first."

"You're absolutely right."

"God, Richard, I hope so."

"Listen, we're getting a lot of business today, and Arthur wants me to keep the store open until eight. But when I get home, we'll pack and be ready to leave in the morning. We'll stay with your parents for the rest of the week, and if nothing's happened here by then, well, we'll see. Your father will probably be sick of having me around anyway. By the way, does he like me yet?"

Lauren laughed, relieving some of her tension. "Sure he likes you. He's just suspicious of any man who sleeps with his baby daughter."

"My intentions are wholesome."

"Well, let's hope they're not *too* wholesome."

Now Richard laughed. "I've got to get back to work. I'll see you tonight. Love you."

"I love you too."

For the first time since all this began Lauren felt that she and Richard had taken charge of the situation. Not completely, of course, but enough to deal with it on their own terms. She knew that going to Lincoln wouldn't actually solve anything, but it was a start. And they'd all be safer there.

Lauren found everyone in the backyard. She sat with Connie on the patio and watched the children splash in the pool under the warm sun. She told Connie that they were going to Nebraska for a few days, possibly a week. She told her not to worry about feeding Amos because she was going to leave him with her friend Susan, who also had a dog and sometimes traded this favor with her. Lauren didn't mention that she hadn't yet informed Susan. She also told Connie not to pick up their mail because, as she put it, "Richard has arranged for some people at the store to look after things." Connie seemed to accept all this, although she did exchange a glance with Benjamin. Of course, Lauren couldn't state the real reason she wanted Connie to stay away from their house—it might be dangerous.

Later Benjamin cooked burgers on the grill, while Lauren helped Connie spread a tablecloth on the picnic table and set out plates and silverware. As they ate, they talked about the upcoming summer vacation and how they would keep their children occupied until school resumed in the fall. Lauren relaxed, comfortable in the company of good friends, until she noticed the pole in the alley with the hidden surveillance camera. She wondered if Zale and friends were watching them now, recording their picnic.

Lauren took Emily home at seven. Emily was tired from swimming and running around with Connie's two boys, and she didn't argue when Lauren suggested she go to bed early. She told her daughter that tomorrow morning they would take a plane ride and visit Grandma and Grandpa.

"Can I bring my dolls?" Emily asked after Lauren tucked her under the covers. Amos was already curled up on the floor on the far side of the bed.

"Not all of them, honey, or we'd have to pack an extra suitcase. You can take your favorite one, okay?"

"But I have lots of favorites. What if they all want to go?"

"Well, you can tell them that they can go next time. But for now some of them have to stay here and watch the house while we're away."

"For how long?"

How long indeed? Lauren wondered. How long could they stay away from their home and wait for Grummund and Novek to arrive? A week? A month? What if they never arrived? Somehow Lauren knew that was wishful thinking. They were coming. The question was when.

"Not long," Lauren said, and kissed Emily on the forehead. "Good night, baby."

"Good night, Mommy."

Lauren switched off the bedroom light and walked down the hall to the master bedroom. The house had grown too cool for her to be comfortable in shorts and sandals, so she changed into jeans and sneakers. She'd decided to wait until Richard got home before she packed her things. And she could pack for Emily in the morning.

Lauren poured herself a glass of wine and carried it from the kitchen to the family room. Just then she heard a voice at the front of the house, a muffled shout.

Frowning, she moved to the living room doorway.

She heard another shout, more distinctive this time, followed by popping noises.

Fear pumped through her veins like acid.

In the next instant the front door burst open with a tremendous crash and two men tumbled in. Lauren stood frozen in terror, her hand to her mouth, unable to move, unable even to scream.

One man dropped in a crouch near the front doorway, pointed a large automatic pistol outside, and fired several times, making sharp cracking sounds that reverberated in the room, hurting Lauren's ears. The other man, the older of the two, also crouched down, but facing into the room. He glared at Lauren.

She'd never seen these men before, but she knew exactly who they were. She realized with sickening clarity that she'd acted too late, that she and Emily and Richard would not be taking a plane ride tomorrow. Perhaps not ever.

Lauren turned and ran for Emily's bedroom.

33

LAUREN RUSHED into her daughter's room.

The light from the hall fell across the bed, spotlighting Emily. She sat up, suddenly wide awake, her mouth open in astonishment and fear.

Lauren fought against a paralyzing panic. She could think of only two courses of action: run or hide. To run, she'd have to pull the screen from the window, lift up Emily and lower her to the backyard, then climb out after her. But was it safe outside? Or were there more men with guns shooting at each other, with her and Emily in their line of fire? But hiding would be no safer because there was no place where they could stay hidden for long.

Maybe not both of us, Lauren thought, but Emily alone . . .

She hurried to her daughter's side and put her hand lightly over her mouth.

"Be quiet as a mouse," she whispered. "You have to hide."

She pulled Emily from the bed and carried her across the dark room to the closet. "Hold real still," Lauren whispered, sitting her down on the floor in the corner, "and don't come out for anyone but me. Promise?"

The little girl was shaking so badly she could barely nod her head.

Lauren dragged a blanket from the top shelf and draped it over Emily. Then she pulled clothes from hangers and dropped them on the floor and on the blanket, trying to camouflage her daughter's hiding place. She didn't know how long Emily could endure being there before she pulled off the blanket and cried out, nor did she know how long she would *have* to endure. But for the moment at least, Emily was safe.

Lauren straightened up and turned around. A man was silhouetted in the doorway.

"Come out here," he said in a harsh voice.

Lauren trembled with fear, but she forced herself not to back away, not to draw attention to the closet. Slowly she stepped forward.

"And bring the little girl," the man ordered.

Lauren shook her head. "There's no one else but—"

"Either you get her out of the closet or I will." He turned sideways in the doorway, and Lauren could see him more clearly in the hall light. He was in his sixties, heavyset, with a jowly face, a round head, and thin, wispy hair. He wore dark slacks and a white shirt with long sleeves rolled up over his forearms. He held a revolver in his left hand.

"Novek," he called. "Tell them we've got two hostages, a woman and a kid, and if they shoot again or try anything, we'll throw out a body."

"NO!"

Peter Grummund turned toward her and barked, "Shut up." Then he reached in and clicked on the bedroom light, making Lauren squint from the brightness. His hair was so thin that Lauren could see beads of perspiration glistening on top of his head. "Get your daughter out of the closet," he said, his voice hard, but perhaps not as threatening as before. "Just behave yourself and nobody will get hurt."

Lauren heard someone shouting, and she pictured the other man, Novek, delivering his ultimatum from the front door.

"Please," she said, "please don't hurt us. We've done nothing to—"

Suddenly Grummund raised his gun and pointed it toward the bed. Lauren saw that Amos had stood and was stretching, finally roused from his resting place. The big dog swiveled his head toward Grummund, his ears up and his eyes glistening, looking like an elongated, tiger-striped attack dog.

"*Don't shoot him!*" Lauren screamed. "He's harmless, he won't do anything." She stepped toward Amos, raised her hand, and tried to speak in a soothing voice. "Amos, you lie down."

Amos whined once and stretched—front paws together, head down, butt up—then squatted down on his haunches with his chest on the floor, his front legs straight in front of him, and his head up.

"Good boy," Lauren said, thankful for his sake that he wasn't aggressive or he surely would have been shot.

"Get that kid out here," Grummund snapped, looking at Lauren but keeping a wary aim on Amos's head, "and I mean now."

Lauren turned to the closet and helped Emily out from under the clothes and the blanket. Emily clutched her mother's leg, too scared to speak or even cry.

"It's all right, sweetie," Lauren said, trying to sound calm. She stroked Emily's hair, then let her hand fall reassuringly on her shoulder. "Everything will be all—"

Novek appeared in the doorway beside Grummund, and Lauren shut her mouth.

Novek was taller than Grummund, a fierce-looking man, dark-complexioned, with curly black hair and low brows. His black sport shirt was buttoned at the neck and stretched tightly across his broad chest. His arms were hairy and corded with muscle, and his fist was filled with a large automatic pistol. He gave Lauren and Emily a passing glance.

"They got the message," he said, his voice deep and gravelly. "It looks like they were *waiting* for us. What the hell's going on?"

"I don't know yet." Grummund turned to Lauren. "Where is he? Where's Donny?"

"Donny? I . . ."

"Your husband, for chrissake." Then he sneered. "Oh, that's right, he's 'Richard' now. Well?"

"He's . . . he's at work." Lauren could imagine the FBI telling Richard what had happened, telling him to stay away from the house.

"He's still at the store?"

"It's Memorial Day. They stay open late."

Grummund smiled out of one side of his mouth and shook his head. "Memorial Day. Jesus Christ."

"What are we going to do, Pete?"

Grummund held Lauren's eyes a moment longer, then turned to Novek. "Don't worry, I'll think of something. Go through the house, pull all the drapes, and block off the doors."

Novek nodded and started away.

"Wait a minute," Grummund said. "You're hit."

Lauren could see that the lower portion of Novek's right pants leg was dark and wet.

"It's nothing," Novek said, and disappeared into the living room.

230

A few seconds later Lauren heard him dragging a piece of furniture across the floor.

"What . . . what are you going to do?" she asked fearfully.

Before Grummund could answer, the phone began to ring. He cocked his head, listening.

"You have two phones?"

"One in the kitchen and one in the master bedroom."

"Let's go." He pointed his gun for emphasis. After Lauren and Emily edged by him, he closed the door, shutting in Amos, and followed them down the hall to the master bedroom. The phone continued to ring. Grummund moved past Lauren to the nightstand, then faced her, raising his eyebrows in mock innocence. "You think this might be for me?"

He held the receiver to his ear, paused, and said, "You're talking to him." He listened quietly for a full minute, looking at Lauren and then beyond her toward Novek, who'd just entered the room. Finally Grummund said, "Okay, now you listen to me. We've got the woman and the little girl, and if you try to send in the troops or shoot us through the windows, these two will die, understand? I want a van gassed up and ready to go, one with doors in the rear. Back it up to the front of the house, open the doors, then get the hell away from it. And I want Donny, er, excuse me, *Richard Caylor*. When he shows up, you can call back for more instructions." He hung up without waiting for a reply.

"What's going on?" Novek asked.

He was standing so close behind Lauren that his breath ruffled her hair. She stepped farther into the room, away from him, pulling Emily with her. Thus far the child had not uttered a sound.

"What do *you* think?" Grummund said, waving his revolver casually. "They've got the place surrounded and they want us to surrender." He looked at Lauren and ran his hand over his forehead, wiping perspiration back into his thin hair. "All right, lady, now you tell me what the hell is going on. The minute we drove up, there were guys waving guns and yelling 'FBI!' Were they waiting for us?"

Lauren nodded.

"I don't get it," Novek said.

"How did they know we were coming here?"

Lauren tried to remember what Jameson had told her and Richard. "They . . . put a tap on your phone."

"*My* phone. You mean at my cousin's house?"

"I think so. They were hoping that . . ."

Lauren stopped, glancing over her shoulder at Novek.

"That what?"

"That Novek would contact you."

"Son of a bitch," Grummund said under his breath. Lauren heard Novek grunt behind her. Grummund looked at him and said, "I guess it's you they really want. Well, no matter." His eyes returned to Lauren. "Where does he have the money stashed?"

"The money? If you mean in my purse, I—"

"Don't play dumb," Novek grumbled from behind her.

"I . . ." Lauren shook her head.

"I don't think she knows," Grummund said, then waved his hand to indicate the room, the house. "By the looks of things he hasn't spent much of it, so maybe there's hope yet. Now you and the missus better go in the bathroom so she can do something about that leg. You're bleeding all over the carpet."

Lauren felt a heavy hand on her shoulder. She jerked away, still holding on to Emily, and backed against the wall. The two men looked at her with neutral expressions. Novek moved a few steps toward the bathroom, his right shoe making a squishy sound.

"You'd better leave the kid out here," he said, "unless she likes the sight of blood."

Lauren turned to Grummund for help, then realized how foolish that was. She squatted down before Emily and held her by the shoulders. "You stay out here for a few minutes, okay?"

"Mommy, I'm scared." There were tears in Emily's eyes.

"It's all right, honey. You'll be all right." She glanced again toward Grummund, who merely stared back. "I'll just be in the bathroom, so you sit here in the chair and wait for me, okay?"

Emily had turned her head and was staring fearfully at Novek. Lauren shook her gently to get her attention.

"Okay, honey?"

"Okay," Emily said in a small voice.

Lauren sat her in the armchair in the corner of the room, then walked past Novek into the bathroom. She opened the medicine cabinet, not knowing what she was looking for, not wanting to face Novek. She took down a box of cotton, some sterilized pads, tape, and a bottle of hydrogen peroxide. The last time she'd used the bottle was a month ago when Emily had fallen on the sidewalk and scraped her knee. As she turned around, Novek was lowering the cover on the toilet seat. He placed his gun on the top of the tank, then sat down and began pulling his wet pants leg up to his knee.

Lauren felt sick to her stomach—she'd never seen so much blood. It was smeared on his lower leg, matting the thick hair, and it ran in rivulets into his sock and leaked from his shoe. There was so much she could smell it. She noticed marks on the carpet, bloody half-moons that led in from the bedroom.

Novek gave her a dark grin.

"It don't hurt," he said. "Much."

"You . . . need a doctor."

"Yeah, right. Just clean it up and put on some of that stuff in the bottle."

The things from the medicine cabinet now seemed ridiculously inadequate. Lauren set them down and pulled a hand towel from the rack. She filled the sink with warm water, soaked the towel, then knelt before Novek and began wiping blood from his leg. She was revolted by her task, and she had to force herself to continue. When she washed out the towel in the sink, she gritted her teeth as blood diluted with water ran between her fingers.

After Lauren finished cleaning Novek's lower leg, she could see that the bullet had passed completely through the back of his calf, leaving a pair of neat holes several inches apart. The skin around them was puckered and discolored, and the holes oozed blood. Lauren guessed that no veins or arteries had been severed by the slug, or the blood would have gushed from his wounds.

She poured hydrogen peroxide over the holes, making Novek wince, catching the runoff with the towel. The smell of blood now was cut by a medicinal odor that helped to settle Lauren's queasy stomach. She held a sterile pad over each hole. They were quickly soaked through with blood, so she pressed two fresh pads over them.

"Hold these and I'll tape them in place," she said.

Novek put his fingers gently over the pads. Lauren saw that his fingernails were dirty and cracked. This surprised her, and she didn't know why until she remembered that Richard had told her Novek had been Grummund's bodyguard and driver. She tried to picture him in a chauffeur's uniform, neatly groomed with manicured nails. The image faded as she wrapped tape around Novek's calf.

He leaned over, examining her work. Then without a word he pulled down his sticky pants leg, picked up his gun from the back of the toilet, and went out to the bedroom, leaving Lauren alone.

She threw the soggy towel in the wastebasket and washed her hands in the sink, scrubbing them until they were nearly raw, until there remained no trace of Novek's blood. As she dried her hands on a clean towel, her eyes moved to the window, a pebbled glass rectangle in the end wall. For a brief moment she thought of cranking it open, knocking out the screen, and pulling herself through to safety.

But Emily was in the next room.

Lauren replaced the towel in the rack and walked out, going directly to Emily's side. The little girl sat rigidly, her mouth partly open, her eyes wide with fear and shock. Lauren could only guess what emotional damage she was suffering.

"Go through the house and turn off all the lights," Grummund told Novek, "and take a look out the windows, see what's going on out there."

Novek nodded and left the room.

Lauren was amazed that Grummund had not even inquired about Novek's wound. And making him show himself in the windows seemed dangerous, even though the federal agents knew Novek and Grummund were holding hostages.

"He needs a doctor for his leg."

"He'll be all right," Grummund said. "Is there an attic in this house?"

"An attic? No."

"Good. I don't want anyone dropping in on us unexpectedly. How about a basement?"

"There's a crawl space," Lauren said, picturing the suitcase under the house, where Richard told her he'd put the gun. She remembered how heavy the revolver had felt when she carried it from this room to the garage. If only she had left it in the dresser where she found it. Perhaps she'd be able to get her hands on it before Grummund knew what was happening. But would she be able to use it? Could she actually shoot someone?

Emily trembled beneath her arm, and Lauren knew she'd do whatever was necessary to save her daughter.

"How do you get under there?" Grummund asked.

"What? Oh, the entrance is outside in the backyard."

"Good. No danger there."

"You're . . . not going to hurt us, are you?"

Grummund pursed his lips. "Not if I don't have to."

"And Richard . . . if he were here . . ."

He gave her a half smile. "If he were here right now, considering what's waiting for us outside, I probably wouldn't harm a hair on his head. I could use him to help us get out of here." Then his face darkened. "But if there weren't any cops around . . . You're god-damn right I'd kill him—for what he did to me and for what he stole from me." Grummund drew a long breath through his nose, reining in his anger. "Of course, first I'd make him give back the money."

"What money?"

"The nine hundred thousand dollars he stole from me."

"*What?*" Lauren shook her head. "He doesn't have that kind of money."

"At least not that you know about," Grummund said. "But believe me, he's got it."

Again Lauren shook her head. "No. I'd know if Richard had anything like that. Besides, he's not a thief. He wouldn't steal from—"

Grummund shouted, *"You bet your ass he—"* He stopped, glancing at Emily. In spite of herself Lauren found this touching—Grummund being mindful of his behavior in front of a child. Of course, she remembered, he'd raised a daughter of his own. Francine. Richard's fiancée.

"You bet he stole from me," Grummund said more quietly. "I hid that money before the feds could get it, hid it someplace where I knew it would be when I got out of prison. Well, I'm out and the money's gone, and there are only two people alive who know where it was hidden: me and your husband, the former Donny Rassitter."

"But he told the FBI where all your money was. They confiscated it."

Grummund shook his round head slowly from side to side.

"Not *this* money, lady. My lawyers gave me an itemized list of all the assets seized by the feds. Donny was very thorough and so were they. They got absolutely everything. Except for my stash—nine hundred grand." His face seemed to harden with determination.

235

"Knowing that money was waiting for me was what kept me from going nuts in prison. And I'll tell you something else—I'm not leaving here without it."

It was difficult for Lauren to believe that Richard would steal anything from anyone, let alone almost a million dollars. But she knew it was possible—anything was possible.

And what if Richard *had* taken the money? Where was it? He'd lived modestly in San Miguel, so, obviously, he hadn't spent it here. Perhaps he'd deposited it in a bank, perhaps a Swiss bank. Or had he merely crammed it in the lining of his suitcase under the house?

And what had he planned to use it for?

Lauren struggled with her thoughts, vaguely aware that the telephone was ringing.

34

GRUMMUND PICKED UP the telephone, then held it at his side when Novek appeared in the doorway. Lauren could hear a tiny voice issuing from the receiver.

"The street's full of cop cars," Novek said, "and I saw some flashing lights in the alley behind the fence."

Grummund nodded, and spoke into the phone. "This is Grummund. . . . Well, speak of the devil. We were just chatting about you, Donny."

Lauren stiffened.

"Or should I call you Richard? . . . Oh, they're just fine. For now anyway," he added, his voice hard. "Maybe you should come over here and see for yourself. Besides, I want to talk face-to-face." He paused, then covered the mouthpiece with his hand and turned to Lauren. "He wants to talk to you. Keep it brief. Don't say anything about Novek's leg or about what weapons you've seen in here, understand?"

Lauren stood. "Yes." She held out her hand for the phone.

"Novek, stay by the kid. And you," he said to Lauren, "be careful what you say." He handed her the phone.

"Richard?"

"My God, Lauren, are you and Emily all right?"

Just the sound of his voice made her feel better, as if she and Emily weren't alone. "Yes, yes, we're fine. They . . . they just burst in, Richard, they kicked in the door and—"

"I know, but they haven't hurt you, have they?"

"No," she said, making eye contact with Grummund, "they haven't hurt us."

"Okay, now listen. I'm going to make them a deal—me for you and Emily."

"No, Richard, they—"

"It's me they want anyway. All of this is my fault, and I'm going to get you out of there, I promise. I'll—"

Grummund pulled the phone away from Lauren. "That's enough," he said to her, then into the phone: "You see? Your family is in perfect health. At least for the time being. . . . A trade? Yeah, we can work that out. . . . Well, then *clear* it with the feds. When you're ready to come in and join the party, call me." He hung up and looked at Novek. "He wants to trade—himself for these two."

Novek was shaking his head. "I don't like it."

"Did I ask you what you like?"

Novek's eyes narrowed. "The woman and the kid are better hostages. The cops might try to take us if we're just holding Donny, but they'd never risk getting these two hurt. They're our tickets out of here."

"Tickets to where?" Grummund said. "You're not using your head, Novek. Without that money we've got nothing. Assuming we can get out of here, we'd be on the run from now on, living like bums. I'm too old for that. I might as well go back to prison. You hear what I'm saying? We wait for Donny and we get the money, then we go."

"Fuck the money," Novek said, his voice low. "I say we take these two and get out of here now."

The room was heavy with silence. Lauren saw the color rise to Grummund's face.

"Now you listen to me. *I* decide what we do, and I'm telling you we're not leaving here without that money."

Novek faced him, arms at his sides, fists clenched, gun jammed in his belt. He muttered something, then turned away and stalked from the room. Grummund looked at Lauren and shrugged, his mouth twisted in a grim smile. A few moments later they heard Novek in the kitchen, banging open cupboard doors.

"You got any booze?"

"There's brandy in the cupboard," Lauren said, "and some wine in the refrigerator."

Grummund nodded. "Maybe a drink will calm him down. Sometimes he forgets himself, forgets who's in charge."

"Who *is* in charge?" Lauren blurted, then immediately regretted it as Grummund glared at her.

"I am," he said, loud enough to make Emily flinch in Lauren's arms. He seemed to notice the little girl's reaction, and when he spoke again his voice was calmer. "I *was* in charge anyway, for years. I had the respect and obedience of a score of men." He gave her a wry smile. "Including your husband. Of course, that was before he turned traitor. As for Novek, well, until I went to prison he was as loyal to me as a trained dog. The trouble is, he's been on his own for too long, away from his master. He thinks he can think for himself."

He started to say more, but he was interrupted by the phone. After he picked it up and listened for a moment, he said, "Ready to surrender? Don't be stupid. I'll tell you what we're ready for—send Richard Caylor in here as a trade for one of these hostages."

"For Emily." Lauren stepped forward and Grummund motioned her back.

"What do you mean, no deals?" Grummund shouted into the phone. "Who the hell am I talking to? . . . Oh, *Special* Agent Howard Zale. Well, listen to me, big-shot special agent, either you send in Richard, or I'm throwing out one dead hostage. And if you think I'm kidding, watch the front door." He slammed down the phone and yelled, "Novek!"

Novek appeared in the doorway. Lauren expected to see him carrying a bottle, but the only thing in his hand was the gun. He looked alert, responding to the urgency of Grummund's voice, his previous anger gone, or at least suppressed.

"Stay in here with the girl." Grummund grabbed Lauren by the arm and yanked her toward the doorway.

"MOMMY!"

Emily tried to follow, but Novek gave her a tiny shove, as if he were brushing away a fly, knocking her sprawling into the chair.

"Don't hurt—"

Lauren voice was cut off by the pain in her arm as Grummund dragged her out into the hall, his hand like a vise above her elbow.

All the lights in the house had been turned off, but the living room was filled with an eerie glow from the strong light sifting in through the front drapes. Grummund shoved Lauren toward the front door, blocked now by a chair. He yanked it out of the way, then stood behind her, wrapped one arm around her neck, and pressed the muzzle of his gun to her temple.

"Open the door," he ordered.

When she did, she was nearly blinded by the light. She saw an unfamiliar car parked at an odd angle in the driveway, its doors open and its windows shattered. The street was filled with police cars, their spotlights turned toward her. She could see no one beyond the lights, but she sensed that policemen and FBI agents were out there, pointing guns at her and Grummund.

Oddly enough, at that moment she feared the police more than Grummund, even though he was pressing a gun to her head. She felt certain he wouldn't shoot her, because he needed her as a hostage. However, the police might risk a shot at him, perhaps hitting her by mistake. And once the shooting started, there was no telling what Novek might do with Emily.

"Please don't shoot!" Lauren yelled. "He's got my daughter in the—"

Grummund tightened his arm around her neck, choking off her words.

"I want Richard Caylor over here right now!" Grummund shouted. "Or I'm going to blow this woman's brains out!"

"No, don't shoot! I'm coming!"

Lauren recognized Richard's voice. And then she saw him as he stepped forward between two police cars and moved into the light. He began crossing the street toward them. Suddenly another man ran into the street and grabbed Richard from behind, trying to restrain him. Agent Zale.

Richard twisted and jerked, frantically trying to break free. Lauren wasn't sure which outcome she preferred: that Richard free himself and join her, or that Zale keep him safely away from the house and the two men inside. She saw Felix Jameson run from between two cars just as Richard broke away from Zale. Zale yelled for Richard to

239

stop. And as Lauren watched, horrified, Zale drew his pistol and aimed at Richard's back. Jameson slammed into Zale's arm, and the gun went off, burying a bullet in the front lawn.

And then Richard was standing before her.

Grummund pulled her out of the doorway.

"Get in here," he told Richard, his voice cold and deadly.

Richard entered the house, his eyes on Lauren.

"Are you all right?"

She nodded as much as Grummund's arm would allow.

"Shut the door and shove that chair in front of it."

"Not until you let her go. That was the deal."

"Not me," Lauren said. "Emily."

"Neither of you," Grummund told them. "We're all together now, and we're going to stay that way."

"But you said—"

"I said nothing. Agent Zale told me no deals, so that's the way it is. Now do what I told you."

Richard hesitated, then closed the door and blocked it with the armchair.

"Move," Grummund said, removing his arm from Lauren's neck. "Back to the bedroom."

Richard took Lauren's hand, and Grummund followed them through the living room, his gun leveled at Richard's back. Novek and Emily were waiting for them.

"Mommy! Daddy!"

Emily tried to climb out of her chair, but Novek put his beefy hand on her shoulder and held her in place.

"Get your hand off her." Richard started forward, and Grummund jabbed him in the back with the gun.

"Sit down on the bed," he ordered.

Novek was smiling at Richard, his hand still on Emily's shoulder.

"I said sit down!" Grummund grabbed Richard's shirt collar, and Richard turned on him. Grummund raised his gun.

"No!" Lauren cried. "Richard, please do what he says." Without waiting for him to move, she pushed past him to Emily's side and took hold of Novek's wrist, thick and hairy and damp with sweat. "Take your hand off my daughter," Lauren said, her voice cracking with fear and anger, Emily's sobs tearing at her heart.

Novek looked at her with hooded eyes, then removed his hand

from Emily's shoulder. Lauren drew her daughter from the chair and held her close, feeling her small body shake with sobs. She wondered if any of them would leave this house alive.

Lauren looked at Richard and saw pain in his eyes—and determination. She knew without doubt that he was prepared to lay down his life to save her and Emily.

"Sit," Grummund said, and shoved Richard in the chest.

Richard sat on the edge of the bed, his gaze still fixed on Lauren's eyes.

"Where's my money?"

"What?" Richard gave Grummund a puzzled look.

"You took nine hundred thousand dollars from me and I want it back."

"I don't know what you're talking about."

Grummund whipped his gun across Richard's face, knocking him back and opening a long gash above his eye.

"No!" Lauren screamed, and started to move forward with Emily still clutching her leg.

Novek grabbed her hair and yanked her back.

"You stay out of this," he grumbled. "Your turn will come."

Lauren was too concerned about Richard to wonder what Novek meant. She watched her husband sit up, his hand to his forehead, blood dripping from his fingers.

"We don't have much time here," Grummund said. "If you want to live, you'd better start talking."

Richard shook his head slowly from side to side. "I swear to God, I don't know anything about any money."

"You're lying." Grummund raised the gun, and Richard put out his hand defensively.

"No, listen to me. How could I take your money? The feds took it all."

"Not the nine hundred grand in the hidden safe in the garage at my estate. I only showed that safe to three people, you and my . . . my two children, God rest their souls. That was a long time ago, when I thought you were going to be my son-in-law. When I *trusted* you, you son of a bitch."

He swung his gun at Richard, who jerked back, catching the blow across his forearm and crying out in pain.

"Nobody stumbled on that safe by accident!" Grummund yelled.

"It hadn't been broken into, and no one knew the combination but *you! You took my money!*" He raised the gun to deliver another blow.

"No!" Richard cried, his arms up to protect himself. "I told the feds about all your assets, including that. *They* took it."

"You're lying. My lawyers got an account of everything the feds took, and that money wasn't listed." Grummund pointed the gun at Richard's chest. "This is your last chance."

"But I *told* them."

"Told who?" Lauren said suddenly.

They all looked at her.

"Who did you tell?" she asked Richard.

He took out his handkerchief and held it to his head, trying to stop the bleeding.

"Half a dozen different agents," he said. "Zale was the case agent in charge of the investigation, but there were always two or three others present during questioning, and they grilled me for days, going over every little detail of the books." He looked at Grummund. "I told them about that hidden safe on your estate, I'm certain of it. In fact, now I specifically remember telling Zale and—"

Richard stopped, his eyes moving away from them, staring into the past.

Grummund said, "What?"

"We were alone," Richard said. "I was in protective custody in some hotel room, and Zale was the only one there. I remember because he'd had lunch sent up, and he and I were eating and he started asking me again if I remembered any more assets you might have hidden. We'd been over it so many times that I automatically said no. And then I remembered the hidden safe. And of course, the combination—Francine's birthday. I don't know why I hadn't thought of it before then. Maybe because I'd never actually seen it. You'd only told me about it, and you never said exactly what was in there."

"There was *plenty* in there before I went to prison."

Richard nodded. "I gave Zale the combination and he said he'd check it out. When I asked him about it a few days later, he told me he'd found the safe—empty."

They all looked at each other, beginning to understand.

Lauren said it first. "Agent Howard Zale took your money."

35

GRUMMUND LOOKED from Lauren to Richard. "Am I supposed to believe that an *FBI agent* stole my money?"

Before Richard could answer, Novek said, "This is bullshit." He pushed Lauren aside and limped toward the bed. She saw that his leg was bleeding again. Novek grabbed a fistful of Richard's shirt and pulled him to his feet, then began striking him with his open hand, slapping his face back and forth, making loud, smacking noises.

"Tell us where the money is," Novek said, grunting from the effort of the blows.

Grummund tried to pull him away from Richard. "Leave him alone, Novek, for chrissake, let him talk."

Novek shrugged Grummund off and shoved Richard back onto the bed. Grummund's face was red from the strain—and from anger. He raised his gun, and for a moment Lauren thought he was going to shoot Novek. The big man faced Grummund, feet spread, fists at his sides.

"You said we weren't leaving until we got the money," Novek said. "Fine. Only now you're twiddling your thumbs while these two tell you fairy tales. You want to know where the money is? Okay, let's quit screwing around and find out."

Ignoring Grummund's gun, he moved past him to Lauren, roughly yanking Emily from her arms. Mother and daughter cried out, and Novek backhanded Lauren across the face, knocking her to the floor. Richard sprang to his feet, but Grummund blocked his way. Novek held Emily easily in one arm, his gun pressed to her temple. The little girl was crying hysterically.

"Tell us where the money is right now or she dies."

"NO!" Lauren screamed.

"Please God, Novek, don't." Richard held up his hands palms forward. "I swear to you, I don't have the money. Don't hurt my daughter, Novek, for the love of God. Don't you think I'd give you the money if I had it?"

Lauren could see that Richard was near tears. Perhaps Novek saw it, too, because he lowered Emily to the floor. She ran to Lauren, who was on her knees and now held Emily to her, hugging her, trying to calm her down.

"So now we know the money's gone," Novek said, sneering at Grummund. "And we only came here for two things, to get the money and to ice Donny." He looked at Richard, but he continued to speak to Grummund. "Are you going to do it or am I?"

"I'll decide when it's time for that," Grummund said.

Lauren could see that the older man was slightly shaken, struggling to retain his commanding tone of voice. Obviously Novek was beyond his control.

"You're through deciding what's best for me," Novek said. "I'm the one who—"

He was interrupted by the ringing of the phone. He snatched it up before Grummund could get to it, listened for a moment, then said, "I'm not interested in what you want, pal. Here's what *I* want. You've got exactly"—he rolled his wrist to check his watch—"fifteen minutes to get that van out front. If it's not there on time, we throw out a body." He slammed down the receiver. The phone began to ring almost immediately, and Novek grabbed the thin cord and yanked it out of the wall, snapping off the tiny plastic connector. The ringing stopped abruptly, its echo continuing from the kitchen.

"That's *my* decision," he told them. "I'm going to watch for that van, and we'd all better hope it shows up on time." He limped from the room, his right shoe making a squishy sound, leaving a trail of bloody footprints behind him.

"You've got to help us get out of here," Richard said to Grummund, his voice a harsh whisper.

"What?" Grummund seemed ready to laugh. "*I've* got to help *you*?"

"I mean the four of us in this room," Richard said, "including yourself."

Grummund's smile was forced. "And what about Novek?"

"He'll kill us all," Lauren said. "Or he'll get us killed."

"She's right." Richard stood. His face was a mess—blood on his forehead, one eye nearly swollen shut, his bottom lip puffy and red.

"Don't you see, the feds will never let Novek leave here—this whole thing was a setup to grab him."

Grummund's eyes narrowed, and he glanced—involuntarily, Lauren thought—toward the open doorway. She and Richard exchanged a brief look.

"Novek doesn't give a damn what happens here," Richard said. "He's got nothing to lose. He knows if he gives up, the feds will take him back to Chicago, where he'll stand trial for murder. So what are his options? Death or life in prison. But you . . . you've got a choice."

"Don't try to—"

"Listen to me, Pete," Richard said with urgency, but also, Lauren noted, with affection. "You can get out of this thing all right. I mean, what do they want you for besides parole violation?"

"How about holding a family hostage at gunpoint."

"We can testify in your behalf," Lauren said quickly.

"Oh, *that* will do me a lot of good."

Grummund had spoken with sarcasm, but Lauren could see he was thinking it over. She also sensed a subtle change in the room, as if there were now an air of conspiracy.

"And there's something else that will help you," she said, beginning to see a chance for them. "You and Richard can both testify against Howard Zale."

"What the hell are you talking about?"

"Don't you get it?" Lauren said. "Zale stole that money. And he didn't steal it from you, not technically. He stole it from the federal government. He could go to prison. You and Richard can put him there."

"She's right, Pete. You can tell the feds about the nine hundred thousand being in the safe, and I can tell them about giving the location and combination to Zale."

Grummund frowned. "If Zale *did* take the money . . ."

"He took it. No one else could have."

"Then why is he still hanging around? Why isn't he retired on an island somewhere?"

"Because he'd do anything to get Novek. I think Zale took the money because it was there—it was easy and the temptation was too great. But when Novek killed his best friend, Zale went on a mission. He'd risk everything to get Novek. Including me and my family. And you."

They were silent for a moment. Grummund rubbed his chin.

"That would explain something . . ."

"What?"

"I shouldn't have been able to find you so easily," Grummund said.

"What do you mean?"

"When I got out of prison, the first thing I did was look for my money. That's all I'd been thinking about for the past four years. That and killing you with my bare hands." Grummund smiled crookedly, as if he were speaking of a college fraternity prank. "When I found out the money was gone, I was certain you'd taken it and I was twice as desperate to find you. I started calling people—my lawyers, some of my old cronies, and so on—anyone who might be able to give me a line on you. It was around then that Novek contacted me, wanting to know what my plans were, seeing if there was something in it for him. And then I got a call from some two-bit hood, a sleazebag named Mo Harrington. Know him?"

Richard shook his head.

"Anyway, he told me, 'Donny Rassitter is now Richard Caylor living in San Miguel.' I asked him how he knew. He's a smart ass, and he said a little birdie told him."

"I'll bet you nine hundred thousand dollars that the little birdie was Zale," Lauren said.

Grummund nodded his head slowly. "It's beginning to figure that way. But at the time I didn't give a damn where Harrington got his information—just if it was accurate." He looked at Richard. "All I cared about was getting to you and getting my money."

"Zale was using all of us to trap Novek," Richard said. "And if anyone got killed in the cross fire, tough luck. But what he *didn't* count on was you and me getting together and figuring out what happened to the money. I'll bet he's out in the street right now sweating bullets."

The phone in the kitchen began to ring again. The one on the nightstand lay mute.

"I think your biggest problem right now is the man in the kitchen," Lauren said, "not the FBI."

The ringing stopped. They could hear Novek's voice, loud but unintelligible.

246

Richard said, "You'd better stop him before he—"

"Shut up and let me think."

"If he says the wrong thing out there, Pete, you'll never be able to deal."

"I said shut up!" Grummund raised his revolver and pointed it at Richard.

Lauren pulled Emily behind her. A moment ago she'd clung to the faint hope that Peter Grummund would let them go and surrender himself to the FBI. Now she believed he might kill them all, beginning with Richard.

Suddenly Novek filled the doorway behind Grummund, his face pale and sickly looking. He leaned against the doorframe for support, and his pants leg glistened with new blood. The phone was ringing again, summoning them to the kitchen.

"Shoot him," Novek said, his voice a low rumble. "I just told them we were going to toss out a body, and it might as well be Donny's."

"No!" Lauren cried, and Richard took a step backward.

They all watched Grummund.

"Well," Novek said, "what're you waiting for?"

Lauren saw a change in Grummund's face, as if he'd made up his mind about something, and suddenly she knew that he wasn't going to pull the trigger. Before she had a chance to feel relieved, though, Novek stumbled forward, raising his heavy automatic pistol.

"All right then." He came up beside Grummund with his gun arm extended toward Richard.

The older man said, "*No,*" and knocked Novek's arm aside just as the gun boomed, filling the room with sound and the smell of cordite and blasting a hole in the plaster wall. Emily began screaming. Lauren held her tightly, while Grummund and Novek yelled at each other. Through it all the phone continued its plaintive call from the kitchen.

"You don't do anything unless I tell you!" Grummund shouted in Novek's face.

"I'm through taking orders from you, Grummund. There's only one way out of here." He lurched forward, grabbed Richard by the shirt collar, and pulled him roughly toward the doorway, pressing the automatic into the side of his neck.

"Don't do it, Novek!"

"I'm going to show them we mean business." He shoved Richard into the hallway.

Grummund took Lauren by the arm and pulled her from the bedroom. Emily clung to her as desperately as if they'd been cast into the sea. Lauren saw Novek struggling to maneuver Richard into the living room, dragging his leg and leaving a trail of blood. She tried to go after them, but Grummund pulled her the other way, through the family room toward the kitchen and the ringing telephone. He shoved his gun in his belt and lifted the receiver.

"This is Grummund. Now listen to me. Novek is on his own. He's going to kill Donny and—"

"No!" Lauren cried.

"—and I can't stop him. I'm giving myself up now, and I'm going to come out through—"

"Hang up."

They both turned to see Novek moving through the family room toward them, his hand on the back of Richard's neck, his gun pointed at Grummund. He'd obviously changed his mind about tossing Richard's body out the front door—at least temporarily. Grummund let go of Lauren and faced Novek and Richard, while a tiny voice squawked from the receiver in his hand.

"I said hang up," Novek said. "You're not going to keep me from getting out of here."

"It's too late. I already told them I was—"

"HANG UP!" Novek shouted from the kitchen doorway.

Grummund hesitated, then hung up the phone. "It doesn't matter, Novek. It's over anyway."

"It is for you," Novek said, and shot him in the chest.

Lauren screamed. Grummund staggered back toward the laundry room, blood billowing from his shirt front. His mouth worked soundlessly as he tried to tug the revolver from his belt. He bumped heavily into the refrigerator, then wheeled slowly around and fell facedown on the tile floor, rattling appliances on the countertop.

Another scream had built in Lauren's chest, but it was choked off when she saw Richard and Novek wrestling for Novek's gun. Richard held Novek's wrist with both hands, and Novek pummeled him with his fist, the two men staggering in a drunken dance through the doorway and into the kitchen. The gun went off, smashing a hole in the ceiling.

Lauren pulled Emily into the dining room as Richard and Novek crashed together to the floor, discharging the gun into the cabinets below the counter, clanging pots and pans.

Still clutching Emily, Lauren stared back at Richard and Novek fighting to the death on the kitchen floor. Novek rolled on top of Richard, pinning him to the tiles. Suddenly Emily yanked free from Lauren and ran in terror toward the bedrooms.

For a moment Lauren was paralyzed with indecision. Should she go after her daughter? Or run to open the front door and hope the police could stop Novek before he killed Richard?

The sound of Emily's bedroom door slamming shut spurred her to action.

Lauren moved quickly into the kitchen, grabbed the nearest object on the counter, the blender, and raised it with both hands over her head. She brought it down with all her might, aiming at the back of Novek's head. But she slipped on the floor, losing her grip on the blender. It struck Novek between the shoulder blades and rolled harmlessly away. He hardly seemed to notice, and continued to fight Richard for control of the gun.

And now Lauren saw why she'd slipped. The tile floor was smeared with blood—some, she knew, from Grummund, but much of it from Novek, whose leg now bled freely. Lauren realized that if Novek had been whole, unwounded, he would have easily taken the gun from Richard and killed him. Even injured, he was more than a match for Richard.

Almost without thinking, Lauren found herself on Novek's back, striking his head with her fists, then scratching at his face with her nails, trying for his eyes. He shrugged and jerked sideways, tossing her sprawling to the floor. The two men rolled against the counter, and Lauren was immediately on her feet again, stretching over them. She pulled open the drawer containing her kitchen gadgets—potato masher, can opener, jar vise, spatulas . . . knives.

The men rolled again, struggling furiously, bumping hard into Lauren, knocking her off her feet. She clung to the drawer, trying to maintain her balance, but it pulled from the cabinet and crashed to the floor, scattering its plastic, wood, and metal contents. Lauren scrambled on her hands and knees and snatched up the nearest sharp object, a steak knife with a serrated blade. She raised it to stab Novek, not caring where—his neck, his back, his face. But he saw her and rolled toward her, forcing Richard up on top of him, using him as a shield. Lauren crawled around on the wet, slippery floor, seeking an opening, and when Novek raised his arm from Richard's back, trying again for control of the gun, she lunged, jabbing the knife into his side. Novek roared like a bear and twisted away from her, snapping off the knife handle against the floor with the blade still in his side.

Lauren reached around frantically for another weapon, and her hand fell on the electric carving knife. She switched it on, the battery hummed, and the long twin blades whirred, moving side by side in a blurred sawing motion. Novek kicked her, slamming the sole of his shoe into her side, knocking her back, then he rolled on top of Richard. Lauren was awash with rage and pain as she crawled toward the struggling men, holding the handle in both hands and pressing the whirring blades to Novek's wounded leg. He screamed and kicked, but Lauren stayed with him as the blades sawed into the meat of his calf. Suddenly Novek let go of the gun and rolled off Richard, bellowing with rage and kicking savagely at Lauren, bowling her over. He rose to his knees, snatched up a cleaver, and towered above her. Lauren was on her back, trying desperately to scramble away, her hands and feet slipping on the bloody floor.

Novek's face was filled with hatred as he raised the cleaver over his head.

Lauren saw Richard behind Novek, the gun in his hands. It seemed to explode in a ball of fire. Novek's mouth opened in surprise. The cleaver dropped from his hand, clattering to the floor. He toppled forward onto Lauren, forcing the air from her lungs.

As she struggled beneath his dead weight, she heard the front door crash open.

36

THE FIRST MAN to enter the kitchen was Agent Howard Zale. He held his gun in both hands, arms extended before him.

Richard rolled Novek's dead body off Lauren and helped her unsteadily to her feet. They were both shaking from fatigue and pain—and from revulsion for what they had just done: killed a man.

Lauren saw that Zale was still pointing his gun. For a fleeting, fearful moment she thought he might shoot them. Then Jameson and several uniformed cops crowded in behind him, and Zale lowered his gun.

"Are they both dead?" Zale asked—eagerly, Lauren thought.

"Novek is," Richard said. His arm was around Lauren, supporting himself as much as her. "I don't know about—"

"This one's still alive."

A policeman was kneeling beside Grummund, touching the man's neck. Grummund hadn't moved, but Lauren could hear him groaning.

"We'd better get the paramedics, fast," the cop said.

Lauren pulled away from Richard and nudged past the men, heading for Emily's bedroom. Richard started to follow. Zale put his hand on his arm.

"Wait a minute, pal, I've got some ques—"

Suddenly Richard swung at Zale, venting the last of his frustration and rage, punching him in the mouth and knocking him to the floor, where he sprawled beside the body of Novek.

"*You're responsible for this!*" Richard shouted.

Zale scrambled to his feet. Jameson stepped between the two men and said, "Hey, take it easy."

"Get that son of a bitch out of my house," Richard told Jameson. Then he smiled sardonically. "And take special care of Peter Grummund. He and I have some interesting things to tell you about *Agent* Zale."

Lauren paused only long enough to see the stunned look on Zale's face. She rushed to her daughter's bedroom. She found Emily on the floor, clinging to Amos. Lauren knelt beside her and held her close.

"It's all right, baby. Everything's all right now."

A San Miguel police cruiser, lights flashing and siren howling, led the small parade to the hospital. Jameson rode behind the cruiser in an ambulance carrying Peter Grummund. Lauren, Emily, and Richard followed in a second ambulance. And behind them, Lauren noticed, was the dark blue car she'd first seen following her nearly two weeks ago. It was driven by an FBI agent in a windbreaker, the same man she'd spotted at Tobey's restaurant and again at Casa Grande.

Howard Zale was not in sight.

Zale had been ordered to stay behind by Special Agent Fredricks, who was in charge of the FBI's Los Angeles office. Fredricks, with background information supplied by agents Hal Ipswich and Monica Sherwood, had a lot of questions for Zale.

Fredricks would also deal with the media, Richard explained to Lauren. The FBI's story to the press would be that Grummund and Novek had been fugitives, fleeing from the police, and the men had broken into the Caylors' house at random, seeking hostages.

Lauren and Richard would repeat this story to their friends and relatives.

"What about Zale?" Lauren asked bitterly.

"He's screwed," Richard said. "Grummund and I will testify about the missing money and Zale's access to it. And the feds should have no trouble laying their hands on that snitch Mo Harrington. They'll squeeze him until he names Zale as the one who revealed my identity. A federal offense. Zale will go to prison for a long time."

"And the money?"

"I don't know. Zale may turn it in and hope for a reduced sentence, not that he'll get one. Or the feds might find it anyway. And if the money stays hidden, Zale will be old and feeble before he gets a chance to spend it—with his friends from the Bureau hounding him every day."

Richard was attended to in the emergency room. His facial cuts were closed and he was examined for concussion. Lauren's wounds were less severe, though just as painful—a hairline crack in one rib and several deep bruises.

Although Emily had suffered the least physically, she was treated with the most care, for she appeared to be in a state of shock, if only a mild one. The little girl was put to bed in a private room. Lauren sat by her side.

Richard entered the room and closed the door softly behind him.

"How is she?" he whispered.

"She's asleep. The doctor said she'll be fine. We can take her home tonight."

"Thank God."

Lauren got up and Richard took her gently in his arms. "Oh, Richard." It was nearly a wail.

"Shh. It's over now."

They stood for several minutes, saying nothing, looking down at their daughter, who seemed to be lost in a peaceful dream.

Finally Richard said, "Lauren, I'm so sorry about this. About everything."

"I know."

"If I'd ever imagined that you or Emily would be in jeopardy . . . I'd never have gotten involved with you."

Lauren held him tighter. "Please don't say that."

"I mean it."

"No. The bad part is behind us. We're safe now. We're together."

Richard hesitated. "It can never be the same between us."

"It will be better."

"I . . . I want it to be."

Lauren smiled faintly. "We have time to make it so," she said. "We have plenty of time."